"In *Dead North*, Hames' lawyer turned accidental sleuth, Sam Williams, finds himself far from home and neck deep in Manchester's seamy gangster scene. But what stands out in this intelligent, intricately woven crime procedural - with a plot to make your brain hurt - is the undercurrent of slick and highly enjoyable humour reminiscent of Raymond Chandler, updated for the twenty-first century. Loved it."

S.E. Lynes, author of *Mother, Valentina*, and *The Pact*

"I really enjoyed it. The characters spring off the page with such natural ease. I was gripped by the story – I love a book that takes turns where you least expect. It's going to leave me with a thriller hangover for some time."

John Marrs, author of *The One, The Good Samaritan* and *When You Disappeared*

"Hames is such a talent that he has created a white-knuckle, breathlessly-paced read that also has heart. Beautifully written and thrilling, Dead North deserves to go to the top of any chart."

Louise Beech, author of *Maria in the Moon, How To Be Brave* and *The Mountain in my Shoe*

"A pacy thriller, rich in voice and with a gratifying degree of complexity. Hames knows how to deliver."

John Bowen, author of *Where the Dead Walk, Vessel* and *Death Stalks Kettle Street*

Also by Joel Hames

Bankers Town
Brexecution
The Art of Staying Dead
Victims
Caged

About the Author

A Londoner in exile, Joel Hames lives in rural Lancashire with his wife and two daughters.

His works of fiction include the novels *Bankers Town* and *The Art of Staying Dead,* as well as the novellas *Brexecution*, *Victims* and *Caged.*

When not writing or spending time with his family, Joel likes to eat, drink, cook, and make up excuses to avoid walking the dog.

You can find out more about Joel and sign up to his mailing list through social media or his very own website:

Facebook: facebook.com/joelhamesauthor
Twitter: @joel_hames
Website: http://www.joelhamesauthor.com

DEAD

NORTH

BY

JOEL HAMES

Cover art by John Bowen

For My Parents

Contents

PROLOGUE

THE DEAD

I DIDN'T WANT to get out of the car, but Gaddesdon wasn't keen on me bleeding all over the upholstery again while he stood shivering outside. I told him my nose hadn't bled since the last time someone had hit it, which was nearly two days ago now, but that cut no ice. So I stood there at the back of the cemetery and watched the gaps between the black-coated mourners as a box with a dead woman in it dropped into a hole in the earth.

There were words, but I wasn't listening. I was thinking of other things, of glaciers and mobile phones, hidden pasts and broken bones. I corrected myself. Almost broken. I'd assumed half Folgate Police Station would be there, and they probably were, but apart from Gaddesdon, and Roarkes, standing there right in the middle and looking nearly as awkward as I felt, I didn't recognise a soul. I took a step back and out of sight. I didn't want Roarkes seeing me. He might ask some awkward questions.

Gaddesdon I could still see. He'd found himself a spot near the front, head bowed, shoulders hunched against the cold, a giant frozen penguin. A whole gang of frozen fucking penguins praying to their penguin god, I thought, and checked the smile before it formed.

I hadn't known Fiona Milton. I'd never met Fiona Milton. I wasn't a police officer, and I wasn't from Manchester or Lancashire or wherever the hell we were. I wanted to know why she'd died, sure, but seeing her corpse buried wasn't going to help me. I cursed Gaddesdon silently. I'd have been better off waiting in the car.

The minister had finished talking and someone else had taken his place, Fiona's superintendent, a fierce-looking man with tiny eyes and a few strands of lank brown hair that flapped idly in the wind as he recalled her bravery, her integrity, her smile, her spirit. I wondered if he'd ever actually met her. I wondered if he'd even known who she was, before someone had come running into his office and told him she'd been gunned down on some godforsaken country lane in the middle of nowhere.

I wondered if I could slip away now, go back and sit in the car, which Gaddesdon hadn't bothered to lock, figuring if it wasn't safe at a police funeral it wouldn't be safe anywhere. I glanced around, searching out eyes. I didn't want anyone to see me. *Bloody Londoner. Bloody lawyer. Sneaking off. No respect.* It wouldn't look good.

And then I heard it.

It shouldn't really have been out of place, not at a funeral, the sound of a sniff, a prelude to tears. But this was a different kind of funeral, a defiant, stiff-backed, fist-shaking funeral. A funeral of suits and uniforms and frozen penguins, legacy and courage and all that bullshit. Not real people. Not tears.

A fat penguin shifted a few inches to the right and I saw the source of the noise. A child. Six or seven years old, I thought, a little boy in a suit that made him look even smaller than he was, his face screwed up to fight off the tears. The tears were winning. There was a girl beside him, a year or two older, holding his hand, turning to whisper in his ear. And behind them both a man, about my own age, one arm on each of their shoulders, staring fixedly ahead, as though he could see something there the rest of us couldn't, lips pressed tightly together. Jaw trembling.

The other victim had already been buried. I remembered what Gaddesdon had told me about Naz Ahmet, Fiona Milton's colleague. Same uniform. Same car. Same death. Another funeral, another superintendent, or maybe the same one, a wife and a child to mourn him long after all the penguins had gone home. I'd been on the case six days and all I'd got out of it were a handful of trips to the hospital and a bunch of leads that took me back where I'd started. I'd been close to giving up a dozen times already. Two people had died, and that was sad, sure, but sad was as far as it went. Finding out who'd killed them might just breathe some life into my dying career, so I had an interest in the whole thing. Beyond that, I hadn't really cared.

The child was still crying, quietly now, hunched into himself, shoulders shaking. I blinked and burned the image into my brain.

Whoever had done this, the bastards would pay.

PART 1

INTO EACH LIFE, SOME RAIN MUST FALL

1: Glutes

"GET YOUR FAT arse out of bed!"

There are nicer ways to wake up in the morning. My bladder was calling out for attention. My bones were aching, with that deep November ache that means you've got a cold coming if you're lucky, and worse if you're not. And now Claire was shouting at me.

I lay there for a moment, trying to figure out which of Claire and my bladder was the more pressing problem. I sneezed. The bladder won. I stood, swayed a little, and made it halfway out of the room and within sight of the bathroom before she spotted me.

"Watch this, Sam."

When I came out of the bathroom she was standing in front of me with one hand on her hip and even at that time in the morning I knew she meant business.

"Look at this."

The TV was on. It was a fifty-five inch flatscreen that took up too much wall and had cost us more than a month's rent, but we'd been on a high when we bought it. We'd just moved in together, and I had a decent case, finally, with proper clients who would pay me and get my name out there. For the first few weeks I'd been unable to suppress a grin every time I walked past those fifty-five glorious inches. One whole month on that high, a hot lawyer with a hot case, reputation restored, a great girlfriend, a big new flat, a big new TV.

I wasn't grinning any more.

Already the TV belonged to a different life, and now when I saw it, it taunted me.

How's work, Sam? it asked me, as clearly as the words bursting out of the eight strategically-positioned surround sound speakers.

What's that? it continued. *Just the one client, Sam?*

I didn't like the way it addressed me by name.

You can't afford the rent, your girlfriend's covered your share for the last two months while you mumble quiet evasions about a 'temporary cashflow problem', Sam.

If you can't see the end of a temporary problem, how long can you go on pretending it's not permanent, Sam?

And all that, past and present, washing through me in the half second it took to focus on the screen.

There wasn't much to focus on. The picture was grainy, but I could see there was a car on it, shaking around, and for a moment I thought I was looking at some eighties disaster movie and wondered why Claire had woken me. Then I realised it wasn't the car that was shaking, it was the screen, the camera, someone's phone, probably, because every time the shot moved to track the car the image went blurry for a moment before finding its target and refocusing.

I sneezed, again, and felt the ache dig itself a little deeper. A thought suddenly hit me.

"Fat arse?" I protested. Maybe a few months ago, sure, but I'd been working on that. I'd joined a local martial arts class. I wasn't exactly Ultimate Fighting material, not yet, not with two decades of beer and kebabs behind me, but I'd learned to punch, roll and kick with a pack of lean and hungry bankers and insurance salesmen. More hungry than lean, most of them. I'd cancelled my membership in the light of that *temporary cashflow problem*, but not before I'd learned the names of all the muscles and tightened some of them up a little. I reckoned my glutes were in decent shape.

She wasn't biting. "They've got him," she said, eyes on

the screen, and that was when I noticed the words across the bottom.

"POLICE CLOSE IN ON SUSPECTED COP-KILLER" blared the scrolling yellow banner. At least they'd got *suspected* in there this time. Poor bastard didn't have a chance, not without the right lawyer, and I didn't think he'd be knocking on my door any time soon.

Which was a shame, because I reckoned I could do a pretty good job for Thomas Carson.

Thomas Carson had been the country's number one news story for the last two days. There was a refugee crisis in Europe and the usual tally of wars on its fringes, but nobody was talking about anything but Thomas Carson. We'd been out the night before, pub, one of Claire's friends and her fiancé, nice enough people, I'd thought. Claire had been working too hard and getting too intense about her work, and that was understandable, given the subject matter was five brutally murdered girls. But two years on one big, horrible story couldn't be healthy, however dedicated the journalist, and I thought maybe a drink would do her good. Me, I didn't need an excuse for a drink. So we'd had the one, and then a few more, and at some point in the evening I'd joked that Carson should get himself sponsored. Thirty-six hours on the run, with every police force in the country on alert and his face on every TV channel and every front page, and they still hadn't got him. *Duracell*, I thought. Or *Nike*. Claire had laughed, her friend had laughed, the fiancé had looked at me like I'd just defaced someone's grave and told me I should have a little more respect for the police officers he'd killed.

"Allegedly," I'd said.

"I beg your pardon," said fiancé, whose name was actually Andrew and who I was starting to think wasn't such a nice guy after all.

"I said *allegedly*. You know, he might not have done it. It's the way the law works."

I knew I was speaking to him the way I'd speak to a child, and I knew we'd all had a few drinks and he wouldn't take kindly to it, but by now I'd decided I didn't like him and I didn't really give a damn.

The evening at the pub had ended shortly after that, and I'd guessed Claire would be after my blood the moment we were alone, but instead she'd opened a bottle of wine, poured us a glass each, and told me she'd never liked that jumped-up little prick anyway.

The thing was, I was only half-joking about Carson and the sponsorship and, most importantly, the "allegedly". Two police officers had been killed, there was no dispute about that, two unarmed officers shot dead on a little country road in the back-end of nowhere. Thomas Carson had been named as the suspect a couple of hours later, and as far as I could tell he'd been named solely because his car had been identified by witnesses near the scene. Not exactly a cast-iron case, but that hadn't stopped the media from labelling him cop-killer and shoving his face front and centre twice an hour ever since. Not the way this kind of thing was usually done, not before a trial and a guilty verdict, at least. But with an armed maniac on the loose it was in the public interest to keep the public informed, apparently.

That was probably true. But the guy wasn't going to be on the loose forever, and when it came to the trial, I couldn't imagine where they'd find twelve people who hadn't seen those "COP KILLER" headlines beneath the guy's face and who could swear they wouldn't be influenced by them. Still, I'd thought, I'd give my left arm to be Thomas Carson's lawyer. My left arm was the weaker one, with a jab like a kitten's handshake, so that wasn't quite the sacrifice it might sound, but you get the idea.

The image had stopped shaking and the car had stopped moving. There were a couple of big buildings in the background, warehouses or factories, some hills behind the buildings, that slanted blur you get when it's raining so hard you can't even see the rain. The image changed, abruptly: four more cars, police, moving slowly forwards. Then back to Carson's little Ford Fiesta, the car he'd been in for the last two days and somehow kept hidden from every cop and every nosy bastard in the country.

Claire had turned the volume up, so now we could hear the girl in the studio describing the scene. It was unfolding just outside Manchester, apparently. There were officers present from the Greater Manchester Police and helicopters on their way, and someone who just happened to be driving home after a nightshift had seen what was about to happen and had the brains and the bandwidth to get hold of Sky News and send them live images at the same time he was filming them. They didn't have the sound from the scene to go with those live images, though, and by the fifth minute of nothing happening the poor girl was starting to get desperate. So it was probably a good thing for her that something finally did happen.

A door started to open.

It was the driver's door on the Ford Fiesta and it opened so slightly and so slowly that if it hadn't been for the anchor gasping, a little, and announcing it like the guy was actually there in the room with her, armed and dangerous and fed up with looking at pictures of a car in the rain, I wouldn't have noticed at all. But that would have been OK, because a moment later the scrolling yellow news feed changed to "CARSON MANHUNT:

VEHICLE CORNERED, DOOR OPENING", and a few seconds after that all the excitement over the door was forgotten in the sight of a leg emerging from the car, followed by another leg, followed by the rest of a human being who might well have been Thomas Carson but was so blurred and distant he could equally have been Dolly Parton.

The figure that might or might not have been Thomas Carson threw itself to the ground, presumably in response to something shouted from one of the police vehicles. I glanced down, half-expecting the yellow banner to tell me this, too, but it still hadn't got past "DOOR OPENING".

The rain had intensified, by the look of it, and the picture was grainier and blurrier than ever. Other figures now appeared in the shot, three of them, walking slowly towards the figure on the ground and waving their arms around. With sound from the scene, no doubt it would all have made sense. Without that sound, it all looked faintly ridiculous.

And that was how Thomas Carson was arrested.

2: Guns and Gangs

"WELCOME TO MANCHESTER," the sign had said. Underneath, someone had written "FUCK OFF" in red paint. I hadn't been anywhere near the place for a decade, I hadn't missed it, and I wouldn't have bothered going back for another decade or two if Roarkes hadn't called.

"I'm in Manchester," he'd said, and I'd pictured him standing there in the cold hard rain, glaring at some suspect or unfortunate detective constable. Every lawyer has one cop who doesn't hate him as much as the rest do, and Detective Inspector Gideon Roarkes was mine. Roarkes was supposed to be based in London, a senior officer in the Metropolitan Police, but he'd been popping up all over the place lately, Cornwall, Lincolnshire, even Wales, his long, tired face caught in the background in a newspaper shot or a TV report into a murder or a kidnapping or a particularly significant drugs bust. A couple of months back I'd asked him who he was really working for, and he'd just grunted and shaken his head, not even bothering with a lie. This time I waited for him to tell me what was so special about Manchester, but instead he'd come up with the last thing I expected.

"I need you up here, Sam," he'd said. Roarkes could get away with calling me *Sam*, or *Williams*, or whatever the hell he wanted, but only someone who wanted his head handed to him would call Roarkes *Gideon*. I'd laughed and waited for him to join in, and found the silence lengthening. Roarkes had got me out of some tight spots in the past, so maybe I owed him. But not enough to go running up to Manchester on a whim.

"It's about Carson," he'd said, and all those witty little barbs I'd been planning had disappeared faster than the free drinks at a wedding. He hadn't been too forthcoming with the details. A place, a time, and it was "about Carson", that was all I knew. Carson had been arrested nearly a week earlier and charged not many hours after that, and since then he'd slipped off the news radar, but not mine. I was still interested, even if there was nothing new to be interested in. I'd probably be swearing at Roarkes in a pub in a few hours' time for dragging me up to this cold wet shithole for no good reason at all, but if it was Carson, it was worth a shot.

There was work to do at home, of course. There was Hasina Khalil, my solitary client, who was seeking asylum in the United Kingdom on the basis of her views on sexual orientation, which were about as popular in her native Egypt as a clown act at a funeral. I'd met Hasina Khalil just once, in the visitors' area at the detention centre she'd been in for two months. I'd been expecting a bold young firebrand with piercing eyes, a shaved head and tattoos in unusual places. Instead I'd found a middle-aged lady with fluent, heavily accented English and perfectly groomed hair, shivering and pulling her coat tight around her despite the heat blowing out of the cheap, noisy fan heater pointing right at her. Something about Hasina Khalil didn't quite add up, but she was the only client I had, and the closest thing to a real human rights case I'd worked on in as long as I could remember.

There was Claire's story, too, which I was supposed to be helping with, which I'd promised I'd help her with as soon as I got finished with whatever I happened to be doing at the time and still somehow not got round to it. Five dead girls, and a gang of people traffickers who'd smuggled them into England to be abused, beaten, and murdered. The three different killers were all looking forward to a lifetime of beatings in the comfort of their maximum security prisons. But the traffickers were still out there, and Claire's files were growing, with new pieces slipped into the jigsaw on a weekly basis. She'd been asking me to take a look at those new pieces and see how they might fit in. I was going to struggle doing that two hundred miles away from the files, but my fault for putting it off so long.

There was also the strong possibility of a job, and if I landed it, it would be the first time I'd been able to rely on a regular income since I'd got myself fired from Mauriers, but it was a job that ran against everything I stood for, or at least everything I'd stood for back when I claimed to stand for anything at all. I hadn't so much as mentioned the job to Claire because I knew that was what she'd tell me.

Atom Industries, my potential future employer, was a large multinational chemicals company whose management thought the idea of invoking European human rights legislation to defend themselves against zealous regulators was a wonderfully clever wheeze, and they were waiting for me to get back to them to arrange a date for an interview. And the remains of the cold were stubbornly clinging on like the smell of week-old fish. But the interview could wait, and I wasn't sure I wanted the job anyway, the cold was just a cold, not malaria, there was nothing urgent going on with the case, and it was the only case I had. The hard-pressed, institutionally-abused citizens of London weren't exactly beating a path to my door. There were lists out there, rankings, a league table of human rights lawyers, and I still harboured dreams of making the top ten. I needed something new. Some attention, a client, some money. Maybe Manchester would be something new.

Manchester was like I'd walked straight into a gritty

seventies TV series set on some northern estate full of shoplifters and pregnant fourteen-year-olds. And it was raining, of course. I swallowed painfully past a lump in the back of my throat, shivered, and started walking a little faster. There were a bunch of kids, seven or eight of them, kicking a ball around on the pavement and not really caring if it hit a car or a house. They'd glanced at me as I'd parked my Fiat, and I'd caught glimpses of sharp noses, narrowed eyes, smirks, one set of rodent features among the whole lot of them. The street looked sad and washed-out and somehow like I was seeing it in black and white. I was less than a hundred yards from a police station but I didn't feel comfortable.

The police station was different, though. Bright, modern, all shiny veneers and functioning coffee machines. It was a police station, so it wasn't somewhere you'd go for fun, but from the little I'd seen you'd rather hang around in there than outside. When I asked for Detective Inspector Roarkes the huge, bald guy at the enquiry desk looked at me like I'd asked for a quarterpounder with cheese and said "Haven't got one of them 'ere, lad."

I checked the message Roarkes had sent me. *Folgate Police Station*, it read, and an address in a suburb of Manchester I'd never heard of before now. This was the right place, this was the right time. I texted him: *I'm here. Where the fuck are you?* The reply came thirty seconds later: *Turn around*, so I did, and there he was, grinning at me like he'd done something clever. I nodded at him and turned back to the sergeant at the desk.

"That's DI Roarkes," I said.

He glanced towards Roarkes and fixed me with a stare. "I'm sorry," he replied, with exaggerated courtesy. "How could I have forgotten?" Roarkes might have been a hotshot back home, but he didn't seem to have made much of an impression in Manchester.

Two minutes later we were sitting in a cold room with dirty white walls and battered furniture that looked like it had been dragged in off one of the skips outside. The whole room had a sense of having been left behind by the rest of the station, and I was reminded of all those shabby, tired rooms I'd met Roarkes in before. Maybe Roarkes was drawn to rooms like this. Maybe he did this to them, accelerated the aging process with his grey hair and his yellow teeth and his general air of weariness. Three chairs, a side table, a desk. The table and the desk were covered in notebooks, scraps of paper, torn-up envelopes. Roarkes indicated one of the chairs and I brushed some crumbs off it before I sat down. He might be a long way out of his territory, but this room had Roarkes written all over it.

"Hello, Sam. Journey OK?" he asked, genially enough, when we were both seated.

"What the hell am I doing here?" I replied. I wasn't feeling very genial.

"We've got nothing."

"You've got Carson."

"Yup. But no motive. Nothing on the forensics. Nothing except his car there when it all kicked off, and no one else to point the finger at."

I was a little surprised. Not on the forensics. No doubt they'd just screwed up, or not looked close enough, and they'd come up with something useful when they had to. But the lack of a motive threw me. Sure, he was a "normal guy", Carson, or at least he'd seemed that way when the press were screaming his name from the front page, but now they'd had enough time to dig something up, if there was anything there to dig. You never knew what might piss a man off enough to turn him from regular Joe into a murderer. Tax demand. Speeding fine. Row with the wife.

I'd seen prosecution lawyers get motive for a shooting out of a lukewarm coffee from Starbucks, and it turned out they were right, too. If they couldn't get motive for Carson then maybe the guy was too regular to be true.

"What's this got to do with me, then? Come to think of it, what the hell's it got to do with you?"

He shrugged, the beginnings of a smile twitching at one corner of his mouth.

"You know me, Sam. There's a dozen Chief Constables with my number on speed dial. I go where the interesting stuff is."

I'd asked the question hoping for better than that, but as usual Roarkes was telling me precisely what he wanted to and no more. For a moment I toyed with the idea of asking him again, directly, *Who do you really work for, what do you really do*, but only a moment. If I ever got an honest answer out of him he'd have me lost in a quagmire of police bureaucracy within minutes. I settled for a gentle dig instead.

"Because you're so clever, right?"

He fixed me with a weary glare, a look of near-infinite patience run dry. After a moment, I laughed. He was a miserable bastard and on a good day he looked like he had a year or two left in him at best, but he *was* clever. If I had to choose a cop for my corner, I'd choose Roarkes. I could see why a dozen Chief Constables might do the same.

"And me?" I asked.

"You're here to advise me. You can be my psychological adviser."

I bit back a line about Roarkes needing more help in that area than he could get from me, and just said "What?"

"It's either that or guns-and-gangs."

I stared at him. He didn't look like he was joking. I waited for him to go on.

"Guns-and-gangs. Special advisers into gun and gang crime. It's a London thing."

"This isn't London."

"You're telling me. But if I want to get you helping me here, it's either psychology, or guns-and-gangs."

Helping me. We were, I felt, edging slowly towards an answer.

"Why can't you get one of the locals to help?"

"They don't like me, Sam," he said, bluntly.

I thought back to the bald giant at the enquiry desk. He'd acted as though he didn't know who Roarkes was, but then he'd looked up and seen him and acted like he knew precisely who Roarkes was and would have been happier if he didn't. The way I'd have acted if Brooks-Powell had strolled past right then. Roarkes had swooped in and taken over their investigation, which was liable to make him unpopular. But not that unpopular, surely? There had to be something more to it.

He was still talking.

"And I don't trust them, either."

He looked away, shutting down a subject I'd have been interested in exploring.

"What about your guys at the Met? What about a psychologist, a real one, if that's what you need?"

I was pushing here, with Roarkes' foot hard against the door. But he'd called me up and asked me to drive two hundred miles in the rain. The least he could do was to tell me why. He gave a long, slow, impatient sigh, without any real malice behind it.

"The unit's gone, Sam. My old unit, at the Met. They disbanded it, gave everyone new jobs, I was travelling so much it didn't make sense having a bunch of people answering to me when I was only there one week in four."

"And the psychologists?"

"I don't like psychologists."

I nodded. He didn't like psychologists. Topic closed. He continued.

"So I've got you instead. You're my adviser. I'll get you in to speak to people, if I can, but remember: you're not a cop. While you're here, you're not even a lawyer."

Not being a cop suited me down to the ground. Not being a lawyer wasn't the end of the world. But *adviser* was vague, even for me.

"So what do you want me to do?"

Roarkes smiled.

"You need to meet someone, Sam."

Serena Hawkes was young, black, more like the rest of the police station than Roarkes, more London than Manchester. Maybe more New York than London, I thought, as I took in the Vera Wang glasses and the Prada shoes and the cheekbones that could cut glass. She smiled at me and shook my hand. Angular. Intense. Unusual.

Carson hadn't appointed a solicitor. Carson hadn't said a thing since he was arrested, except his name and his address and whether his wife and son were OK, which he'd asked a dozen times a day for the first three days, and then gone silent. The family didn't have any preference, they didn't know any criminal solicitors, they'd never had the need, so when Serena Hawkes had been appointed to represent him nobody had objected.

Thing was, he hadn't said a word to her, either. Nothing to the police, nothing to his lawyer, and eventually the local police had realised they were out of their depth and needed a specialist in getting people talking. Someone had called in Roarkes and Roarkes, for reasons he still hadn't fully explained, had called in me, even though it was clear Carson already had a solicitor and from what she was saying, Serena Hawkes had no intention of giving him up.

"I told Serena you were good at this sort of thing."

"And what sort of thing is that?"

"Don't be modest. You know what I mean. The old Sam Williams magic. You get people talking."

I started to laugh, and then I realised he wasn't joking. I'd had some luck in the past, cases cracked, silences broken, lies untangled. A decade back I'd had a photographic memory, a great job at a great firm, a passion for justice, and ambition to match the passion, but a lot can change in a decade. I still had the photographic memory, when it felt like working. Maybe Roarkes was mistaking luck and the remains of a freak-show act for talent. If I was half as good as he thought I was I wouldn't have been sitting at home waiting for him to call and summon me to Manchester. And if he expected me to snap my fingers and get Carson spilling his guts, he was going to be disappointed. I stared at him, and he stared back, unreadable.

Maybe he was right. It hadn't just been luck. I'd been good at this, in the past. Good at sniffing out that one key fact that unlocked a man, that put him in a place where he was better off talking to me than lying or keeping his mouth shut. Good at getting under his skin. And certainly better than the blunt and aggressive Roarkes.

I'd been feeling quite positive about myself and my abilities for all of three seconds when I noticed that twitch at the corner of Roarkes' mouth again, and the truth hit me. Roarkes knew precisely how good I was and where my limits lay. Roarkes also knew the state of my client list and how significant a case like this could be. Roarkes was doing me a favour, I decided. All this bullshit about "getting people talking" was for the benefit of Serena Hawkes, who probably needed a better reason for another dog in her kennel than Roarkes feeling tender-hearted.

"Fact is," she said, "we've got nothing to lose."

You might not, I thought. I'd just driven two hundred miles into the rain and the cold and my car had probably been stolen or separated into a thousand little pieces by now. I bit back the words and tried being polite instead.

"You really don't mind this, Ms Hawkes?"

"Not a bit. As long as you don't forget this guy's my client you and I are going to get along fine. Do your thing."

If I can remember how, I thought. And then something more pressing came to mind.

"So who's paying me?"

They looked at one another, the ageing DI and the sharp young lawyer. They hadn't thought of that. Maybe money wasn't an issue for a jetsetting police officer and a designer solicitor, but it was a burning one for me. Even a big-name case had to bring some cash with it, because Claire couldn't go on funding my less-than-extravagant lifestyle forever. Fuck it. I stood up and looked around for my coat before I remembered I hadn't taken it off.

"Sit down."

Roarkes had an authority that came from decades of dealing with crooks and bullshitters. I sat down. I couldn't have driven back to London anyway. I'd shoved two days' worth of painkillers and cold remedies down my throat on the journey up, and now whenever I looked in the same direction for more than a few seconds, things started moving around.

"We'll sort something out," said Roarkes. "Won't we, Serena?"

She nodded. She didn't look happy about it, but she nodded. The nod was good enough for me. I didn't plan on sticking around long enough to run up much of a fee.

The corridors might have been stuffed full of the same uniforms you saw all over the country, but I was getting the feeling this wasn't your usual police station. Carson's cell, for a start. It had a slab of smooth, authentic-looking wood instead of the regular door with a hole in it and a metal slider to slam shut when you wanted to scare the living shit out of some teenager who'd passed out on the street with half an ounce of damp weed and a stupid grin. There was a bed in there, sheets, a pillow. And we were looking at the guy through a glass window which, Roarkes assured me, was a one-way thing. I needed the assurance, because Carson didn't stop staring at the window he couldn't see through the whole time I was watching him. Average height, blond hair, that weather-beaten look that comes from spending all your spare time on a bike or chopping wood, good-looking enough in an everyday sort of way. Apart from the fact that he was in a cell charged with the murder of two police officers, there was nothing unusual about Thomas Carson. And he kept staring at me, so long and so intent I had to ask Roarkes, again, if he could see me. Roarkes rolled his eyes and shook his head and I believed him, but that didn't make me feel any less nervous. Something about this guy didn't add up. Carson might not be talking, but he wasn't dumb.

While we were watching three men walked by, officers in uniform. They fell silent as they approached and kept their eyes straight ahead, down at their feet, on each other's faces. Anywhere but us. As they turned the corner I heard laughter and a muted curse. Roarkes wasn't wrong. They didn't like him here.

"What have you done to piss them off?" I asked him. Roarkes was good at pissing people off, it was his specialty. It looked like he'd outdone himself.

He shook his head, as if he didn't know and it was just some strange peculiarity of Manchester cops, and then he started explaining anyway.

"Look, they don't like me being here. I get that. It's

their patch, and whenever I get called in it's like the Chief Constable's turned to his own men and told them they're not even smart enough to catch Jack the Ripper."

I thought about that, for a moment.

"Jack the Ripper never got caught."

"They didn't have me on the case," he returned, quick as lightning. "But it's not just that. It's two of their own. Two officers dead, and they might not have been Folgate police, but they were police, and it hurts. They were all set to beat the living shit out of Carson when I turned up and stopped it, and they took it like I was on his side."

"Are you?"

"I'm not on anyone's side. I just want to find out what the fuck's happened here and get home. So the whispers started right away, and when they found out I'd been talking to the suspect's lawyer, those whispers just got louder."

I turned towards Serena, who responded with a tight little smile as Roarkes continued. "I had a nice little chat this morning with the superintendent upstairs. As far as he's concerned, the sooner I'm out of Manchester, the better."

I could see their point. Roarkes had a habit of making himself unpopular, but he couldn't have done any more here if he'd tried. A thought struck me.

"You haven't made any effort at all to turn it around with them, have you?"

He grinned at me. "Why the hell should I? I don't like cops who beat up suspects. They make everyone's life harder. Juries don't like it when a suspect gets wheeled into court covered in police-administered bruises. Defence lawyers love it, though. Right?"

I nodded.

"So no," he continued. "I haven't made nice with the lovely policemen. I don't like them and I don't give a toss if they don't like me. Now take a look at Carson."

Looking at Carson took a couple of minutes. I might be allowed to talk to him in due course, apparently, once the formalities had been dealt with and I'd been processed as a psychologist or whatever the hell Roarkes had decided to call me. Roarkes wasn't guaranteeing anything, given how popular he was in Folgate, but talent or no, I wasn't getting Carson to talk if I couldn't get the other side of that glass window. I shrugged and reminded Roarkes and Serena that they were paying, and Serena started to say something, but Roarkes got in first with a "Don't worry. It'll be sorted soon enough."

Carson hadn't had much on him when he was found. No murder weapon of course, because that had been recovered at the scene. Wallet, cash, cards. Three photos. A young boy, four or five years old, his son, Roarkes told me. An older family shot, a husband and wife, smiling, two sullen-looking kids, and no one knew who they were or what they were doing in his wallet. Some people on horses halfway up a mountain that sure as hell wasn't in Manchester.

"What's this?" I asked, holding up the last one, and Serena finally piped up with something useful.

"Argentina," she said. "He lived there for a while. Ran a business out there."

I turned to Roarkes.

"And you didn't think it was worth telling me this?"

He glanced briefly at his feet, which was as close to an apology as I was likely to get. Argentina. There might be something in that. South America. Cartels, maybe, or was that further north? Argentina was Nazis and the Falklands and angry people setting fire to tyres. Nothing obvious to connect it with a shooting in the north of England, but it was off the beaten track, and that meant it was worth looking into.

Roarkes handed over some copies of the photos and I shoved them in my back pocket. I didn't think the photos we had would tell me very much. The photos we didn't have were a different story. Carson was a married man, and there was nothing anyone had found to suggest the marriage was anything other than happy. There was a photo of his son, a photo of a family of strangers, and a photo of a bunch of middle-aged tourists, by the look of it, halfway up a mountain in Argentina. But not a single photo of Carson's wife.

Which, I thought, was something else worth looking into.

3: Little Dead People

WE WERE BACK in Roarkes' temporary office, the three of us. Serena Hawkes was sitting down looking bored. She'd been through all this already. It wasn't like she was learning anything new. Roarkes was fiddling with some bits of plastic on the little side table.

"We reckon it played out like this," he said, and picked up one of the bits of plastic. Lego. He was holding three red Lego bricks stuck together in one hand and he was talking to me like this was a totally normal thing.

"So this is his car, right."

"What?"

"This is the Fiesta. Carson's car."

As a reconstruction, it left a bit to be desired, but I thought I might as well play along until I figured out where he was going.

"And he's driving along here."

He put the bricks down on the table and slid them forward. It struck me that Carson's Fiesta was blue, not red, but I didn't think that really mattered.

"It's about ten minutes from his house, little country road, usual bends and hills but nothing special about it. Milton and Ahmet are in their car here."

He set down another clump of bricks. These ones were white. Sergeant Fiona Milton and Constable Naz Ahmet were the officers who'd been killed. They'd been driving a standard police Volvo. At least Roarkes had the colour of the car right this time.

"They come up behind Carson and flag him to stop. He stops—"

"Why?"

"Why what?"

"Why did they flag him down? Was he on his phone or something?"

"No. Someone called in, described the car, colour, plates, driver, said he was carrying a weapon."

Another minor detail no one had bothered filling me in on.

"Who made the call?"

"We're still looking into it. One of those pay-as-you-go phones. It's taking a while."

Maybe. Maybe Roarkes had another "psychologist" sorting that out for him. I doubted it. And if someone *had* called it in, why hadn't they come forward by now?

"And why the hell did a pair of unarmed cops stop someone who they thought might have a weapon?"

"I asked the same thing. Apparently it was all a bit vague. They thought maybe it was a knife or something. And it's not like they're swimming in armed police out there in the sticks."

I nodded. They probably needed all the armed police they had just to handle the kids outside the police station. Meanwhile, the whole thing had been triggered by a call and no one knew who had made it.

"Carson stops on the left here, the road's a bit wider, room to pass by, not so bendy. Milton's driving, she stops about twenty yards back on the other side of the road. So here they are."

Roarkes was certainly well-equipped. He had two Lego figures, now, the old-fashioned ones with the yellow heads you could twist round and pull off and shove a helmet on if you wanted to assemble your very own Village People. Except one of the heads wasn't yellow. It was brown. Roarkes was using a brown Lego figure to represent a dead Asian police officer. I looked up, briefly, at Serena

Hawkes, and wondered what she made of it all. She saw me looking and grinned, not a tight smile this time, but a wide, on-the-verge-of-laughter smile, softening her face, smoothing away the corners. I grinned back. Roarkes was too old to know any better.

"The way we figure it, Milton approaches, Carson gets out of the car, walks round the back of it and comes at her from behind."

"Why did she let him get out of the car?"

"How's she going to stop him?"

I nodded. Roarkes continued.

"So she turns around to face him and he fires at her, hits her right in the forehead, she's dead."

He pushed the yellow-faced Lego figure down so it was lying on its back next to the red bricks.

"Ahmet doesn't have time to react. Carson's already there with him, makes him turn around, shoots him in the back of the head."

"Christ!"

I couldn't help it. The press had been calling it a cold-blooded execution from the start, but I'd assumed that was just their way of drumming up some excitement. I'd have put money on a difference of opinion that had got out of hand. The brown-headed Lego figure was face down next to the white bricks. This was about as cold-blooded as it got.

"Witnesses?"

"The actual event?" Roarkes shaped his hand into a gun, made a popping noise and shook his head. "No one saw a thing, no one heard a thing. But a minute or two earlier, yeah, we've got something."

"What?"

"Not much. Couple of cars on the same road. Wanted to get past. Got waved back by Ahmet, had to drive back the way they'd come. Both of them remembered Carson's blue Fiesta, one of them even had the plates, and of course that matched the vehicle that had been called in about the weapon."

"Who were they?"

"One local. Farmer, driving a trailer-load of sheep around. He's the one who remembered the plates. Other one's a woman from Bolton, she's got a friend with her in the car, just been to one of those posh country pubs for an overpriced meat pie and they've both overdone it on the mulled wine, so I was surprised she could remember anything at all."

"Anything else?"

"Not really. Farmer thinks he passed another car after he got turned around. Land Rover. Dark blue. Remembered a bit of the plate on that one as well, but not enough to get a match. Whoever was driving it, they'd have been turned around, too. They'd have been the last ones there, before Carson started shooting. But no one's come forward."

"And the woman?"

"No use. Even when she was sober she didn't have much to say for herself. Saw the Fiesta, that would have stuck in her mind because of the police. But she didn't even spot the farmer."

I looked back at Serena and she shrugged. Hardly the strongest foundation for a case, but that was all good news as far as she was concerned. She didn't have to make a case. She just had to pick holes in one.

I looked down at the table. Why had Carson walked round the back of the car in the first place? Maybe Milton had asked him to open the boot, check there was nothing in there. Maybe there had been something in there, something Carson had dumped before the police caught up with him two days later. So he'd shot her, and that hadn't been planned, it had just been necessary, and because he'd shot her he had to shoot Ahmet, who would have seen the whole thing. All very quick, though. Ahmet hadn't had a chance to call for assistance. The last communication from either of them was Milton saying they'd stopped the Fiesta and were going to investigate.

So it was possible, the way Roarkes was setting it out with his little Lego men. It was awkward, it had to be squeezed and twisted round a bit to fit it in, but it was certainly possible, and if the bodies had been found the way Roarkes had described them, it was probably the only way it could have happened. I ran through everything we had, everything Roarkes had, or Serena, it was difficult to tell who was on what side at the moment, or whether there were any sides at all. There wasn't much. Maybe getting a real gun-and-gangs expert in wouldn't be such a bad idea.

"Too much to hope for CCTV around there, I guess?"

Roarkes smiled wearily.

"You'd imagine, wouldn't you? Why would anyone bother? As it happens, we thought we'd got lucky, because there's a track up to a farmhouse right where it happened, and there's cameras on the house *and* cameras on the track, but the bloody farmer doesn't bother switching the bloody things on. Says there's no point because he's not got anything worth nicking, there's no one around to nick it, and if there was the police wouldn't care so why should he?"

I laughed, then coughed, then laughed again, my head a fog of painkillers and phlegm. Roarkes went on.

"You should hear the guy. Miserable bastard. Not that I can blame him. You think it's cold and wet round here, just wait till you get up there. Course he didn't see anything, and he didn't hear the shots either, because he's half-deaf."

This was useless. They really had nothing at all.

"What about Carson? Anything unusual?"

"No. Runs a local business, outdoors stuff, small time. We've got some people looking into it, but there's nothing particularly exciting."

I thought about that. Local business. My experience of local business was confined to dodgy landlords and small-time drug dealers, but that was just the circles I moved in. I imagined it was a little calmer out here. Not the kind of thing you'd expect to lead to murder, really. But then, people could get upset about all manner of things. I remembered a case back at Mauriers, where I'd started my career, a guy who'd gone crazy and stabbed the woman who ran the nail bar across the road because her customers kept blocking his drive. Small-time business could make some big-time enemies. And, I reminded myself, that wasn't confined to other people. David Brooks-Powell had started at Mauriers three weeks before I did, and never bothered hiding his disdain. Brooks-Powell was Knightsbridge, St Paul's School, tall, good-looking, reasonably clever, very smooth and extremely arrogant. He'd gone on to get me fired, although I hadn't exactly made it difficult for him. But Mauriers had been a good firm with high profile clients, and I'd been a young, ambitious lawyer, when I started, at least. Right time, right place, it wouldn't have taken much for me to hurt David Brooks-Powell, physically. Could I have killed him? I couldn't say no for sure.

Now it was probably the other way around. Not six months back I'd sued him and the firm, and Mauriers had settled, but not before David Brooks-Powell had been utterly destroyed in that courtroom. Beating Mauriers had turned out to be a temporary bounce on a long slow fall, but beating Brooks-Powell was something I wouldn't have given up for all the Carsons in England. Mauriers had downgraded him from partner to "part-time consultant", which meant they'd fired him but didn't want to spell it out. Right now, he'd probably be quite happy to put a gun to my head and pull the trigger.

I smiled at the thought. Roarkes coughed, and when I looked back up at him he was glaring at my left hand. I followed his gaze and saw why. I'd picked up one of the figures, without thinking about it, without even meaning to, and I'd been sat there grinning away like a fool and rotating the head of the figurative corpse of Naz Ahmet between finger and thumb. I put it back down on the table and forced my brain back to Carson.

"Nothing else?"

"Nothing. The science boys are still looking, but if they were going to find anything they'd have found it by now."

I nodded, and turned it all over again. Forensics. No photo of the wife. Layout of the cars. Land Rover. Argentina. Local business. Any one of those things might be the key to what had happened. But I doubted it.

The key to what had happened was sitting there in that cell staring through a blank bit of wall at people he couldn't see, and I'd have given anything to crawl inside Thomas Carson's head and find out what the hell had happened to Fiona Milton and Naz Ahmet.

4: Through the Window

IT WAS TEN in the morning and I was standing in the bathroom going back over an uncomfortable telephone conversation with Claire and trying to shave in a cracked, warped mirror that made one of my nostrils look twice the size of the other. A good night's sleep would sort me out, Roarkes had informed me, and directed me to the nearest First Quality Inn where he'd booked a room for me but not bothered suggesting we meet up for a drink or something to eat. There was no one in Manchester I particularly wanted to see, with the possible exception of Serena Hawkes, who had shaken my hand and left as soon as she politely could, so I'd ended up in my room, alone, with a slice of something that claimed to be a pie but seemed to be filled with the same sludgy pastry that held it together, two cans of warm beer, and a cold, empty bed. I'd sat on the bed and called Claire, and she'd told me breezily that everything was fine and she had some new information for me to look at.

"What, about Carson?" I'd asked, before I could stop myself, and there had been a pause during which I remembered that Carson wasn't the only thing in the world and that Claire had absolutely nothing to do with him anyway.

"No," came the reply, still breezy, but with that faint trace of an edge I recognised from all those times I'd ended up on the wrong side of the conversation. "No, of course not. Tanya and Xenia."

Tanya and Xenia were two of the murdered girls. Tanya and Xenia weren't their real names, nobody knew their real names, but there had been some suggestion in court that one was Russian and the other was Greek. The police had referred to them as "Girl A, Blonde" and "Girl B, Brunette", and once the killers were locked up, they'd closed the files and moved on to something else. Claire had been clawing her way towards the truth for two years now, alone and with the grudging consent of her editor, writing real, printable stories every week or two to keep him happy. She'd decided the girls deserved names.

"OK," I said. "That's great. I'll take a look as soon as I get back."

"Right. Thanks."

There was still an edge to her voice. She might have got used to that *as soon as*, but it didn't mean she liked it.

Somehow or other I managed to change the subject, and a few minutes later we said our goodbyes in a tone that was frosty, but not quite frozen. I put down the phone and tried to remind myself why I'd come up in the first place. I needed a big break. I needed a major case, and I needed it now, not in six months or two years or whenever it decided to pop up. Carson was here, and now, and so big that even hanging off the ends of Serena Hawkes' four hundred dollar shoes I might make a name for myself. Fearless lawyer, scourge of the corrupt, defender of the righteous. Not a guns-and-gangs expert. And not a psychologist either; the helpful people who ran Folgate Police Station had seen right through that before I'd even presented myself for processing.

I'd marched up to a little second floor office just before leaving the station, as per Roarkes' instructions. There was a woman sitting behind a window, middle-aged, dark roots showing on her blonde hair, a look on her face that suggested she'd woken up chewing on a lemon and only taken it out to knock back a pint of vinegar. She glanced up at me as I approached, alerted by my footsteps, and then returned to the contemplation of her fingernails.

"I'm with Detective Inspector Roarkes," I said. I forced a smile onto my face and tried to look as friendly as I could, but she wasn't budging from those nails.

"I know who y'are," she replied. "Sam Williams. Human rights lawyer."

She said those last three words in the same way you'd expect someone to say "child abuser" or "estate agent".

"Yes," I replied. "I'm here to help in the investigation. I'll be working as –"

"Legal adviser. You're Roarkes' legal adviser."

I'd been about to say "psychologist", like Roarkes had told me to, but she looked up now, finally, and her face was set. I nodded, instead, and filled in the forms she'd pushed towards me. So I was Roarkes' legal adviser, which I knew he wouldn't be happy about. If the closest I was getting to Carson was the wrong side of that glass window, I couldn't see myself getting the facts out of him any time soon.

Alone in that hotel room, with the evening stretched out in front of me like a bed of nails, and desperate for something to do, I'd called Maloney. Ex-gangster, ex-crime lord, ex-client, one of those clients whose connection with human rights was difficult to put your finger on, but when you've lost your job, you take what you can. Maloney and I were bound together by a complex web of favours and gratitude so multi-layered I doubted either of us knew who owed what to who any more. When I'd engineered his acquittal nearly a decade earlier, the result of a half hour of Sam Williams magic and two pints of bitter in a dirty Walthamstow pub, that was just me doing my job. What counted came later, when I told him which of his staff he could trust, and who was running dirty drugs and underage girls behind his back while he tried to keep his operation as clean as organised crime could get. On the other side of the beam, Maloney was handy with information, and he'd looked after me more than once when I'd got myself into more than the usual amount of trouble.

Maloney was retiring, going straight, but he'd been retiring and going straight for the last ten years and there was always something keeping him in. He joked that they'd be engraving *Almost Ex-Crook* on his headstone, but I could tell the bastard didn't mind one bit. And nor did I, because while he was still in, Maloney knew crime and criminals like I knew North London kebabs. But even he couldn't help with Carson. Only Carson could help with Carson, and Carson wasn't in the helping mood. Maloney said goodbye with a friendly expletive, and it was just me, and that empty bed, and too many hours left in the day for me to call it a night.

Just as I was starting to make peace with the silence and the occasional burst of noise from the evening traffic, my phone rang. I didn't recognise the number, but I answered it anyway, and there was Hasina Khalil, wailing and wheedling and about as welcome as an American in Pyongyang.

The lesbian story was, as I'd suspected, Grade A bullshit. Hasina Khalil had decided to come clean.

"I am sorry," she said, "but it was not like I have much choice."

"Why are you here, then, really?" I asked. She'd already spent two minutes ranting incoherently about the dangers of Egypt and how the English people loved the gays and the lesbians so much that she had to pretend to be one if she wanted to survive.

It was all about politics, she told me. Her husband had been a high-ranking official in the Mubarak administration. He'd been seized "by the scum that took over", and executed, and things didn't look good for

Hasina Khalil if she was sent back to Egypt.

I sighed and told her that if she wanted me to represent her, she'd have to be straight with me. I'd decided not to dump her even while she was still ranting, because a lying client was better than no client at all, and politics wasn't a bad angle, either. Of course, this whole story might just be another lie, but I had ways of finding things out.

I put the phone down and sat on that cold, narrow bed. The best thing I could have said about the whole day was that my Fiat had been where I left it when I emerged from the police station, with no obvious new marks on it.

Despite Roarkes' pronouncement, there was no chance of a good night's sleep in the First Quality Inn. I woke, periodically, with an uncomfortable sense that there was something there in the room with me, something sliding in through the window and curling malevolently under the curtain towards me. Morning brought a thin, watery sun and a familiar headache, but my cold, at least, seemed to have faded into the background. The room was freezing, though; the chill outside had crept in overnight despite my turning the thermostat up to maximum. The double glazed window (blown, view over dual carriageway) hadn't put up much resistance, but that wasn't particularly surprising since the damn thing wouldn't even shut. There was half an inch of clear air when there should have been solid glass, and I thought this might account for the weird images that had come to me during the night. I tried to wedge a towel in there but the angles weren't right and it kept falling back into the room. I called down to reception to ask about getting the window fixed or changing my room, and the woman who answered sighed in frustration, like it was all my fault, and told me they'd see to it as soon as they could but that they might not get to it today. It sounded like something she'd had to say before, many times, a flat, bored tone that suggested they probably wouldn't get to it this week, either. "Quality" clearly meant something different up here.

I decided to give up on the shave. Better stubble than blood. I backed out of the bathroom, four steps to the bed, sat down, and asked myself again what the hell I was doing here when just a couple of hours away in London there were any number of rooms that offered complete insulation from the outside world.

The big break. That was it. Crack Carson, get famous, surf that fame for the whole week and a half it lasted all the way to a client who would pay me more than Hasina Khalil and lie to me a little less, and wouldn't make me hate myself as much as Atom Industries would. Top ten. There were other things, too. There was Roarkes, who I liked, however rarely I might show it, and who'd clearly gone to some trouble to get me in. And there was Serena Hawkes. I was intrigued by Serena Hawkes, there was no point denying it, unless it was Claire asking, of course, in which case I'd deny it as long as I had breath. I'd looked her up when I'd got to the room (it was *the* room, not *my* room, because I didn't intend to be in it any longer than I had to), using the slow and intermittent hotel wifi. Serena Hawkes wasn't top ten, either. She was no closer to it than I was. But she seemed to be taking Carson in her stride. She'd made half a dozen TV appearances already – local, which was why I hadn't seen her before she walked into Roarkes' office with her designer face and her surprising smile – and even on the tiny smudged screen on my phone I could tell she'd handled them like she'd been on TV all her life. I couldn't figure Serena Hawkes out at all. What did she really feel about my involvement, about her own relationship with Roarkes? There was something in the way she'd acted at the police station. Alert, involved, but somehow removed from it all. Like she was in control, but in control from a great height and a vast distance. It was certainly an interesting style.

Finally, there was the silent man in the cell, the everyday guy with two dead cops on his hands. He was the challenge, he was the test I'd set myself. Was I a fool or a genius? A fool would be wasting his time. A genius would open up Thomas Carson's head like a book. Carson was facing the distinct possibility of life in prison, and he wouldn't talk to a soul.

I might not have got past the glass yet, but I wanted him talking to me.

I reminded myself of that two hours later, sat outside the room, watching through that big glass window, with Roarkes in there opposite the guy and Serena Hawkes smiling quietly to herself beside him. Carson hadn't said a word. I wasn't sure he'd even opened his mouth. Since they'd walked him to the interview room from his cell straight past the hidden window, he could hardly have missed it. He knew someone was watching him. Maybe that was why he wasn't talking.

Today's adventure at Folgate Police Station hadn't begun well at all. Roarkes had strolled past the custody desk, Serena and I trailing in his wake, and the custody sergeant had jumped up instantly, as though she'd been waiting for this very thing, had run around us and stood in the corridor blocking our path.

"We need to speak to Carson," Roarkes had announced, sharp and authoritative. The authority hadn't meant a thing. The custody sergeant, a woman with short dark hair and an elfin face who might have been pretty if she'd chosen to smile instead of glowering at us, had shaken her head.

"I don't think so. I'm the custody officer and you have to go through me. I've got to consider the suspect's fitness to be interviewed."

Roarkes turned and stared at me, and then at Serena. I shrugged. Serena, who'd looked like she was on the verge of a smile herself, wiped it clean off her face the moment Roarkes' eyes fell on her, and copied my shrug.

"She's right, you know," she said. "Police and Criminal Evidence Act. Code of Practice."

I nodded. I'd used PACE myself, often enough, to delay an interview, to make things awkward enough for a custody sergeant to give up and send my client home. Roarkes turned back to the woman standing in front of us, who had watched our short discussion in silence.

"What's your name?"

"Sergeant Forrester, sir."

"What grounds do you have for suspecting that the suspect may not be fit for interview?"

She smiled, now, suddenly, and I was right, she was pretty. Still hard as nails, though. The smile didn't reach her eyes. This was all about Roarkes. Sergeant Forrester didn't give a damn about Carson's fitness for interview.

"He's not talking, is he, sir? There's a good chance we could class him as mentally vulnerable. I mean, does he even understand what you're saying to him?"

"He understands all right," growled Roarkes. Sergeant Forrester was undeterred.

"And even if he does, I have to consider the risks to his mental state."

It was like she'd learned the bloody code off by heart. Which suited me down to the ground. Time to start paying my way.

"You do understand, Sergeant Forrester, what the implications might be if Detective Inspector Roarkes is not permitted to interview the suspect?"

She turned towards me, head tilted to one side.

"Tell me, Mr Williams."

"You know PACE, Sergeant Forrester. And this isn't a burglary or a bit of joyriding. If there's any chance this delay could hinder the investigation – well, we can always go and talk to your superintendent about that, can't we?"

The smile dropped away, and for the first time she faltered. I'd taken a chance – for all I knew the super would take her side, take the same side as everyone else in Folgate, by the look of it, which was whichever side Roarkes wasn't on. But I was gambling on this little stunt being Sergeant Forrester's own game, and at a certain point, the game stops being worth playing.

She took a step to the side and nodded.

"OK," she said. "You can go in. Not you," she barked, pointing at me and clearly bitter at being beaten. "You're not a psychologist, you're not Carson's lawyer, there's no provision for you to be in there at all. You can wait outside."

I opened my mouth to argue, and then realised she was right. I had nothing.

"Is there any way I can see what's happening in there?" I asked. "CCTV or something?"

There were cameras all over the station. It was a fair question, but Sergeant Forrester just laughed.

"Most of the cameras don't work. The one in the canteen does, and in medical, but you can't interview him there. You can watch through the window."

So I stood there and watched Carson ignoring Roarkes and his own lawyer, unable to hear a word they were asking him but not really caring. They could have asked him the capital of Mongolia or whether he took sugar in his tea. Either way, they weren't getting any answers.

After fifteen minutes of this Roarkes decided to take a break, and he and Serena left Carson alone in the cell.

"Can we do this somewhere else?" I asked as Roarkes closed the door behind him, and Serena shrugged. I knew what that shrug meant. It meant he hadn't said a word to anyone for days, no matter where he'd been or who'd been watching him. We could move to the Black Hole of Calcutta for all the good it would do. Thomas Carson still wouldn't talk.

A suspect not talking isn't exactly an unusual thing. When the other side has nearly enough to send you down, the worst thing you can do is open your mouth and hand over that last little detail to complete the job. I advised half the people I acted for to keep their mouths shut, and I'd have given the same advice to the other half if they hadn't already blown it. But with Carson it was different. The police had close to nothing. All he had to do was say "I didn't do it," and sit quietly in his cell until they gave up and sent him home. And he wouldn't even say that.

But I couldn't think of any other way to get him talking. I left them to continue their one-way conversation, and retired to Roarkes' office to think.

There were crumbs on the desk and the usual heap of papers. I sat down and closed my eyes, and waited for a flash of inspiration. After five minutes I caught myself dozing off to visions of Sergeant Forrester slapping me across the face with a copy of the PACE Code of Conduct.

I blinked, frowned, blinked again.

When Serena and Roarkes broke off for a second time, just twenty minutes after they'd restarted, I was waiting for them. I walked past them to the cell door and put my hand on its handle and Sergeant Forrester was up and shouting before I'd even started turning it.

"What the hell do you think you're doing? You can't go in there."

I turned to her, slowly, concentrating on keeping my face straight and my voice level.

"I think you'll find I can, Sergeant Forrester."

She shook her head and I continued.

"You need to read your PACE, Sergeant. You've stood there and told us Thomas Carson's vulnerable or mentally disordered, and sure, he's got his lawyer here, and I'm certain Detective Inspector Roarkes means him no harm, but where's his appropriate adult?"

Sergeant Forrester turned and looked behind her, as if expecting to see an appropriate adult walking towards us. There was no one, of course.

"Don't be ridiculous," she said. But she didn't try to back it up. It was another long shot I was playing, but I was starting to feel the odds moving my way.

"And really, it's not up to you, is it, Sergeant? You know the rules. If the detainee is mentally disordered or vulnerable, he can't be interviewed without an appropriate adult present. Since the suspect's wife isn't here, and I am, and I'm not employed by the police, I'm perfectly placed to perform that role."

She hesitated, and I played my ace.

"If you take a look at my client history, you'll see I'm very experienced in dealing with vulnerable people."

There was an element of truth to this, but the vulnerable people were more likely to be my clients' victims than my clients. I was counting on Sergeant Forrester not going into that kind of detail.

She frowned at me, started to say something, stopped, started again.

"I'll have to think about it. Got to get Carson checked out by the doctors, first."

The smile was back on her face. She didn't care about Carson's mental state any more than she cared about mine. Roarkes had left it to me so far, but now he stepped in.

"We've already been through that. We need to do this

interview now. Do you want more dead cops on your hands while we fanny around poking Carson's head?"

Sergeant Forrester stared at him, and I rejoined the fray.

"And if Carson's own lawyer isn't objecting..."

We turned, the three of us, to look at Serena. I could see her mulling it over, and for a moment I wondered why. Then she nodded and I decided it had just been for show. She was local, after all. She'd have to carry on working with these people long after Roarkes and I were gone. There was a long silence, twenty, maybe thirty seconds, and then Sergeant Forrester gave a short, fast nod.

"OK," she said, and stomped back to her desk.

"Good work," said Roarkes. "But don't forget what you're here for. You're not a lawyer now, Sam."

No, I thought. I wasn't a lawyer, and I wasn't a psychologist, either. I was an *appropriate adult*, and that meant I could join in the interview as much as I damn well wanted. I was back on a high. Maybe a few minutes of carefully-chosen questions would be enough to prise open Carson's mouth.

Fifteen minutes later I was thinking there wasn't a crowbar in the world tough enough to prise that mouth open. Roarkes had gone in all guns blazing, threatening the kinds of punishment traditionally reserved for witches and traitors. Carson had turned to me with a *see what I have to put up with?* look on his face, and for the briefest of moments I'd thought *Yes!*

But that was all I got. The look. An instant later the look was gone, replaced by the blank, uninterested mask of a man watching something he didn't care about happening to someone he didn't know, and I was left wondering whether I'd seen it at all. Clearly just sitting there with Roarkes wasn't enough.

"You and I know Detective Inspector Roarkes is exaggerating for effect, Mr Carson," I said, smoothly. "But I have to tell you, as someone with your interests at heart, that he's not exaggerating as much as you might think he is. If you can't dig yourself out of this I don't reckon much for your chances."

He turned to me. The mask didn't move. I continued.

"Because you'd think someone who's killed a couple of cops is going to have an easy time of it in prison, wouldn't you? I mean, the screws aren't going to be too friendly, but they never are. But the other cons, they'll like you, won't they? They'll all want to be your friend."

Nothing. That was a leading question. I'd expected a nod, at least. That was the idea. Leading question, basic response. Get him used to that response. Get him engaging with me. Then move on. But I hadn't even got the basic response.

"And at first, for a week, maybe two, that's just how it'll play, Mr Carson. But give it that week, and they'll start looking at you and wondering if you really are as tough as a cop-killer should be. You'll be the man with the crown, and every other con in there is going to want to take it off you. And I've got to be honest, Mr Carson. You don't look that tough to me."

A hint of a shrug, I thought, although again it was gone so fast I might have just imagined it. A twitch in a shoulder. A phantom hint of a possible shrug. That was the best I was getting out of Carson.

"Let's go to the pub," said Roarkes, as we watched Carson making the same walk back to the same bright little cell. Serena nodded, and I asked him to repeat himself, because coming from Roarkes a social invitation was as likely as a warm and loving hug. I agreed, warily, caught between my desire for a decent drink and the suspicion of someone who knew Roarkes well enough to know nothing with him was ever straightforward. When we got there and I saw the huge windowless dirty-walled formica-tabled plastic-chaired hangar of a place with a tiny bar in the corner and the grease so heavy in the air you could almost feel it pushing you down, I saw the rub: even the First Quality Inn might have something better to offer. Serena took it in her stride. This was probably her local.

"So, you've had your little chat with Serena's client," said Roarkes, his voice neutral, his expression deadpan. "Helpful sort, isn't he?"

Serena sighed, wearily. She'd known Roarkes for a matter of days, and already she was sick of him. I fought back a grin and shrugged instead, silent, a passable imitation of Carson himself. Roarkes nodded.

"Any ideas?" he asked.

I shook my head.

"Might as well go home, then," he continued. "No point wasting any more time. You gave it your best shot."

I was astonished.

"Hang on," I said. "I've only just got here. Let me get my feet under the table, figure out what's going on."

I stopped, wondering what I was talking myself into, thought about backtracking, and remembered how much I needed to make something of this.

"Give me a chance," I finished, somewhat desperately.

Roarkes nodded. That was what he'd been hoping for. Serena was drinking and watching in silence.

"So what do you need?" asked Roarkes.

I didn't know. That was the problem. I couldn't unlock Carson without a key, and I had no idea where that key was. Unless…

"What's with the wife?" I asked, and Serena lifted her face from the vodka tonic she was slowly sipping to fill me in.

"Nothing," she said. "Nothing you wouldn't expect. Poor woman's scared out of her mind, doesn't understand what's happened, keeps saying things like *he's never shot anyone before, you know*, trying to keep it together in front of her lad, not really doing a great job of it."

"Any point me seeing her?"

Serena shrugged.

"Not really. But if you want to, knock yourself out."

"Go if you want," said Roarkes. "But go easy. Don't upset the woman. I'll send someone along to keep you company."

5: Into the Forest

I DIDN'T WANT the company. But I didn't fancy any more time in the room with Carson until I knew a little more about him, and Roarkes wasn't sending me alone. I wasn't stupid enough to think the wife would give me anything obvious. But there might be something indirect, something personal, something I could use to chip away at Carson's mask and get under his skin. I almost admired him, the way he sat there, locked inside his own head, just watching the world roll on outside and refusing to take part. But there had to be a reason. The guy wasn't catatonic, he wasn't in shock, the doctors had checked and double-checked and there was no physical reason for his failure to interact. He was eating and drinking, putting one foot in front of the other when he had to, using the toilet. The *vulnerable person* line was bullshit, but they'd started it. Thomas Carson was no more vulnerable than I was. He just wasn't talking. There had to be a reason.

The chaperon Roarkes had assigned me was a detective constable named Gaddesdon. It took nearly an hour to get to the house, from Manchester, but Gaddesdon seemed delighted at the chance to get out of Folgate for the afternoon.

"Never been round here," he said, big round face beaming at the patterns of sunlight and shadow bouncing off the hills. "Nice, in't it?"

After the rain and misery of the city, I couldn't disagree. The last vestiges of my cold seemed to have disappeared, although that might have had something to do with the triple dose of ibuprofen I'd knocked back before we set out. The place was called Bowland. The Forest of Bowland, although I couldn't see much evidence of trees.

"It's not that sort of forest," he explained, still smiling. For all the glamour of the Criminal Investigation Department he was still more *Police Academy* than *Life on Mars*. Folgate hadn't been willing to help Roarkes, to deploy any of their "local resources", but they'd been happy enough to lend him Gaddesdon. I thought I could see why, It took me a few minutes to get used to his vowels, that grunted "u" and short, sharp "a", a harsher version of the sounds Serena Hawkes made. Most of what he said was either irrelevant or so blindingly obvious there was no point saying it at all. But when it came to the Forest of Bowland, Detective Constable Gaddesdon had done his research. "Kings and that used to go hunting round here. That's what forest meant in the old days."

I nodded. I didn't care. It looked nice enough, and Gaddesdon was driving, so I could look as much as I liked. Turned out fifteen minutes was as much as I liked. It was the countryside. It was pretty. That was it.

The Carsons lived in a small detached cottage in a village called Bursington, nestled between gently rolling hills, with a brook running through the middle of it, and a pub, and no doubt a wicker man for burning strangers who asked too many questions. They'd lived there for three years, straight off the plane from Argentina. Place like this, I imagined they could call themselves locals in another fifty.

Sally Carson was a dark-haired, fine-featured woman in her mid-thirties with one son, one husband, and a touch of colour in her face from the years in South America, and apart from the tiny detail about that husband being stuck in a cell accused of murdering two police officers, there was nothing unusual about her in the slightest.

That wasn't strictly true. There was something. I just couldn't put my finger on it. She was nice enough, fidgety, nervous, but that was understandable. She recognised Gaddesdon from the police station, which meant she clearly had an eye for detail and a half-decent memory, and she was happy to talk to me even though she understood Serena Hawkes was her husband's lawyer and she didn't quite understand what my role was.

I thought I'd be honest, for once.

"I don't really know myself, Mrs Carson."

She relaxed a little and laughed.

"Call me Sally, please. Fancy a brew?"

We stood in the kitchen while she made three cups of tea and I tried to explain why I was there and what I was hoping to achieve.

"I want to get enough out of Thomas to be able to show the police they're wasting their time with him, Sally. But he won't speak to me."

She turned to me, a teaspoon in her hand, and the bright, flighty nerves were gone. She just looked tired, wasted, done in. Exhausting, surely, keeping up the front, acting like everything was fine, or would be fine once a misunderstanding or two was sorted out. And she'd been doing it for a week.

"He won't speak to me either. He's allowed calls, he's even allowed visitors, but he won't speak to anyone. Anything at all that you can do to help us, well, it would be wonderful."

There was no point going through the same questions the police had been through. She knew nothing about the shooting and could think of no reason her husband would be involved in something like that. Instead I asked her about her son, Matthew, and saw her face light up at once, as I'd known it would. There were photos of the boy on the walls and the mantelpiece and the kitchen table, the same tousle-haired four-year-old in school uniform and swimming shorts and a football kit several sizes too big.

Sally Carson talked about him for ten minutes straight, with only the slightest of interruptions and prompts, but she didn't give me anything I could use.

I steered the conversation onto Argentina, where Sally had met Thomas on one of the wilderness trips he ran down there. She was from Manchester, she explained; he'd been raised in Blackburn. Two English northerners in the hills of Patagonia, with horses and campfires, glaciers and mountain lakes, bitter tea and the smell of charred chorizo. They'd hit it off immediately, and since Sally had no job waiting for her back home, she'd decided to stick around for a while. A while turned into thirteen years, during which time they'd moved in together, got married and had a child. But they'd never intended to stay there forever. Once they started thinking about schools, they realised it was time to come home.

"What was it like out there?" I asked. It was about as general a question as they got, and Sally Carson could take it pretty much any way she wanted. She assumed I was asking about parenthood, doctors, that sort of thing. I gave her a couple of minutes on the state of Argentina's public services, and guided her onto business.

"Oh, the tourists were still coming, even after the recession. It was cheap, for them. Of course the money we made didn't stretch so far when we decided it was time to come back, but it could have been worse. And by then Thomas was his own man, sole proprietor, he could make all the decisions, and I think that was good for us, good for him, it meant he'd been able to move the business in the right direction."

"So he'd been working for someone else before, right?"

Sally turned to Gaddesdon, a confused frown on her face.

"I thought you knew all this. I'm sure I've already told

the police all of this."

Gaddesdon looked over at me, lost, and I apologised.

"I'm sorry. It's just, anything at all we can use to get through to your husband, you know, it might help get him out."

She nodded.

"He'd been in business with a local guy. Partners. They put in half the cash each, and Alejandro had some land for the horses, and Thomas did most of the work, so it seemed a fair split. It worked well enough, but they did argue, especially when Alé…"

She stopped, and looked at me closely for the first time.

"Do you really need to know all this, Mr Williams?"

I paused for a moment and remembered what Roarkes had said. *Don't upset the woman.* But I was there and he was in Manchester, and I was there for a reason. Find the fact. Get under Thomas Carson's skin.

"It's Sam. Please. And I'll be honest with you, Sally, I have no idea what I need to know and what I don't. The more you tell me, the more chance I'll hear the one thing that'll help me get through."

She pulled out a stool and sat at the kitchen island. Gaddesdon and I remained standing, and I tried to think myself into that still, steel-walled room in my head where I could remember every word she said, where the photographic memory I'd once possessed replaced the tired blur I tended to live in these days. Easier said than done. The brain wasn't what it had been, and I was still a little light-headed from all the painkillers. If I ended up remembering half it would be a decent result.

"OK then, Sam. His partner, Alejandro, he was a nice enough guy, but he was lazy. And – you know where Patagonia is, right?"

I gave a half-nod. It was in Argentina. It was in the

middle of nowhere. Like the Forest of Bowland, I thought.

"Well it's huge. It's in the south of the country and it extends right up to the border with Chile. And sometimes things happen round that area that shouldn't."

Borders can only mean one thing.

"Smuggling," I said. It wasn't a question. Sally nodded.

"Anything and everything, and it goes both ways. There's big business taking the right things through the mountains."

"What did this have to do with Thomas?"

"Well, it wasn't Thomas, it was Alé. He was a local, he grew up in the area, he had friends up to all sorts. Friends in the police who ignored things they didn't want to see, friends at the borders who didn't search people they knew they were supposed to search, and friends crossing from one side to the other five or six times a week with something they shouldn't have hidden away in their pockets or their backpacks or their saddlebags."

"So Alejandro wanted to help out his friends?"

She nodded again. There was an expression on her face I couldn't quite put a name to, her own unique border country where wistful, frustrated and resigned all met.

"Just lending them horses, letting them camp in the field, it wasn't much and it wasn't like anyone was getting hurt. But Thomas didn't like it, and neither did I. We were foreigners. We hadn't grown up in the area. If people started looking into us – well – I just didn't think...."

She tailed off. She didn't need to spell it out. The local guy would get the benefit of the doubt. The foreigners would get the benefit of a cell and whatever the Argentine equivalent of porridge might be. I nodded for her to continue.

"So they argued about it. Alé said OK, it would stop, and the next week Thomas turned up with a tour group who'd been booked in for months, and five of the horses were off with Alé's friends halfway to Chile. Thomas had to borrow some horses off a neighbour and he was furious, and Alé promised nothing like that would ever happen again."

"Don't tell me, the same thing a week later?"

"No, a week later something very different. Alé disappeared."

"What?"

"He disappeared."

I turned to Gaddesdon, who was looking out of the kitchen window at the sheep in the field next door with the expression of a man who'd never seen a sheep before.

"Did you know about this?"

He shook his head. "Doesn't mean Roarkes didn't, though. Doesn't tell us much, the detective inspector."

Typical Roarkes. The man kept his cards so close to his chest he probably couldn't read them himself. Mind you, I thought, if Gaddesdon was the one person I had to confide in, I probably wouldn't be telling him much either.

"I did tell the detective inspector," Sally continued. "I told him all about it. Alé disappeared and no one's seen him since. The local police spoke to Thomas and me. Some of them were his friends. They sent out search parties into the mountains, they looked everywhere. They found two of his horses on one of the mountains, some food in the saddle bags, but no sign of Alé."

"So what, he had an accident?"

"That's the most likely explanation. The conditions out there can be treacherous. Seems bright and sunny one moment, and the next there's a blizzard and you can't see two feet in front of you."

"And the business?"

"Alé had an ex-wife and two kids in Buenos Aires. She'd married again and she'd done a lot better second time round, so they were living on this huge estancia and playing polo with businessmen and diplomats. A million miles away from Alé and the life he led – he had led. They weren't interested in him or his business. They had him declared dead, and said Thomas could keep the land and his share of the business."

"So it all worked out quite well for you?"

She glared at me, shocked. The shock looked genuine.

"Alé was our friend! There might have been difficulties, but we were close. He helped Thomas get on his feet, and we helped him when he was struggling himself. So no, Mr Williams. It didn't work out well for us at all."

"Sorry," I said, wincing at the Mr Williams. But only on the outside. Sally Carson might have been shocked, but she was defensive as well, more than she needed to be, and in my experience people who were more defensive than they needed to be usually had something to hide. And I was annoyed. It wasn't Sally Carson I was annoyed at, but she was the one in front of me, so I didn't really mind that glare. The one I was annoyed at was Roarkes, who'd told me he wanted my help, who was at least pretending he wanted my help, but hadn't bothered to mention the missing business partner. *Everything's normal,* he'd said, Serena Hawkes had said, they'd all said. Normal bloke, normal wife, normal life. I might not have cracked Carson but there was a crack in that *everything's normal* line, a crack so big you could stuff a whole dead Argentinian in it.

"Anyway, it's true, Thomas did well with the business after that. Brought in enough so that we could sell it and buy this house when we decided to move back home."

"And Thomas runs an outdoor business here, too, is that right?"

"Yes. We both do. I do the admin. Thomas takes

people climbing, in the hills, camping, does trips with schools, stag weekends, some of those corporate bonding activities."

It all sounded innocent enough. But everything sounds innocent the first time you hear it.

"And how's business?"

"Unbelievable. I never realised so many people would be happy to sleep outside in the rain. We can barely keep up with demand. We've bought one of the fields just outside the village – you can see it, that one, there, with the oak tree in the corner."

I looked as directed. It was a field. There were sheep in it. Couple of farmhouses and a barn or two nearby. Could have been any other field within fifty miles.

"We've got to get rid of the moles first, it's a bloody nightmare, full of hills and holes, they've been digging the place up for years. Then we'll try for permission to use it for camping, and maybe some training exercises, perhaps a little climbing practice for the younger ones."

It was a field. It was horizontal. I had to ask.

"What would you climb?"

"You can get a decent outdoor climbing wall cheap enough. But that's down the line. We need to get rid of the moles and get permission for the camping first. And yurts. People like yurts these days. Makes them feel like they're not in England any more."

It would take more than a yurt to make the place look like Mongolia, I thought, but there wasn't much point saying it. And, I'd noticed, she was speaking in the present tense. Sally Carson didn't seem to think her husband's arrest was going to stop him putting people in yurts.

I hoped she was right.

6: Half a Million Ifs

WE DROVE BACK in silence. For about three minutes. After three minutes, with Bursington dropping out of sight in the rear-view mirror and the rain still holding off, Gaddesdon started talking, and talking was pretty much all he did for the next hour. Roarkes, Manchester, Carson, the police station, his ex-girlfriend, his pool club, his mates, his favourite beer and favourite curry, the guy couldn't stop. And the whole time I was trying to think, because there was something about Sally Carson that didn't seem right to me, and I couldn't figure out what the hell it was.

The defensiveness, I decided. The way she'd reacted when I said the wrong thing about the business partner. The expression on her face when she spoke about him. There was something there. It could be anything, maybe she and this Alé had been sleeping together, maybe the relationship had been more than just business. And in that case, even if it wasn't important, it might have made her nervous. Or it could be something big. If Alé had carried on helping his smuggler friends and Carson and his wife hadn't been able to talk him out of it, maybe they'd tried to stop him some other way. I remembered the photo the police had found in Carson's wallet, the men and the horses. All pale and young and very European, except one, the guy at the front, a little older and darker and wearing a hat with the ease of a man who wore that hat every day, not just when he was on holiday. A decent-looking guy. Not that Carson was ugly himself. But who knew what might have happened way down in Patagonia. I'd drop

Alé's name in next time I spoke to Carson. And Roarkes hadn't seen fit to mention it to me. I'd have a word with him, too.

He kept me waiting for fifteen minutes while he finished a meeting, which didn't do much to improve my mood. The moment he walked back into his office I was on my feet, finger in his face, asking why the hell he'd thought the small matter of the suspect's ex-business partner disappearing in suspicious circumstances wasn't worth telling me about.

He placed his hand around my finger and guided it gently down to my side, smiling the whole time. Like most of Roarkes' smiles, it said a lot, and what it said wasn't all that friendly.

"I said I'd told you everything that was important, Sam," he said, still smiling. "This wasn't important."

"How do you know?" I asked. I wanted to shout it in his face but it came out petulant, the pitch and volume falling as I spoke so that even as the words dropped out I could tell I sounded more like a moody teenager than a crusading lawyer. That wasn't the impression I'd been aiming for. At least Serena Hawkes wasn't there to see it.

"Because the Argentine police are satisfied the chap's dead, they're satisfied he died in an accident, and they're more than satisfied he has nothing to do with our case."

I sat back down. The Argentine police could be as satisfied as a cat with a dead bird. So could Roarkes. I wasn't, but it looked like I was on my own.

"So what else have you got?"

I couldn't believe he was asking me that. What did *I* have?

"Oh, we've got leads coming out of our ears, haven't we, Gaddesdon?" I replied. Gaddesdon opened his mouth and stared at me like I'd just grown an extra head. I carried on.

"We've got nothing, Roarkes. If you say Argentina's a dead end then I guess I'll have to let it go. Have you looked into Carson's business?"

"No. Anything there?"

"Nothing I can point to, no. But he's got a field and he wants to build stuff there and you know how uptight people can get about their villages."

Roarkes laughed, suddenly and unexpectedly, and the anger I'd brought into the room with me dropped away.

"I'll get some people to look into it. Gaddesdon, you can make a start, can't you?"

The DC nodded and trotted out of the room like he'd been told it was time for his walk. I liked Gaddesdon, he seemed a nice enough guy, but I didn't think he was going to be the one to crack this case. And I didn't see much sign of Roarkes' other "people".

"How's Claire?" asked Roarkes, as he handed me a drink. We were in a different pub this time, more beer, less bacon and eggs. The beer was a local one, and after a tentative sip I found, to my relief, that it wasn't bad at all. Earlier, in his office, Roarkes had played me a recording of the call that Milton and Ahmet had responded to, the call that had sparked everything off. Forgettable, all of it, the voice, the accent, even the words. And they still hadn't found the phone. So it was beer and crisps with Roarkes in a half-decent pub, and for a little while this was Roarkes at his best and we could have been anywhere.

I eyed him carefully. Even at ease, Roarkes always had another question hidden under the one he was asking. I decided to answer them both.

"Yes, she's fine, thank you very much, and no, she doesn't know how bad business has got."

Roarkes raised one eyebrow, like he didn't approve, and shrugged, like he didn't know what I was talking about. Even his body language had undercurrents. A smile came unbidden to my lips, and I asked after his wife. I'd never met Mrs Roarkes, all I knew about her came from the occasional complaint from her husband, the month she'd risen at six every morning to pick the egg out of his egg-and-cress sandwiches, the mysterious disappearance of the cigars he kept for a special occasion, the way his scotch seemed to taste weaker every time he drank it. Mrs Roarkes wanted to prolong her husband's life as far as possible, even at the cost of his enjoyment of it.

"Mrs Roarkes is supposed to be visiting her sister in Winchester," he said, a frown on his face.

"Supposed to be?" I asked, and he leaned forward and lowered his voice to a whisper.

"If I bolt all the doors and get uniform to search everyone in here, I'll bet you fifty quid they find her in a wig at the next table noting down every drink I've had."

He sat back, wearing the look of someone who'd just solved the *Times* crossword in ten minutes and was about to tell me how, and I rolled my eyes. Sometimes I wondered if Mrs Roarkes really existed, or whether she was just a convenient fictional wife for the man Roarkes pretended to be. And then he'd say something surprising, a moment of concern, a rare flash of honesty, her loneliness, her long, slow recovery from breast cancer, the constant, nagging worry over money, even when there was no need for it.

We slid, from there, into easy recollections, people we both knew, cases we'd worked and the fools on the other side. Most people saw the miserable Roarkes, the man who made their lives hell until he got what he wanted. This was the other Roarkes, the rare one, the one who told jokes with actual punchlines that weren't about bankruptcy or divorce or a dead pet. The one who opened up, a little, not like normal people open up, but Roarkes wasn't normal anyway. The one who brought a bonus pair of whisky chasers back from the bar when it was his round. For about forty-five minutes I forgot about the fact I was two hundred miles from home on a case without any decent leads. And then he asked me what I thought of Sally Carson, and I opened my mouth to tell him she seemed straight enough and certainly pleasant enough but there was something about her that jogged something somewhere else and made me feel just the tiniest bit uneasy, but before I got a word out Gaddesdon was stood in front of us, panting like a dog on a hot day.

"What brings you here, detective?" asked Roarkes, and Gaddesdon grabbed for the nearest drink, which was mine, took a great gulp, wiped the sweat off his forehead, and stopped panting long enough to speak.

"It's Carson, sir. He's tried to top himself."

Carson was in hospital. He wasn't dead, he wasn't going to die, but what he'd be like when he woke up was anyone's guess. He'd tried to hang himself using a belt, a chair and a door handle, and the moment Roarkes heard about the belt he changed from a calm, middle-aged detective inspector into a spittle-flecked madman.

"How the fuck did the stupid fucker get hold of a fucking belt?" he roared. We were standing in the corridor next to the custody desk back at Folgate, just a dozen gleaming tiles from the cell Carson had come close to dying in, and four police officers were stood in front of Roarkes looking at their shoes and trying not to catch his eye. I'd slipped into the station behind Roarkes and Serena, flashed the card they'd given me at the woman on the enquiry desk, and she hadn't batted an eye. The same woman had made a big show of checking that same card when I'd arrived that morning, nearly ten minutes of grunting and staring at me, but right now the officers of

Folgate Police Station had more on their minds than pissing off a lawyer from London.

"You!" shouted Roarkes, pointing to the big bald sergeant who'd greeted me the previous day. "You're in charge, right?"

"I'm the shift custody sergeant, sir," he replied, with a quiet deference that didn't suit him.

"So what the fuck was Carson doing with a belt?"

The sergeant didn't blink. "Didn't have it when I booked him in, sir. Don't know where he got it."

"And he did this himself?"

"Reckon so."

Roarkes narrowed his eyes. I could see his jaw trembling. I didn't think he was buying it.

"What's your name, sergeant?"

"Tarney, sir. Sergeant Russell Tarney."

"Sergeant Tarney, you were the fucking custody sergeant when Carson first arrived, and you were the fucking custody sergeant when he tried to kill himself, and you're telling me you don't know how he got hold of the fucking belt?"

By the end of the sentence Roarkes was all but screaming, and even though I was standing behind him and well away from the direction of his anger I found myself flinching. Tarney just nodded. The guy hadn't been particularly friendly when I'd first arrived, but I felt sorry for him now. I was impressed by his stoicism, too, his complete refusal to react, like an iceberg with an angry ship bouncing off it. I'd never seen Roarkes like this. I hoped I never would again.

Gaddesdon was running around the place looking for access records and CCTV footage. Serena Hawkes had rushed in looking shell-shocked, her face blank, her head turning from side to side whenever anyone spoke, like she knew something was going on but couldn't figure out where. One of the constables took her to Roarkes' office to make her a cup of tea. I joined her a few minutes later, with Gaddesdon and Roarkes just behind me.

Gaddesdon couldn't find anything, and somewhat surprisingly, that wasn't his fault. The CCTV wasn't functional – just like the CCTV at the farm, commented Roarkes with more than his usual growl, while Gaddesdon confirmed what I'd already guessed: it had been down for a while, but it took a lot more than a while for things to get fixed in Folgate. Sergeant Forrester had hinted as much that morning. They'd spent all their money building the place. There was nothing left to actually run it. The access records weren't much better. The last people to see Carson had been me and Roarkes, and I knew neither of us had given him a belt.

"You know, I was never searched," I pointed out. Roarkes nodded. It didn't sound like anyone had been searched, except for Carson himself, and he'd only been searched on arrival, which meant as long as he could find somewhere decent to hide it, he might have had that belt for up to a week. If there had been a belt at all. If Folgate's friendly officers hadn't decided to take matters into their own hands.

"What kind of a fucking police station do you run here?" shouted Roarkes, again, and this time it was Gaddesdon I felt for, as the only local officer in the room, but hardly responsible for what had gone wrong. Gaddesdon looked sheepish and didn't try to answer, and Roarkes collapsed into a chair, sighing but calmer already.

Serena Hawkes had finished her tea and was twirling a strand of long dark hair about her fingers and shaking her head.

"I don't understand it," she said. "I'd never have thought. I mean, it wasn't like he told us anything. But whatever it was, we could have helped, right?"

I shook my head.

"I don't think Thomas Carson wants our help, Serena," I said, and she stared at me for a moment before picking up her empty cup and focussing on that.

"So how does it work round here?" I asked Gaddesdon. "Big station, lots of cops. You have half a dozen who take turns on custody desk, right?"

Gaddesdon shook his head. "No. There's only two. Russell Tarney and Elaine Forrester. If neither of them are around then we just kind of fudge it, do what needs to be done between us, make sure everything's OK."

I heard a muttered "for fuck's sake" to my side, and saw Roarkes shaking his head.

"This Tarney, what's he like?" I asked. Gaddesdon shrugged.

"OK, I suppose."

Shrugs and shakes. The most high-profile criminal suspect in the country had just come within an inch of taking his own life and all we had were shrugs and shakes. I thought I'd look into Elaine Forrester, with her elfin face and her PACE and her generally obstructive behaviour. But I thought maybe I'd look into Tarney first. My brief sympathy for the man had evaporated quickly enough. I didn't like him. Someone round here had done something very wrong indeed, and I wouldn't have been at all surprised if it were Russell Tarney.

I'd left my car in the same spot as the day before. The police station had its own car park, and Roarkes had assured me I could use it, but I'd seen what happened to vehicles identified as frequent visitors to police stations, and I didn't fancy tracking down bits of my car all over Manchester. Besides, the boys were out on the street again and they hadn't done any harm last time.

"Right, lads?" I ventured as I strolled past them.

Nothing. Not even a nod. They could smell the London on me.

I'd left the building with Gaddesdon, who was so completely unshaken by Roarkes' outburst that it was like it had never happened. Without thinking to ask why I wanted to know, he'd told me when Tarney's shift would be over and described the Peugeot he'd be leaving in, but better than that he'd told me which pub he'd be in later that night and what time he'd be there. Russell Tarney, apparently, had a routine, and when he wasn't on duty he could be counted on to spend the best part of every night knocking back pints in the Bull out on Blackmoor. Being shouted at by Detective Inspector Roarkes wasn't the kind of thing that would shake that routine. The Bull, clearly, was a pub. Blackmoor was "a bit of Manchester", added Gaddesdon, in a way that made it clear it was a bit of Manchester he didn't think much of. I moved my car forward and across the road so I had a better view of the station car park, and now the boys on the street were watching me. I couldn't blame them. It was obvious enough what I was looking at. Maybe they thought I had a bomb in the car. They were going to be disappointed.

My eyes were fixed firmly on the car park, so the sudden tap on the passenger window took me by surprise. I glanced up, expecting bad news. Serena Hawkes was there, looking at me and smiling. Even through the rain-streaked window in the semi-darkness I could tell that smile wasn't real. I leaned over, opened the door and she climbed in.

"What are you waiting around here for, Sam?"

I thought about it for a moment, and decided what I was planning on doing probably wasn't appropriate behaviour for a Solicitor of the Senior Courts of England and Wales.

"Just thinking. Are you OK?"

She nodded.

"Because, you know, you don't look OK."

She smiled again, a little more realistically this time, and I gave myself a mental pat on the back for making her feel that tiny bit better. Serena Hawkes, I decided, was looking at all this the wrong way. She was seeing the glass half-empty when from where I was sitting it still looked three quarters full.

"You know this isn't your fault, right?"

She nodded. "I know. It's just – this case. I was so happy when I landed it, you can't imagine, I was over the bloody moon."

I could imagine it all right. I'd spent most of the previous week imagining it. She went on, the words tumbling out so fast I couldn't have interrupted her if I'd wanted to.

"And then it turns into nothing, just some bloke sitting there with his mouth shut and the police running round in circles. I mean, they got killed, two of them, I was expecting all kinds of grief, all kinds of shit from them, and shit from the police I know how to handle. But instead no one knows what the hell's going on, and the pricks at Folgate are the usual pricks but Roarkes is bloody *helping* me, and I've *still* got nothing done, I've messed up so badly they've had to call you in, and now this."

She trailed off. The smile was gone. She turned away from me, but not quickly enough to hide the fact her eyes were glistening.

"Serena. Listen to me, Serena. This isn't your fault. There's nothing you could have done that would have made this turn out any different."

She nodded, but she didn't look round. I carried on.

"And it's not like he's dead. Chances are he's going to be fine. And the police have nothing. Which means eventually they're going to let him go, and it doesn't matter what you did or didn't do, you'll be the lawyer whose client was plastered all over the news and then released before he even got to court. Have you started thinking about going for the press?"

She turned to look back at me, a frown on her face. It was a nice-looking face, I decided. Unusual, sure. But definitely nice-looking.

"What do you mean?"

"I mean suing the bastards. They're ripe for it. Bound to get something out of one of the tabloids, at least."

She nodded. "Yeah. I guess we'll cross that bridge when we come to it. Got to get him out first. That's if he ever wakes up. And he might want someone else acting for him after that. At least they can't pretend he's not vulnerable now."

She smiled, a sad little smile, and sighed. Her glass wasn't just half-empty. It hadn't seen a drop for years.

"I don't know, Sam," she continued. "I don't remember the last time I had a client I actually wanted."

I didn't know Serena Hawkes well enough to say if she was an empty-glass person or this was just an empty-glass moment. I took a chance, reached across, put my hand on her shoulder. She looked at it for a moment, and I thought she was going to object, but she didn't. Instead she let it rest there, shivered, slightly, and settled down into the seat. Neither of us said anything for a minute. We looked out of the windscreen at the gloom and the drizzle and let the silence grow around us, feel its way through the car, build a space where nothing could disturb us.

A van sped past, sending a spray of dirty water against my window, and my hand felt suddenly wrong where it was. I couldn't work out whether moving it away would make it worse. She turned to me and smiled, an uncertain sort of smile that only added to my unease. And then she reached up, took my hand off her shoulder and held it between both of hers.

"Thanks."

I smiled back at her. She hadn't let go of my hand. I wasn't sure what was going on, but I certainly didn't hate it.

"Well, I do my best," I said. I couldn't think of anything else to say. Defusing the moment. I didn't want the moment defused, or at least I didn't think I did, but my mouth was ahead of me on the same track it always picked when it went off on its own, glib, comic, deeply unserious.

"Really. I feel better now. Much better. You're a good man, Sam Williams."

"You don't know me well enough to say that."

Shit. What was I saying? This wasn't glib. This was worse. And she was buying it, too.

"Hmmm," she said, and glanced quickly away. I could still see the smile, though, reflected in the windscreen. "Well, if we're going to be working together, don't you think we should get to know each other a little better?"

Just in case I hadn't got the message, she squeezed my hand between hers, hard. I got the message. I couldn't speak.

"What do you say, Sam? Fancy a drink?"

Her phone rang. She flinched, reached into her bag with her other hand, checked the display, switched it off. But the moment was gone. She'd turned back towards me and released my hand, and the smile was just a nice, normal, friendly smile between colleagues. If I said no, if I was too busy or too tired or desperate not to miss *Game of Thrones* then that would be fine, it was just a nice, normal, friendly drink between colleagues that hadn't happened today but might happen tomorrow.

But the words were still there, and the shiver, and the smile, and the squeeze. If I said yes, it was a lot more than a friendly drink between colleagues.

She was still smiling. Half a million *if*s passed through my head in the second it took me to open my mouth and say something.

"Sorry. I'd love to. But I've got a client back home who's going to be deported in the morning if I don't get off my arse and do something for her. Tomorrow, maybe?"

The smile didn't flicker. I wouldn't have liked to take Serena Hawkes on at poker. She took my hand again, gave it a gentle pat, turned and opened the door, and I wondered whether I'd done the right thing. Nothing was happening in the Hasina Khalil case and she had no more chance of being deported in the morning than I did. I could have told Serena about Claire, but something was stopping me, and I didn't want to look too closely at what it was. I could have told her the truth, that I was planning on spending the evening watching Russell Tarney. I could have forgotten about Tarney and Claire and spent the evening with Serena Hawkes, who seemed, as she walked away from me through the rain, to be sensitive, intelligent, interesting and far from unattractive.

It was too late for any of that now.

7: Tarmac

I DIDN'T HAVE time to dwell on it. It was dark enough now for the streetlights to come on, but they hadn't – either the council was broke or the streetlights, probably both. As luck would have it a car was turning the corner by the police station as Tarney came out of the main door, headlights straight onto his face just long enough for me to be sure it was him.

Even from that momentary glimpse I could see Tarney wasn't a happy man. He was caught mid-snarl, a snarl at the lights shining in his eyes or the memory of Roarkes screaming at him in front of all his colleagues or the world in general – Russell Tarney seemed the kind of man who didn't need much excuse for a snarl.

Maybe the snarl was his default expression. He was out of uniform, in jeans and a thick black coat that might have been hiding anything from spandex to a shotgun.

Then Tarney was gone, and a battered green Peugeot was nudging its way out of the car park and onto the road. The boys on the street had vanished – once it was clear there wasn't going to be any action between Serena and me they'd given up and headed off. I turned the key and started to follow.

Manchester was busy and Tarney was heading right into the middle of it. Christmas markets, even though it was barely November, road closures, half the world on its way home from work and the other half on its way to a bar. There was so much traffic on the road that not being spotted by Tarney was easy, even for an amateur like me.

Keeping track of him was something different. I'd lost him by the time I hit the half dozen shops and restaurants they called China Town, and I pulled into a taxi space to work out where I was and where he was going. By the time my phone had woken up and told me, Tarney and his Peugeot were long gone. It didn't matter. I knew where he was headed.

There was a moment's concern, when I pulled into the near-empty car park in Blackmoor twenty minutes later and saw no green Peugeot there, but then I spied it in the cul-de-sac across the road. Blackmoor didn't seem so bad, despite Gaddesdon's dismissive tone. The bits I'd noticed in the glow of the streetlights looked comfortable enough: quiet, wide pavements, tidy terraces and good-sized semis. And those streetlights were glowing, unlike the ones in Folgate.

The pub wasn't as quiet as the car park, fortunately, or Tarney would have spotted me the moment I walked in. He was sat with two other men, three pints on the table, all bald and fat and all looking like they'd stepped straight out of an audition for a low-budget gangster movie. I headed in the direction of the slot machine and then veered off to the bar, where I ordered a pint of bitter in my most inconspicuous accent, but made the mistake of saying "please". The barman stared at me for a moment before turning to get a glass. People didn't say "please" round here when they ordered a drink. There was a sign next to the bar that said "No Weapons, No Drugs, No Figting". I decided not to point out the missing "h".

There was an ancient-looking jukebox next to the slot machine, grinding out the dying bars of a Bowie number, and in the background the usual ambient pub noise of muttered conversation, glass on wood, doors opening and closing from time to time. I took a seat at a table in the corner furthest from Tarney and kept my eye on him.

"Major Tom" floated into silence, and no one bothered to pick a new tune. I sipped at the beer. It was dark and weak, local brewery, stupid name. For a few minutes nothing happened, and then my phone rang. I looked down and saw it was Maloney. I couldn't take the call, not without raising my voice and drawing attention to myself. I didn't want to risk walking out to take it, either. I hit the big red IGNORE button and hoped Maloney could wait.

The door beside me opened and a woman the size of a small car staggered out, giggling. I hadn't even noticed the door. Ladies toilet. I was sitting outside the ladies toilet, and, I noticed as I glanced to my left, just a few feet from the gents. No wonder this was the quiet end of the pub. The phone started to ring again and this time I found IGNORE without even looking at it.

I looked down at the beer and decided it wasn't worth another sip. I got up and walked back to the bar, and ordered a pint of lager. I didn't say "please" and I didn't comment on the fact that I was only a quarter of my way through my last drink, and this time I didn't get any stares.

Someone fed a coin into the jukebox and it cranked back into life, some awful eighties soul I couldn't even bring myself to feel nostalgic for. One of Tarney's drinking partners got up and ambled towards me, and for a moment I thought I was about to get my head kicked in. Then he opened the door to the gents and I breathed again.

Half a dozen teenagers walked in. Fifteen years old, I thought, sixteen tops, but the barman didn't blink when they asked for their beer and vodka. They brought a bit more noise in with them, and even though they had that same feral look I'd seen on the kids by the police station they still made the pub seem friendlier. I took a sip of my lager and glanced back at Tarney.

Tarney wasn't there.

I felt a hand on my shoulder and turned. The reason Tarney wasn't at the table drinking bitter that tasted of piss with his cannonball-headed friends was that he was standing next to me, looking down at me with an expression that mixed sinister smile and angry snarl and was much nastier than the sum of its parts. I swallowed.

"Sam Williams," he said. It wasn't a question. I nodded anyway.

"I know why you're here, Williams," he said, and I thought I might as well say something, because if he knew I suspected him I didn't have much to lose.

"Wait, Sergeant," I said, but that was as far as I got, because at that point he leaned down and whispered in my ear.

"I don't give a fuck what you think you know, Williams. You don't know anything. You and your mate Roarkes. We don't want you here. Now get the fuck out of my pub before you find yourself waking up next to Thomas Carson."

I could smell his breath, the beer, the sweat glistening on his head. The words hammered at me. *Fook. You don't know anything. Fook.* I swallowed again, and nodded. He didn't move, still bent at the waist with his mouth next to my ear. I nodded again, stood, took a quick gulp of my lager and walked quickly towards the exit. I glanced behind as I left. Tarney was already sitting back with his friends, his beer in his hand, laughing at something one of them had said.

Outside it was still raining, and it was cold, but not cold enough to explain the way my hand shook as I unlocked my car. I swore silently. I'd allowed myself to be bullied by some fat bastard of a cop, and there was nothing I could do about it. The shaking was over soon enough, but I could still feel it inside me, a cocktail of rage and humiliation, at Tarney for threatening me, at myself for failing to stand up to him. What was I afraid of? What did I think he was going to do to me, in a pub, in public, with witnesses? I pictured the witnesses, Tarney's friends, the barman, the teenagers. I remembered the sign at the bar. I'd probably done the right thing.

Right now I was tired and cold, and stuck outside in an endless drizzle. What I wanted was a whisky, but there was no way I was going back in the Bull to get one. I opened the glove compartment and found the emergency cigarettes where I'd put them a few months back. "Emergency" was probably a little strong. Every now and then, once a month or so, I really wanted a cigarette. If I couldn't find one, that was an emergency.

I got out of the car and lit up, because I knew if I smoked inside Claire would still be able to smell it days later with the windows open and the air conditioning on full blast. I fished out my phone to look at the time and remembered the call from Maloney. He wasn't the type to call without a reason. I was about to hit the call back button when I heard a shout.

"What the fuck are you still here for?"

I looked up and saw three figures walking towards me. The pub door was still falling shut, so they were little more than black shadows against the light, but I didn't need to see their faces to know who they were.

"Just having a smoke," I said. Surely even Tarney couldn't have a problem with that.

The pub door closed. There was a little light in the carpark, spilling in from the road, just enough to see that Tarney did, in fact, have a problem with that. He was a couple of yards away, a yard, right in my face, his mates behind and either side of him like a pair of henchmen in a Bond movie, and his problem was rapidly becoming mine.

"Bollocks you're having a smoke. You can have a

fucking smoke anywhere. You're spying on me, aren't you?"

"No. Seriously. I was just having a smoke."

"Where is it, then?"

I looked down at my right hand. It had been there, the cigarette, I was sure of it, I'd only lit it a minute earlier and taken, what, two, maybe three drags, reached down for the phone, where the hell was it?

There. I could see it still glowing on the wet tarmac. I bent down to pick it up.

A second later something hard was driving my face into the back of my head. The pain was excruciating, like something had gone seriously, permanently wrong, but even as it shot through me I was trying to figure out what had happened and worrying about what was coming next. I could feel hard wet tarmac on my back. Tarney had kneed me in the face as I bent down, that was it, he'd kneed me in the face and now I was lying there with blood streaming out of my nose and my eyes barely able to open.

I heard movement beside me and then I was sitting up. I hadn't meant to sit up, I didn't think I *could* sit up, but it was an instinctive reaction to the boot that had just slammed into my kidney. Sitting up brought my face into closer range, and as I opened my eyes I saw another boot heading my way. They hadn't covered boots in the face at the martial arts class, but I managed to drop back down in time, and I thought it had missed me entirely until I felt it smashing my right arm into the ground. A battered arm, I reflected, in a brief, bootless moment, could hurt a lot, but not as much as a battered face.

The pub door was open again, I could see light in that direction, and I tried to shout, but my throat wasn't playing ball. Now the henchmen were either side of me and lifting me to my feet and Tarney was saying something. I couldn't hear him. There was a ringing in my right ear, and I worried for a moment that Tarney might have done me some permanent damage. Then the ringing cleared, suddenly, and I wasn't worried about my ear any more. My ear was the least of my problems.

"I don't think Mr Williams has quite understood us," he was saying. "I get the feeling we need to make ourselves a little clearer."

I was pushed up against a car. My car. Driver's side. I could have turned and climbed in, driven away, gone back to London and Claire and the fifty-five inch television, and Atom Industries, with all their money and their regular, normal job which involved neither murderers nor psychotic police officers. I could have forgotten all about Thomas and Sally Carson and Serena Hawkes and Detective Inspector Roarkes, who I was starting to think had a lot to answer for, not least the state my face was going to be in by the end of the night. Except I couldn't do any of that, because there was a fat bald man holding each of my arms and another one in front of me smiling like he knew something I didn't, and when I found out what it was I wasn't going to like it.

I found out what it was half a second later. It was Tarney's fist, and behind it the surprising fact that Tarney wasn't just a fat bald copper who liked his beer, he was someone who knew how to punch a slightly-tougher-than-he-used-to-be lawyer and make it hurt. I crumpled to the ground, or halfway there, because the goons either side weren't letting me go, and amid the explosions going on in my stomach and shooting through to my head I tried to remember whether being hit that hard in the solar plexus was dangerous or merely intensely painful. I opened my eyes and Tarney was still smiling, drawing his fist back, ready for another crack, and if my throat had been on my side I'd have said pretty much anything to stop that fist where it was, but I couldn't say anything at all. I tried mouthing the word "please", but the bastard just smiled a little wider and brought the fist back in, hard and sharp, a left hook to the right side of my head and that same bloody ear again.

A split second later my head smashed against the car and the ringing was back, with shouts and footsteps and the baseline from "Groove Is In the Heart", which had me worrying about concussion and brain damage until I remembered the jukebox. I was on the ground, the impact of my head against the car had been enough to shake off the goons, and now the music had come to an end, but the shouts hadn't, those same Manchester vowels that had been bouncing relentlessly through my head for most of the last two days. I was starting to really hate those vowels.

I opened my eyes. There was a shape in front of me, leaning over me. I closed my eyes, resigned to whatever pain was coming, and prayed it wasn't going to kill me.

Nothing came. I opened my eyes again and waited for the shape to come into focus, but even before it had progressed beyond a blur I could see it wasn't Tarney because it was half his size and there was a dark patch that looked like hair on top.

"Are you OK, sir?"

A woman. Dark hair. A uniform. A police officer.

I turned my head. Tarney was on the ground, on his belly, arms behind his back, a big guy in uniform on top of him. One of his friends was in a similar position. The other one was nowhere to be seen, and from the distant shouts coming at me through my still-ringing ears it sounded like he'd made a run for it.

"Sir?"

I looked back to the police officer. She was wearing that expression that forces itself onto your face when you don't want it there, the one I usually try to hide from my clients when the prosecution pulls a zinger out of the bag, the one that says, "You're screwed, mate". I didn't know why she was asking if I was OK. I only had to look at her to know I wasn't.

Time to get up, I thought, and stretched out my right arm for support. My right arm was the one Tarney had just put his boot through, and didn't seem to want to play ball. I tried the left, and the police officer shook her head and told me to stay down until the paramedics arrived, "Just in case."

I tried not to think about what "just in case" might mean, and concentrated on what was happening a couple of yards away. Tarney wasn't behaving like he was supposed to. He was on his feet now, one hand palm-out in front of his face in that "calm down" stance that says *I'm going to do what you want me to* and is about as believable as a Volkswagen emissions test. I didn't trust that expression and a moment later I knew I was right, because his other hand, the one that wasn't in front of his face, was heading to his pocket. I tried to say something but the nerves in charge of my mouth still weren't up to the job.

It didn't matter. The police officer who'd brought him down had spotted the same thing I had, and pounced on the hand before it had a chance to get where it was going. One hand on Tarney's wrist, the other round the back of his head, pushing down in a goose-neck grip, and turned slightly to the side in case Tarney decided to use a knee. Part of me was impressed with myself for seeing all this. Another part was saying if I knew so much about self-defence I might have tried actually using it when it was me Tarney was beating the shit out of, but it was too late to worry about that now.

Tarney was down again and the police officer was digging around in the pocket looking out for whatever weapon the bastard had been planning on using. Out came the hand. The contents of the pocket followed. A knife, I guessed.

Only, it wasn't a knife. It wasn't a weapon at all.

It was money. It was a roll of bank notes. And it was thick enough to make a short man tall.

8: Dead Man's Name

TWO HOURS. TWO hours just to get out of the bloody hospital when right from the start they'd told me I probably didn't need to be there and it didn't look like there was anything broken anyway. Two hours sitting there, the first hour with a uniformed constable from Blackmoor, the one who'd brought down Tarney's mate with, he proudly told me, a reverse flying scissor-kick. I didn't know what a reverse flying scissor-kick was, I didn't remember them from my class, but that didn't mean he'd made it up. There was a lot I couldn't remember from that class, like how to avoid boots and knees and fists, so I sat there and looked suitably impressed while trying to stem the flow of blood to my nose with a few strips of toilet roll.

After an hour Gaddesdon had shown up, sent by Roarkes, who appeared to value his own leisure time more than the well-being of his tame "adviser". Gaddesdon had glared at the uniform and the uniform had glared back before he realised that anything was better than sitting in the waiting area at Manchester Royal Infirmary's Accident and Emergency department with a bloody-nosed Londoner who didn't want to be there either. *Good*, I'd thought, *Gaddesdon won't care whether I stay here or not*, but I'd been wrong, because Detective Inspector Roarkes had, it emerged, given very clear instructions as to what I was to do and when I was to do it, and that included not being allowed to step outside the hospital until I'd been seen and given a clean bill of health.

Gaddesdon was taking his duties as chaperon more

seriously than I'd expected, and this annoyed me more than it should have done, because unless he fancied pulling his lazy arse out of the pub, turning up and arresting me, Roarkes had no more right to keep me here than he'd had dragging me up to Manchester in the first place. I told Gaddesdon this, and he seemed to find it amusing, which annoyed me even more. I didn't tell him the other thing that was annoying me, which was that I could have been having a quiet drink with Serena Hawkes instead of sitting here with blood all over my clothes surrounded by vomiting drunks.

I'd resigned myself to a long wait, so two hours shouldn't have pissed me off that much, but it did. The doctor who finally saw me spent all of ninety seconds asking me questions and prodding at my nose before he told me there was nothing wrong with it, nothing he could do anything about, anyway. Tarney hadn't broken it, which demonstrated a particular skill that shouldn't have surprised me. He poked at my stomach a couple of times and said there was nothing wrong there either, and the best thing I could do would be to go home, clean out my arm, and take some painkillers and some antibiotics, in case of infection. I laughed when he said that, "painkillers," like I hadn't just built up a tolerance for the things on the strength of a mild cold, and he frowned at me and shook his head, then looked me up and down and frowned again, more deeply, as if there were something else he wanted to say. Whatever it was, it couldn't have been important, or at least not any more important than the line of more seriously injured people waiting their turn outside, because he shook his head again, turned away, and opened the door for us to leave, while Gaddesdon stood there smiling at me like all this was good news rather than no news at all. I got up, ignoring the box of pills the doctor had placed on the table in front of him, and walked out without saying another word.

I stopped outside the waiting area. I had no idea where I was or how to get back to Blackmoor, where I assumed my car was still waiting in the car park for me to come and drive it away. It was raining, worse, it was hail, hard, vicious little balls of ice, and it was dark. There was a line of ambulances waiting to drop off the sick, injured and dying, but there was no sign of a bus-stop or a taxi rank or anything that might get me away.

"Wait up!" shouted Gaddesdon, unnecessarily loudly for someone standing just a couple of feet behind me. I turned to him, wondering what on earth Roarkes had planned for me now. "Don't you want to see Carson?"

I frowned. The last I'd heard, Carson wasn't far off half-dead himself. I couldn't imagine what seeing him would achieve, unless Gaddesdon thought I'd get a kick out of looking at someone even worse off than I was.

I shrugged. Maybe that wasn't such a bad idea.

"He's just upstairs."

So it was a lot more than two hours, in the end. And Roarkes, to his credit, wasn't in the pub at all, but standing outside yet another room with a big glass window in the wall and Thomas Carson inside it.

Carson was hooked up to a machine and there was a screen with green lines flowing smoothly up and down. Everything looked calm and ordered and you'd never have guessed the chaos this guy had thrown everything into just a few hours earlier.

Carson might not be saying much – which wasn't a huge change from when he was conscious, I thought – but Roarkes was full of news. Once he'd satisfied himself that I wasn't about to drop dead in front of him – and asked Gaddesdon to confirm every point, I noted – he started in on what the hell I'd been doing following Tarney in the first place.

"Trying to get under his skin, were you?" he asked, with what looked suspiciously like a sneer. "Looks like he got right into yours."

And then a lecture on the state of Carson's health in the kind of medical detail I neither needed nor understood. After a couple of sentences I cut him short.

"Just tell me if he's going to die."

Roarkes shook his head slowly, and reminded me suddenly and forcefully of my old English teacher, who'd given me exactly that look when I'd informed him that Macbeth was just a Scottish Maggie Thatcher.

"No, Sam. He's not going to die. In fact, the doctors tell me he's probably going to wake up quite soon and when he does I'm going to have that bastard's story out of him one way or another."

I pointed through the window, at the screen and the mass of wires and tubes that was keeping Thomas Carson alive.

"You think all this is going to turn him into Mr Chatty, do you?"

Roarkes leaned forward, face so close to the window he was practically touching it. A cloud formed on the glass and he wiped it into an oily smudge with his sleeve.

"I don't give a damn whether he wants to talk or not any more. We've been too easy on him."

"He tried to kill himself, for Christ's sake."

"Nothing to do with me. I've hardly been waterboarding the bastard."

That was true enough. Whatever had prompted Carson to hang himself, it wasn't police brutality. Roarkes had put a stop to any hint of that the moment he'd arrived in Manchester.

"Oh, something else, Sam," he said. There was a look on his face I didn't recognise.

"Yes?"

"What do you make of this?"

He passed me a piece of paper. I kept my eyes on his face as I took it, and his expression clicked into place. He looked awkward. Sheepish, almost. Maybe he felt bad about the battering my face had taken. It wasn't like he'd told me to follow Tarney to the pub, it wasn't like it was his fault at all, but if he wanted the blame he was welcome to it. I nodded to myself and looked down at the paper.

It was grey, but it looked like it had spent a lot of time in someone's hand or someone's pocket and it had probably once been white. It was A4 sized, folded three times, and there was a single line of writing on it, one letter, one word, twelve numbers, in faded blue ink.

A Lopez, it read. And beside the name – because it was obvious at once that it was a name, and I had a pretty good idea whose name it was – were the numbers.

41 12 17 71 50 00.

I handed it back. Awkward and sheepish were right, but it wasn't my beating Roarkes felt bad about.

"Lopez," I said, and looked hard at Roarkes. He must have known what was coming, but he didn't blink. "You assured me none of this had anything to do with Argentina. You told me it was a dead end."

He nodded.

"This Lopez," I said. "It's the business partner, isn't it? Alejandro?"

He nodded again, folded the paper up and put it in his pocket. "I'm sorry, Sam. This is probably nothing."

"Don't give me that, Roarkes. Where did you get it?"

He sighed. "Found it in a book. In the house."

"What are you doing searching the house now?" I asked, because this was something that should have been done a week ago. He shook his head.

"We're not. They searched the house and found it

while he was still on the run and filed it in the wrong bloody place. First time I saw it was an hour ago. They're muppets up here. If they're not keeping things from me on purpose." He shook his head, lost in thought, contemplating the depths of Mancunian incompetence, and for a moment I was right there with him until I realised he was just trying to change the subject. I wasn't about to let that happen.

"So? What else is there?" I asked.

"Well, normally we wouldn't have thought twice about it, people write things, put them somewhere, forget about them, years later they turn up and it's not exactly a big deal."

"So what's the difference now?" I asked.

"So the difference is, the book was *No Prayer for the Dying*."

"Sorry, don't know it."

"Neither do I. Wife tells me it's a cracker. The important thing is it only came out last year."

I thought about that for a moment, and why it should matter. It only took a moment, which was longer than it should have taken, but I was tired and I'd been smashed about a bit, and I was starting to regret having turned down those painkillers.

"Which means whoever put that bit of paper in that book, they did it back in England. Years after the business partner went missing."

"Exactly," said Roarkes. "It's probably nothing. Probably started out as a bookmark in some other book and ended up getting used for the next one, too."

It was possible, I supposed.

"Did you ask her about it? The wife?"

He nodded. But Sally Carson hadn't known a thing. His handwriting, she'd said. Her husband's. And his book, too. Not her sort of thing.

"Any ideas on the numbers?"

He grinned at me. "Gaddesdon thought it was the lottery, didn't you?"

Gaddesdon was still there, staring through the glass at Carson as if he was expecting the guy to stand up and walk out. He turned and nodded at us, and went right back to staring at Carson. There was none of the usual big blank nothing on his face. Instead there was an expression so out of place there it took me a few seconds to put my finger on it.

It was hatred.

Roarkes was still talking. He hadn't noticed Gaddesdon's face.

"Didn't seem quite so likely to me. Not with the 00 there."

I'd been thinking about those numbers for all of a minute so far, and lottery numbers hadn't crossed my mind. But even with the mystery of Gaddesdon's expression taking up half my mental capacity, something else had.

"Coordinates?"

Roarkes raised his eyebrows and nodded again, impressed.

"Not just a pretty face, are you, Sam? Mind you, you're not much of a face at all right now."

I gave him two fingers. He raised an eyebrow again – just the one this time – and went on.

"But you're right, of course. South and West. Got one of the uniforms to look it up for me. It's a glacier. A great big bloody glacier halfway up a mountain in the middle of nowhere."

"But in Argentina, right? The middle of nowhere *in Argentina*? Near where they used to live?"

Roarkes nodded.

"So this bit of paper has a dead man's name on it, or at

least a man who's been missing for years, and a location in the middle of nowhere, and it turns up on the other side of the world in a book that only came out last year that just happens to be owned by a guy who's suspected of murdering two police officers, and you're still telling me it's a dead end?"

Roarkes opened his mouth to say something, but he didn't get a chance. My phone was ringing. I looked at the display, a mobile number, not one I recognised. I answered it anyway.

"Sam Williams?"

It was a female voice. Manchester accent. Last week I wouldn't have known it from Leeds or Preston, but it was pretty much all I'd heard for the last thirty-six hours.

"Yes," I said, and instantly regretted it.

"This is Mia Arazzi. I write for the *Daily Mirror*. I understand you're involved with the Carson case and I was hoping you might have something to say about it to our readers. We haven't had a sniff out of the police for days."

The press had been pretty quiet since the arrest, and I'd assumed it was because they were doing the right thing and keeping a discreet distance until the trial came round. I couldn't have been more wrong.

"No," I said, and killed the call. One word. Probably more than she deserved. I turned back to Roarkes, anxious to get the bastard back on the ropes and explaining himself to me like he'd been on the verge of doing before the journalist had called, but before I could say anything my phone rang again. I picked up, ready to give Mia Arazzi a piece of my mind, and heard a very different voice.

"Sam? Are you OK, Sam?"

Claire. I hadn't spoken to her since the day before. A lot had happened since then.

"I'm fine."

"Roarkes told me you were in hospital."

She sounded upset. I glared at Roarkes. When I'd finished this call, Roarkes was going to be getting more than a little grief from me.

"I'm fine, Claire. I really am. Just a bruise or two. Probably better-looking than when you last saw me."

She didn't laugh.

"I don't like you being involved in this, Sam. Not if it's going to end up with you in hospital."

And that was it. *Claire didn't like it.* I felt that sudden shift, that slip, that step forward into empty space and anger. It wasn't fair, it was hardly Claire's fault, she hadn't dragged my sorry carcass two hundred miles up the M6, she hadn't smashed my face up or allowed my almost-client to almost-kill himself, she hadn't withheld key facts from me or refused to say a thing to save her own skin, and she hadn't phoned me and asked for a comment for the *Daily Mirror*, but she was the one on the end of the phone when it all came out, and that was her bad luck.

"Who the fuck do you think you are?" I said. I said it quietly enough, and my voice was level and calm, but nobody who heard me would have thought I was calm underneath.

"Sorry, Sam?"

That edge was back in her voice. I knew Claire well enough not to speak to her the way I'd just spoken. I ignored the edge, and the voice in my head that was telling me to stop.

"I said who the fuck do you think you are, Claire? My mother? My fucking boss?"

"No, Sam, I just—"

"Don't give me the *I just*, Claire. I've come up here to do something. I'm going to try and do it. When I've finished I'll drive down to London and you can go back to telling me what to do all day, but while I'm here I'll do what the hell I want to and you will not tell me otherwise. Do you understand me?"

My voice wasn't level any more, and it wasn't quiet either. A nurse turned in my direction from the station at the end of the corridor, and I glared back at her until she looked away. Roarkes and Gaddesdon were staring the other way and pretending they couldn't hear me. I didn't care.

"Fuck you, Sam," she said. I could hear the tears in her voice, but I could hear that edge, too. I wasn't surprised. I let her go on.

"I was going to come up, thought you might want some help. Thought you might want to see me. Guess I was wrong about that."

And suddenly, like water draining out of a sink, all the anger was gone. It wasn't just Carson and Roarkes and Tarney, I realised. It was me. It was my toilet-bowl of a career, my overdrawn bank account, my shiny new flat full of shiny new toys Claire was paying for.

But that wasn't her fault. I couldn't think what to say. Sorry. Sorry was probably best. I started to say it but I didn't get past the "s" before she cut back in.

"I'll see you when you get back. If I'm still here," she said, and hung up. I toyed with the idea of ringing straight back but I knew she wouldn't answer. I wouldn't if I were her.

9: Shogun

GADDESDON GAVE ME a lift back to the hotel. What I wanted was a lift to the pub car park so I could pick up the Fiat and drive somewhere else, not home, not to Claire, but not the First Quality Inn either. Roarkes shook his head and that was it. I had my orders, Gaddesdon had his, and what I wanted was no more relevant than what I'd had for breakfast that morning. I was too tired to argue. Instead, I settled for telling Roarkes that he was a useless piece of shit and if he didn't follow up on the Argentina lead then I'd make sure someone knew about it. He said he'd think about it, which was an improvement, at least, and reminded me we had more pertinent leads.

"Oh yes?" I said, wondering what else he hadn't bothered telling me.

"Yes," he replied, and pointed at my nose. It took me a moment to figure out what he meant, but only a moment. Tarney. My hunch on Tarney had paid off, even if it had cost me a bleeding face and several wasted hours in the hospital. The money.

Where had the money come from?

Roarkes didn't know. No one knew. Tarney wasn't saying a word, and in normal circumstances no one would be able to do a thing about it. But these weren't normal circumstances. Tarney had been kind enough (I tried to snort at that "kind", but it hurt too much) to beat the crap out of an innocent member of the public (Roarkes almost choked over the "innocent" as he was saying it), and straight after that he'd pulled out a wad of banknotes in what looked very much like an attempt to bribe a police officer, with enough witnesses to keep him locked up till he got bored of saying nothing.

I wasn't so sure. Carson hadn't got bored, and he had a lot more at stake than assaulting a lawyer. Tarney had a reason or two to talk, sure, but he might have all the reasons in the world not to.

As I sat in the passenger seat next to Gaddesdon, yawning and screwing my eyes shut every time the pain shot through my nose, which was every time Gaddesdon touched the brakes or the gas or turned the wheel more than a couple of degrees, I remembered the call I'd rejected at the pub. Maloney. He'd left a message. I lifted the phone to my ear and found myself listening in astonishment to a voice that was about as different from Maloney's as a human voice could be.

"Sam," it said. It was a female voice, one I hadn't heard for years and hadn't thought I'd hear again. There had been two calls, of course. I'd assumed the second caller had been the same as the first. I'd been wrong.

"It's Elizabeth Maurier."

Like I didn't know.

"I appreciate there have been some difficulties between us, Sam, but there are some things we have to talk about."

A bit late for that, I thought. Maybe if she'd called me before I'd taken her stupid bloody firm to the cleaners – or not. I doubted it would have made much difference. And "some difficulties" was putting it mildly. She'd thrown me out, egged on by that bastard Brooks-Powell. She hadn't tried to speak to me once since then, not even after I'd squeezed a seven-figure sum out of Mauriers on behalf of nineteen former employees who'd all been bullied out of the firm by Brooks-Powell himself. Employment law wasn't really my thing, but a six-year-old could have handled the case. "Some difficulties" my arse.

"You've got my number, Sam. Please call me back when you can."

I let the phone fall to my lap and wondered what the hell she wanted to talk about now. No doubt she was annoyed with me, with what I'd done to her firm and its precious reputation, but if that was the case it wasn't me she should be angry at. Brooks-Powell had been the villain. And she'd hired him.

I picked up the phone and listened to the message again, and this time it all flooded back, the heady first months at her firm, the thrill of a big win in court and the sudden realisation that a win did nothing for a victim's pain. And all that followed: the slow decline, the mistakes, the parting of the ways. That gentle, slightly breathy voice, all country houses and champagne flutes, just as it had been when she'd told me she didn't want to see me in her offices again. She didn't sound annoyed, but she never really did. Maybe she wanted to talk about something else. Maybe she just wanted to build bridges.

The way business was going, a bridge back to Elizabeth Maurier might not be such a bad thing. But there were other matters to take care of first. Elizabeth Maurier could wait.

As I deleted the message the phone started to ring again. I looked down. This time it *was* Maloney.

"Nice of you to pick up," he said by way of greeting. I couldn't be bothered to explain myself.

"Got anything for me?"

"Very well, thanks, Sam. And how are you?"

That was too much.

"Oh, fine. I'm in Manchester, Claire won't talk to me and I've just had my nose broken by a dodgy cop, but apart from that, I'm just fine."

We were stuck at a red light and I could see Gaddesdon frowning at me out of the corner of my eye.

So I'd exaggerated about the nose. And Gaddesdon knew precisely why Claire wouldn't talk to me and whose fault that was. I didn't care. Maloney was laughing.

"Yeah, I just spoke to Claire. I couldn't get hold of you, wondered if she might be able to. She doesn't seem very happy with you. If I were you I'd give her a call and straighten things out."

I exhaled slowly. I didn't need a lecture on relationship management from a gangster. Maloney must have realised he wasn't getting anything else out of me, because after a couple of seconds silence he went on.

"But I think you're going to be happy with me. Or at least your friend Roarkes will. I've got something very interesting on Thomas Carson."

And suddenly the pain and the weariness were gone and I was sitting up, frowning into the darkness, waiting for whatever it was Maloney was going to say with all the patience of a four-year-old at a birthday party.

"So?" I said, after all of half a second's pause.

"So Thomas Carson doesn't exist."

Whatever I'd been expecting, it wasn't this. I thought back to what I'd just seen in the hospital.

"For someone who doesn't exist, he's done a decent job of wrapping a belt round his neck."

"Eh?"

I filled Maloney in on the day's events, and waited for him to elaborate.

"I checked out his background, Sam."

"And?"

"And there isn't one. All the documents, all the school records, the family stuff, even the passport and the driving licence, it's all fake."

For a moment I was too stunned to say a word. But only a moment.

"How come the police didn't spot this?"

I sensed Gaddesdon watching me again, glancing to his left, and then back to the dual carriageway he was hurtling down at a speed that would have got anyone else pulled over.

"I didn't spot it myself. But you know my people. They do these things better than anyone else, and they can see when something's not quite right."

I'd come across Maloney's people before. I'd come across the man who "did" his documents for him. If he said Carson wasn't real, then Carson wasn't real. Maybe this was why Roarkes wanted me here. Forget the talent. Not a cop, not a lawyer, just a guy who knows people who know how to get things done.

"So who is he?"

"Don't know. I'm looking into it. Your Thomas Carson must have got himself created before he went to Argentina, because he flew out there under that name. But before that – well, there are records with Thomas Carson on them. They're just not real."

"Shit."

It wasn't the most eloquent of responses, but I couldn't think of anything else. There was a great big gap in my brain. Maloney tried to fill it.

"So it looks like your guy, Carson, whatever his name is, he's born aged eighteen or nineteen or something like that. Your real guy, how old he is, who he was before he was Carson, it's anyone's guess. But we'll find out."

"How?"

"We will. I'll keep you posted. And call that girlfriend of yours and promise her you'll stop being such a cunt. OK?"

"Yup," I said, and hung up before I remembered to tell him precisely how much I valued his input into my personal life. It didn't matter. For a few minutes my mind was racing faster than Gaddesdon was driving and nothing mattered, not even the tiredness or the pain in my nose. Carson was a fake. And I didn't care what Roarkes thought, or the Argentine police, or anyone else. I was right about the business partner, Alejandro, he had something to do with all this, the bit of paper with the glacier coordinates proved it.

"Turn around," I said.

Gaddesdon carried on driving.

"Turn this car around or I'll get out and walk."

Gaddesdon turned to glance at me, briefly, and went back to driving. I stretched over to take a look at the dashboard. We were doing close to ninety, and it didn't look like we'd be slowing down any time soon. I wasn't going to get out and walk. I tried changing tack.

"Whose car is this, Gaddesdon?" I asked, as if nothing had happened.

It couldn't be his. It was a Mitsubishi Shogun, *POLICE* all over it. Gaddesdon wouldn't have a Shogun. And he was CID. From what I knew, CID didn't drive marked patrol cars.

"One of the sergeants from the station. Briggs. You haven't met him."

I knew I hadn't met him. When it worked, I still had that photographic memory, after all.

"Nice bloke?"

Gaddesdon shrugged. "He's OK, I suppose. I wouldn't want to piss him off."

Perfect. I smiled to myself.

"OK then, Charlie," I said. I'd heard someone shouting "Charlie" at him from the custody desk when we'd been running around chasing our own shadows in the aftermath of Carson's suicide attempt. I hoped it was his name rather than an insult. "How do you think Sergeant Briggs would feel if I bled all over his nice clean Mitsubishi?"

It *was* clean, too. No crumbs, no crisp wrappers or coffee cups, no bits of crap scattered about the back seats. I suspected Sergeant Briggs wouldn't be too happy with blood on his upholstery. I doubted he was pleased Gaddesdon was in it at all.

Gaddesdon was looking at me. I could see him weighing up whether to upset Briggs or Roarkes, and coming to a decision.

"Your nose isn't bleeding any more, sir," he said. I smiled again.

"You don't have to call me sir, Charlie," I replied, reached up to my nose, and twisted. The pain came instantly, sharp and brutal, a swarm of angry wasps roused without warning and stinging blindly in every direction. I tried not to scream. I felt the blood dripping onto my hand. Still dripping, not pouring. But that was just the first twist. And a gentle one.

My eyes were closed but I could sense the car slowing and hear the gentle tick of the indicator alongside Gaddesdon's gasp. When I opened them a moment later we were pulling off the dual carriageway and Gaddesdon was looking at me and slowly shaking his head.

"You're mad, you are," he said. "Roarkes is going to kill me. So where do you want to go?"

10: Fake

I KNEW IT was a long drive, and I knew it was late, but I also knew there was no point going back to my hotel room and sitting there while a bunch of half-baked ideas flew in wild circles around my head like a flock of drunken geese. And late was good, anyway. Catch someone by surprise, they might say something they'd planned on keeping to themselves. Roarkes would be treating me like an ill-behaved ten-year-old by morning, but I'd gone beyond being afraid of Roarkes' words. Tarney's fists had put them in perspective.

But Sally Carson didn't seem that surprised to see us. She was red-eyed, standing in the open doorway wearing a dressing gown and indoor shoes with the news playing quietly on the TV behind her, and ushering us inside with the look of someone who'd been waiting for that knock on the door all evening.

"How is he?" she asked, as soon as we were in, and I understood. Roarkes had let her visit her husband, or at least see him from behind a pane of glass and then step inside the room to hold his hand for a minute, but then she'd been told to go home and reminded that her husband was still under arrest on suspicion of murder. All while I'd been getting my nose turned to jelly by Russell Tarney, and she hadn't heard a thing since. I was there to force answers out of her, not to play nice, but I couldn't ignore the fear in those red eyes.

"He's OK, Sally," I said, and she smiled and took my left hand and squeezed. The second woman to squeeze that hand in one evening, I thought, inappropriately, and went on before she could get too excited.

"He hasn't woken up or anything, not yet. But the

doctors say he will soon and he should be fine when he does."

"Apart from a bruised neck," added Gaddesdon, and I shook my head at him as Sally Carson's briefly beaming face fell back into the desolate lines it had been wearing when she'd opened the door.

Five minutes later we were sitting in the kitchen drinking hot, sweet tea and I was trying to explain the state of my face without letting too much information slip out. I didn't want to get distracted. Tarney wasn't important. Not right now. With someone to fuss around, someone with a bleeding nose – I'd twisted too hard, I realised, and the blood wouldn't stop coming – Sally Carson was looking a little more composed.

"Take this," she said, and shoved a bowl of warm water in front of me with a wad of cotton wool. I dabbed away for a minute, while Sally tutted at the state of my face and my shirt, which had sustained more damage than I'd realised when Tarney had stamped on my arm.

"Is your arm hurting?" she asked, and I took a proper look at it for the first time. There was some tenderness, a little blood, an uncomfortable spot or two where the stone from the car park and the material of the shirt had been driven into the skin. It didn't hurt. Compared to my nose, my arm was Terminator. I shook my head and took another sip of tea.

It was time.

"Can you help me with a couple of things, Sally?" I asked, as gently as I could. I knew she was suffering, but I had a job to do, and I had more chance of doing it if I could catch her off guard. I didn't feel bad about it. Not yet. I thought I'd save feeling bad about Sally Carson for later, when it could join feeling bad about Claire and my nose and have a nice little misery party.

"Sure," she said, and smiled at me. I decided to start

with an easy one.

"That bit of paper the police found, the one with the numbers on it."

She frowned, as if she were trying to remember what I was talking about. It seemed a little unlikely that she could have forgotten it already, but after the suicide attempt it was always possible.

"In a book," I prompted, and she nodded like it had suddenly come back to her.

"Yes, I remember. One of Thomas' books. Thriller, wasn't it? I don't really go in for thrillers."

She laughed, and I smiled back at her, but at the same time I was thinking to myself, *I didn't ask whose book it was.*

"And you don't know what these numbers are?"

She shook her head.

"41 12 17 71 50 00," I said, just like that, and even though it was Sally Carson's face I was watching I could sense Gaddesdon's mouth fall open beside me. I'd be lying if I said I didn't get a little bit of a kick out of it.

But Sally Carson gave me nothing. A shrug, a slight frown. I was staring at her, I knew I probably looked strange enough myself, bloody nose, bruised face, eyes wide and unblinking. I didn't care. Nothing. If this was a test, she'd passed it with flying colours.

But, I reminded myself, that had been an easy one.

"Tell me," I asked, "when did you and Thomas get married?"

"2005," she said, immediately. The ghost of a smile returned to her lips as she spoke. "I wanted to do it at one of the smart hotels in Bariloche, it would have been beautiful, but Thomas wanted something that was more *us*, so we had a load of people from the town out in one of the fields and got some wine and beer and a huge asado going."

"What's an asado?" I asked.

"It's a barbecue," she said, and spent the next couple of minutes explaining what a barbecue was like in Argentina, which sounded a lot like a barbecue in England only with more meat and better weather. I let her go on. She was back there, with Thomas, with her friends, enjoying the day, enjoying herself. It was cruel, but if I was going to get anything at all from her I'd have to pull the rug out while she was still dancing on it.

She tailed off, still smiling, and looked at me expectantly. That threw me, for a moment, and I wondered what it was she was expecting. I doubted it was what I was about to say.

"And when did you find out your husband was a fake?"

She didn't blink.

"I beg your pardon?"

"A fake. You know, a fraud, a liar. When did you find out?"

She frowned at me, stood, swayed slightly, and held out an arm to steady herself against the kitchen island. The frown deepened. I could almost see the outlines of thoughts chasing each other through her head. I'd have killed to know what those thoughts were.

"What the *hell* are you talking about?"

I glanced over at Gaddesdon, whose mouth was hanging open and who looked almost as shocked as Sally Carson. It was, I realised, a risky move. All I had was the word of a career criminal, and I hadn't even mentioned it to Roarkes, who'd warned me not to do precisely this sort of thing and was already on thin enough ice himself. I hoped I hadn't put a crack in it. It was a bold step, which was lawyer-speak for a stupid one. But I'd taken that step, and there was no going back now. I tried to ignore my tiredness and the tension, and spoke slowly and calmly.

"Thomas Carson is a false identity. Thomas Carson

doesn't exist. He never has existed. Your husband made him up."

Sally Carson sat back down, bit her lower lip and slowly shook her head. She took a long, deep breath, as if she were gathering herself for something, and spoke.

"I don't know what you're talking about, but I can assure you it's nonsense. Now please, if you don't mind, I'd rather you left."

I couldn't fault her reaction, but something was still nagging at me. I nodded at her, stood, and picked my four years out-of-date Samsung phone out of my pocket.

"Do you mind?" I asked, and she frowned at me.

"Do I mind what?"

"I need a photo," I replied. I was hoping she wasn't going to ask why, because I didn't think a sense of déjà vu or something equally vague would cut it.

"No," she said, "I don't think so. I think you've got a damn nerve, to be honest. I thought you were here to help me."

I'd thought much the same, until Maloney's call. I wasn't sure why I was there at all now. I looked at her, trying to keep the guilt and confusion off my face, and she stared right back at me. She was furious, and if she was faking it, she was good. The seconds ticked by, and just as I was about to turn away and leave she took a deep breath and relented. "Oh, OK. It's not like I've got anything to hide."

One photo, with Sally far from her best, but it would have to do. Her reactions had been spot on, close to perfect, but something about Sally Carson still didn't seem right. Her comment about the book. That brief, expectant pause. It wasn't much. It wasn't anything at all, really. But somewhere, something was jarring, even as it rang a bell somewhere else. Something wasn't quite right.

I was barely out of the door before she slammed it

shut. Bursington by night was cold, wet and windy. I had the feeling that we'd just been lucky, earlier, and Bursington by day was usually the same. We hurried back to the Mitsubishi.

A man was waiting for us there. Round, smiling face, glasses, white hair. He didn't look like a farmer, I thought.

"Hello," he said. "Daniel Cullop. I live just over there."

He didn't sound like a farmer, either. He pointed back over his shoulder, into the darkness, where I could just make out a different shade of darkness that might have been a building or might just have been another cold wet hill.

"How can we help you, Mr Cullop?" I asked. Maybe it was being with Gaddesdon, standing next to the patrol car, but I knew I sounded like a police officer even as I said it. I knew precisely what Roarkes would have to say about that, too. I didn't care.

"Just wondering what the latest is. We heard about Thomas, this afternoon."

No surprise there. I doubted Sally Carson had been shooting her mouth off, but Mia Arazzi and her colleagues would have been all over it. Gaddesdon took over.

"I'm afraid we can't say anything about that, sir," he announced, and moved past Daniel Cullop to open the driver's door. I went to the passenger side and was about to climb in before I had a sudden thought.

"Mr Cullop," I said, and he turned to me, smiling, eager, ingratiating.

"Yes, erm…"

I ignored the unspoken question. He didn't need to know my name. He certainly didn't need to know I wasn't a police officer.

"Can you tell us anything about the Carsons? Anything out of the ordinary."

Cullop shrugged, still smiling.

"Not really. They seem pleasant enough. My other half has tea with Sally from time to time. Of course they're not so popular now they're trying to turn the place into some kind of Glastonbury Festival, but what can you do about that?"

For a moment I didn't understand what he was talking about, and then I remembered the moles and the yurts. Hardly Glastonbury, but this was a small village in the middle of nowhere. Half a dozen families with kids in a field would be Armageddon as far as they were concerned. Daniel Cullop was still talking.

"I mean, we've all spoken to Thomas, and he tried to reassure us, but he would, wouldn't he? And as for the council, well, everybody knows if you throw enough money at them you can build whatever you want."

Daniel Cullop sounded like he could go on for the rest of the night if we gave him the chance. I thanked him, said goodbye and climbed into the car where Gaddesdon was already waiting with the face of a bored teenager enduring a long and dreary family dinner.

"Let's go," I said, and moments later we'd left Bursington behind to its wind and rain and curious neighbours. I had a photo of Sally Carson, who still reminded me of something and I couldn't think what. I had a fake husband, and all I could do about that was wait for Maloney to tell me who he really was. I had a scrap of paper with the coordinates of an Argentine glacier on it that had turned up eight thousand miles away with no good reason – and the name of a dead man next to those coordinates. I had a suspect in hospital and a police station full of people who wanted me two hundred miles away. And now I had a bunch of angry neighbours – no, not angry, just disgruntled, I thought – and council officers who were happy to let you do whatever you wanted as long as you threw them a big enough bone.

No leads indeed, I thought, and smiled into the darkness.

11: No More Than a Flicker

"JUST FUCK OFF," said Claire, and hung up on me. She lingered a while on that first "f", stretched it out like the string on a catapult, long enough that I had time to take it in while she was still on it, to wonder how serious she was, how serious all this was, whether I'd made the kind of mistake that couldn't be put right.

I'd texted the photo to Claire the moment I'd got back to the hotel room, which didn't show much sign of having been tidied, but I was past expecting any kind of "quality" from the place. I'd included a cryptic little message alongside the image, *this face could blow the case,* it said, enough to whet her appetite and, I hoped, gloss over the way our last conversation had ended.

I called her at ten in the morning, and it didn't take me long to realise that hope was a little ambitious. A frosty greeting, a vaguely disparaging comment about the woman in the photo (she couldn't possibly think there was something between me and Sally Carson, could she?), and that was just the start. OK, I thought, I can work with this, I can bring her round. I asked her how she was doing, whether she'd made any more progress on her story, an obvious enough trick to make it sound like I was genuinely interested in what she was doing, and I could almost see the frown on her face as she replied "Fine" in a voice that sounded anything but. I pushed on regardless.

"Thing is, that Sally Carson – suspect's wife, the woman in the photo – she rings a bell and I can't figure out why. Reckon you can dig through the files on my laptop? See if I've come across her before?"

I was prepared for a sigh and a *why the hell didn't you take the bloody thing up there with you?*, I'd even rehearsed a cute, self-mocking response, but Claire's answer, her obvious, inevitable answer, was the one thing I didn't see coming. So that "Just fuck off", with its long deep crescendo on the "f", hit me like a hammer in the dark.

A uniformed officer from Blackmoor turned up twenty minutes later to take me to the Fiat. I had time, while the constable drove me in silence through some surprisingly colourful parts of Manchester, to hammer out an apology to Claire on the Samsung, redraft it three times, and delete it anyway because the mood she was in, there wasn't anything I could send her that would work. A text hit my inbox while I was crafting the final round of abject apologies, from Michael Slaney, an old Mauriers colleague who'd taken up a Government policy post at the Home Office a couple of years back.

Re Hasina Khalil, it read. *Politics my arse. Speak later.*

Now I was intrigued. But Hasina Khalil could wait. We were turning into the pub car park, and there was the Fiat, right where I'd left it, no more battered than it had been, certainly better-looking than its owner. Even while I'd been staring at my phone with my mind full of Claire and Hasina Khalil, I'd realised what I needed to do about Carson, and I knew Roarkes wouldn't like it.

So Roarkes wouldn't find out until it was too late.

Getting back to the hospital wasn't exactly a breeze, what with all those road closures and Christmas markets and no Tarney to follow this time round, but I got there only twenty minutes after my phone had said I would, and kept my smile serious enough and my stroll brisk enough to smuggle me past anyone who might have wondered who I was and whether maybe they ought to stop me. Idiots. The guy had tried to hang himself, and someone had helped him, so it wasn't like no one knew security was an issue. Serena Hawkes was right: there was no doubt he was vulnerable now. And there I was, not a cop and not his lawyer, could have been anyone, standing in front of him and watching him sleep.

Most of the wires and tubes had gone. He was breathing on his own, at least. There was an IV into his hand, but they put an IV in your hand if you graze your knee, so that didn't mean a thing.

"Mr Carson?" I said, softly. Nothing. "Thomas" – a little louder. He twitched, shoulders jerking minutely and so quickly I wouldn't have noticed if I hadn't been looking right at them. It might have been nothing, it might just have been a sleeping reaction to a voice in the room, but I didn't think so. The bastard was awake.

"I know you can hear me, Thomas. I'm sure someone'll be along soon and tell me you can't be disturbed or some crap like that so I'll be quick. Two questions for you."

Nothing. My eyes were stuck on him so tight you'd have needed white spirit and a blade to peel them off. I could see every tiny bead of sweat on his forehead, but I couldn't see a hint of anything else. I carried on.

"What's with the glacier, Thomas?"

Still nothing.

"Is it your mate? Alejandro? That where you buried the poor sod?"

No more sweat. No more twitching. But he was awake. I was sure of it. I tried the other line.

"And while we're on the subject of buried, where's the real Thomas Carson?"

This time there was movement. A tiny one, no more than a flicker round one eye and a cheek, but it was there. I hadn't imagined it.

"Did you just make him up, or is he some other dead

bloke you thought you'd turn into?"

The flicker went out. Thomas Carson – I couldn't help thinking of him as Thomas Carson, even though I was sure he wasn't – was marble again, a statue, immobile bar the steady rise and fall of his chest.

"OK, Thomas. Have it your way. But we'll find out soon enough. It doesn't look good, though, does it? Two dead cops and the man who might have done it isn't who he claims to be. Doesn't look good at all."

I turned and left the room and made it all the way to the end of the corridor before I walked round a corner and straight into a very unhappy Detective Inspector Roarkes.

Gaddesdon was standing next to him, avoiding my gaze, looking rather like a dog who'd been caught with half the fridge in his mouth. I was wearing an old t-shirt and a sweater and Roarkes had grabbed a lump of the sweater, and the t-shirt, and, I thought, possibly a little skin underneath, and twisted, and pushed me back into the wall. I heard a quiet tear, felt the sweater give, and mentally consigned it to the same bin as the shirt I'd been wearing when Tarney had gone for me. Unlike Tarney, Roarkes was supposed to be a friend. I didn't like to think what he did to people who weren't his friends.

"What the FUCK do you think you're doing, Williams?" he hissed. Another hospital corridor, another scene. Visitors and nurses scurried past behind him. I shrugged, or came as close as I could with half my upper body in his hand.

Five minutes later we were sitting in the hospital canteen drinking coffee with the consistency of chicken fat and the taste of burnt wood. It turned out Roarkes wasn't particularly angry about me going to see Carson, or if he was, it was in the background. What had really pissed him off, he said, was our little visit to Bursington. A barely-coherent Sally Carson had woken him at seven in the morning with a story he'd found difficult to believe, he said, until he remembered the level of stupidity I was capable of.

"Her husband's just tried to top himself, and you go round there with this nonsense, this pile of crap, and you expect she's going to be pleased to see you?"

I shrugged again. Gaddesdon was still looking at the floor. I hadn't much cared how pleased Sally Carson was. It was what she had to say that interested me.

"And you were, what, surprised she didn't just cave in and say *oh yes we're Bonnie and Clyde how clever of you to find us Mr Williams*?"

I glanced over at Gaddesdon. Maybe that looking-at-the-floor thing wasn't such a bad idea. I'd been ready to stand my ground, because Maloney's information was always good. But what had we really got out of our trip to Bursington? A photo of a distraught-looking woman; some gossip from an inquisitive neighbour. And on my part, a girlfriend who was so angry with me she probably wasn't my girlfriend any more. I'd missed the point. *It's not the quality of the information. It's what you do with it.* Something Roarkes had told me, I remembered, back when I'd asked him how he'd cracked an apparently motiveless murder without a single witness on an estate whose residents would rather have thrown themselves out of a twentieth-floor window than be seen talking to the police. That was all he'd told me, too. Typical Roarkes. He was still talking. Not quite so loud, now. He'd got that out of his system.

"Of course I'm not one to dismiss a lead out of hand, however absurd it might be and however dubious its source. So I asked Sally Carson what might have given you the impression her husband was – what did you call him – a *fake*, that was it, I asked her if she could think of anything that might have led you to believe her husband was a fake, and of course she couldn't."

"No surprise there," I said, and immediately regretted it.

"I'm doing the talking here, Williams!" shouted Roarkes, and slammed his fist down on the table so hard the coffee would have been all over me if it had been normal coffee. Instead it just wobbled. *Williams*, this time. Roarkes wasn't messing around.

"I asked Sally Carson if she could vouch for her husband's past – following up every angle, I said, just doing my job, had she met his family or his friends from before he went to South America, and of course she hadn't, because he was an only child and his parents were dead and he'd gone to South America to get away from all that and start again."

"Denial," I said, and saw his jaw tighten. I shut my mouth. It was the wiser choice.

"And where precisely did you pick up this little gem of information, Williams?"

I carried on saying nothing.

"Gaddesdon!"

Eyes still on the floor, Gaddesdon mumbled something that sounded like "I don't know, sir. It was someone on the phone."

"It was Maloney, wasn't it?"

I did my best impression of Thomas Carson, sitting there – lying there, right now – giving as close to nothing away as I could.

"Fine. Have it your way. Some idiot calls you up in the middle of the night and tells you Carson's not who he says he is but – and tell me if I've got this wrong – he's not who he says he is but your *source* can't tell you who he actually really is. And armed with this superb, impeccably-researched nugget of intelligence, off you go to have a word with a woman who's just a few hours and the width of a belt away from being a widow. You're not a cop, remember. Don't try and act like one. And don't make me look like a prick."

He shook his head. I didn't think it was worth trying to justify myself. I wasn't sure I could.

"And you call yourself a lawyer, Williams. Christ. I pity your clients. I really do. As for you," he turned to Gaddesdon, who met his eye for all of half a second before looking back down, "you're just an imbecile, but I wouldn't worry, because that makes you smarter than everyone else in that bloody station."

Roarkes took a sip of his coffee and grimaced.

"Lawyers and Manchester cops," he said, and shook his head. I tried not to laugh, failed, and noticed Roarkes failing to stifle the beginnings of a beaten-down grin himself.

"Come on, you pair of bloody morons. Let's get back to the station."

The main entrance to the hospital was a large revolving glass door, into which Roarkes strode without looking back. The other moron and I were left to the compartment behind. As I stepped onto the zebra crossing outside I heard a shout from behind – Gaddesdon – and looked up to see a car coming towards me, yards away, with no sign of slowing down. I jumped back and watched it shoot past, dark green and nondescript and driven by a mop of bushy blond hair. Gaddesdon was laughing. So was Roarkes, from across the road.

I was shaking.

"Fuck off!" I shouted. A woman who had just emerged from the revolving door carrying a toddler with his arm in a sling stopped and stared at me. I wasn't sure who I was shouting at, the driver, Roarkes, Gaddesdon, Carson, Claire, the bastard who'd beaten me up the night before. They all deserved it.

Roarkes had crossed the road and put an arm on my shoulder. He was still laughing.

"It's not funny," I said. He stopped laughing and folded his arms.

"Yes it is," he replied.

"That bastard tried to kill me!"

Roarkes started laughing again. Gaddesdon joined him, the two of them laughing and shaking their heads and looking at me like I was about to see their side of it and laugh along with them.

I wasn't.

PART 2

THE WHITE HILL

12: Get a Grip

WE AGREED NOT to discuss the incident outside the hospital any further, which meant that I very much wanted to discuss it, I wanted it looked into and properly investigated and I wanted serious consideration given to whether I should be granted police protection, and Roarkes didn't want to discuss it at all. It was an accident, he said, walking away as I unlocked the Fiat and slid into the driver's seat, and then he corrected himself, because it wasn't like I'd been hit.

"It wasn't even an accident. It was a bit of careless driving."

I started to argue, and he turned and glared at me. Maybe he was right, I thought. And even if he wasn't, it didn't look like there was much I could do about it. I decided to chalk it down to bad luck and look after things I did have some control over instead, and before I could talk myself out of it, I'd punched out a short and humble apology to Claire and hit *send*.

Serena Hawkes was waiting for us in the office Roarkes had taken over and made his own. She had her back to us as we entered, but I could tell what kind of mood she was in from the way she sat, straight up, rigid, elbows out. She spun to face us, eyes blazing, and I knew I was right. I braced myself for the onslaught.

"What the hell gives you the right to keep me from my client?" she asked, and I took a step back before I realised she wasn't talking to me. I glanced to my left. Roarkes was wearing a frown which told me he was as confused as I was.

"I'm sorry?" he said.

"You will be," she replied, just three words in a low, steady monotone, but somehow as intense and unpleasant as the verbal assault Roarkes had inflicted on Tarney.

Gaddesdon was despatched for hot drinks and crisps while Roarkes tried to explain why Serena had been held at bay, and she started to calm down. Seguing seamlessly into a description of the near-miss outside the hospital and my "ridiculous" reaction to it helped improve her mood, too. It didn't do much to lift mine, but Roarkes was never one to let someone else's feelings get in the way of an opportunity to steer the conversation his way. I opened my mouth to argue and he silenced me with three words of his own.

"Get a grip," he said, shaking his head, and suddenly I felt like a child trying to argue with the grown-ups.

Serena was smiling, again, that slightly sympathetic, slightly knowing smile. Roarkes, it seemed, was at least partially forgiven. A shame, I thought, because I'd been rather enjoying the venom. It was a novelty. Someone was furious and it wasn't with me.

Serena's frustration had all been down to one poorly-briefed constable. There *had* been someone keeping a watch over Thomas Carson, and that someone had been told to keep everyone away, no exceptions, which, Roarkes insisted, wasn't his doing. Serena Hawkes had tried to face the watchdog down, but it had been like trying to face down a brick wall. And to add insult to injury, he'd got bored and disappeared for a coffee an hour later, allowing a barely-connected lowlife like me – an entirely inappropriate adult – to stroll in and have his own somewhat one-sided conversation with the purportedly-comatose murder suspect.

Serena was looking at me strangely. I didn't like it. After a couple of minutes I asked her if something was wrong and she pointed to my face.

"Tarney," I said, and she looked blank. No one had told her. There had been other things happening, things more important than some B-list lawyer getting his face smashed in. So I told her, and she tutted and shook her head, but once the brief look of shock had had its moment I couldn't fail to spot the hint of a smile flitting across her lips. Yes, it was funny, I supposed, in a sick kind of a way. And no doubt she was thinking this was why I'd blown her off the night before, that it wasn't down to finding her unattractive or dull or anything like that, and of course she was right. I thought I'd better wipe that smile off her face, so I filled her in on what I'd found out from Maloney – omitting any background on the source. She seemed sceptical, which was fair enough, if slightly less sceptical than Roarkes.

"Doesn't add up, Sam," she said, and out of the corner of my eye I saw Roarkes grinning a rare, smug grin, "but if you think it's worth looking at, I'm not going to stop you."

Roarkes sighed in frustration. Sure, he didn't want me wasting time on it, and he might even be right, but I didn't care. All those leads he hadn't bothered with were bothering me. There was something out there that would help me get into Carson's head, if he ever woke up. I didn't know where it was or what it was, and maybe I'd never find it at all, but a bit of time wasted on a dead end and a bit less of the smug grin might do Roarkes some good.

One of the leads Roarkes had bothered to follow up, or at least tried to, was the mysterious third car that might or might not have approached the murder scene but hadn't shown up anywhere else. A dark blue Land Rover, a Defender, that was all anyone had, PK11 on the plate, which was half the bloody Defenders in Lancashire, no

CCTV or ANPR or anything other than one local farmer with a trailer full of sheep who'd been turned round himself and swore blind he'd seen this guy heading the other way a minute later. Couldn't describe the driver, thought it might have been male. And this was the witness who'd remembered Carson's plates to the last letter, so if he didn't have anything more than that, it was hardly surprising no one else did either. This one looked like a bona fide dead end.

But so was Carson, for now. When I got a minute away from prying eyes to call Maloney, he told me to hang tight. I knew Maloney. I could be hanging a while. Carson still wasn't saying anything, and neither was his wife, now, and whatever it was I thought she reminded me of, Claire wasn't going to help me find it any time soon. I asked Roarkes about Tarney, but it turned out Tarney had taken the same vow of silence as Carson. I wondered if maybe I might shake something out of Tarney myself, but Roarkes said no, and given the nature of my relationship with Tarney, he probably had a point.

"Come on," said Gaddesdon, and grabbed me by the arm. It was my right arm, the arm Tarney had marked so elegantly with his size twelves, and I hadn't noticed till now how sore it was. I winced, and Gaddesdon looked at me like I was some kind of soft southern bastard. Maybe I was, but this time I had an excuse.

"Tarney's feet," I said, and Gaddesdon gave a sympathetic, know-what-you-mean kind of nod, as if the custody sergeant had stamped on half the arms in Folgate.

"Come on, sir. Let's get some lunch. You haven't seen the crime scene yet, have you?"

I shook my head. It wasn't like Gaddesdon to take the initiative like that, I hardly knew the guy but even I could see taking the initiative wasn't really his thing. Maybe lunch was his thing.

I'd been in some bad pubs in my time, but the King's Head was a new kind of awful. A nice enough bar, and then a huge cold conservatory with the rain beating so hard on the roof you could hardly hear the waiter apologising for what wasn't on the menu today. He'd have been better apologising for what was: I found myself confronted with a great grey block of fish that dissolved into water and bone the moment my fork hit it, and Gaddesdon's chicken was so badly burnt it might just as well have been a lump of coal. That didn't stop him tucking in with gusto and grabbing a handful of soggy chips off my plate when I sat back and pushed it away in disgust.

Maybe it was just me. The place was packed, after all, elderly ladies by the bus-load, tourists with a liking for the cold and the wet, little knots of farmers gathered in sullen pockets like Victorian mourners.

As my eyes washed over the crowd I spotted a mop of bushy blond hair and went suddenly cold. I blinked and looked again, and it was a few strands of combed-over white. Roarkes was right. I had to get a grip.

One thing the King's Head did have going for it was a decent mobile signal. I had three texts, two from insurance claims handlers fishing for a non-existent accident, and the third an extravagantly polite message from Atom Industries inviting me to get in touch to confirm a date for my interview. I hovered over the delete button for so long they could have burnt another couple of chickens for Gaddesdon to eat in the time it took me to make up my mind, and finally put my phone in my pocket and left the decision for another day.

Three texts. Not one, I noted, from Claire. Maybe I hadn't been humble enough.

As we made our way towards the exit we found the

route blocked by one of the farmers, either a stout man or a slim man in a stout coat, it was difficult to tell which. Gaddesdon tapped him on the shoulder and asked politely if we could squeeze past, and he turned so slowly I wasn't sure if I was watching a man moving or an oil tanker changing direction. "Thanks," said Gaddesdon, and the farmer replied with one of those nods that passes for a smile in those places where a smile's a sign of weakness.

On the way out we walked past the table he'd been sat at. His friends were grumbling, and I could just about make out what it was they were grumbling about.

I turned and stared at them, but they were back to their bitter and the weather and whatever it was the farmers usually talked about round here. I waited until we were back in Gaddesdon's car before I mentioned anything.

"Did you hear them?"

He hadn't. I gave him my best impression of what I'd heard. *Cops and journalists. Thieves nicking anything that's not nailed down and we're left to it, but the moment someone kills one of them, here they all are.*

Gaddesdon shrugged.

"Not really the same, is it?" he said. "Someone nicking a lawnmower and someone shooting two officers."

Which was fair enough, but wasn't really the point.

"The guy with the CCTV."

Gaddesdon didn't know what I was talking about. I wasn't sure his memory stretched back more than twenty-four hours on a good day. I reminded him.

"The farmer. Near the scene. Said his CCTV was switched off because there was no crime round here."

"What about him?"

"From what I've just heard, there's plenty of crime round here. Enough to leave a few cameras running, at least."

Gaddesdon turned and looked at me, which was

disconcerting, because he was doing forty and the road wasn't as straight as I'd have liked.

"Don't listen to that lot, sir. Farmers. They'll moan about anything."

"Sam," I said. "Enough of the *sir*. Let's visit the scene, OK?"

Gaddesdon shrugged. I took it as a yes.

13: Chicken Jalfrezi

THE CRIME SCENE could have been anything, anywhere. The forensics officers had packed up and gone home and taken all their masks and yellow tape with them. A narrow road, a couple of lay-bys, on either side, twenty yards apart. Six-foot hedges bordering the road, fields, a wood in the distance. There was nothing to tell you two police officers had been murdered here. I walked up and down for a few minutes, taking it all in, not that there was much to take in, and trying to ignore the drizzle that was soaking its way steadily through everything I was wearing. Gaddesdon stood with his arms folded, impervious to the rain even though he had neither a coat nor an umbrella, staring fixedly at nothing.

A few yards further on there was a track, just as Roarkes had said, and it took us to a farmhouse where a tight-lipped man in his fifties told us he'd already told everyone everything he knew so we should stop bothering him or he'd make a complaint.

"Do you mind if I take a look at your CCTV system, sir?" I asked. He stared at me. I hadn't introduced myself, so I was guessing he thought I was police, just as Daniel Cullop had. I wasn't going to tell him otherwise. Being mistaken for police wasn't so bad, anyway. People tend not to like the police, but in my experience, they like lawyers even less.

"Over here," he said. I'd spotted a camera on a pole at the entrance to the track, and another one high on the wall of the farmhouse. The computer running it all was in the corner of a barn tacked onto the side of the house, with a power cable running through a glassless window to feed it. It was switched off, but it was still plugged in. I turned it on.

It whirred for a minute, and the monitor flickered to life. Blue screen. The whirring stopped, started again, died. "No disk," read the screen. I stared at it.

The farmer was outside with Gaddesdon, both of them silent.

"Did you know there's no hard drive in your PC?" I asked him. He looked at me like I was talking a foreign language.

"The drive. The bit of your computer that has everything on it, all your data, your programmes, your system, everything you've recorded. It's not there."

He shrugged.

"Nick anything, they will," he said, turned and walked back inside the house, letting the door fall shut behind him. This was the farmer who'd claimed he had nothing worth stealing. Gaddesdon followed me back into the barn and bent over the computer.

"He's right, you know," he called out a minute later.

"What? How?"

"It's been nicked. Look. Someone's unscrewed the back, pulled out the hard drive, left everything else there."

"Why the hell would someone do that?"

Gaddesdon shrugged.

"Dunno. Storage. It's what everyone wants, right?"

Right, I thought. Top marks for Gaddesdon. They want it so bad they'll come to a farmhouse in the middle of nowhere to steal it out of a computer so old it's never heard of Facebook.

Roarkes was looking pleased with himself when we returned, that smug grin back on his face, which usually meant someone else was wearing a frown. I hoped the someone else was Tarney.

"Got one of the bastards talking, have you?" I asked, and he shook his head.

"Nothing that good, no. But we found the phone the original call was made from."

Nothing that good? From where I was standing the phone was a miracle. And for all he was using the plural pronoun, I didn't see anyone in that "we" except Roarkes. I raised an eyebrow and Roarkes filled me in.

"Well, not the phone itself. But we tracked down the owner. Says it was nicked."

"That's convenient. Did he report it?"

"No, he didn't report it. But he doesn't look the type to talk to the police unless he has to."

I nodded. Roarkes went on. The owner of the phone – Brian Betterson, the guy was called – claimed to have lost it outside a football ground the day before the killing. Turf Moor. Burnley.

"They're used to losing things round there," said Gaddesdon, and laughed. No one joined in.

Betterson had already been pulled in and interviewed by a detective sergeant who'd had the bad luck of a free half hour at the wrong time, with Serena Hawkes allowed to sit in as an observer. Nothing useful, said Roarkes, and showed me the transcripts. He wasn't wrong.

"Did the guy seem convincing?"

"Serena certainly thought so. Give her a call."

I did. She agreed with Roarkes. The phone was starting to look like yet another dead end.

"Mind if I speak to the guy?" I asked her.

"No skin off my nose."

Brian Betterson was halfway back to Burnley when Gaddesdon got hold of him, and his response to being asked to return to Folgate was loud and fairly predictable. But he agreed to come in, and that was the important thing.

Except maybe it wasn't. I sat there, in what Roarkes insisted, for the tape, was an "advisory role", with Betterson muttering darkly about *all the fucking observers and advisers* and *no wonder they can't catch any real criminals*, while Roarkes asked him most of the same questions the DS had asked an hour or so earlier and got the same answers, preceded each and every time by "I've already fuckin' been through all this." Brian Betterson was a tall, thin man in his late twenties with cheap, fading tattoos on his upper arms and the distracted look of someone on his way down and already thinking about his next fix.

And Brian Betterson was nervous. That was certain. He had his story straight enough, phone taken from his bag when he'd put it down to have a smoke before the Burnley game. He hadn't reported it to the police because it was a cheap phone, a crap one, and what were the police going to do about something like that when there were people getting raped and stabbed all over the place? It struck me that Brian Betterson probably wouldn't have gone to the police even if he'd lost something expensive, because, as Roarkes had indicated, Brian Betterson didn't look like he enjoyed talking to the police. But that was fair enough, I thought. He was a junkie. He had, as Roarkes informed me just before we went in to see him, a short and modest record for handling stolen goods. The biter had been bitten. He wasn't going to come moaning to the police about it.

One last try, I thought, and asked him to read out some words.

"Why the fook would I do that?" he asked, but he did it anyway.

"Hello, listen, I think I've seen a man with a weapon."

"Yes, in his car."

"Dunno. Dark hair, late thirties."

"Blue Fiesta. Driving out of Charborough, up towards Bursington."

He didn't sound anything like the man who'd made the call, and I didn't think he was acting. I didn't think he was clever enough to act. Brian Betterson was nervous, but not because he was lying. He was a dead end. I was sure of it.

Ninety-nine per cent sure, at least.

Back in Roarkes' office we sat in silence staring into space, a pair of plastic gnomes fishing an empty pond. I cast my mind back through the day, event by meaningless event, until I hit my morning call to Claire, which probably had more meaning in it that I wanted it to. I wondered what Roarkes was thinking, whether he was considering the case, or his wife, or just what he was going to have for his dinner. He looked tired, strained, more than just the usual unhappy, and I'd opened my mouth to ask if he was OK when my phone rang. I answered without looking at it.

"Mr Williams? Mia Arazzi, *Daily Mirror.* I know you don't want to get into some long conversation but can you just confirm one thing for me?"

I was about to kill the call without saying a word, but something stopped me. I didn't have to confirm anything. But it wouldn't hurt to hear what she had to say.

"Go on," I said. "I'm not promising anything."

"I've been hearing there's a chance this Carson thing is all to do with planning and development."

I nearly dropped the phone. How had she heard that?

"Mr Williams? Is this true?"

"What have you been hearing, then?"

"I gather there's some suggestion of impropriety. People taking money to make certain decisions. And, of course, other people being very unhappy about that."

I nearly asked her what her source was, and then I

stopped. Daniel Cullop, probably, or someone like him. All too eager to talk to the press. That plus some digging through the local papers and the planning application records. She might have a source, a proper one, but I didn't think that was likely.

"I'm sorry, Miss Arazzi."

"It's Mrs."

"Either way, I'm afraid I can't comment on that. Sorry."

I ended the call. I hadn't learned anything. But I hadn't given anything away, either. Planning could get people angry, sure, but cold, calculated murder? It was a very long shot.

Roarkes had heard my side of the call and guessed the rest. He was muttering under his breath about *fucking Folgate cops can't keep their stupid mouths shut*. I hadn't considered that possibility. Maybe it wasn't Cullop at all. What better way to get Roarkes off your back than getting the press onto his?

I was thinking about Mia Arazzi, and Betterson, and Tarney, and what Serena Hawkes might make of it all, and then, entirely by accident, about Serena Hawkes in general, when my phone rang again and there she was on the other end.

"We need to talk," she said, which wasn't what I expected at all.

"OK," I replied. "I'm at the station. When can you get here?"

"Forget that. I'm starving. Meet me at the Maharaja. It's on Turner Street. Should take you about fifteen minutes from Folgate."

I looked at my watch. It was nearly eight and I hadn't noticed myself getting hungry. Suddenly, I felt very hungry indeed, and that had nothing to do with the fact that the woman I was going to break bread with was someone I very much wanted to see.

"Is this a date, Serena?" I asked.

"I don't give a stuff what you call it, I just want a chicken jalfrezi, a keema nan, and a pint of Kingfisher."

I might have been talking to myself.

"See you in fifteen," I said.

I was there in ten, waiting at a table when she walked in looking a lot brighter than the last time I'd seen her. I'd been thinking about how I should play this, what I should say, whether I should really be here at all. I'd decided to park that last one. I was having a meal with a colleague, we had important matters to discuss about the case we were working on, and the fact that I was in a long-term relationship with a woman who wouldn't talk to me two-hundred-and-something miles away in London was entirely irrelevant.

I'd almost convinced myself that was true.

She smiled at me as she hung her jacket on her chair, sat down, and ordered a beer. I decided to jump straight in.

"What's up, Serena?"

She smiled again, and shook her head.

"Let's order some food and have a drink before we get down to business, Sam."

I wasn't arguing with that.

This was a different Serena from the one who'd sat in my car and looked like she had every case in the world weighing her down. This was a Serena Hawkes who could knock back a pint of Kingfisher like it was water, order another, and manage half an unusually-hot chicken jalfrezi before the drink arrived. I knew it was unusually hot because I was eating the same thing, but a lot more slowly and cautiously than she was, the heat filling my mouth and rushing up and into my head. I could taste every last sliver of chilli. She spotted me trying to pick the red bits off my fork as subtly as I could, and grinned.

"Bit much for your southern stomach?"

"No," I protested, "it's just—"

"Just what?"

I sat back and returned her grin.

"Just nothing. You win. You can take it spicier than I can."

"That's all I wanted to hear."

"Excellent. You've made me feel half the man I was. Happy now?"

"Delighted."

She told me where she was from and how her life worked. Her father had disappeared when she was four, and her mother had brought the two of them up alone, Serena and her sister, kept them out of trouble, landed herself a job at the biggest law firm in town as a receptionist, trained by night and turned herself into a legal secretary. She'd saved enough to send the girls to university. Pauline was a doctor, now. Serena had followed her mother into a legal career.

"She must be very proud of you."

She shrugged. "You wouldn't know it to hear her talk. It's all about the next thing, the next case, why aren't I representing this one, she keeps seeing lawyers on TV, why am I not on TV, all that."

I laughed. She joined me.

"What about you, Sam Williams?"

It was my turn to shrug.

"Nothing much to say."

She gave me one of those looks, face down, eyes up, *who the hell are you trying to kid?*

"I looked you up, you know. You're not the chump you pretend to be, Sam."

Chump. I raised an eyebrow. There was a compliment

buried in there somewhere, but it would take a big spade to dig it out. Serena ignored the eyebrow and went on.

"No, really. The case against Mauriers, that wasn't bad, was it? And back in oh-four? They were calling you 'one of the brightest legal stars of the future', weren't they?"

I couldn't help smiling at that one. The zenith of my career. We'd freed a man who'd served twenty years for a murder someone else had committed, and I'd been the one who found the key to get him out. But I'd seen the parents, their faces, at the moment of my victory I'd turned and looked at Bill and Eileen Grimshaw watching the release of the man they'd spent twenty years blaming for their child's death. The faces of people going through the whole thing all over again. I'd tried to forget those faces and stuck the cutting on the inside of my desk drawer, and I'd looked at it whenever things weren't going so well, which was once a month, then once a week, then a couple of times a day as Brooks-Powell turned his own screws until they kicked me out of the firm and I said goodbye to that desk for good. The faces of Bill and Eileen Grimshaw had stuck around a lot longer.

I looked up from my food and saw Serena was grinning at me, expectant, so I gave a modest shrug.

"It's better than *the bloke who can't take a chicken jalfrezi.*"

"It could be worse," she said, and laughed, and I laughed too, and we slid back into an exchange of easy, comfortable truths and disclosures. Nothing important. Nothing dangerous.

Once we'd finished our main courses – or once she had, with mine pushed to the side and still half a dozen forkfuls to go – the conversation started to lag. I took a long, deep drink and sat back.

"So what did you want to talk about?"

The change was so swift you'd think they were two different women. One moment she was laughing, teasing me, chatting happily about her life, the next she was frowning, smile gone, the frustrated sigh of someone resigned to discussing something she really didn't want to.

"It's Roarkes. I think he's trying to block me."

I hadn't really known what to expect, something about the case, probably, something about Carson, no doubt. But not this.

"Really?"

"I – I think so. He's not getting very far, is he? He hasn't got any leads and if he has he's not sharing them with me. I mean, I know I'm supposed to be on the other side, but this case is so fucked up I don't think there *are* any sides. And then he calls you up – and no offence, Sam, but I still can't figure out why. He tries to question the suspect without me there, like he thinks *I'm* blocking *him* when all I've done so far is be as cooperative as possible."

I thought about it for a moment. I thought about what Roarkes had done since I'd arrived. Not a lot, I decided. There was a lot of waiting around and reacting to events, which wasn't like the Roarkes I knew, and not very much of anything else. He'd brought me in to help, the so-called expert, but I knew Roarkes well enough to realise he'd never expected a miracle. Even a genius couldn't get inside Carson's head. And as for leads, maybe she had a point. I'd asked to speak to Tarney, got nowhere. I'd asked him about Argentina and he'd told me to drop it. I'd mentioned the planning angle to him and he'd pretty much laughed in my face. I'd given him Maloney's line on Carson's background, or lack of it, and he'd shut me down so fast I didn't have time to blink. I'd come within a couple of feet of being run over, and he'd told me to get a grip.

And he'd found Brian Betterson, a dead end with a mobile phone.

It wasn't that Roarkes didn't have any leads. It was just that he wasn't following up the leads he did have. Maybe Serena was right. But it only made sense if he had something of his own.

I took a sip from my drink and realised what I was thinking. It was ridiculous. I knew Roarkes. He might not be the most charming copper out there, but he was on the level. Serena wasn't right. She couldn't be right. I sure as hell hoped she wasn't right. But whatever the truth, arguing with her wasn't going to help.

"Maybe. I think he's under a bit of stress himself. The locals aren't making it any easier for him. And don't worry. I don't blame you for questioning my involvement. But I promise I'll tell you everything I find out. Think of me as your assistant, OK?"

She smiled.

"I think I can live with that. But I wish I'd never taken this case on."

Even behind the smile, I could tell she meant it. We'd already had this conversation, in my car. I took a deep breath and prepared to revisit the arguments I'd made last time round, and opened my mouth to kick things off, and her phone rang.

She flinched, again, the same flinch she'd given when it had rung in my car. The phone was sitting face-up on the table. She looked down and registered the caller ID, then back up at me.

"Sorry," she said. "Won't be a minute," and I gave her what I hoped was a winning smile. She picked up the phone.

"Pauline? Everything OK? Is Bella OK?"

I couldn't hear the voice on the other end, but clearly everything was OK, and so was Bella, whoever Bella might be, because the next thing Serena said was, "Listen, hon, I'm just talking to a colleague about the case. Can we chat in the morning?"

A short pause.

"Good. Give me a call between patients, OK? Bye love."

She put the phone down and grinned apologetically at me.

"Sorry. She's been having trouble with her daughter. Just wanted to make sure there was nothing serious going on."

Maybe that was true, maybe it wasn't, but the way Serena reacted every time her phone went off reminded me of someone with too many things on her mind. She was nervous, I decided. On edge. Tense. She needed a break.

"You need a break," I said, and her head flew up. She fixed me with a glare. I'd seen that glare. She'd used it on Roarkes. I didn't like it on me.

"Why? Want to take the case on yourself?"

Her eyes were narrowed. I was reminded of a cat. And not a sleepy, friendly one. I put one hand up in a gesture of conciliation – the same gesture, I realised, that Tarney had made as he'd reached into his pocket.

"No. Sorry. That's not what I meant. I meant you're on edge. You need to get this case done, which it will be soon, seriously, and you need to take a break. You're like a rabbit in headlights."

I glanced down at the table. Her hands were resting beside her empty glass, her fingers curled into fists. I'd gone too far. I never had learned to stop myself.

"What are you, some kind of bloody psychiatrist?" she spat.

"You're jumping at shadows, Serena. I'm just trying to help. I'm serious."

She relaxed, suddenly, looked down at her near-empty plate for a long time, long enough for me to register the full insipid horror of the music they were piping in. When she looked back up there was a rueful smile on her face.

"I'm sorry. You're right. I do need a break. I just wish all this was over."

"Me too. It will be soon. Count on it. That's a promise. A cast-iron, Sam Williams promise."

14: Initiative

BY NOON NEXT day I was regretting that promise already. The evening had begun to peter out as our plates had been cleared away, and had floundered on an awkward moment where the waiter had asked if we wanted coffee "or something a little stronger", and we'd sat watching one another try not to be the one who said *no* first. It had ended five minutes later with the two of us walking out to our separate cars and a handshake – a damned *handshake* – as she thanked me for coming and assured me, with that big, warm smile, that it had done her the world of good.

I didn't believe her, smile or no smile. I drove back to the hotel and tried to congratulate myself for not ending up in bed with someone who wasn't Claire, but I didn't believe that, either. The car park was full, which meant I had to park on the other side of the road, and that shouldn't have meant a thing, but I still found myself looking both ways before I crossed and waiting longer than necessary for an innocent taxi to crawl past. Back in my room, with the air still cold and the window still open, I fell quickly into an uneasy sleep and dreamt about Claire, but halfway through she turned into Serena and I woke up late, a dull ache in the arm Tarney had rearranged, and more tired than I'd felt when I'd gone to bed.

There was a missed call from Michael Slaney, my contact at the Home Office. When I called him back he answered on the first ring and laughed loudly for a full ten seconds before he managed to say anything.

"Hasina Khalil!" was what he said when he finally

finished laughing, and then he filled me in.

Hasina Khalil's husband had been a minor bureaucrat in the Egyptian Ministry of Agriculture under the Mubarak administration. He'd been arrested – not for his views or his allegiances, but because he'd been caught with his hand in the till. He hadn't been executed, either. He was currently in prison, awaiting trial.

I called her immediately and confronted her with what I'd learned.

"Is it true, Hasina?" I asked, and she stopped sobbing long enough to admit that yes, it was, all of it.

"And the reason you don't want to go back is because you'll be arrested for helping your husband steal from the state?"

"Yes," she muttered.

"How much money are we talking about here?"

"A lot of money. I am sorry. I should have told you. But I was so afraid. It is not like England, over there, it is not like your prisons, it is like death."

I sat on the bed as she painted me a picture of the Egyptian penal system, and tried to work out what I was going to do. She'd lied to me, sure, but that wasn't reason enough to send her back. And there was that thing about the money. *A lot of money.* If I was going to act for a crook, at least I might get paid for it.

I interrupted her and told her I'd need a little time to consider whether I could continue to represent her. I expected another outburst, but all I got was a quiet, resigned, "Yes, I understand."

As I hung up I saw a text had come through and felt a brief moment of fear and elation, but the number wasn't Claire's. It was a number I'd seen recently and it took me a moment to place it. Mia Arazzi. The journalist. There was no message, just a web link. I pondered the possibility of malware, decided the phone had survived long enough already, clicked the link and found myself reading an article on the *Daily Mirror* website. She'd written the article and texted me to tell me about it, and if I couldn't figure out why straight away, it was clear as neat vodka by the time I'd read it.

The article focused on the planning angle, which seemed more of a dead end the more I thought about it. But not to Mia Arazzi. Hints, suspicions, sources, nothing concrete, of course, because there couldn't be anything concrete unless she was prepared to simply make it up. And a nasty sting in the tail: the police weren't getting anywhere. So-called experts had been brought in from London. Roarkes was named, fully, *Gideon* and all; I, thankfully, wasn't. All he'd achieved so far was to put his own chief suspect in hospital. Roarkes was right, I realised. If anyone was spilling the beans to Mia Arazzi, they were doing it from under a Folgate police uniform.

The text was a threat. She hadn't named me yet. She might, if I didn't give her anything. I added Mia Arazzi to the list of things I didn't like about Manchester.

The easiest way out of Manchester was getting Carson cleared. He might be guilty; he probably wasn't. The important thing was the evidence, and there wasn't any, just a bunch of half-leads that led nowhere. I decided I wasn't going to let the dead ends get to me any more. I decided to embrace them. Planning applications. Glaciers. Tarney. Sod Roarkes. He was probably right about the leads, he was usually right, which didn't make him any easier to work with. But that wasn't the point. I'd follow each lead to its inevitable locked door, try the handle and say *fuck it, I did my best*. I got in the car and drove to Folgate, where I met Detective Sergeant Priya Malhotra, who blew all my plans to hell in five minutes.

Detective Sergeant Priya Malhotra was short, spiky, tough, clearly bright, everything Gaddesdon wasn't. She reminded me of a cactus. She looked at me with the wariness of a cornered dog when Roarkes introduced us, and I already knew about the toughness and the intelligence from the transcript of her interview with poor Brian Betterson. Roarkes hadn't got anything more out of Betterson second time round because Priya Malhotra had already got everything there was. She strode into Roarkes' office, where he was sat at the desk flicking through bits of paper that looked like they'd been there for decades, and I was sitting with my feet on the side table trying not to fall asleep. She strode in, holding a file and looking like she'd just caught Jack the Ripper, and stopped short when she saw Roarkes wasn't alone.

"It's OK, Priya," said Roarkes. "He might be a lawyer, but he's on our side. You can speak in front of him."

Priya, I noticed. He hadn't called her Detective, or Malhotra, or just insulted her the way he insulted pretty much everyone who wasn't a Chief Constable or a Chief Constable's spouse. I filed that little insight away as she told us what she'd found.

What she'd found was that the story of Carson's field was a little murkier than we'd been led to believe. For a start, there had been trouble when he'd come to buy it. It was up for auction from the estate of a farmer who'd died the year before, and everyone had assumed it would be going to the neighbour who'd grazed his sheep on it for decades. When Carson put his bid in there was the closest thing to uproar Bursington had seen since the Civil War, words were exchanged in the pub and, it was alleged, threats were made. Carson had laughed it off, apparently, but still. Someone had threatened him. And when it came to the planning applications, there were objections and insults, and if the villagers had bothered to coordinate their efforts they'd probably have worn Thomas Carson down, but they hadn't, and they didn't, and that had upset them even more.

DS Malhotra had spoken to the landlord of one of the local pubs, and a clerk at the council, and the development consultants who'd handled the applications on Carson's behalf. No one suggested anything that might conceivably have led to the cold-blooded murder of two police officers. But Carson's field was starting to look like it might be getting promoted from dead end to country lane, and country lane was the closest thing we had to something that might actually lead somewhere.

And there was something else. Something that might fit in with the Cullop comment and the insinuations of Mia Arazzi. DS Malhotra had been given the job of running through the Carsons' financial affairs to see if there was anything useful there, and at first it seemed there wasn't. Credit card bills, utilities, flirting with the edge of the overdraft, payments back and forth between personal accounts and company accounts that probably weren't entirely above board but weren't anything to shout about. Mortgage. Life insurance. They all checked out except the life insurance, which turned out to be nothing of the sort. Two hundred pounds every month, out of the Carsons' joint current account, straight into some other account in the Bahamas that certainly wasn't the Provident Union Life Assurance Company, whatever the reference on the standing order said.

It was noon and she'd been chasing the money for three hours, Malhotra said. Give her a week and she'd find out where that money was really going. The Bahamas were a hard nut to crack, but she'd spoken to some people who'd spoken to some other people who knew where the nutcracker was. But for the time being, it was another lead. Maybe Carson really was throwing money at someone on the council to get his applications through. Maybe this was something else entirely. She'd called Sally

Carson and asked her about it, but Sally had told her she wouldn't be saying another word to the police without her solicitor present. Her solicitor wasn't Serena Hawkes – no one knew who her solicitor was, or if she'd even appointed one, so I didn't think we'd be getting much out of Sally Carson for a while. Malhotra gave me a sideways look when she'd finished telling us about that particular conversation. It appeared she knew about my little visit to Bursington.

I rather liked Malhotra. When she left the office to grab some more files I asked Roarkes about her and how he'd managed to acquire another local officer, and he mumbled something about the article.

"What's that?" I asked, even though I knew precisely what he'd said.

"That bloody article. The Arazzi woman. Bloody hammered me. Wankers upstairs thought I could do with some help. Whether I wanted it or not. And I don't. Not from this lot. Someone else to go running to the press whenever her brain ticks over. Just what I need."

I nodded, in feigned sympathy. He *could* do with some help. He wasn't going to get very far with Charlie Gaddesdon and Sam Williams as his only backup, and from the little I'd seen of her, Malhotra didn't look the type to spill her guts to Mia Arazzi. But I was used to Roarkes moaning and this wasn't Roarkes moaning, not really. He was pleased about Malhotra, Folgate or not, and he didn't really care about Arazzi, and the ridiculous notion I'd had the night before that he might be hiding something was just that, a ridiculous notion. Roarkes was trying as hard as anyone to solve the case. He just needed some proper help. Now, hopefully, he had it.

"So that's one and a half officers you've got in your little army now," I said, cheerily, and Roarkes scowled at me.

"What?" I demanded. It was Roarkes who insulted Gaddesdon every time he laid eyes on him, not me. A bit rich for him to take the high ground now.

"Do you know why Gaddesdon's on this case?"

I shrugged. "No one else wanted him, I guess. They had to give you someone. They gave you someone they could do without."

Roarkes shook his head slowly, and sighed.

"Gaddesdon volunteered. He insisted."

"Why?"

"Because, my brilliant, incisive friend, Gaddesdon and Ahmet were friends. They trained together. Known each other for years."

I remembered the flash of hatred, the expression on Gaddesdon's face as he gazed through the window at a sleeping Carson, and then later, the figure standing motionless in the rain staring at the crime scene. Gaddesdon made a little more sense now.

Still, for all his motivation, he was no Malhotra. The woman had initiative. When she returned, the first thing she asked was whether she could have a word with Tarney, but Roarkes had bad news on Tarney. He'd been taken elsewhere, a police station in Chetwood, the other side of Manchester, and charges were being prepared. If there was any suggestion of corruption it couldn't be investigated by anyone from Folgate, and that meant Roarkes and Malhotra, and Gaddesdon, for what he was worth, were *persona non grata*, which was a shame, because talking to Tarney seemed like a very good idea. Roarkes had spoken to Superintendent Adams at Folgate and asked him to have a word with his opposite number in Chetwood, to push against the ban, but he didn't think Adams had pushed very hard.

"No surprise," he said. "He's one of them, Tarney's one of them, everyone except me and you, Sam."

I glanced over at Malhotra, who'd had to endure this little rant in silence, a frown playing across her face, and wondered whether it was time to present Roarkes with his own tinfoil hat. And for all the anger and paranoia, it didn't really matter, because Tarney wasn't talking anyway. He and everyone else.

By the time we were done going through Malhotra's findings it was past two and I was starving. I'd skipped breakfast, I remembered, and not eaten a great deal of that chicken jalfrezi. I'd been surviving on police station coffee all morning, which was a bit like trying to survive on rehydrated dried grass with sour milk thrown in. The pubs weren't serving anything except beer and crisps now the lunchtime rush was over, and the idea of a pub didn't grab me anyway.

"Try the canteen," said Roarkes. I didn't like his smile as he said it, like he knew something I didn't.

Five minutes later and two mouthfuls through a barely-digestible jacket potato, I knew it, too. Any alternative to the station canteen was worth trying.

Roarkes' latest choice of pub wasn't much better than the first one he'd taken me to, but at least it was a real pub. The other customers were a mix of middle-aged alcoholics and underage street thugs, but no one seemed to be looking for trouble, so I allowed myself to relax. There was a stained paper menu on the counter, a long list of pies and sandwiches and supposedly "unique" burgers, but we were too late to order anything off that – when I asked them they looked at me like I'd asked for two pints of Guinness and some heroin. They were happy to sell me a packet of crisps and butter me a couple of slices of bread instead. I had a Coke, Roarkes tutting alongside me as he dipped his face in a pint of local bitter and tucked into his own crisp sandwich like he'd lived in the north all his life. *Butty*, I'd seen on the menu. That's what they called a sandwich up here. A *crisp butty*.

I was sick of it. Sick of the rain, the people, the traffic, the shit food. *Fook the crisp butty*. Roarkes glanced up at me, fragments of crisp stuck to his moustache, and laughed. I hadn't realised my expression was so obvious. I sighed, and took a bite. Soft white bread, thick coating of butter, nice crunch in the middle. I really was starving. I took another bite.

I wouldn't admit it to Roarkes, but a Coke and a crisp butty wasn't such a bad lunch after all. I finished it in a couple of minutes and asked for another one, and while I was waiting for them to make it I looked around at the alcoholics and the thugs and realised they probably weren't alcoholics or thugs after all, just normal people enjoying a normal drink at a slightly unusual time of day. One of the youths nodded at me, like I was his mate.

I was worried. I was worried that maybe Manchester wasn't such a shithole after all. I wasn't having the best of times up here, no point pretending otherwise, and try as I might, I couldn't blame Serena, who still fascinated me, or Roarkes, who was only trying to help me, or Carson, who might not be saying much but still drew me on like a distant glow in the darkness. If I couldn't blame Manchester either, then maybe the problem was me.

15: Violence In The Air

BACK AT THE station I was starting to feel like a spare wheel on a car that wasn't moving. Roarkes took a call in his office the moment I sat down, and I watched as his expression switched from *annoyed* to *bat-shit furious* in the space of a second. He raised one arm, pointed at the door and mouthed "fuck off" at me. I remembered how he'd handled Tarney. I didn't need to be asked twice.

There was no sign of Serena, but Gaddesdon was hovering around, smiling at nothing in particular, and I wondered whether this spare wheel sensation was what he felt all the time. Plus the hatred, of course. I couldn't forget the hatred. I went to find Malhotra and asked her if there was anything we could do to help.

She glanced up at me with a smile, then noticed Gaddesdon standing behind me. The smile faltered.

"Er, no, it's OK. I've got everything under control here. It's mostly just waiting."

I looked past her, at the piles of paper carefully balanced on what looked suspiciously like a card table. If Gaddesdon couldn't be trusted to deal with any of that then maybe he really was a liability.

As I walked back into Roarke's office my phone rang. I checked the display before I answered. It was Maloney.

"Got anything for me?" I asked, feeling slightly dirty for having hoped it would be Serena.

"We've found him," he replied.

"Found who?"

"Carson. Who Carson was."

I waited for a moment, assuming Maloney was about to go on and tell me. He didn't.

"So?"

"So you've got to come and meet someone."

"Why?"

What Maloney had actually found, it turned out, was a man who claimed to know who Carson had been before he was Carson. Maloney's informant – he wouldn't give me the name, however many times I asked – was prepared to tell me what he knew, for a price, if we met face to face that evening.

I looked at my watch. It was nearly four. Roarkes was looking at me and shaking his head. He knew who I was talking to, and I knew what he thought of Maloney, but Roarkes wasn't my boss.

"Where?"

"Pub. East End of London."

The drive would be hell on four wheels. Everyone in Manchester would be trying to get out of it the same time I was.

"I can't be there till late."

"We'll wait."

Maloney gave me the name of the pub and the location. The Mitre. I'd heard of the place. Someone had been stabbed there a few weeks back. There was one other important detail.

"How much?" I asked.

"I've got it," said Maloney, and I didn't push it any further. I wasn't exactly rolling in cash and I didn't think Roarkes would be advancing me expenses for something like this. If Maloney was going to take the hit, good for him.

The drive was slow and uneventful, and inching closer to London didn't bring with it any of the relief or euphoria I'd hoped it would. I thought about calling Roarkes and letting him know what I was doing, and then I pictured him, either shaking his head mournfully at my stupidity or spitting teeth at me for wasting good petrol. He knew I'd spoken to Maloney, but no more than that. And for all that Roarkes had brightened up that morning, the further I got from him, the more I heard Serena's words, her worries, her suspicions. I called her instead. I told her where I was heading, and why, and even though she didn't say it I could tell she was thinking the same things Roarkes would have said out loud. I told her I thought I might pay Tarney a visit when I got back, and she had no problem with that. She just didn't know how I was going to manage it and why I was talking to her about it.

"You're a local lawyer. Surely you know who's acting for him? And you must know Chetwood, right?"

"Ye-es," she replied. "I know the super there. But latest I heard, he hasn't got a lawyer."

"Oh," I said. I hadn't thought of that. And then I had one of those rare but beautiful Sam Williams brainwaves.

"What about you? You know the super, right? Get yourself in there. Act for him. He won't complain, will he?"

"He might."

"I know I wouldn't," I said, and instantly regretted it. There was what sounded like a stifled laugh from the other end of the line, and then it was back to business.

"I'll see what I can do," she said. It wouldn't be easy, I thought. If someone suggested there was a conflict of interest between Tarney and Carson, she wouldn't be able to take on Tarney. But who'd care enough to bother doing that?

I called Claire three times on the way, and three times she didn't answer. I didn't know how things were going to pan out tonight, but I wasn't going to be driving back before tomorrow and I didn't have the money for a hotel or any great desire to sleep in my car or borrow a bed off Maloney. All of which meant Claire was going to be seeing me tonight, whether she wanted to or not. Elizabeth Maurier phoned again, and I let it go through to voicemail. When I played it back she was telling me I couldn't just put the past behind me and forget about it. I thought about the Grimshaws and their murdered daughter, and I hoped she was wrong.

And I still hadn't decided what I was going to do about Hasina Khalil.

It was raining in East London, but not like it was raining in Manchester. I didn't care. I'd be in my car, in the pub, in the car again and home. It could be raining blood for all it would bother me.

The Mitre, the dirty East End pub Maloney's contact had picked, was just the kind of place you'd expect to meet someone who didn't always walk the right side of the law and was prepared to tell you things he shouldn't for the right fee. I'd been in enough of them myself. I was usually the one paying the fee. It was dark, there was a bit of loud metal playing and about thirty drinkers, all men, one woman behind the bar, two people playing pool silently and seriously, a smell of damp and piss and spilled beer and a general feeling that if you said the wrong thing you wouldn't get much chance to apologise. I kept my head down and tried to convince myself that the people staring at me weren't staring at me at all, or if they were then it had nothing to do with Carson and Tarney and the nondescript green car that might have tried to run me over the previous morning. I wasn't buying it. There was violence in the air. The Mitre made the Bull on Blackmoor look like the Ritz.

Maloney was sitting at a table in the corner furthest from the pool table. He wasn't alone.

The man sitting with Maloney was grey-haired, and even from the far side of the room I could tell he was nervous. Maloney had obviously said something to him, or just looked significantly in my direction, because he was smiling at me with that *everything's cool* smile people wear when nothing's even close to cool but they don't want to let it show. I recognised that smile. I'd worn it myself often enough. I was probably wearing it now.

Fine. If the guy was nervous, that was fine, that was my role decided for me. I was the guy who wasn't nervous. I walked right up to the table, stood next to the guy, held out my hand and said, "Sam Williams."

"Boris," he said. "Boris Crick."

I frowned. I couldn't help it. The handshake was weak, but it was firmer than the name. I didn't know what a Boris Crick would look like but it wasn't this guy. I remembered that Maloney hadn't given me the name either, and decided to act like it didn't matter. This wasn't one of those crack-the-case, get-inside-the-head deals. This was pay to play. There were two near-empty pint glasses on the table, which made my next move obvious enough.

"What are you drinking?"

"Two pints of Stella," said Maloney. "You're buying."

I went to get the drinks. I glanced back at the table as casually as I could while I waited. Maloney and "Crick" were sitting in silence. This wasn't going to be a sociable evening.

Crick grabbed his drink with the eagerness of a man who was getting uncomfortable and wanted something in his hands. He sipped slowly, staring at nothing, and then he turned to me and said, "So what do you want to know?"

I'd assumed Maloney had been through all of this already. I didn't really know why I had to be here, but if that was the way Crick wanted to play it, well, he was the one with the information.

"Thomas Carson. Who is he, really? What can you tell me?"

Crick took a long drink, dragged the back of his hand across his mouth, and nodded.

"Carson. Had no idea, till I saw the pictures in the papers. I thought that guy was dead."

I waited.

"Used to know him, though. Francis, his name was. Is. Francis Grissom. Just a kid, really, but handy with his fists. That was, what, fifteen years ago? Twenty?"

I looked closely at Crick. He was grey and there were lines, sure, but he wasn't as old as I'd first thought. Early fifties, I guessed. Younger than Roarkes, anyway. I nodded.

"He used to work with some people I knew. Up north. I didn't like them. Didn't like any of them. But that one I remembered. They were proud of the guy. Used to boast about him. Liked the way he did what he was told to, no questions asked, and the people he worked for did very nicely out of it."

Crick bent back down to his drink and I took advantage of the pause.

"What did they do, the people he worked for?"

Crick shrugged, and for a moment I thought he didn't know, but it wasn't that.

"What didn't they do? Drugs, mainly, and people, a bit of protection, guns, I heard, but I don't know if that was true."

Another pause, another sip. Crick was letting the facts out slowly. Maybe he thought he'd get more money that way.

"Where were these guys?" asked Maloney, and Crick turned to him with a frown on his face, like he was trying to remember.

"Lancashire. Burnley and Blackburn, you know, those

places where they have so many stabbings no one notices one more."

Maloney pushed. "So how did *you* know them?"

Clever, I thought. Wouldn't have occurred to me. Whatever his name really was, Boris Crick was one hundred per cent cockney. This place was probably his local. Not a hint of a northern accent.

"People I worked with back then, they had arrangements with the people he worked with. I used to go up there once a month, for a year or so. They never came down here, though. We always had to go to them."

I opened my mouth to ask precisely what these *arrangements* were, and then closed it. Better I didn't know, unless I had to. I had another question, though, a more pertinent one.

"So what happened to Francis Grissom? Why did he change his name?"

Crick shrugged and I thought *here it is, the bit where he pretends he doesn't know until a fat bunch of tenners turns up*, but it didn't come out like that.

"You hear rumours, you know. I mean, these guys were nasty. I thought I was hard, but they were something else. They had a line, a motto, 'In For Life' they said, it didn't matter what happened, you couldn't leave. And if you pissed them off, they killed you. No second chances, no apologies, no excuses. Story was they even got one guy to top himself, let him know they'd come after his family if he didn't. So Grissom, if he wasn't happy, he couldn't exactly tell anyone. And a lot of people were getting killed back then. I'd open the paper and there'd be a fire some place no one else has ever heard of, somewhere in Lancashire and I'd be saying *bloody hell I was only there last week picking stuff up* and there's a couple of bodies there and no one ever finds out who did it. So I show up one day and there's no Grissom, he'd always been there, always him and a couple of others, seemed to get on well enough, all of them, but this time he's not there, and I say *where's Frank then?* and all I got was nothing."

It hadn't been the easiest thing, following Crick's narrative line, but I just about understood it.

"And that was it?"

"Right. They said nothing, I thought *better keep your mouth shut, Boris,* and that was it. No more Frank. Thought they'd be pulling his body out of some ditch in a few weeks' time. Did a few more runs for them and then, well, I had my own bit of bad luck."

I frowned, expecting more, but Crick was back to his pint. Maloney stepped in to explain.

"Boris had a bit of a run-in with the police. Grievous Bodily Harm. Wrong time, wrong place. Did his stretch."

"Seven years."

"Seven years, Sam. Fair stretch."

I nodded. I'd had clients who'd done less than that for killing people, and that wasn't because they had the world's best lawyer. Whatever Boris Crick had done, I wouldn't have fancied being on the receiving end.

"That's me done then," he said, suddenly, and stood, empty pint glass in one hand.

"Really?" I asked. I couldn't help it. It was all so abrupt.

"That's all I've got, mate. Seriously. You want anything else, you're going to have to ask some other guy."

"No names, then?"

"You fucking kidding?"

He'd turned to face me, and even though he was the same man, past his prime, nothing to worry about if you looked at him, there was suddenly a hint of menace. Maybe it was because I'd just heard about the seven years. But I didn't think so.

"I've given you Grissom. You think I'd give you the

other names even if I had 'em? You're not paying me enough for that, mate. Not even close."

He turned, again, and found his way blocked by Maloney. Maloney was smiling, but I knew Maloney. This wasn't a happy smile.

"Sit down, Boris. You've had your money. Have yourself another drink."

Boris sat. That was all it took. A few words from Maloney.

But there were no more names. He'd given us Grissom and Grissom was all he had, and Grissom's face was all over the news anyway. "Someone's gonna tell you who he is. Might as well be me." Crick had another drink and entertained us with the tale of a rival dealer who'd been shut down using a nail gun and a bucket of acid, and a family suspected of talking to the police, burnt to death in their own home, just in case. Nice people Francis Grissom had mixed with.

No more names. When Crick got up to leave a second time, neither of us tried to stop him. He nodded, wished us good luck, advised us to leave it there. And then something else, just as he was about to go.

"No names, right? No people. But there was something. They called themselves the Corporation. Haven't heard a word about them for years. They'd been getting smaller for a while, you know how it is, the Poles were coming in, the Pakistanis, new suppliers, new products. They were losing turf. But I can't believe anyone took them down. They're still there. You can count on it."

Part of me thought that was the best piece of information I'd got since I'd been dragged into this mess. But that was a small part. For the rest, it was just a word, a stupid word, and a name from the past that might turn out to mean something, but probably wouldn't. Boris Crick wasn't the kind of man I'd trust to give me the time of day, let alone the name behind a murder.

Maloney didn't agree. We got one more drink each, which was enough to put me over the limit, but you couldn't drink lemonade with Maloney. He was convinced Crick was on the level. It wasn't like he knew the guy. It wasn't anything more than a hunch, with a light dusting of arrogance on top: he was Maloney, and you didn't lie to Maloney. Me, I came at it from a different angle. Most of the people I spoke to lied to me. My clients lied to me because it was second nature. The police lied to me because I was on the other side. Witnesses lied because they were scared or greedy or just didn't care enough to tell the truth. When I spoke to someone, I started with the assumption they were lying. Crick hadn't done much to change my mind.

Maloney had to go after ten minutes, which meant I could leave my half-drunk pint of lager and drive home. The Mitre was no more inviting than it had been when I'd walked in, less so now my companions had left. Boris Crick didn't seem the kind of person you'd rely on in a tight corner, but if I had to be here I'd rather be drinking with him than by myself.

But who could you rely on in a tight corner? I thought back to Roarkes. *Get a grip*, he'd said. I'd bought it, for a time, but now I wasn't sure. I wasn't sure about Roarkes at all. Nothing was as clear as it should have been. I sat in the driver's seat, shut the door, closed my eyes and took a long, deep breath. I was tired, I decided. It had been a long day. That was all.

I took it slowly; on top of the tiredness, I didn't know the East End well enough to drive through it without concentrating. For all the money and the banks and the Queen Elizabeth Olympic Park within spitting distance, this little stretch of East London wasn't much more than a slum. Crumbling tenement blocks, screams in the distance, men lying in the gutter, bins emptied across the street, no lights except the ones on my car. I thought about Crick, the bullshit name, the bullshit handshake, the story which gave us just as much as we needed and no more. He was lying, I decided. I was all but certain of it. Maloney was too used to people fearing him to notice when they were only telling him what he wanted to hear. I sat waiting at a red light and felt a surge of anger, but it didn't last long, because however angry I might be it wasn't angry enough to hold back the cold, black wave of depression that followed. Crick was lying, I'd wasted my time coming down here, and Maloney had wasted his money. I was all but certain he was lying and I'd go back to Manchester tomorrow and follow the rest of the half-leads until there was nothing left to follow.

And after that?

I didn't know. The one thing I was sure of was that I didn't want to work for Atom Industries.

All but certain.

The tiniest sliver of doubt.

What if Crick was telling the truth? If Carson was Francis Grissom. If he'd been part of a crew who did things that disgusted even Maloney, because I'd glanced at him, briefly, during the story about the dealer and the acid, and there was an unfamiliar look on his face. If there was anything in that sliver, anything at all, then it would change everything.

But that was one hell of a big *if.*

16: Nose

CLAIRE WASN'T HOME. I checked my watch before I rang the buzzer, and then I rang it anyway, because the last thing she'd said to me was still ringing in my ears. I didn't think she'd take kindly to me just showing up in the bedroom and waking her.

But she didn't answer, and I let myself in, and the place was a mess, but the usual kind of mess. No one in the living room. No one in the bedroom or the kitchen or the bathroom either. It was eleven, so it wasn't like she had to be in, but Claire always told me when she was going out, even if I wasn't going to be around.

Till now, anyway.

I panicked, for a moment, and threw open the wardrobe where she kept her clothes. Still there. Panic over. There was a scotch egg in the fridge, a packet of watery, wafer-thin chicken slices and an almost-empty carton of orange juice. Loaf of bread on the counter, hard but not yet green. It was bad, but better than when I'd been living alone. I was hungry. It would have to do.

I was sitting on the sofa watching a repeat of an old US sitcom when I heard the door open – I'd left it unlocked so Claire would know I was in and awake – and turned just in time to see a fist coming at me. I ducked, but I'd been drinking and I was tired and I probably wasn't that good at dodging a fist at the best of times. It hit my left temple and I was sure I felt the contents of my head come uncoupled from whatever was holding them in place and start to slide around.

"Get your nose out of Thomas Carson's business,"

said a voice in a bland, nondescript accent, and then the fist came swinging back, straight for the same nose that had only just started to recover from its last beating, and everything went black.

Claire woke me by screaming. I opened my eyes, shut them because it hurt, the light and the scream and the general state of being awake, counted slowly to three, and opened them again. She was standing in front of me and even through the tears and the light I could tell she was torn between *are you OK?* – which I clearly wasn't – and *what the hell are you doing here?*

"Someone beat me up," I said. I was surprised how clearly the words came out. "Again," I added. I reached up, felt my face, my nose. It stung. That was all. I couldn't really tell without a mirror, but it didn't seem much worse than Tarney had left it. I explained what had happened. My eyes were still stinging and I couldn't keep them open for more than a few seconds at a time, but I was sure I saw her wince in frustration when I got to the bit about leaving the door unlocked.

"We need to call the police," she said.

I shook my head. I didn't want to speak to the police. Not yet. I didn't want to speak to anyone.

I didn't know who I could trust.

"I'm going back to Manchester tomorrow. I'll sort it out then."

"A doctor, then."

My head was still ringing from the shake I'd just given it, so I had to make do with words.

"No. It's nothing serious."

She shook her head, gave an exaggerated, exasperated sigh, then hugged me and helped me onto my feet. We staggered together into the bathroom, where she cleaned me up slowly and carefully, undressed me, pushed me into the shower ("because we might have got rid of the blood, but you still stink, Sam"), turned it on and left me there to soak in the steam and the hot water and try to forget about Roarkes and Carson and Tarney and the grief my nose had been through over the last couple of days. I couldn't get it out of my head.

After five minutes the bathroom door opened and Claire stepped into the shower. Suddenly, my head was utterly, beautifully clear.

She was still pissed off with me next morning, and I couldn't blame her, but I apologised, repeatedly, and after the seventh or eighth time she said, "Just forget about it, OK?" and I decided that was as good as I was going to get.

"How's your nose?" she asked. I'd almost forgotten about my nose. It was hurting, a little, but a little wasn't so bad. The arm was aching, too, from time to time, a niggling reminder that boots could do just as much damage as knees and fists, but the arm could wait in line. I had more important things to worry about than the arm.

There was a moment of uncomfortable silence when she asked me when I was heading back, and I told her as soon as I could. But it was just a moment.

"Then you'd better get on with these," she said. "Let's see if that photographic memory can extend past a takeaway menu these days."

There was a file in her hand, and I opened my mouth to argue with her, because I'd only just had my face smashed in and surely she could let it go, just this once. Then I remembered a smashed-in face hadn't stopped me running around after Sally Carson, blood dripping out into Sergeant Briggs' Shogun, and I'd been owing Claire this for a while now, *as soon as* I had the time, and the fact was, I was interested, too. If she had anything new, anything that would take her a step closer to finding out who the traffickers were, then I wanted to be the one to slot that something new in its place. Maybe a couple of hours' work wouldn't kill me.

She'd made good progress, even if her files were a mess, scraps of paper of different sizes and colours placed seemingly at random. I spent half an hour putting them in order, and there it was, staring me in the face. One man, two places, and I'd been working with criminals too long to believe in coincidence. I called Claire over from the kitchen where she was brewing strong, dark coffee, and showed her what I'd found.

She checked and double-checked until she was sure there was no mistake. The man, Jonas Wolf, ran a business on the site the traffickers used to bring the girls in. Jonas Wolf had been in the apartment block where one of the girls had died. It wasn't exactly proof, but it was more than just a crack in a case, it was an opening a mile wide. Claire kissed me, and smiled, and told me I was allowed to go back to Manchester after all.

I took five minutes to flick through my own files before I left, but there was nothing there that screamed Sally Carson at me. Whatever bells she was ringing, they weren't on my hard drive.

"You don't have to do this, Sam," said Claire, and I remembered I hadn't got round to telling her how desperate things were. Just a cashflow problem, I'd said, and she'd nodded like I was offering her cheese on her spaghetti. And she didn't know about Atom Industries, either.

"I do," I replied. That was all I could think to say.

She shook her head.

"No you don't. You just think you do. You just think this is what Sam Williams does, or at least, the Sam

Williams you've decided you want to be, and you're Sam Williams, so off you trot. You do have a say in this, you know."

I froze for a moment, and wondered whether maybe she was right. Then I remembered it didn't matter. I needed Carson. I needed that sliver to come good. I smiled at her. I'd given up having a say in anything a long, long time ago.

17: Solid Smoke

I HAD ANOTHER message from Atom Industries, a little less polite, a little less patient, and a voicemail from Hasina Khalil informing me that it might take some time to obtain the funds since her bank accounts had been frozen. I hadn't managed to figure out what was bothering me about Sally Carson, and the source for the lead I'd counted on breaking her husband's case was as trustworthy as a shark with a smile. I'd been punched in the face, again, and when I'd reluctantly called Roarkes and told him about it, he'd laced his sympathy with a healthy dose of patronising sarcasm. But I drove back into a cold wet Manchester feeling a lot better than I'd felt leaving it. I didn't know who'd hit me and who'd sent him, but it meant I was on the right track. I was on half a dozen tracks, so that didn't narrow things down as much as I'd have hoped, but it was a start. Something was going to happen. Something would turn up.

And if it didn't, I'd be heading back to London soon enough.

Serena Hawkes was sitting in Roarkes' office when I walked in and before I'd even sat down she was staring at my face.

"Beaten up again," I said, and she gave me that look again, a sad shake of the head plus a hint of a smile.

"You've got to stop pissing people off, Sam."

Roarkes had run clean out of sympathy.

"Had a nice little jaunt, have you? Pleased to see you're back. I take it we can forget all this crap about Carson being someone else?"

"What's got into him?" I asked. He'd been curt with

me earlier, but that was just Roarkes. This was more than just Roarkes. Serena pointed to the newspaper on his desk. I picked it up.

Mia Arazzi, again. It was a brief article, just a few short paragraphs, but one of those paragraphs threw in something new.

"Questions are now being raised within Greater Manchester Police regarding the competence of Detective Inspector Gideon Roarkes to oversee this investigation. In particular, the failure of the force to probe Thomas Carson's history in Argentina, including the mysterious disappearance of his one-time business partner, has set alarm bells ringing at a senior level."

Another bloody Folgate leak. Roarkes named, again, but not me, I noticed with relief, and then I looked back up at Roarkes and the relief was gone. He was wearing the expression of someone who'd been forced to watch while his car was set on fire and driven into his house. And he was looking at me like I was the driver. He stood up and walked around the desk until he was standing no more than six inches away from me, and then he lowered his head and stared into my face.

"Was this you, you bastard?" he growled.

I was at a loss, for a moment, and then I remembered my threat. If he didn't follow up the Argentina angle, I'd make sure someone knew about it.

"Don't be ridiculous," I said, staring right back at him with a boldness and conviction that didn't extend past my eyes. He frowned and stepped back, and I decided it was my turn.

"Sorry you've got your name in the papers again – both your names, in fact – but it's not like it's anyone else's fault, *Gideon*."

I was warming to the battle. Roarkes glared at me, lips pursed, and I glanced down to see the fingers of his right hand tapping rhythmically against his palm, a silent countdown to a very loud explosion. Roarkes was ready for a fight.

I was more than happy to give him one.

"See my face?"

He nodded. "Seen a bit too much of it lately, to be honest."

That was weak. I decided to let it go.

"I told you someone was after me. I told you that car wasn't an accident, and now they've gone after me in my own home."

He nodded again. "You're right, of course."

The tapping had stopped. He was frowning, still nodding, gently, like he was thinking things through and starting to see my side of it. He walked slowly back to the desk and sat down.

"Obviously there's something going on here and your life's in serious danger."

I hadn't expected that.

"I mean, they walk into your flat – how did they get in, Sam?"

I paused, trying to remember, and then it came back to me.

"I'd left the door unlocked," I replied, quietly.

"Right, so they walk in through an open door – how many of them?"

"Just one, I think. I didn't get a good look at him."

I thought I could see the faintest hint of a smile under that frown.

"So this one person walks in through an open door, and – blimey, this is serious – he punches you in the face."

I could see where this was going and I didn't like it. I opened my mouth to say something, but Roarkes was on his feet talking before I could get a word out.

"Now, don't take this the wrong way, but on the one

hand we've got a couple of police officers getting shot in the head, and on the other hand we've got a sneaky little lawyer getting punched in the face."

"He said something about Carson. He said I should drop it."

It was true, but I could hear the words as I said them, and they sounded more like a plea from a psychiatric patient than the testimony of a solid, reliable witness. Serena had sat silently throughout the exchange, watching and listening. I forced myself not to glance in her direction.

"I see," said Roarkes. "I'm quite tempted to punch you in the face and tell you to piss off myself, Sam. Maybe he was just a nice, friendly police officer. Maybe he was my guardian angel."

I opened my mouth again, and again Roarkes stopped me.

"What he wasn't, I can assure you, was an emissary of the South American mob or the local planning department out to silence a dangerous witness."

I felt the blood drain from my face. White was a good look for rage, but by now I was so angry and so humiliated I didn't have any words to pair the colour with. All I could do was shake my head, slowly, and hope the message was getting through.

Roarkes was still talking, and from what he was saying, the message wasn't getting through.

"I'll get uniform to take a statement from you, because something's going on, sure, I won't deny that. But you've got to stop overreacting. You've got to calm down."

Calm down. I'd already reached boiling point and come down the other side. *Calm down* was too much. I turned and walked out of the office. I stood in the corridor for a minute, breathing slowly, thinking through everything Roarkes had just said, and then I remembered Serena's comment in the restaurant, Roarkes ignoring the best leads he had, and the phone call he'd taken, mouthing "fuck off" and waving me out of the room with a face like a plum tomato. He'd dragged me up to Manchester for whatever talent he thought I had, and now he was shutting me down every time I tried to use it.

What was he hiding?

I stood for another minute, just breathing and turning things over, and then I walked back in without knocking and started talking before he could say anything to stop me.

"Here's the deal, Roarkes," I said. "You want me to stick around?"

He shrugged, then nodded, then grunted.

"Yeah. S'pose so."

I'd expected more of a fight. I'd been ready to threaten a full-page spread, just me, Mia Arazzi, and whatever I decided to tell her. I tried to keep the surprise off my face and went on.

"I'm not ready to drop the question of Carson's identity. I'll look into any other crap you want to throw at me, but I want someone looking at some names for me."

He nodded.

"I'll give you Gaddesdon."

"I want Malhotra."

There was a pause, while Roarkes frowned and sucked the air between his teeth. I hated it when he did that.

"OK," he said, at last. "But you take Gaddesdon too."

I thought about it for a moment. As far as I could tell that left Roarkes with Roarkes and no one else, but given he didn't have any leads, he didn't exactly need the manpower.

"Done. So what have you found out while I've been off sampling the delights of London?"

Roarkes looked at Serena. She looked back at him, at

me, down at the table. Maybe she was right about Roarkes. So many possibilities, so little action.

"Nothing?"

Roarkes nodded. I looked down at the newspaper, still open on his desk.

"Mia Arazzi's right, you know. What about Tarney? What about the glacier? If Alejandro Lopez isn't six feet under the snow right where those coordinates point then I'm Buffy the fucking Vampire Slayer."

Roarkes stared at me, blank. Clearly he'd never heard of Buffy the Vampire Slayer. His voice, when he spoke, had the flat, restrained tone of someone saying something for the last time.

"Forget the glacier, Sam. This is Manchester. The glacier's in Argentina."

I stared at him. He shrugged and gave a long, slow sigh.

"For Christ's sake. Alright. You've got Gaddesdon. You've got Malhotra. You want to bang your head against a fucking glacier, be my guest."

I'd just seen Roarkes back down twice in the space of five minutes. I wasn't sure I'd seen him back down once before. I decided to ignore his less-than-gracious tone, twisted my stare into a conciliatory smile, and wondered how precisely one would go about investigating Argentine glaciers anyway. Maybe Malhotra would know. She seemed to know everything else.

As I turned to go, Roarkes laid a hand on my shoulder. I glanced back round at him, ready for a fight, conditioned by all my previous encounters with the man, but all I saw on his face was that strain, again.

"Look, Sam, I'm sorry about your face," he said.

I waited for the punchline, but there wasn't one.

Gaddesdon might have been the free gift I didn't want,

but he was the one who found what we were looking for. Roarkes had ushered us into a tiny room with a computer and space for one person at a time to sit down and told us to get on with it, and I'd cursed his spirit of generosity before I remembered he was lucky to have got even this. Once we got started it took all of fifteen minutes for Malhotra to hit the first seam of gold with a list of old newspaper reports and CID notes, some digitised, some just references to papers in folders in boxes that hadn't been opened for twenty years and were now stacked six deep in the basement. I'd been exaggerating when I'd mentioned looking at "some names" – there were just the two, *Corporation*, and *Frank Grissom*, and Grissom didn't show up anywhere at all, but there were half a dozen references to the Corporation on the system. Nothing solid, though: informants who claimed to know something but never really said what, a sentence in white paint on the ruins of a burnt-out house, a victim babbling a word that might have been "Corporation" in the moments before he bled to death on a Burnley back-street. If it was gold, it was the shit sort of gold they sell tourists in North London markets: snitches looking for more money, kids pissing around with a can of spray-paint, a couple of drunk witnesses trying to make sense of a dying man's last gurgles. The Corporation could be anything, but the chances were it was nothing at all.

And then Gaddesdon followed one of those references to one of those boxes and came back from the basement clutching a memo written by a barely-literate detective sergeant following a fire at an Italian restaurant in Burnley in 1995. He found the article from the local paper ten minutes later. Four dead – the owners and their two children, a sixteen-year-old girl and a boy of just eight. In the handwritten note Gaddesdon had found, the DS attempted to make sense of what had happened.

"Luca Moretti called at station May 18 10am. Spoke to me. Said thretened by corperation. I said what corperation. Luca Moretti said corperation again. At this point."

The memo appeared to end there. To my amazement, Gaddesdon had unearthed what followed.

"DI Peterson needed holp on Op Blackbird so I told Luca Moretti to come back tomorrow. May 19 2am fire service attend Moretti restorant, kitchen fire, no suspicous circs."

Malhotra got to work straight away. The DS, an exiled Scot named McTavish, was long dead, as was DI Peterson. Blackbird, the operation Peterson had wanted some "holp" with, was an investigation into cigarette smuggling that had ended a year or so after the fire with no charges being brought. I didn't think Blackbird was relevant, but I asked Malhotra to dig a little deeper, just in case. The glacier could wait.

Crick had mentioned something remarkably similar. A family suspected of talking to the police, then burnt to death in their own home. Luca Moretti had spoken to the police, or at least he'd tried to. *No suspicious circs.* That was McTavish's view of the matter, and he knew his patch and the people on it better than I did. But if there was nothing to it, why write the memo? Was he covering his back? Had he suspected something after all?

And then I reminded myself how flimsy this was and what McTavish had actually done with this memo. He'd addressed it to nobody, shoved it in a file and forgotten about it. He might not have been sure everything was as clean as it looked, but he certainly wasn't convinced it was murder or that anything like the "Corperation" was involved.

Twenty years later I was in the same position. There was a gang that might have existed, there was a man who might have been in that gang, and there was the word of one ex-con that he was Thomas Carson. Roarkes was right. I needed to start looking elsewhere.

Serena was still in Roarkes' office. There was a slightly frosty silence between them, and I wondered for all of five seconds what was behind it before Roarkes set it out.

"Serena here's got the Tarney gig."

I smiled. It had worked, then.

"Good for you."

She didn't smile back. Whatever was going on between her and Roarkes clearly needed resolving.

"Thanks," she said. It didn't sound heartfelt. I was about to walk out and leave them to it when Roarkes slammed his fist down on the desk.

"Dammit, Serena, you've got to let me in with the bastard!"

She shook her head and looked at me. Of course she wasn't going to let him speak to Tarney. She didn't trust him. But, I thought, there was probably a more diplomatic way to put it than that.

"I don't think she can," I said. "Not yet. It's too soon. Too much risk of conflict."

"I'd be kicked off the case," she added. "It's not like I'm on solid ground myself, acting for Carson and taking on Tarney when it's perfectly possible there's a connection between them. Nobody seems to mind very much with me, though. With you, Detective Inspector, it's a very different matter."

"Why?" he asked, one of those long, slow, falsely-patient *why*s that are anything but. Serena smiled sweetly back at him, and I didn't think a smile like that was likely to calm him down. I remembered how furious she'd been when she'd been prevented from seeing Carson. It looked like payback time.

"Because I tend not to shout at people, bang my fist

169

on tables, scream abuse at beleaguered custody sergeants."

I thought back to Tarney, standing there while Roarkes hurled word after pointed word at him. Just standing there. He hadn't been laughing about it, but he hadn't looked particularly beleaguered, either.

"Anyway, it doesn't matter," she continued. "Chetwood won't let you in. And even if they did, he wouldn't talk. He won't talk to me, and he certainly won't talk to you."

"Can I see him?" I asked. "I'm not *officially* connected with this guy." I jerked a thumb towards Roarkes and saw his face twist into a scowl. Roarkes in the dark, and his pet lawyer off getting the goods, if he could. He might have given me Gaddesdon and Malhotra, and let me loose on the Corporation and the glacier, but I wasn't in a forgiving mood. I was, I realised, rather enjoying this.

Serena shrugged. The state of mind she was in, that was about as positive as it was going to get.

I turned around and left them to it. A defence lawyer and a police officer. Up to now, things had been going pretty well between them, but the truth was they had different jobs to do and different ways of doing them. She had two clients who didn't want to speak to her. He had a local force who wanted him packed and gone, and journalists exposing his first name and questioning his competence in the national press. I thought about that scowl, the tension etched all over his face. Roarkes was always pissed off about something, that was the way he woke up in the morning, it was probably the way he'd been born. But I hadn't seen him look so angry before, or so cornered. Roarkes wasn't telling me everything.

And I was in the middle, called in by him, doing her job. I was answerable to no one, but I'd had my nose smashed in twice in three days. I wasn't so sure I had the best end of the deal.

Back at the First Quality Inn there was a new girl on reception, bleached blonde and friendlier than the last one, which wasn't saying a lot. Most snakes would have been friendlier than the last one. Upstairs my room was still cold, but someone had finally managed to force the window shut after I'd complained for the fifth time. As I pulled off my shirt I heard the phone ring. I glanced at the display.

Elizabeth Maurier, again. She wasn't going to stop calling until I answered. My finger danced a jig between the green "ANSWER" and the red "REJECT".

I hit the red. I knew I was only delaying the inevitable. I knew I'd end up speaking to her sooner or later. There might even be something in it for me, and it wasn't like I didn't need it. But hearing her voice on that voicemail had brought it all back, painfully, dug up memories I thought I'd burnt and buried the ashes, and now they were out there, swirling around, waiting to flood in the moment I took a breath in their direction. Bill and Eileen Grimshaw, the bereaved parents, their pain not one tooth less sharp for all my genius. The pompous, smiling face of David Brooks-Powell. The longer I held off speaking to Elizabeth Maurier, the longer I could look the other way.

I should have been asleep the moment my head hit the pillow, but something was going on outside. Male shouts, a door slamming, more shouts. *Drunks*, I thought, and then, rising like smoke, *What if they're not?*

Thirty seconds later there was a knock on my door, three knocks, then three more, a rhythmic rat-tat-tat that turned the smoke solid and pinned me to the bed. I hadn't heard any footsteps, but a hand couldn't knock on my door by itself.

My breath was coming in short bursts and I was sweating, in spite of the cold. Three more taps, and then the footsteps. Moving away. My breath slowed.

I waited five minutes and called down to the girl on reception, who apologised and explained that some country lads on a stag weekend were a little the worse for wear.

18: Dead Teeth

I MANAGED WHAT I thought was a decent night's sleep, undisturbed by the chaos outside, but I was awake at eight, exhausted before I'd even moved, with the kind of headache that should have cost me half a bottle of Scotch. My arm was aching again, and I was surprised to see the scrape had turned the colour of boiled lobster and felt warm when I touched it. It must have been the arm and the head that had woken me, because without something getting in the way I'd have slept till lunchtime – and fragments of the night's dreams tumbled together in my mind into a disconcerting vision of Boris Crick, with a mop of blond hair and a knowing smile, telling me to get a grip.

The smile didn't need much explanation. As I strolled across the car park at Folgate the first thing I saw was Serena Hawkes, frowning at her feet as she walked towards me and spoke on her phone.

"You shouldn't have done that," she said into her phone, and then noticed me and flashed a weary smile. I smiled back.

"Client," she mouthed silently at me, and then I saw it, behind her, heading for me, for both of us, moving too fast. An Astra, a red Astra, a balding man with glasses at the wheel staring straight in front of him.

We were straight in front of him. There was no way he hadn't seen us. But he hadn't slowed down, either. Without thinking I reached out my right arm and dragged Serena to the side, up against the row of parked cars. She moved like a ragdoll, too surprised to offer the slightest resistance, which was a good thing, because that arm was still aching and wouldn't have shifted her an inch if she'd fought it.

I looked back up and the car was gone, except it wasn't. It had turned and was slowly backing into a narrow space four cars down. Serena was gaping at me like I was a lunatic, her phone still pressed to one ear. I recognised the balding man with glasses. He'd stopped for a brief chat with Roarkes in the corridor when we'd returned from our crisp butty lunch. He was a police officer, parking his car, in the car park outside the police station.

"Yes, OK, you're the boss," said Serena into her phone.

I smiled at her, weakly, and whispered, "Sorry."

Get a grip.

Roarkes seemed happier than he'd been the day before, but not a lot happier. He was putting down the phone as I walked in, shaking his head and breathing slowly out through his teeth.

"What's up?" I asked, trying to sound as cheerful as I could, and wondering if I'd get the truth.

"Upstairs. No progress, they get pissed off, crap in the papers, they get more pissed off. Nothing I wasn't expecting. Nothing I haven't dealt with a hundred times before. Doesn't make it any nicer, though."

I nodded. It was convincing, it was probably true, but Serena's doubts were beginning to infect me. I didn't think it was the whole story, but I didn't have the energy to press for more.

"What's the latest with Serena? I just saw her on the way out."

He looked back down at his desk. "Ask her yourself. She won't even talk to me."

This was turning into one of those conversations where nothing gets said, and even that gets said badly. I tried a different tack. A more direct one.

"So what have you got on the attacks?"

Roarkes looked up. It was a start.

"What attacks?"

"On me, Roarkes. Three of them."

He frowned and looked back down.

"Two."

I opened my mouth to argue, and then thought better of it.

"Tarney's in custody. I've reported the love tap you got in London. I told you. Uniform are sending someone to talk to you about it."

"When?"

He shrugged. "When they get to it. It's not exactly a red-hot lead, is it?"

"Fair enough. So I guess that means you're working on all the other red-hot leads, right?"

He grimaced, and nodded at me.

"OK. You're right. From what you've said, there's clearly some connection between the attack on you in London and our investigation. If Carson's our man, he's not working alone. But it's a punch in the face, Sam. If you want to go and get yourself shot, then you'll be our number one priority. Until then, it's a minor assault."

I took a deep breath and exhaled through my teeth. On one level, he was absolutely right. On another, though, it was a lead, and it wasn't like we were rolling in leads. And less than five minutes with the man had me adopting his mannerisms, the bitter sarcasm, the hissed breath through the teeth. Roarkes wasn't good for me. I'd do better looking elsewhere.

Malhotra, it turned out, wasn't done with the day job. There were other crimes committed by real criminals who hadn't yet been caught, and there were plenty at Folgate who'd rather have her processing traffic offences than helping Roarkes. Gaddesdon was available, but he was

175

bored and whining, and successful as he'd been with the McTavish memo, I didn't think he'd hit a hole-in-one again any time soon. I had the feeling we'd got all we were going to out of the Corporation. I could sit and wait for Serena to defrost and sort out an interview with Tarney, or I could go and do something else.

I ran through the options in my head. The piece of paper, the glacier: I still didn't know where to begin. It wasn't like I had contacts in the Argentine police. Sally Carson wasn't going to be opening up for a while. There was the planning angle, the locals and the council, there were possibilities there, but I was damned if I was digging through the minutes of council meetings and trying to figure out what wasn't being said. Tarney, the Land Rover, the missing CCTV, the Corporation, all dead ends or bumps in the road so big I didn't see myself getting over them. Malhotra had someone looking into the bank accounts and Operation Blackbird, but that would take time and effort and I didn't really believe it would give us anything we didn't already have. Brian Betterson had lost his mobile phone and didn't have anything useful to tell us.

I stopped there. Brian Betterson. The one lead Roarkes had followed up on, and then declared dead. I was inclined to agree with the diagnosis, I'd been ninety-nine per cent sure of it and I still was, but the way things were going, one per cent was worth a shot.

Gaddesdon was sitting in the canteen drinking coffee with a pair of pretty young community support officers. I couldn't hear what they were saying, but from the colour of his face it looked like they were teasing him. He was wearing a white, uncreased shirt and a dark tie, which wasn't like him at all, and his smile suggested he didn't mind the teasing.

"Can you get us a car?" I asked, and he nodded. I had

the feeling a marked patrol car might shake things up a little.

"And grab Brian Betterson's address, will you?"

He stared at me.

"Betterson. The guy from Burnley."

He carried on staring.

"The one whose phone was stolen?"

Nothing. The girls were starting to giggle, now, quietly, but clearly enough.

"Come on, Gaddesdon. The phone that was used to call in about Carson, the call that Milton and Ahmet responded to, the call that got them killed?"

"Oh," he sighed. "That phone."

"I'd better let the DI know where we're going," he said, reaching for the radio, as we headed out of Manchester in the same Shogun I'd bled in a few days earlier.

"It's OK," I lied. "I've already been through it with him."

I knew what Roarkes would have said if I had done. *You're not a cop. Leave it alone. Don't push it.* But I'd been through everything else. There was nothing left to push. I crossed my fingers and hoped Gaddesdon wouldn't check.

"OK," he said, and put both hands back on the wheel. "It's in the right direction anyway. Dead north." He pointed at the Shogun's satnav. "We'll stop on the way."

"Why?"

"The funeral."

What funeral? I nearly asked, and stopped myself just in time. Someone had mentioned it, I couldn't remember who or when, but I'd heard it already that day. Fiona Milton. Half the reason I was here, and her funeral was this morning in some town I'd never heard off halfway between Manchester and Burnley. Hence the suit and tie, I

177

realised.

The other half of the reason was Naz Ahmet. Gaddesdon's friend. I'd done a decent job of avoiding the subject so far, but we were heading to his colleague's funeral. It was time to break the silence.

"You knew Naz Ahmet, right?" I asked. I tried to make it conversational, incidental, more *fancy another pint?* than *I'm sorry for your loss*, but it came out closer to the loss than the pint. Sometimes words make you say them the way they're supposed to be said. And without taking his eyes off the road, without tears or even a break in his voice, Gaddesdon told me about his friend.

They hadn't just trained together. They'd worked together, in Manchester, before Naz had married and become a father and moved his young family to a village outside Blackburn. Gaddesdon had been there when Naz had met the woman who would become his wife, a night of alcohol-fuelled dancing and gambling the day they'd graduated police training. He'd been there at the wedding, at the celebrations after the child had been born, at the wheel of a rented van when they'd moved out of Manchester. At the small, private funeral after his friend had been shot.

Naz had been buried as soon as his body had been released, in accordance with Islamic tradition. The family, he told me, as he turned into the cemetery car park and nudged his way into a space between two other police cars, were still in a state of shock.

I doubted Fiona Milton's family would be much happier.

They weren't. The widower and the children, the funeral tears, both shed and unshed, the anger that sparked inside me as I witnessed their grief. And that little chat I'd had about Naz Ahmet had turned him, too, into something more than just another dead victim. I was tired and hungry, and possibly a little unwell, but that didn't account for the sense that this was about more than making a name for myself and avenging my nose. I didn't think Roarkes had spotted me, and he'd given Gaddesdon no more than a nod, so our visit to Brian Betterson was still on. As we pulled out of the cemetery car park, I noticed the red Astra again, the one I'd fled from back in Folgate. Same man at the wheel, bald, glasses. It was a police funeral and he was a police officer. I couldn't see his clothes through the car window, but he was probably dressed like a penguin, too. Gaddesdon turned onto the main road and I closed my eyes. I must have been asleep moments later, because next thing I knew we were coming to a halt on a road that looked like somewhere no one bothered cleaning up between riots.

Betterson's flat was on the ground floor of a three storey house that had once been white but was now the dirty grey-brown of dead teeth, with splashes of unaccountable black thrown in like the flattened remains of giant insects. There was a buzzer by the door, and the letters "BB" scratched onto the wall beside it, but nothing happened when I pushed it. I tried again, held my finger down. It probably wasn't even connected. I tried banging on the door and shouting Betterson's name through the letter box, and after a couple of minutes the door was opened by a squat, angry-looking woman with a cigarette in her mouth.

"What ya want?" she spat. I took a step back, almost colliding with Gaddesdon.

"Brian Betterson. Do you know him?" I asked.

She narrowed her eyes and puffed up a cheek and I had the uncomfortable feeling of being observed by a predator. I sensed Gaddesdon, behind me, edging away. She was wearing a blue towelling robe, but there was nothing fluffy about her.

"'E's gone. Packed up 'is stuff and gone. Yet'day night."

"Oh," I said. I couldn't think of anything else. Gaddesdon, amazingly, could.

"Do you happen to know where he's gone, ma'am?" he asked, and to my surprise, she smiled. It was the *ma'am*, of course. I'd used that trick often enough myself. A bit of deference. Everyone likes to think they're better than they are.

"Sorry, son. 'E's paid up, and when they're paid up I don't know aught about 'em and I don't care neither. Can't help ya."

"Thanks anyway," I said, and she smiled again. I didn't like the smile a whole lot more than the narrowed eyes, but when she shut the door on us, she didn't slam it.

Gaddesdon was already across the road and climbing back into the car. I stood there, for a minute, thinking through the implications. Betterson hadn't said anything about leaving. We hadn't asked him anything that would have led him to say it, true, but it wasn't the kind of thing that would slip your mind. We call him in, twice, to ask him about the phone, and two days later he's gone. I wondered if there was a connection. That one per cent was starting to look a little bigger.

I turned and started across the road, only to find my way blocked by a tall gentleman with grey hair and a stick. He was wearing a suit jacket and a shirt buttoned right up to his neck, and although the jacket and shirt looked nearly as old as he did, he didn't quite fit in with the street.

"Took yer time," he said, and I stared at him. He pointed his stick at an open door two houses down.

"That's my place. I called, last night. Your lot said you were too busy."

Another one taking me for a police officer. Given my

mode of transport, it was hardly surprising.

"I'm sorry, Mr—"

"Lennox," he said. "It's Lennox. I'd have thought they'd have told you that before they sent you out, at least."

I couldn't help noticing that in a street of grey and brown, Mr. Lennox's house was still white.

"Well, Mr Lennox," I began, but that was as far as I got.

"I've got all the details down here," he said, rummaging in his trouser pocket and bringing out a sheet of notepaper folded neatly in half. "The noise they were making, enough to wake the dead, it was."

Gaddesdon had finally noticed my predicament and wandered over, a stupid grin on his face. He stopped a few yards away, watching and clearly enjoying himself. He didn't look like he was going to do anything to help.

"Honestly, the things they get up to, and they call it fun, that lad sounded like he was having his teeth pulled out but I suppose that's a night out for young people these days."

"Mr Lennox," I said, again, but having waited all night Mr Lennox was going to have his say now.

"And in a car, they were, I mean, the car's what you use for getting to a place, isn't it? You don't just sit in it all evening and shout."

"Yes," I replied. Agreeing was probably the best way to get through this quickly.

"So here it is," he said. "Dark blue Land Rover, I've got the plates, they can do whatever they like as far as I'm concerned but I don't want them doing it outside my house."

I held out my hand for the piece of paper and opened my mouth to say *thank you very much* or *I can assure you we'll look into this* or whichever platitude sprang to mind, and then I stopped.

A dark blue Land Rover.

I opened the paper. The writing was small, neat, proudly vertical.

"Land Rover Defender," it read. "Colour: dark blue. Registration: PK11 VAX".

I passed it to Gaddesdon, who stared at it for a moment with a quizzical look on his face. Only a moment, though. Then his mouth fell open.

Betterson in. Betterson gone. PK11. Land Rover Defender. The mysterious third car we'd all but given up on.

This was one coincidence too many.

Even Roarkes couldn't ignore a lead like this one. He didn't give me any of the shit I'd been expecting over our trip to Burnley, and before we were off the phone I could hear him barking orders to some poor sod to organise a full house-to-house and pass on Betterson's description to the local hospitals. It sounded like the Land Rover had finally unlocked Folgate's resources. Gaddesdon and I went back and spoke to the landlady, a Mrs Skilling, still in her blue towelling robe, who now seemed rather gratified to find herself so close to the centre of something so very exciting, and made us sit down and drink hot sweet tea while she explained that yes, she had been in the previous night, but no, she hadn't heard anything unusual, but she did sleep very soundly these days. Gaddesdon, with all the subtlety of a nuclear bomb, pointed to the half-empty bottle of gin I'd already spotted beside her armchair. I didn't think Mrs Skilling was going to be much help. Maybe something would show up in Betterson's room, but I doubted it.

Details filtered through over the next hour or so. Roarkes was all energy, no trace of that tension and sullen hostility that seemed to have been haunting him lately. Serena was elsewhere, she had other clients after all, ones who'd actually appointed her and were prepared to talk to her, too.

Betterson had driven, or been driven, to Liverpool, it emerged, because he'd been on the six o'clock ferry to Ireland that morning. There was a grainy still from the one-frame-a-second CCTV at the ferry port showing him making his way out. Even with a resolution that would have made me look like George Clooney, you could tell it was Betterson. He was holding a piece of cloth to one side of his head, and although the still was black-and-white, my bet was that cloth was very red indeed.

But at least he was alive.

The car was registered to a businesswoman from Preston by the name of Abigail Starke, except it wasn't, because the car she owned with the registration PK11 VAX was a bottle-green Jaguar and she could see it in her driveway even as she patiently explained to Gaddesdon that yes, that was her car, and no, it wasn't and never had been a Land Rover Defender.

Another dead end, I thought. Betterson was in Ireland and we'd track him down eventually, but given the little we could say about him I didn't think the police over there would be putting him top of their priorities. He'd been threatened and beaten, outside his own home, and he'd run away rather than run the risk of saying the wrong thing and getting worse treatment next time. Which meant Betterson knew something we didn't, and if that secret was worth fleeing the country for, chances were it had something to do with the people who'd taken his phone and made the call that had put bullets in the heads of two police officers. The car might have helped, but now it didn't look like the car was going to show up either.

I wandered down to the canteen and called Claire, to

kill some time, if nothing else, and she sympathised in an emotionless, heard-it-a-thousand-times sort of way. I'd been droning on for seven minutes solid about the case and my nose and arm before I realised she wasn't really responding, and it was another minute before I realised why.

"So, more importantly, how are you getting on with Jonas Wolf?" I asked, with a big emphasis on that "So", as if that had been the reason for the call in the first place. It didn't work.

"Oh, finally remembered something that isn't about Thomas bloody Carson, have you?"

There was a pause, but I wasn't stupid enough to jump in and defend myself. I knew Claire's pauses by now. She wasn't finished with me yet.

"What with that photographic memory of yours, I'm surprised you forget anything at all. But then, you only remember the *important* things, don't you?"

Not long after we'd moved in together I'd explained, by way of apology, how I could recite minute details of cases I'd worked more than a decade back, but had forgotten every single item she'd asked me to pick up from the supermarket that afternoon. It was one of many things I wished I'd never said.

"I'm sorry," I muttered. There was no defence. There wasn't much chance of mitigation, either. *I'm sorry* was the best I had. She ignored me.

"Wolf's going very well, thanks for asking. I've tied him to Rosa's import," – I shuddered, briefly, at that, the idea of a human being *imported*, but that was what these girls had been, commodities, and disposable ones at that – "and I'm building a connection with the guy who got convicted for Xenia."

"Well done," I said. "That's brilliant."

I should have been impressed. I *was* impressed. I just

wasn't very good at putting that into my voice, and Claire wasn't particularly disposed to find it there.

"Look," she replied, with a sigh that made me think for a moment that we were turning into Roarkes, all of us, old and weary and permanently dissatisfied. "Why don't you just run along and crack your case, and let me know when you've finished and you're ready to have a proper conversation, OK?"

"I'm sorry," I said, again, and got a *hmmph* in return, a grunted acknowledgement that wasn't as good as a friendly goodbye but was a lot better than nothing. At least she hadn't told me to fuck off this time.

I toyed with the idea of calling Serena, but what did I have to say to her? Maybe I could ask her to get me in with Tarney. Sit in front of another silent face and restrain myself from punching it until it finally had something to say. Shout "I know about the Corporation!" a few times, see if that did anything. It probably wouldn't. But it was better than sitting there drinking police station coffee and exploring the pointless twists and turns of my own mind. I'd picked up the phone and was scrolling through it for Serena's number when Malhotra burst into the canteen and stopped in front of me panting like a fat man on a big hill.

"What?" I said, after thirty seconds, because she still hadn't caught her breath. These Manchester CID weren't the fittest bunch I'd come across. She gasped a moment longer and finally spoke.

"We've found it, sir."

"Found what?"

"The car."

Another dead end had just opened up a little.

19: Across the Line

SHE HADNT FOUND the car itself, or at least, not its current position. But she knew where it had been, and that was something.

The answer lay in ANPR, the national automatic number plate recognition system. The plates had already been fed into the database, and nothing had turned up except Abigail Starke's bottle-green Jaguar shooting up and down the M6 half a dozen times a month. ANPR data was stored for two years, and there were plenty of cameras, including nine between Burnley and Liverpool, which led to a couple of reasonable conclusions: Betterson hadn't been driven to Liverpool in the Land Rover Defender, and the plates had been cloned recently enough that they weren't likely to show up anywhere at all.

Until they did.

The database was divided into motorway, urban, high-intensity and "other" sections. High-intensity meant ports, airports, power stations, sensitive spots that needed monitoring. "Other" was for places that didn't need ANPR in them at all, but some local police officer or politician with too much power and too little brain had decided they did. "Other" was always the last place to be searched, if anyone bothered searching it at all. If your target didn't show up in urban, motorway or H-I, it wasn't likely to show up outside the 7-11 on the village high street.

But Malhotra was both persistent and rigorous and she wasn't giving up on the Land Rover until she'd exhausted all possibilities. Which is why she'd asked for access to the "other" data, been granted it, reluctantly, and trawled through it herself until she got a hit even she hadn't been expecting.

Right up in a remote part of the Forest of Bowland that no one ever visited, even by Bowland standards, there were some birds. White Hill, the place was called. Every year the birds came back to their nests in this cold, grey bit of England and every year their numbers got fewer and fewer until, as Malhotra informed me, there were only three nesting pairs in the country and all three of them nesting in that same spot.

The local farmers hated the birds, because they blamed them for attacking livestock. The local thieves loved them, because their eggs sold for a fortune on a black market populated solely by rich lunatics. The upshot was that these six birds lived their lives under constant threat of being shot or poisoned or having their eggs stolen, and they weren't smart enough to just move somewhere else.

When that kind of thing happens in city estates, to actual humans, when there's a family getting harassed and threatened and spat at and beaten and occasionally stabbed or shot or just burnt to death, usually by my clients, they can complain as much as they like, nothing ever gets done. But if it's three pairs of nesting birds in some protected site an hour from the nearest pub, everyone gets indignant and there's CCTV and regular sweeps in the 4WD and occasionally even a helicopter. And following a particularly heinous spate of egg-snatching, someone had decided to link the CCTV on the road nearest the nests to the ANPR system, and got about as much joy out of it as I'd got out of being punched in the face. In the six weeks since the link had been installed, precisely zero birds had been assaulted. But the camera still ran and the data still got sent and the matches still got made. And around the same time as Thomas Carson was getting himself arrested, a dark blue Land Rover Defender with the registration number PK11 VAX was driving through this particular spot on its shitty little single-track road, and back again forty minutes later.

I went over the ANPR stills three times with Malhotra. There was no doubt at all. Up the hill and down again, the Grand Old Duke of York in a Land Rover, and when I asked her what was there, apart from some rare nesting birds, all she could tell me was there were some farms and some barns and nothing anyone could possibly be interested in. I doubted that. The people who'd threatened Betterson, the people who, I was starting to think, had almost certainly been involved in the deaths of Ahmet and Milton, wouldn't have driven all that way to look at a bird.

"Off we go," I said, and Malhotra looked at me like I'd just suggested we strip off and make love on the canteen floor.

"Why not?"

"I don't think you realise what it's like up there, sir," she said, and I smiled and shook my head.

"You can tell me while we're driving."

"No," she said. "We need to think about this first."

I couldn't imagine what there was to think about. We were going to stop at every building within a mile or so of the camera until we found what we were looking for. Neither of us actually knew what it was we were looking for, but I figured we'd know it when we found it.

She waited till I'd finished, shook her head at me, and laughed.

It turned out I really didn't realise what it was like up there. In a mile or so there might be a barn, there might be twenty, there might be another half-a-dozen ruined outhouses that didn't figure on a map and never had. But a mile wasn't what we were looking at. Google might tell me there was just the one road up there, but Google didn't know about all the side tracks and farm tracks and fords and paths that your average family car could probably handle without much difficulty. A Land Rover Defender could have gone anywhere. Our potential search area was half the size of London, and it would take a dedicated team of a dozen officers up to a week to search it properly. Malhotra and I driving up there to take a look would be like hunting for a sober Scotsman on Burns Night.

"What else can we do?" I asked. For a moment we'd had a lead, a proper lead, and I'd been the one that had found it. Already that lead was starting to look like all the others. I couldn't see Roarkes getting a dozen officers, or lending them to me if he did, and I had the feeling a week was too long anyway. Malhotra frowned.

"We could watch the CCTV?" she said, hopefully. I remembered the way she'd raced in, eyes gleaming, close to bursting with excitement. Now she probably felt as shit as I did, but at least she'd come up with a suggestion. It was better than nothing.

Other than the stills with the number plates on them, the ANPR database didn't hold any useful footage, but the Bowland feed was uploaded daily to an online site monitored by lonely bird-watchers with too much time on their hands. So now I was sitting with Malhotra in the little room Roarkes had given us, perched uncomfortably on a chair designed for one large person, or two tiny ones, watching forty minutes of CCTV footage in real time in case we missed something.

We hadn't missed a thing, because apart from the Land Rover coming up the hill and down it forty minutes later, not a thing had happened. We couldn't see enough of the Land Rover to tell who was driving it or how many people were in it. All we had were the car and the general location.

"Let's widen it out a little," said Malhotra, and I looked at her in amazement.

"You can do that? You can search different places?"

She shook her head at me, slowly, the way you shake your head at an adult struggling with a child's toy.

"No, sir. It's not magic. I mean widen out the time frame. Search half an hour before, maybe, half an hour after."

"Oh."

We watched the half-hour from before the Land Rover had driven past, in real time, again, and saw nothing at all. By the time it came to looking at the half-hour after we were both bored and convinced we were wasting our time, but we did it anyway, at four times normal speed.

After two minutes – eight minutes of real time – we hit pay-dirt. A car sped by, too fast to see clearly.

Neither of us spoke. There were farms and homes out there, after all, not many of them, but enough to account for the occasional car driving past. Malhotra reached forward, adjusted the speed, turned back the clock. We waited. After thirty seconds a car entered the frame, moving slowly, pausing to handle potholes or dead rabbits or whatever the hell they put on their roads up there. Malhotra had grabbed a pen and paper to make a note of the licence plate, but there was no need.

"I know that car," she said, after a moment.

I nodded. I knew that car too. I'd followed that same battered green Peugeot through half of Manchester, lost it, found it again just in time for its owner to put his fist through my face.

It was time I had a conversation with Russell Tarney.

Serena wasn't in a cooperative mood. Or, as she put it, she wanted to help as much as she could, but she didn't have the authority to just let people in and out of a police station whenever they wanted.

"It's all we've got, Serena," I said, and she sighed and told me to meet her at Chetwood in an hour's time and she'd do what she could. I didn't mention the ANPR. I thought it would be a nice surprise.

Tarney stared at me when I walked in. He was sitting behind a table with Serena next to him, his lawyer, technically, although the way she told it they'd hardly exchanged a word. I ignored the stare and sat down opposite him, where the police usually sat, only there weren't any police today because they'd got bored of being stared at by a silent Tarney.

He wasn't silent this time, though. He was laughing. He laughed at my face, for a moment, then stopped and stared again.

"I didn't do that," he said. If nothing else, he was a good judge of facial injury.

"You started it," I replied. "But that's not why I'm here."

He looked at his watch.

"I'm going home in a couple of hours, Williams. I don't have to say a thing to you."

I looked at Serena and she nodded. It shouldn't have come as a surprise. You can't lock people up indefinitely for punching someone in the face. Even if that someone's me.

"Tell me about the Corporation," I said, and he didn't so much as flinch. "Come on," I pressed. "Tell me about Carson, then. We know he's not who he says he is. We know he's Francis Grissom."

Tarney shrugged. "Seems you know more than I do," he said. "Any idea why he killed those officers then, Williams?"

"Where did you get the money, Tarney?"

"Dogs," he said, and grinned at me. I turned to Serena.

She nodded again.

"Sergeant Tarney insists that the money found in his possession at the time of his arrest was his winnings from a greyhound meeting the previous night."

"Was there a meeting?" I asked, and she nodded again. I paused for a moment, and thought about what she'd just said. *Sergeant Tarney insists. At the time of his arrest.* Stiff. Formal. Not the Serena Hawkes I'd been getting to know. She was in a difficult position, I realised. She wanted to break Tarney as much as I did, but she was still supposed to be his lawyer, and that meant she had to protect him from bastards like me. If I pushed things too far, she'd have to stop me.

Serena Hawkes was getting in the way, I realised. She didn't want to be in the way, but she didn't have anywhere else to go.

I got to my feet and walked out of the room. She followed me into the corridor.

"I'm sorry," she began, but I cut her off.

"Don't be. I wouldn't want to be where you are. Haven't got much room to move, have you?"

"No," she said, and smiled at me, and it occurred to me that there might be a way round this after all. For a moment I felt a little guilty, but only a moment. It had to be done. I excused myself to visit the bathroom.

I'd been back in the room with Serena and the still-grinning Tarney for less than a minute when her phone rang. She spoke quietly, for thirty seconds or so, nodded, looked concerned. Tarney didn't stop grinning at me. I tried not to care.

"Got to go," said Serena when she'd finished the call. "That was Detective Gaddesdon, from Folgate."

"Yeah, I know the guy," I said, sympathetically.

"Says Roarkes needs to see me. Urgently." She'd already stood and put on her jacket.

"Any idea why?"

"Gaddesdon didn't know."

"No surprise there," I said. Again, a twinge of guilt. All for the greater good. I got up to leave with her and she gestured for me to sit back down, just as I'd hoped she would.

"No. He said just me."

"Oh," I said.

"You might as well stay here. Talk to Tarney. I doubt he'll tell you anything, but you never know."

The grin on Tarney's face didn't shift a millimetre. It was like he couldn't even hear us talking about him.

"You sure you don't mind?"

"Just don't beat up my client," she said, and laughed. I might have imagined it, but I thought Tarney's grin had just got a little wider.

Tarney was still grinning. Serena was right not to worry. I had more chance of winning a Nobel Prize than intimidating her client. I'd bent the rules just to get in alongside Serena. Staying behind with Tarney was like snapping them in half and setting fire to the stumps. I had to work fast.

"Come on, Russell," I began. "It's just you and me now."

"And the tape," he said.

The tape wasn't running. I held up the machine to show him.

"Out in a couple of hours, right?" I asked. He grinned again.

"And all that time in a cell without saying a word to a soul. Your friends will be delighted."

"If I knew what you were talking about, maybe I'd agree," he replied. I carried on, as if I hadn't heard him. He was starting to piss me off.

"And if you had told us a little, well, I'd imagine they'd be pretty angry, wouldn't they?"

The grin didn't shift.

"Like, if you'd told us about Grissom and the Corporation? I mean, how else would we know about that?"

He leaned forward and put his head in one hand, the way you do when you're having to explain something very simple to someone very stupid.

"Listen, Williams, let's get this straight. I've never heard of this Grissom. I've heard of the Corporation, because I've been a cop round here for years, and you hear things. You could have picked that up anywhere, Williams. No one's going to believe it was from me."

He sat back again and took his hand away from his head. He was smiling. He was right, too, and time was running out. I had twenty minutes, if I was lucky, before Serena got to Folgate and realised I'd set her up. She'd be on the phone straight away, and I'd be out of Chetwood so fast they'd be testing me for performance-enhancing drugs. Serena wouldn't trust me again, not after this, and neither would Roarkes, and Gaddesdon would be in trouble himself and not particularly inclined to talk to me. Malhotra was waiting outside in her own car and if she knew what I'd just done she wouldn't be very happy, either. If Tarney had nothing to give me, I'd just pissed off a lot of people for very little payoff.

Twenty minutes.

"But I'm right, aren't I? You took some money from someone who works for this gang that call themselves the Corporation, and you gave Carson a belt so he could hang himself. I know you did it, you know you did it, so why are you pissing around?"

Tarney shook his head. No doubt he'd been in enough interviews to realise how badly I was handling this one. I'd been in enough of them myself. There's a line, at a police interview, and on one side there are the things you can say without breaking the rules, and on the other side there are the things you can't, and if you do say them the lawyer – who's usually me – will be down your throat before you've finished your first sentence. The moment that happens you've lost all your momentum and all your authority and the guy you've just arrested is doing all he can not to laugh in your face. The best interviewers flirt with that line all the time, dancing along it, putting one toe the wrong side and drawing it back in again before anyone can cut it off. I was playing it too safe.

Particularly given there was no brief there to stop me.

I sat back and eyed Tarney for a minute. He shrugged. There was no point playing silent mind games with the man. I wasn't sure he had enough of a mind to join in. I leaned forward again, and spoke clearly and quietly.

"Where do you think I found out about Grissom?"

He shrugged again. "I couldn't give a fuck."

"And the Corporation. Where do you think I heard about them? Here I am, some soft little brief from London, and I've got the name of a gang so secret no one in your station's ever heard of them."

"For all I know, Williams, you could have shat the word out on a bit of paper and read it there."

I didn't seem to be getting to him.

"Because the people who told me about Grissom, and the Corporation, they can put the word out, Russell."

He leaned forward himself, now, and suddenly I was right back there in the pub with his *I know why you're here, Williams*, and feeling uncomfortably like I wanted a police officer there to look after me.

"You don't frighten me, Williams. You've got some mates. They can spread some bullshit and say I've been shooting my mouth off. But if all they've got to spread is one word any old twat could come up with and some name no one knows anything about, well, let's just say I don't think I'll bother locking the door at night."

Ten minutes. I sat back again. I'd strolled right up to the line, stepped across it, and for all Tarney cared I might as well have rubbed the whole bloody thing out. Last try.

"What if word got out about something else?"

He smiled. He didn't think I had anything else. He didn't know about the bird-watchers and their camera.

"What if word got out about White Hill?"

The smile shifted. It was back again, half a second later, a tenth of a second, and if I hadn't been staring at him like a starving man eyeing a wounded rabbit I wouldn't have noticed a thing, but for a moment, it had disappeared. The moment I said *White Hill*.

I knew that shift, that moment when the fact you've been saving for the right moment opens up the guy you're talking to like a blade in a pumpkin, and he doesn't want you to see it. That's when you twist the blade a little harder. I had him. I had the bastard.

"I mean, we could head down there, me and a bunch of your old colleagues, look around, we'd find something eventually. We'll tie you in, one way or another, what with your car showing up just around the time Carson got nicked. But that'll take time, won't it? So I was thinking of something else."

Tarney was leaning back again, impassive, like you could smack him in the mouth with a demolition ball and he wouldn't even notice, but I'd seen that smile shift. I knew it was an act. I leaned back myself and twisted the blade.

"I was thinking, what if we send you home early, make a big deal out of it, why wait two hours, send you home and tell the press we're letting you go because you've been so cooperative?"

He twitched. The left side of his mouth, my left, his right, curled up and then down again.

"And at the same time we announce we're shutting down all routes into White Hill because of some highly sensitive information we've received from a well-placed source. Maybe in the same press conference."

I sat forward, and spoke quietly.

"Don't worry Russell. We wouldn't actually say it was you. Not in so many words."

I waited. I glanced at my watch. Five minutes. Silence. I could almost feel the seconds ticking by. I looked at my watch again. Tarney didn't know what I'd done, he didn't know about Gaddesdon and the call and the wild goose chase we'd sent Serena Hawkes on. I had to look like I was as relaxed as a billionaire behind bullet-proof glass.

Still nothing. The smile was still there, like it had been for all but a fraction of a second since the moment I'd walked in the room. Four minutes.

I didn't feel like a billionaire behind bullet-proof glass.

Three and a half minutes.

"What do you say, Russell?" I asked. A last, feeble twist of the blade. I had to say something. What Russell Tarney said was precisely nothing.

Three minutes. The phone buzzed in my pocket. I fished it out and read the text from Gaddesdon.

Srna here, it read. *getting the hell out. You should too.*

Two minutes. Probably less. It hadn't worked. I stood up, put on my jacket, wondered how long it would take me to get back to London and whether Serena would report me to the Law Society. Tarney was staring at me now. He'd won. I'd lost the case, lost Serena, Roarkes, got Gaddesdon into all kinds of shit, probably Malhotra too, even though she didn't have the faintest idea what I'd done. I'd failed to crack the top ten and moved one painful step closer to Atom Industries. And Tarney had beaten me.

Thirty seconds. I nodded at him, once, and turned around, and as I reached out for the door handle he spoke.

"I want a deal."

20: Where Falcons Nest

I'D BEEN WRONG about the thirty seconds. I got six more minutes before a flustered-looking sergeant banged on the door and asked if he might have a word. He wasn't entirely sure what was going on, he said, but he'd been asked to remove me from the cell. Someone was on their way over, someone with questions; I was to wait for them at the station.

"Am I under arrest?" I asked, all wide-eyed and innocent.

"Oh no," he replied. "It's just – if you could possibly wait."

"Sorry," I said, and two minutes later I was in the passenger seat next to Detective Sergeant Malhotra and praying for a set of green lights. I knew who that *someone with questions* was, and after what I'd seen her do to Roarkes, I didn't fancy being on the wrong end of an angry Serena Hawkes.

He'd asked for a deal. He must have known I couldn't give him one, but what I'd said had clearly scared the cockiness right out of him and he was suddenly, and very obviously, quite desperate.

I'd told him we didn't have long. I'd told him to give me everything he had, and I'd argue his cooperation with Roarkes and the Crown Prosecution Service. He might have been desperate but he wasn't stupid.

"I'm not telling you anything till I've heard from that bastard Roarkes," he said. Clearly he didn't know Roarkes very well. The only thing he'd get out of Roarkes would be a determined prosecution and, if he was unlucky, a set of minor internal injuries to go with it. One thing he wouldn't be getting was a deal. I shook my head.

"This isn't about Roarkes. Not yet. Give me something and then I'll see what I can do."

I thought I could hear footsteps outside, banging, shouting, but this was a police station, I reminded myself. Footsteps, banging, shouting, they were part of the furniture. No reason they should have anything to do with me.

Tarney was staring at me.

"You don't have long," I told him. He had a couple of hours, still, which was a hell of a lot longer than I had, but he didn't need to know that.

A new set of footsteps approached. Purposeful, I thought. Purposeful footsteps. Or were they the same as any other set of footsteps, and it was just that I was expecting someone to barge in any second and kick me out?

"Come on," I said, and looked at my watch again. I was betraying my nerves. Tarney had to realise there was something else going on.

The footsteps passed by and faded away.

"In a hurry, are you?" he asked. A couple of minutes ago he'd been desperate for a deal and I'd been in control. I wasn't in control any more.

I looked past him, at the wall, dirty-green tiles and smears from the years of coffee thrown at it. I looked down at the table, same green, same coffee. Anything not to look at Tarney and have him stare into my eyes. My phone was on the table, in front of me, and as I reached out for it, an idea took root and grew and sprouted fully-formed into the light.

I picked it up and scrolled through the latest calls until I found the one I wanted, dialled, put it back down again and turned the speaker on. It rang twice before it was answered.

"Mia Arazzi here."

"Hello Mia, this is Sam Williams. Remember me?"

"Of course, Sam. How can I help you?"

"You wanted some information on the Carson case?"

"Have you got any? All I hear is dead ends."

"Oh, I've got something for you."

I had nothing for her. There was no way Mia Arazzi was getting a thing from me. But this particular deception was entirely guilt-free.

Tarney was looking at me with an expression on his face I couldn't read. I had no idea if he was buying it.

"I'm all ears."

I hit the mute button and gave Tarney my toughest stare. Tarney was a career police officer in a not-particularly-nice part of Manchester, so I doubted my toughest stare would have much impact, but it was the best I had.

"Mia Arazzi's been bugging me for days, Tarney. She writes for the *Mirror*."

Nothing. Silent and unreadable. I was losing him.

"Your friends back at Folgate have been feeding her nice juicy lumps of meat for days, but they seem to have run out. This is a *very* juicy lump of meat, Tarney."

He nodded. I couldn't tell what the nod meant. I reached down for the phone, to take it off mute and drag the bluff a little further, but for the life of me I couldn't figure out what I could say that would keep both of them on the hook.

So it was a good thing Tarney spoke first.

"OK," he said.

I took the phone off mute.

"I'll call you back, Mia. Something's come up."

I killed the call before she could say anything that

might change Tarney's mind.

"I don't have much, Williams," he said. Footsteps, again, approaching and passing by.

"Names, Tarney. Who paid you, what they paid you to do, I want the lot."

"I don't have names. I don't know anyone's name. I got a call, got a location, went there, got paid. Got another call a while later, went back, picked up a belt."

No names. It was Boris Crick all over again, useless or close to it, except that a cell in Chetwood was still a nicer place to be than The Mitre. "Who paid you?" I asked. "Who gave you the belt?"

"No one. It's an old barn, on the White Hill. I go in, there's a table there, first time there's cash on it, second time there's a belt."

"What, so someone just calls you up and you go there, you don't know who they are, why they're calling, what they want, but you go there anyway and you take their money?"

"Something like that, yeah."

Tarney was lying to me. He had something else, he must have something else, no one would do what he'd done without knowing who was paying them.

"How did you know what to do with the belt?"

"Told you. Had a call. They said pick up the item and give it to Carson."

"Voice?"

"Male. Middle-aged. Probably."

This was going nowhere.

"So what exactly do you have for me, Tarney?"

He smiled and picked up my phone. I couldn't see what he was doing with it, but after thirty seconds he handed it back and it was on Maps.

"There," he said, and stabbed his fat index finger at the screen. I could see the White Hill, or at least the words

White Hill, in the top-right corner. Tarney had put a flag down in the middle of the screen, about a mile to the south and west of the peak, if that was what the words meant.

"That's the barn," he said. "There's a track off another track off the road. Use your phone. You'll find it."

The barn. We'd have found the barn ourselves, eventually, but we might not have known it when we did. If he was telling the truth, at least he'd saved us some time. And I hadn't given him anything for it, yet.

Footsteps approached. Stopped. A bang on the door. The sergeant. *Someone was on their way over.* And I wasn't hanging around long enough to say hello.

"You'd better have something better than that, Tarney," I said as I left. He grinned at me.

"There's more where that came from," he said. "But do me a favour, will you? Keep it between us."

My nose gave a convenient twinge as I walked out of the room. It still wasn't right. It might never be right. The arm was still hurting, too. I didn't think I'd be doing Tarney any favours.

Priya Malhotra was a careful, patient driver, the kind of driver we're all supposed to be but never are. A careful driver wasn't what I wanted just then.

"White Hill," I said, and she started to explain what she'd already explained once before, that there was no point going just the two of us, we needed numbers and a plan of action, the land properly squared off, kilometre by kilometre, maybe dogs, maybe even the bomb squad. I stopped her before she'd hit the second sentence.

"Look at this," I said, and passed her the phone. She indicated and pulled over. Detective Sergeant Malhotra wouldn't look at a phone while she was driving.

"What am I looking at?" she asked, and I explained,

leaving out the bit about Gaddesdon's phone call and Mia Arazzi. Malhotra wasn't stupid, though. She'd seen Serena Hawkes leaving in something of a hurry, and she'd seen me come running out of the police station in much the same style, only more so. She gave me a look that said *you haven't told me half of what happened in there, but you will*, and hit the gas, and suddenly, mercifully, Priya Malhtora wasn't such a careful, patient driver after all.

She wasn't a quiet driver, either. "I need my beats," she said, as the needle flew past sixty, and hit some buttons on the console without looking at them. The music was hard and fast, Bob Marley sampled and remixed into something else, heavy on the bass but light on the peace and love. For five minutes or so I thought I quite liked it, and then I realised it wasn't going to slow down or get any quieter, and I changed my mind. I glanced in the mirror, thought I saw that red Astra again, blinked and it was gone. It wasn't until I noticed the cars in front of us slowing down and moving out of the way that I realised she'd put the lights on. I must have said something, because she turned to me – driving straight into a blind corner at close to eighty miles an hour – and said, "Give me my beats and the lights and Steve McQueen couldn't touch me."

She had a point. She was fast all right. Ten minutes later we were out of Manchester.

I recognised a hill or two, I thought, and a village in the distance that might have been Bursington but really, they all looked the same. Very nice, very pretty, very peaceful, if you weren't in a car with Priya Malhotra and her beats, at least. Within forty minutes we were slowing down, a little, and the road wasn't something that a civilised part of the country would have called a road at all.

The clouds were massing, and the sun was finding the gaps, feeling its way through, lighting up the hills in patterns that changed so fast they felt like something viewed at double speed. Or maybe that was just the way we were moving. Malhotra turned off the music, reached over, took the phone off me, and frowned at it. She didn't seem to have such a problem driving and looking at a phone any more.

"OK," she said. "We'll have to guess, a bit. What did he say about the tracks?"

"Track off another track off the road."

"Not much help, was he?" she replied. But she was smiling. It looked to me like Priya Malhotra was one of those detectives who like a challenge.

We passed a track to her left, and paused while she stared down it, and at the phone, and back at the track again. Then another one, on the right, thirty yards further on. Four more, in quick succession.

"Any of these might be ours. But I'm going to find the one that leaves the road closest to this spot where he says the barn is, and keep my fingers crossed."

"Isn't there a map somewhere with these tracks on?"

She shook her head.

"Not really. Half of them are on the Ordnance Survey as footpaths or bridleways. Half of them aren't there at all, farmers have just cleared the way themselves to make it a bit easier to get from one field to another."

On we chugged, slower and slower as the road got worse and worse. Malhotra was driving a decent modern Nissan. I was surprised Tarney's Peugeot had made it this far at all.

"Recognise it?" said Malhotra, suddenly. I looked around. The sun had disappeared again, and the rain was starting, drop by heavy drop, driven onto the windows by a wind that had sprung up out of nowhere. There was nothing outside, nothing at all, not even a tree. It looked the same as it had looked for the last twenty minutes.

Malhotra was looking around herself, with the air of

someone who had something specific in mind.

"There," she said, and pointed. There was a grey post by the side of the road, propped up by narrow bits of wood that looked far too flimsy to put up any real resistance to the wind. There was something black on top of the post, and for a moment I thought it was a bird perched there, maybe one of those falcons or kestrels or whatever they were that someone had decided were so important.

"The bird-watchers' camera," she said. "So he must have gone past here. Forty minutes, the Land Rover took. There and back, but we don't know how long they were in the barn. We'll keep going for a bit."

We went past another half dozen tracks before she finally picked one, but after half a mile it bent round the wrong way and the only thing leading off it was so wet and rutted there was no way Tarney would have got his Peugeot down it. Turning was impossible, so Malhotra just reversed all the way back to the so-called road, with the rain now heavy and the clouds low enough to turn afternoon into evening before its time.

The next track petered out after a couple of hundred yards. The one after that opened out into something so wide and flat the locals probably called it the motorway, but that ended in a farmhouse with nothing beyond it and nowhere near Tarney's elusive barn.

I was starting to think he'd played me, and wondering whether I might give Mia Arazzi a little information after all, because if I couldn't get anything useful out of the bastard I had no qualms about making him suffer. The next track took us uphill, then turned sharply down again and back to the road, only we couldn't be sure precisely where or whether we'd missed any other tracks in between, so we had to drive all the way back along the track again, just in case.

Malhotra was glancing at the clock in the dashboard. The grey was thickening into something closer to dark, and in the dark I didn't think we'd be able to achieve anything at all. It was probably time to head back to Manchester. We could come back in the morning, find the place then.

Or rather, Malhotra and Gaddesdon could. If Gaddesdon hadn't been kicked off the case himself. Unless I came up with something that justified what I'd done to Serena, I'd be heading back to London and off the Carson case for good.

My phone rang. I looked down and recognised Gaddesdon's number. I hadn't expected a signal this far out of town. I picked up.

"Hello Sam."

He sounded fine. He sounded positively cheery. And he was calling me *Sam*, now, which I'd asked him to do repeatedly, to no avail.

"What's up?"

"Serena's furious. She knows it was you. I just said there must have been some kind of mix-up and Roarkes backed me up, but she's not stupid."

That didn't make sense.

"Why did Roarkes back you up?"

"Because he's still pissed off she wouldn't let him in to see Tarney. Think he's quite pleased you got one over on her. He's wondering where the hell you are, though."

I laughed. No doubt he was spitting teeth over the stunt I'd pulled, but maybe Roarkes was on my side after all. I doubted he could protect me for long, but at least I wasn't going to be getting the treatment from him.

"Got anything juicy then?" he asked cheerfully

I hesitated. We didn't have anything at all, yet, and what we might have wasn't exactly juicy.

"I'll tell you later."

"I've got something for you though," he began, and embarked on a long and not particularly funny account of Abigail Starke, the driver of the bottle-green Jaguar, calling the station, getting put through to Gaddesdon (*poor woman*, I thought) and begging him to be discreet. All those trips down the M6 had ended in a hotel near Warrington, where she'd been meeting a gentleman for activities entirely unrelated to the import and distribution of electronic components, the core business of Starke Products, Limited.

"Starke naked," giggled Gaddesdon, and even though he wasn't with me I felt like slapping him. Abigail Starke's husband didn't know a thing. She very much hoped he never would.

I told him I'd call him back later, and said goodbye. I realised immediately that I'd forgotten to thank him, because whatever he'd said on the phone to Serena, it had worked. He might be a child in the body of – well, a large child, really – but he'd done me a favour, and he'd done it well. I hoped I'd get the chance to thank him in person.

"Shall we call it a day, sir?" asked Malhotra. While I'd been talking to Gaddesdon she'd tried and abandoned yet another nasty little track.

"Yeah," I said. "OK."

She manoeuvred the car carefully around so we were pointing the right way, and after a couple of minutes the post with the camera came back into view. Half a dozen yards before the post there was another track leading off the road. We hadn't noticed it on the way up, it had been obscured by the contours of the hill, and unless you knew it was there you wouldn't see it until you were driving back the other way.

Malhotra stopped the car.

"Might as well," she said. It was a question. I nodded.

We drove on for five minutes, five slow and painful

minutes, and then an even smaller track appeared on the left. Malhotra stopped again, picked up the phone, smiled and passed it to me.

There was a flashing blue circle in the middle of the screen. That was us. Over to the top-right were the words *White Hill*. And not far from the blue circle – about half a mile, the map indicated – was the flag Tarney had put down.

We were there ten minutes later. The barn wasn't just old, it was derelict, the walls coming down, the wooden door reduced to four rotting planks, the roof one good storm away from collapsing entirely. It was dark inside, but Malhotra had a flashlight, and I knew right away this was the place Tarney had been talking about. The room was empty. It was a single room, not even a room, really, just a giant blank interior with wooden boards on the floor and nothing in it at all.

Except right in the middle, alone and looking like it owned the place, sat a heavy oak table.

The table was empty. Nothing on it. No meetings or drops planned, by the look of it. Malhotra pushed the light around, all the corners and edges and bits that had been blown in by the wind, but that was all there was. One empty table. Tarney had been telling the truth, I assumed, although I couldn't even be sure about that. But unless he had some better information, I'd just blown the chance to work the biggest case of my career on a lead that had taken me precisely nowhere. I caught a glimpse of myself in a suit and tie, sitting behind a desk in a tall glass building emblazoned with the logo of Atom Industries, and shuddered.

We made our way silently back out. There was no need to talk, nothing to talk about. As I approached the doorway I tripped in the darkness and put my hand out just in time to prevent yet another bloody nose. Malhotra turned and shone the light on me.

"Sorry."

"It's OK," I said. I could have let loose at her, for being selfish with the light, not letting me see where I was going, but I knew I'd just be taking everything else out on someone who wasn't to blame. That hadn't been a problem for me lately, but this time I held myself back.

I climbed back to my feet and I'd reached the door when it suddenly hit me.

"Hang on," I said.

"What?"

"Pass me the torch."

I took it from her and shone it back the way I'd just walked. The wind had dropped and I could see the dust still rising where I'd hit the floor. I walked over, pointing the torch down.

"What is it, sir?"

"I tripped over. But there's nothing here. So what the hell did I trip over?"

She was beside me a moment later, breathing fast with excitement. The torch was picking out pebbles, wood shavings, a paper cup. Nothing big enough to have made me fall. A couple of little sticks. Another cup. A ring of rope, nailed into the floor.

That was it. That had to be it. I walked over, carefully, as if it were a dangerous animal I didn't want to disturb. I passed the torch back to Malhotra, bent down and picked up the rope.

A square of wooden floor came up with it. I heard someone gasp, and realised it was me. Malhotra shone the light into the gap where the floor had been.

It was bigger than the opening had suggested, wide enough to squeeze in a couple of people, and it went down far enough to stack them two deep. Four bodies.

There were no bodies in there, no sign there ever had been, I didn't know why I was thinking about space in terms of bodies, but I couldn't help it.

There were a couple of empty polythene bags and a briefcase, unlocked and also empty. And in one corner, dark and small and looking like the fossilised remains of some ancient, unknowable creature, was a mass of metal and plastic, all shiny surfaces, dark recesses, lumps and wires.

I heard another gasp. This time it wasn't me. Malhotra reached in and pulled it out, this thing, whatever it was, held it up, breathed in slowly like she was savouring a fine wine.

"Well, staple my tongue to the floor," she said. I hadn't heard that one before. I waited.

"Know what this is, sir?" she asked.

I shook my head, realised she couldn't see me, said "No."

She shone the torch on it, the thing, turned it around, passed it to me. It was cold and surprisingly heavy. It seemed vaguely familiar.

"It's a few years old, by the look of it. It's been kicked about a bit, too, but I don't think it's too smashed up."

She paused.

"It's a hard drive, sir."

21: The Killings

THE WAY MALHOTRA handled the track and the so-called road on the way back, in what was now quite definitely the dark, you'd have thought there was someone after us, and I couldn't help glancing back from time to time to check there wasn't. I couldn't blame her. She was excited. She wasn't the only one. Back came the lights. Back came the beats. If I needed someone to get me somewhere fast she'd be the person I'd pick to drive, but I'd ask for a different choice of music. I did ask for a different choice of music. She told me I could pick the tunes when I was driving.

"Can I drive, then?" I asked.

"No," she said, and turned the music up.

I turned it back down and called Roarkes as soon as we were on a more civilised surface. As I dialled I remembered how I still wasn't entirely sure what he wanted out of this investigation, but I couldn't keep something like this from him. Malhotra would tell him if I didn't. It wasn't far off six o'clock now, and there was a chance Roarkes would have left for the day already, but I figured this was important enough to bring him back in.

"Williams," he said. The tone of voice was enough to remind me I wasn't in his good books, even if he had rather enjoyed the stunt I'd pulled on Serena. Plus the fact that he was calling me *Williams*.

"Hello, Roarkes. Got something for you."

"Yes, Williams. You've got an angry defence lawyer who wants you run out of Manchester, possibly out of England, and you've got a detective inspector who doesn't really see why he should get in her way. And where the hell have you been, anyway?"

He might have asked me a question, but he didn't stop to let me answer it. On he went. I could tell he was annoyed, but I could also tell *annoyed* was as far as it went. He wasn't going to kick me off the case, and if Serena Hawkes tried to get me kicked off, he wasn't going to make life easy for her. I let him talk for another thirty seconds, and then I hit him with it.

"I've got a hard drive," I said.

That shut him up.

The Land Rover might have unlocked Folgate's resources; it took the hard drive for them to open the door and invite us in for tea. There was an IT suite in the station's basement, and it was a lot smarter than Roarkes' office and a hell of a lot bigger than the tiny room he'd shoved me in with Gaddesdon and Malhotra. It was full of glass and computers and extraordinarily young men and women with pencils behind their ears. It reminded me of those underground research facilities you see in the movies, where top-secret scientists conduct experiments on aliens who are never quite as dead as they look.

This time the corpse was a hard drive, and I wasn't the only one praying it was alive.

It was alive. All that clicking of teeth and shaking of heads when Malhotra handed it over wasn't the sign of a patient too far gone, just contempt for our technical incompetence in ever thinking it dead. Five minutes fiddling around with some wires brought a thumbs up from the senior techie, and five minutes after that we had a USB stick full of video files neatly laid out for us to pick over.

We watched it back in Roarkes' office, me,

Gaddesdon, Malhotra, Roarkes. He'd called Serena, because whatever bad blood there was between them this was too important to leave her out, but she hadn't answered. He left a message instead.

The files were neatly labelled, time, date and location. There were half a dozen cameras but only two pointing at the road. We'd been told about just one of them, but it was starting to become apparent that we hadn't been told the whole truth by a whole lot of people. Maybe the hard drive had been stolen, like the farmer said. But more likely he'd just been frightened into handing it over.

Malhotra put herself in charge of the computer, and it took her a few minutes to find the right files and work out how to align them side by side displaying the same time and date. Just a few minutes, but we begrudged every second, Gaddesdon hopping from one foot to another like he needed a piss, Roarkes sighing theatrically, me pacing up and down as if I were trying to remember something vital.

"Got it," she said, and we all stopped what we were doing and gathered round the tiny screen. The footage had been captured by a pair of modern, high-definition cameras, placed perfectly so as to cover as much of the road as they could without losing quality, so if the whole thing had been staged by a film director the view couldn't have been much better. The road was empty as the file opened, but there was a time stamp on the screen, and we knew exactly when the call from Betterson's phone had been made and almost exactly when Carson had been stopped. A few seconds of two hundred times normal speed, and we were there.

"Are you sure you want to see this?" asked Roarkes, and I was about to ask him why the hell not when I realised he wasn't talking to me. I turned to Gaddesdon, whose friend was about to be shot dead on the screen in front of us. He gave a short, jerky nod, silent, his usually ruddy cheeks the white of a November sky. Malhotra hit play.

The blue Fiesta comes into view first, slowing already, and pulling into a lay-by just in shot. A moment later the reason it's stopped becomes clear, as Fiona Milton's patrol car stops in the other lay-by on the other side of the road, a little further back.

Milton and Ahmet get out of their car. Carson stays in his.

Ahmet stays with the patrol car. Milton approaches. Carson still hasn't got out.

"I don't get it," said Roarkes. Malhotra paused the recording.

"What?" I asked.

"Carson has to get out of the car. He has to get round the back. Otherwise it doesn't make sense, the way they were shot, the way Milton was shot."

I was thinking the same thing. These people weren't following the script, weren't doing what their Lego counterparts had promised. Carson had to get round the back, maybe check the boot, maybe Milton had just asked him to. Maybe all that was about to happen. It was beyond grotesque, I suddenly realised, what we were doing, watching these people, knowing they were about to die.

"Sod it. Start the tape, Malhotra," said Roarkes. "Let them get shot their own way."

I grimaced and glanced at Gaddesdon, but he didn't seem to register the words.

A vehicle comes into view behind the patrol car. It's a little Mazda. Green. The woman from Bolton. It slows as it sees the flashing lights, stops. Ahmet has turned around to face her, walks over, ducks down to the driver's window, gestures and speaks. A moment later the Mazda reverses, stops, starts again, slowly and jerkily conducts an eight-point turn to face the other way and drive off.

Milton is still approaching the Fiesta. She's not in any hurry. Carson still hasn't got out, but his window's down and you can just see the side of his head as he nods and appears to say something to the approaching police officer. Milton is now standing beside the Fiesta, talking through the open window. For someone who's investigating a report of a weapon, she seems remarkably cool, but she's not stupid. Still looking at the car, she slowly backs away as the door begins to open.

"Here it comes," said Roarkes, and I heard Malhotra sigh. I wasn't the only one getting annoyed by the running commentary.

Naz Ahmet has been watching events unfold from beside the patrol car, one hand still inside through the open window. I'm guessing that hand is on the radio. Now he retrieves his hand and steps away. Another vehicle is approaching. It's a battered 4WD, so old I can't even tell what make it is, and it's carrying a trailer stuffed so full of sheep we can see the wool edging out through the gaps. Ahmet puts his hand out, the car stops, Ahmet walks over to explain. Despite having a trailer attached, the farmer manages to turn around in half the number of moves it took the woman from Bolton. As he drives away, Carson emerges from the Fiesta, his hands in clear view. In a moment, he's going to move to the back of the car to get the gun, or she's going to tell him to open the boot, and we'll finally get to see how it happened.

Carson puts his arms up in the air, and Milton approaches and frisks him, quickly and efficiently. She reaches into the car and takes the keys from the ignition, and then leans further in. I'm guessing she's checking the glove compartment. She emerges a moment later, turns and says something to Ahmet, who nods, and then to Carson, who walks past her to open the rear driver's side door.

And then another car approaches.

"Who the fuck is this?" asked Roarkes, which was pointless, because as he was well aware, none of us had the faintest idea. And he shouldn't really have been surprised to see it.

It's a dark blue Land Rover Defender. We can't see the plates from the angle of the second camera but I'd bet my last penny they say PK11 VAX. Ahmet does his usual, steps out into the road, holds out his hand, the Land Rover stops.

You can half-see the man inside, not clearly enough to know what he looks like, but clearly enough to identify his gestures. He's speaking to Ahmet, nodding, and pointing at something in his other hand. As the hand comes up and out of the window you can see it's a phone.

There's no sound and I'm no lip-reader, but it's obvious what he's saying.

I'm the one who called it in.

Ahmet nods, then gestures at him to turn around and go. He's right. The guy's got to go, no matter what he's seen or who he's called. Instead, the guy opens his door and steps out, and Ahmet shrugs in a resigned sort of way and turns back to Milton to ask her something.

He never gets the chance. The man from the Land Rover raises one arm, whatever's in his hand isn't a phone any more, and an instant later Ahmet's on the ground.

"Jesus H Christ," said Roarkes. Gaddesdon swallowed loud and hard, his eyes fixed on the screen. No one sighed. No one else made a sound.

Fiona Milton has turned to talk to Carson again, but the sound of the shot jerks her back round to face her fallen colleague. Carson's looking, too, but neither of them are facing the camera so we can't see their expressions.

The man from the Land Rover is looking at the camera, though, or at least in its general direction. He smiles, briefly, and I can see he's a well-built man, not short, not tall, not fat, just solid and well-built, he's in his late fifties, probably, or early sixties, a little grey, a lot bald. He raises his arm again, and Milton's down. Carson bends over her, and then straightens back up and looks at the man with the gun. The man with the gun smiles at him and says something, it's not clear what, even though his lips are in full view, he shakes his head, and walks back to the Land Rover. He reaches in, pulls out a piece of cloth, wipes down the gun, and throws it casually into the hedge across the road. He takes a moment to look around, staring briefly right at the camera and nodding to himself. Then he gets into his car and drives away.

He doesn't drive straight onto the main road, though. He drives up a track and out of sight, and I know without following him that this is the track to the farm where the CCTV footage is held, and that in the brief visit that now comes, the hard drive will be removed and the farmer will be terrified into complicit silence.

Carson has bent back down to Milton. There's no point. Both officers, the medics say, died seconds after being shot. He stands up and runs over to Ahmet, puts his head to the dead man's chest, gets back up, walks over to the Fiesta, sits on the ground with his back against it. Nothing happens. Two minutes later, he pulls himself back up, walks over to Milton's body and retrieves something from her hand.

His keys.

He walks back to the Fiesta, gets in, and drives away, in the direction he was already facing.

Three minutes later another car stops. A woman, alone, in a gleaming white Mini with 2015 plates. She sees the flashing lights, gets out of the car, spots Ahmet's body, runs over to it and bends down, sees Milton's, runs to her and does the same thing. She's a paediatric nurse returning from her shift on the children's unit at the Royal Blackburn Hospital, she's done stints at Accident and Emergency before, if anything could have been done she'd probably *have been able to do it. But nothing could be done. She runs back to her car and makes the phone call.*

Malhotra hit stop. For a moment, there was silence. Then everybody was talking at once, including me, and no one could hear a word anyone else was saying.

"Shut the fuck up!" shouted Roarkes. It worked.

"You," he pointed to Malhotra. "Back it up to the shootings. I want to see the bastard that did this again and I want his face on every TV channel between here and Outer Mongolia by the time the main news bulletins go out this evening. And get this over to facial recognition. I want to know who this man is. You," and now he was pointing at Gaddesdon, who was already returning to his red-faced self, "get hold of Serena Hawkes. I don't give a damn if she's sulking. I want her here now. Tell her what we've got. That should make her jump. I'm going to have a nice quiet word with the super at Chetwood and explain to him that if I don't have Tarney in this station within the hour I will have him shot. If Tarney isn't shot first."

"What do you mean?" asked Malhotra.

"Once this bastard sees himself all over the news it won't take him long to realise someone's landed him in it." Roarkes was pointing at the screen, where Malhotra had frozen the tape on as clear an image of the killer's face as we were likely to get. "If they let Tarney out and it turns out he does actually know something useful, he's as good as dead. I want him here, and I want one of us watching him every second of every day until we're all dead or he's dead or the case is closed."

Malhotra nodded. I remembered what Tarney had said, *keep it between us.* He wouldn't actually be named, but it was far too late for that now. Roarkes was right. He might have smashed my nose up, but we couldn't just let him die.

"What about me?" I asked. He looked at me and smiled, suddenly, unexpectedly, almost warmly.

"Go back to your hotel, get some sleep. I brought you up here to crack Carson and find out why he did it. You've cracked Tarney instead, and you've got Carson off the hook, so I reckon you can feel pretty pleased with yourself. Meanwhile you've been beaten up twice and you claim to have some kind of magnetic attraction to moving vehicles. Claire might think I'm the acceptable face of British policing, but I'll never hear the end of it if I send you back even uglier than you arrived. I reckon you're done, Sam."

I started to argue with him, because disagreeing with whatever Roarkes was saying had become second nature over the last few days. I opened my mouth to tell him he was talking shit again and suddenly realised he wasn't. Carson might have been as helpful as a florist in a fist fight, but he hadn't killed Ahmet and Milton and as soon as he could stand up and walk around, he could go home.

Or maybe not go home, not quite, because even if he hadn't pulled the trigger, it looked like he knew the man who had. One way or another, Carson was involved. He was off the hook, but he was still in the lake, and there were some pretty nasty sharks in there with him. I wasn't ready to give up on Carson.

But more than that, I was tired and hungry – I couldn't recall eating a thing all day – and fed up with worrying where the next fist was coming from or who was going to try to drive their car into me. Maybe the hotel wasn't such a bad idea after all.

22: A Terrible Mistake

I WAS MOST of the way back there when my phone rang. I glanced down, recognised the number, thought about it for all of two seconds. I'd have to speak to her eventually, I realised. It might as well be now. I pulled over and answered on the fourth ring.

"Hello, Mia," I said. I didn't get the chance to say anything else.

"Don't you *hello Mia* me, you piece of shit. I had everyone lined up waiting for your big story, and it turns out you've got fuck all!"

"I can explain –" I began.

"Don't bother. I'm more interested in what you're doing about all those nice little leads. There's a glacier in Argentina that might have some secrets, I hear."

Those bastards. Again. I wondered whether they actually solved any crimes at all, or just spent their days chatting to journalists and beating up lawyers. Folgate had more holes in it than Carson's mole-ridden field.

"I can't talk about that, Mia. You know I can't."

"No great surprise there. You're a tight-lipped bastard, even for a lawyer. What about the planning angle? Has to be one or the other, right? Planning or Argentina?"

She was persistent, I had to give her that. And I did owe her an apology, or something.

Or something. I had something. It would be news in an hour or two anyway, and sure, it would be old news by the time she went to press, but the *Mirror* had a website, which meant she wouldn't have to wait till morning.

"As it happens I have got something for you, Mia."

"Sure you do."

"Really. But you have to promise me one thing."

"What?"

"When I give you this, you don't go hassling Roarkes or Serena or any of the others, not until the story's out with everyone else. Then you can ask whatever you want. Till then, it's just you and me and however many people look at your website. And don't go telling anyone who your source is, either."

"Source? You? Like you've got anything worth printing."

I waited a few seconds before replying. Mia Arazzi was all dressed up in cynical and angry, but the clothes didn't fit. She'd paused herself, for a moment, before replying, and it might have been the quality of the signal but I thought I could hear a faint tremor in her voice. She was still keen.

"We know who killed Ahmet and Milton," I said, as calmly as I could, and the sharp intake of breath on the other end of the line told me I'd been right.

"Who?"

"I don't have a name, and I can't give you the photo. But I can tell you it wasn't Carson. I can tell you there's footage of the killing taking place, that Carson was deliberately set up, and that the killer drove a dark blue Land Rover Defender with cloned plates. That enough for you?"

"Why should I believe you?"

I thought about that for a moment.

"OK, here's the deal. You publish and it turns out to be bullshit, you can name me. I'm the bastard that put you up to it, I'm the lawyer Roarkes brought in, I've fed the press a heap of crap, that's a story itself, right? But you'll want to be fast. The guy's face'll be all over the news by nine."

That gave her a little over ninety minutes, which wasn't much of a scoop. But if she was the journalist she thought she was, she could write it in ten, get it approved and uploaded in five more, and all over Facebook an hour before anyone else knew a thing about it. I knew how it worked, Claire had explained it all to me. Juicy story, lots of clicks, happy advertisers, happy editor, happy journalist. I reckoned I'd paid Mia Arazzi back.

I pulled back onto the road and continued towards the hotel. It was raining, as usual, and even though rush hour was supposed to have ended a while ago, it looked like I'd picked the wrong time to drive, again, with what felt like half of Manchester headed the same way. Plenty of time, stuck in the fumes and the red lights, to think it all through. The planning angle, Argentina, Carson, Grissom, there might be a connection, but nothing that explained what had happened to Milton and Ahmet. And Carson might not have killed them, but if he was Grissom then he'd been part of a gang who killed routinely, who killed anyone that got their way and didn't care how they did it. You pissed them off, you died, or – what was it Crick had said? They threatened your family, and they were convincing enough that you'd do their own work for them. Charming.

You'd top yourself. That was it. That was what Crick had told us. The man who was so afraid he killed himself to protect his family.

I heard car horns behind me. The lights had changed, they were green, there was a rare patch of empty road in front, ten whole beautiful yards of it.

I couldn't move. The horns went on, there were more of them now, two, three, a dozen?

It didn't matter.

To protect his family.

They'd sent Carson a message. Two messages. What had the killer said? I tried to think back to the footage. Now I was starting to understand what was going on, I thought I could guess what the man from the Land Rover had said to Carson before he'd got back in his car and driven away.

"Over to you."

That was the first message.

The second message was just as straightforward, and a little more practical.

It was a belt.

By the time I'd come back to the real world the lights were red again, and the noise from the car horns behind me had stopped. I didn't realise why until I heard a click and the door swung open. A tall, thick-set man with no hair and boxer's nose stood there in the rain, arms crossed, staring at me with a look that blended superior with violent and was oddly familiar.

"What the fuck do you think you're playing at?" he asked. Familiar accent. A fellow Londoner. I glanced down from his face to his arms. There was a lot of muscle in those arms.

"Get out the car," he said. His voice was still level. I looked back at his nose. My own wasn't in the best of nick, but it was still some way short of the mess his was in. I recognised the expression on his face, now. Tarney and his friends had been wearing it while they smashed me to pieces.

"Sorry," I said.

"Not good enough," he replied, and reached towards me. I held up one hand to stop him.

"Walk away and get back in your car," I said. "Do it now, and I won't have you beaten so badly that nose'll be the prettiest thing left on you."

I watched as the smile formed on his face. I smiled back. He didn't seem to be expecting that. He frowned. I picked up the phone beside me. He walked away, shaking his head. I was tempted to call him back and ask him to shut the door, but that would have been pushing my luck. There was a quieter side road to the left. I drove in and parked, and as I glanced in the mirror I thought I saw a red Astra cruise slowly past along the main road. But how many red Astras were there in Manchester? Hundreds? Thousands, maybe? It didn't matter. There were more important things to worry about than my paranoia. Real things. I dialled Roarkes, who answered on the first ring, and I explained what I'd realised. Carson had been given the chance to kill himself before the man with the Land Rover went looking for more people to kill. He'd tried to take it, and failed, and it wouldn't be he who had to face the consequences.

Roarkes understood. He was sending a unit to Bursington even while he was talking to me. Whoever the man with the Land Rover was, he'd killed Milton and Ahmet just to make a point. If he wanted to make it again, Sally and the boy would be top of his list.

"Get them there before the news bulletins go out, Roarkes. Whoever this bastard is, seeing his face on TV isn't going to make him any happier."

"Go and get some sleep, now," he said, and I agreed, but there was no way I was going back to the hotel. Not yet. There was someone I had to speak to.

The sergeant at the hospital looked familiar. I approached her with my hand outstretched and in it the card I'd been issued at Folgate. She frowned as I drew closer, and then she nodded, and her features settled into something closer to a smile. She knew who I was, at least. I just hoped the patient's lawyer hadn't been in touch and made sure no one let Sam Williams within a mile of her client.

I was lucky.

"Go on through, Mr Williams," she said. There was another police officer sitting on a hard plastic chair outside the door to Carson's room, but he'd seen his sergeant wave me through, so his contribution to the security arrangements was to stand up and open the door for me.

Carson was awake. His eyes were closed as I approached the bed, but I'd seen him close them when I'd glanced through the glass window before the constable had opened the door. I walked up to the bed, past all the machinery that wasn't really necessary any more, because Thomas Carson was doing just fine on his own, breathing and eating and pissing and shitting without anyone needing to do it for him. I bent down to whisper in his ear.

"I know who you are, Grissom," I said, watching for the slightest movement. Nothing. Just the gentle rise and fall of his chest as he went on pretending to sleep. He was good, Grissom, or Carson, or whatever his name was, but, I figured, he'd had plenty of time to prepare for this.

"And we know who killed Milton and Ahmet. We know it wasn't you."

Not even a twitch. I tried a different tack.

"We even know why you tried to kill yourself, Grissom," I said. "We know why you did it and we know what's going to happen now you've failed. They're going to go after Sally, aren't they? Sally and…"

For a moment the boy's name escaped me, and I paused, and then I remembered. But I didn't say anything.

"Matthew," he said. He said it quietly but clearly, through a throat that sounded like it had been cleaned out with a wire brush. It was the first word I'd ever heard the man say.

He opened his eyes and turned towards me and smiled, and spoke again.

"If you know who I am, Mr Williams, and you know who *they* are, then surely you must realise that speaking to you would only make things worse."

He turned away, and closed his eyes, and I realised suddenly that I'd made a terrible mistake. Grissom had always known his wife and child were in danger. He'd tried to keep them safe by keeping his mouth shut, permanently, if he had to, but that hadn't worked. And now we knew a little more of the story, there would be round-the-clock protection, policemen with guns and radios and infrared motion-detecting devices screaming if the wrong person got within a hundred yards. There was no rush. Eventually the police would find the killers, and things would return to normal. Until then, Sally and Matthew would be safe. As far as Thomas Carson was concerned, nothing else mattered. I'd taken the key and turned it, but I'd turned it the wrong way. Carson was locked up tighter than ever.

I left without saying another word.

I'd just sat down on the bed at the First Quality Inn and started trying to work out what I was going to do with the rest of my evening when a text came through.

You'd better be on the level, it said. It was from Mia Arazzi and it included a link to the *Mirror* website.

I briefly scanned the article. It had been live for less than forty minutes and there were already more than a hundred comments. It had everything I'd told her, and no more, apart from a basic recap of all that had happened since Ahmet and Milton had been found dead. She hadn't given away my name, either. I hoped she'd keep it that way.

As I put it down on the bed, the phone rang again. I checked the display. Another caller I didn't want to speak to. Another one I had to.

"Hello, Serena."

"Hello Sam."

"Look, I know you're pissed off and I'm sorry."

"Don't worry about it."

That wasn't what I'd expected.

"You're not pissed off?"

"Well, I *was* pissed off, and then I found out you'd actually got something useful out of the bastard, and my other client looks like he's not going to be convicted of murder, so I think I can bring myself to forgive you. But do me a favour, please, Sam? Can you try to trust me?"

"I did trust you," I said. "I just didn't think you'd trust me. I wouldn't have done."

She laughed.

"Maybe not," she said. "But I do now. And by the way, you're fine to go and talk to Carson whenever you feel like it, but I'd appreciate it if you'd let me know."

"Thanks," I said. I meant it.

"Don't worry about it. It's all turned out for the best, hasn't it?"

There was a script, in which Serena would yell at me for a minute, and then calm down, but not enough to say anything like *it's all turned out for the best*. Mia Arazzi had followed the script: anger, mistrust, grudging acceptance. Serena was making hers up as she went along. Extraordinary woman, I thought.

"Thanks," was all I could think to say, again.

"So where are you?"

"Back at the hotel."

"Fancy that drink?"

She'd given me the name of a bar she thought I'd like,

a nice place, she said, with the emphasis on the *nice*, like I was some half-man of a southerner who wouldn't be able to handle the dirtier side of Manchester. I guessed she was judging me on that chicken jalfrezi.

It was just a drink, I kept reminding myself, as I sprayed on the deodorant, splashed on some aftershave and changed into a shirt almost identical to the one I'd been wearing all day, only a little less creased, plus the trousers I'd been wearing when I'd first driven up here and which had been resting over a chair ever since. My arm had started pounding, suddenly, a new and surprising reminder of Tarney and his part in everything that had happened, but I figured a drink would help fix that. A drink and the company.

When my phone rang again I assumed it was Serena, checking where I was or making sure I knew where I was going, and I answered without looking at the screen.

"Sir," said an anxious voice.

"Gaddesdon?" I asked. He sounded a little breathless and he was calling me *sir* again, but it was him all right.

"Sir," he said, "there's a problem."

"What have you done now, Gaddesdon?"

He's said the wrong thing to the wrong person, I thought. He's upset Sally Carson. He's broken a vital piece of equipment. He's pissed off Roarkes. He's lost something.

I was almost right with the last one.

"It's Sally Carson," he said.

"What about her?"

"She's gone. She's just – gone."

23: On The Road Again

THERE PROBABLY WASN'T anything I could do to help Sally Carson, but the idea of sitting in a bar with Serena Hawkes while half Greater Manchester Police were out there hunting for her client's wife didn't feel right. I dropped her a text apologising and explaining why, and then realised she probably already knew.

It wasn't just Sally Carson that had vanished. Gaddesdon had gone into the kind of detail that blind panic produces, the name of the sergeant in the protection unit who'd been sent to pick her up, the name of the constable who'd gone with, which route they'd taken to Bursington and how long it had taken them to get there. None of that mattered. What mattered was that when they'd arrived, there was no sign of Sally Carson and no sign of her son, either. None of the neighbours knew where she'd gone. Her car was missing from the driveway. Apart from the occasional visit to Folgate, and then the hospital, accompanied by uniformed police every time, she hadn't left the house since Thomas had been arrested. One of the neighbours was standing outside when the unit had arrived, clutching a stock pot full of Bolognese sauce. She'd told Sally she was coming round, she was sure of it. Just that afternoon. Barely four hours ago. Where could Sally be?

Nobody knew. Sally Carson and her son had been missing a matter of minutes, and already, all avenues had been exhausted.

Nobody knew.

That, I thought, was bullshit. Somebody knew. And I

knew where that somebody was.

As I walked past her desk, the bleached-blonde hotel receptionist gave me a smile and told me to have a nice evening. The clean clothes and the aftershave, I thought. What a waste.

Getting back into Manchester was a lot easier than getting out. I remembered the old joke about places like this. *A good place to come from.* As long as you were going somewhere else. But I was starting to recognise things, even by night, even at this speed. Roads, buildings, hills, rivers. As I drove past one I was looking forward to the next. Manchester, I realised with horror, was growing on me.

Same sergeant at the hospital. Same constable. They smiled and let me through and I wondered, briefly, whether they knew the man in the room they were guarding had turned from cop-killer to witness in the space of an afternoon. Either way, I wasn't supposed to be here. No one wanted me talking to Thomas Carson by myself. But no one seemed to be stopping me. As I approached I could see him through the window, asleep, or resting, utterly relaxed, and utterly unaware that the one thing keeping him that way was gone. I remembered, just before I walked into the room, what Serena had said, and paused to drop her another text. *I'm going to try to talk to Carson.*

"Hello, Francis."

He sat up immediately and smiled.

"Not pretending to be asleep now?"

"No point. You know I'm not telling you anything."

He was right, of course. He had no reason to say a word. In his world, his wife and son were sat in front of the TV eating their dinner with the fire lit and half a dozen police scattered around the house staring at the night. In his world, everything was fine.

His world no longer existed.

"Sally's missing," I said. He grinned at me. I tried again. "She's disappeared. Matthew too."

"Sure she has," he replied. I couldn't blame him. Telling him his family were still in danger was the only way to get him talking. Maybe if I'd realised that earlier, and lied to him, she might not have disappeared at all.

I slammed my fist down on the table beside his bed. There was a folder there, some flowers, a glass half full of water. The glass shook.

"I'm not bullshitting you, Carson," I said, and it was that slip, that word, *Carson* instead of *Grissom* that swung it, because the moment he heard it he knew I wasn't lying. Grissom was my trump card, the ace that told him I knew more about his hand than he wanted me to. Carson was me, desperate, pleading for his help.

The grin was gone. The world inside Carson's head was gone, flattened into nothing by the truth.

"Where are they?"

"I've told you. I don't know."

Now he was shouting, his voice hoarse, the words tearing their way out the throat he'd tried to shut forever.

"Find them! Get out there and fucking well find them!"

He was on his feet, his head twisting from side to side, as if Sally and Matthew were in the room with us, hovering just out of view. The door opened, the constable came in, started towards me, and then stopped when he saw I wasn't on top of Carson at all and certainly not close enough to be causing the kind of pain that would produce a noise like the one he was making now.

"Ohmygod ohmygod ohmygod," it went. "Ohmygod ohmygod ohmygod," louder and quieter and louder again, his head in his hands, and then his hands up and above him, shaking, supplicating. After all those days of silence, he was making up for it now. The constable was standing by the door, open-mouthed and utterly bewildered. I waited for Carson to go quiet, or at least relatively quiet, because he was still gasping the same three words, over and over.

"Where is she, Carson?"

He ignored me. Or maybe he just couldn't hear.

"Thomas?"

On he went, "Ohmygod ohmygod ohmygod."

"Please. You have to listen to me. We want to find Sally. We want to find Matthew. Do you know where they might be?"

I spoke gently. He looked right at me, now, and frowned, as if he were surprised to see me there. He stopped talking. I took a step towards him, reached out to put an arm on his shoulder, saw the constable take a step into the centre of the room.

"Please, Thomas. You've got to help us."

He shook his head.

"It's possible the people who did this have got your wife and your son, and they're not nice people, are they, Thomas?"

He shook his head again, but this time he spoke, and it wasn't gibberish, it was an actual word, and he was looking at me as he said it, so there was at least a chance it was supposed to be a reply.

"Restaurant," he said.

For a moment my mind was blank. Of all the things he might have come up with, *restaurant* wasn't getting me any closer to his family. What the hell did *restaurant* have to do with anything? I opened my mouth to ask him again, and then I remembered.

"The Italian restaurant?" I asked. "In Burnley?"

He stared at me. There was nothing there, nothing in

his eyes, he didn't seem to be looking at me at all, just the space in front of him where there was sound and movement and colour.

"Please, Thomas. Help me. Is it the Italian restaurant? The one that burnt down?"

Carson took a step back, to the bed, sat down, dropped his chin to his chest, and closed his eyes. I felt a tap on my shoulder.

"I'm sorry, sir," said the constable. "The doctor'll be here in a moment. But I think you should go. Carson can't hear you now."

He was right. Carson didn't look like he could hear anything at all.

I had my phone out and Gaddesdon's number on the screen before I'd even left the room. The sergeant who'd let me through earlier was walking towards me with a young man in green scrubs with a pinched look and an expression of controlled fury. As Gaddesdon answered the phone, the man grabbed my right arm and asked me what had happened. I winced, hard, shook my head, mumbled, "Sorry," and hurried away, blinking at the pain that had just shot through me.

Three things I needed from Gaddesdon. Just three things. The first was to call Malhotra, tell her what I was telling him now, what had just happened, the clue Carson might or might not have given me, and tell her to get down to the hospital as fast as her Nissan would let her and be there when Carson started making sense again. The second was to make the same call to Serena. The third was to give me an address, because I was already in my car, the phone on speaker, the maps app open and the word "Burnley" keyed in. But *Burnley* alone wasn't enough. I needed an address.

Gaddesdon wasn't in his sharpest mood.

"An address for what, sir?"

"The Italian restaurant, for Christ's sake. Haven't you been listening to a word I've just said?"

"Yes, yes, sorry. But it burnt down, didn't it?"

He had a point. Whatever was there now, it wouldn't be the restaurant Luca Moretti had burned to death in with his wife and children.

"I know. I guess I'll start there and move outwards, see who's there now, what they know, ask some questions. It's all we've got."

"It's not much to go on, sir."

He was right there, too. But apart from *ohmygod* it was the only thing Carson had said, and he'd said it in what had looked remarkably like a moment of sudden lucidity. For the instant in which he'd been granted the time and temporary sanity for a single word, that was the word he'd chosen. If it had been me, I'd have made sure that word was pretty damned important.

As I approached the barriers that guarded the car park exit, I noticed a red Astra slide into place beside me. *Thousands of them*, I thought to myself, again, and then I opened the window and looked closer and saw the face of the man who was driving it.

Bald head. Glasses.

And sure, thousands of them, too, but in the same car? Here?

Gaddesdon was still talking. I felt in my pocket for the car park ticket and decided to give up on making him call me Sam.

"And the address wasn't in the memo, sir, or the local newspaper article. It just had the name of the place, and the family."

Even struggling to find the ticket, even with the Astra beside me and a man in it who I was convinced was following me, even with all that on my mind, I couldn't quite believe what I was hearing.

"So, Gaddesdon, all you've got is the name of a restaurant, and the people that ran it, and the date of the fire in which they all died, and searchable reports from the fire brigade and all the local press, and the internet?"

"Sir."

I felt in my other pocket for the ticket. There were two lanes at the exit, two barriers. There was a car behind the Astra, and there had been one waiting behind me, too, but I was taking so long he'd reversed and moved across and now there were two cars lined up behind the Astra. I hadn't finished with Gaddesdon.

"I can see your problem, Gaddesdon. I imagine it'll be the nearest thing to impossible to find out where that restaurant actually was."

"OK, sir."

My fingers brushed against a piece of card and I pulled it out, triumphant. The ticket. Another car had joined the queue behind the Astra, I noticed, three of them now, and the one at the front suddenly let loose with the horn, a shrill blast into the cold night air. I turned and stared at the bald man, who was looking straight ahead, unmoving. I remembered something important.

There was another exit to the car park.

"I'm in the car now. Get hold of Malhotra. Get hold of Serena. Call me as soon as you've got the address. Phone's telling me I'll be in Burnley in forty minutes. Let's see if I can make it thirty."

I flicked on my hazard lights and opened the door, because if you can't find your exit ticket it stands to reason you'll get out and start looking on the floor. Astra man glanced in my direction, saw me staring right at him, and looked away. The car behind him gave another blast, and as I watched he shook his head in defeat, opened his window and fed his card into the machine. Before the barrier on his side had fully lifted I was back in the Fiat with the gearstick slammed into reverse, and ten seconds after the Astra was through I'd turned around and was on my way to an exit that would take him at least ten minutes to reach on the roads outside the hospital.

Gaddesdon was still talking, but by now I'd zoned him out completely.

"Call me when you've got the address," I barked, and hung up as I shoved my ticket into the barrier, tapping the steering wheel impatiently as I waited for it to rise. Thirty long seconds later I slid onto the main road on the far side of the hospital. Traffic was light and the directions were clear enough, which gave me time to consider what had just happened.

Who was Astra man?

He was a police officer, I was sure of that, I remembered seeing him more than just the once in Folgate. I'd seen the car at Fiona Milton's funeral, too, but I hadn't spotted the driver among the mourners. Not that I'd have worried if I had done. The man was a police officer, after all. I'd assumed that put him in the clear, but that assumption had been little short of stupid.

Tarney was a police officer too.

I'd seen Astra man talking to Roarkes, I remembered, and I added that to the strain on his face, and the mood swings, and ignoring the leads, and kicking me out of his office. I'd told Gaddesdon to contact Malhotra and Serena, but I hadn't mentioned Roarkes, which had been an oversight, not a deliberate omission.

But maybe keeping Roarkes in the dark wasn't such a bad idea.

The motorway round Manchester was quiet, unlit, relatively dry, and let me hold a steady ninety the whole time I was on it. No sign of the Astra. Hardly another car on the road. The next turn took me dead north, and as the relics of the old mills approached and disappeared either side of the road I realised this was the same route Gaddesdon had taken to drive us to Bursington the first time. So different by night, I thought, the huge old buildings and the hills and the sudden splashes of light in the darkness. Not just different. Extraordinary, somehow. And then I realised I hadn't had a decent night's sleep for weeks, and I hadn't eaten all day, so my head was full of that weird long-haul flight sensation where nothing seems quite real. It wasn't the road or the hills or the mills. It was just me.

The next motorway beckoned, and as I skidded my way round another misjudged roundabout my phone rang. I couldn't answer it, not without killing myself or at least slowing down more than I wanted to, so I waited until I was doing seventy in a straight line before I looked down. Below the missed call notification (from Gaddeson, of course) was a text (also from Gaddesdon). *Called Mal and Srna,* it read. *Srna not happy.*

Any number of reasons for that. Could even be because she'd missed out on a drink with me, but I doubted it. I'd done what she'd asked me to, anyway, I'd let her know I was coming to see her client, and it might have been a bit last-minute, but she hadn't actually said *in advance*, had she?

She'd probably meant it, though. She'd probably meant she wanted the kind of warning that would enable her to be there, in the room, while I spoke to her client, so she could give me signals and take me outside and stop me doing the kind of thing that might plunge that client into a catatonic vacuum. I didn't think Serena on hand would have helped. It hadn't helped much with Tarney. It wouldn't have brought Carson out of his shell.

Good thing Gaddesdon hadn't called Roarkes as well, I thought. Sam Williams questioning Carson, alone, and speeding off to Burnley still alone to dig up the past. Roarkes would have had a field day with that.

Below the terse little message was an address. And below that an urgent plea. *Pls call ASAP when you can,* it read. I would, too. But not until I got where I was going.

Still doing seventy, I typed in the new address and found myself guided straight back off the motorway. There were rows of terraced houses, shops, a supermarket, a cinema, a vast building site where signs emblazoned with random catchwords like "Regenerate" and "Future" sprouted like styrofoam boxes in a Friday night gutter. It might have been anywhere.

It was Burnley.

My phone guided me past the football ground and a handful of signs for a stately home. I'd slept all the way to Burnley that morning – I couldn't believe it was still the same day we'd set off to find Brian Betterson – and on the way back I'd been staring at the numbers on my phone, talking to Roarkes, trying to work out where Betterson had gone, paying not the slightest bit of attention to what was outside the car. Betterson's bit of Burnley had been what I'd expected, dirty, run-down and tense, hemmed in on all sides by bookies and nail bars. This bit, in contrast, was almost nice. The terraces were clean and the bins laid out in neat, ordered rows. The streetlamps were working. The people outside the pubs were standing and talking like normal people outside normal pubs. Maybe all that *regeneration* bullshit wasn't total bullshit after all. I was, according to my phone, three hundred yards from the restaurant, or whatever was left of it. A barbers, another row of terraces, a Chinese takeaway. Two hundred yards. A set of traffic lights, a large primary school. One hundred yards. More terraces. A tiny, narrow playground, thrown in between the houses like an alleyway with ideas above its station. A field.

That was it. I stopped the car. This was the address. Number 46.

I'd stopped on the other side of the road, the odd numbers. Across from where I parked, behind a double yellow line so faded it was hardly there at all, was what should have been a burnt-out Italian restaurant, or whatever had been built on its remains. Instead, there was a big, empty patch of grass surrounded by barbed wire.

There was nothing there.

24: The Jar

I HIT REDIAL, and when Gaddesdon answered I jumped in before he could speak.

"There's nothing here. Are you sure this is the address?"

"Yes, sir. It adds up. Old phone book and the fire brigade logs. Both said 46."

"Shit," I hissed.

"There's some news, sir. About the woman."

Hope flared. I waited.

"Well, we haven't actually found her."

Hoped died again.

"But we've found the boy."

That was something. It was more than something, it was half of everything, and it might get us closer to the other half.

"Where? Where was he?"

"One of the other neighbours brought him in. There's a police station in Clitheroe, she took him there."

Clitheroe was the nearest town to Bursington, which wasn't saying much. It was still far enough away that your pizza would be cold by the time you made it home.

"Why? How come she had him?"

"It's all a bit confusing, sir, but she said Sally had turned up banging on her door like a madwoman a little before eight, said she had to finish it, and she said *finish what*, and all she said was *it's on the web*, and asked if the woman could look after the boy for her."

I tried to untangle it, the *her* and the *she* from *Sally* and *the woman*, flying around my head like bats. I tried to take

241

refuge in the grammar and the syntax, and I failed, because I knew perfectly well what Gaddesdon had said, and I knew at least a little of what it meant, and what it meant was that it was my fault.

"Sir?" said Gaddesdon.

"Hang on," I replied. I needed to clear my head. "No. Tell me again, what did Sally Carson say? Exactly, Gaddesdon."

"It's here, sir. One moment. Oh yes. She said, *I've got to finish it off.* Then she said, *It's all out there on the web.* And then she said *Take Matthew* – that's the boy's name, sir – *I've got to sort it out before it's too late.* The neighbour couldn't make head nor tail of it and neither can we, sir, but that's basically it."

I couldn't make perfect sense of it either, but one thing stood out clearer than the rest. "*It's all out there on the web.*" I'd given the story to Mia Arazzi and told her to publish it, and she had. A minute later I'd realised something like this might happen, too, I'd warned Roarkes, I'd told him to get to Bursington before the news reports went out. But it was too late. I'd already leaked the story myself. I'd endangered Sally Carson and her son, and she'd realised it before I had.

It was my fault. My fault she was in danger. My fault she'd disappeared.

"Sir?"

Gaddesdon wanted something. It no longer mattered. I had nothing, no leads, nothing at all. Just a patch of grass and mud surrounded by barbed wire. And a woman who was missing and might already be dead.

"What?"

"There's something else, sir."

"Yes, Gaddesdon. I know. Serena isn't happy. Wants her client treated with kid gloves, right?"

"No, sir. I mean, yes, she does, she's pissed off with

you, but that's not it. It's the restaurant."

I waited.

"There's been a mistake, sir."

I could guess precisely who'd made that mistake.

"The article, sir. Did you read it?"

"What article, Gaddesdon?"

He coughed.

"Gaddesdon?"

"Sorry sir." He sounded like someone who really didn't want to say what he had to. "The article about the fire."

"No, Gaddesdon. You showed me the memo you found. From the illiterate sergeant."

"Yes. Well, there was an article, and it said there'd been a fire, and they were all dead."

He stopped.

"Yes?"

"And it turned out they weren't."

It was a dry night, but cool. Dry and cool didn't explain the finger of ice suddenly pressing against my spine.

"What do you mean, Gaddesdon?"

"It wasn't my fault, sir. It's just, they went to press while the fire was still being put out and I suppose they didn't check their information, they just asked someone at the scene. Anyway, there was a correction in the following week's paper."

He paused, again.

"Go on, for Christ's sake."

"I'm sure it's not important, sir."

The build-up he was giving this particular piece of information said otherwise. So did his tone of voice. I'd had enough of prompting him. I waited.

"It's just, the girl, sir. She didn't die. She was taken to hospital suffering from smoke inhalation, and she was out again next day. Rest of them burned up, they could hardly

ID the bodies, sir. But the girl was fine."

The sixteen year old. Something hovered just at the edge of my mind, an idea, but I couldn't reach it. I was too tired. My arm was throbbing, suddenly, and my brain was stumbling slowly from one thought to another like a drunk man in a fog. Gaddesdon was still talking.

"Thing is, it's probably nothing, right, sir? I mean, this was all about the Corporation, wasn't it? Fact they killed three people instead of four, it's neither here nor there, is it?"

Was it? Was he right? I was standing in the dark in front of a field. Was this whole thing another dead end?

"I've taken photos of the two articles. I'll send them to your phone now. Maybe you can get something out of it all."

"Thanks, Gaddesdon," I said, still staring at the field. Without realising what I was doing, I'd started to walk around the perimeter, looking for a gap in the barbed wire fence. I didn't know what I'd do if I found one. It wasn't like I expected to see anything useful in there.

"I'll leave you to it, sir. Let me know if you want me to come out there, though. I can give you a hand, if you want."

"No, Gaddesdon. You stay put. I'll call you if I need you. Go to the pub or something. Just stay close to the station."

Thirty seconds later my phone beeped. Gaddesdon's message. The articles. Difficult to make out, bad copies badly digitised in the first place, bad photos taken by Gaddesdon, a dirty, smudged screen I was trying to read them on.

I'd walked from one end of the field to the other alongside the road. Houses either side, narrow strips of land between them and the wire. No gaps yet. My phone rang and I glanced down at the little notification above the article I was trying to read. Elizabeth bloody Maurier. Again. Her timing, as ever, impeccable. Fuck off, Elizabeth Maurier.

There was a photograph beside the first article. The restaurant, or what was left of it, a smouldering husk in the morning light. It had taken nearly twelve hours to bring the fire under control.

The second article was shorter and more formal, an apology and a correction, and usually that would have been where it all finished, but it had been a big mistake about a major tragedy, so space had been made for another photograph, and when I saw it I nearly dropped the phone.

I pinched the screen to zoom in and get a better look at the image, but the definition was so poor all I got was a slightly bigger blur. It didn't matter. I'd seen that photograph before.

I reached into my back pocket and pulled them out, three photographs. Matthew, the son. The tourists, together with the man I thought must be Alejandro.

And the family shot. The photo that had made no sense. Husband, wife, two children. A girl, early teens. A boy, a lot younger.

I read the caption beside the newspaper article. The photograph had been taken in 1993, two years before the fire. Three of the people in that photograph had died in the fire. One hadn't. The girl. Chiara Moretti.

She'd been sixteen when the fire took her family, and twenty years had gone by. I glanced back at the photograph, at the mother, and the girl, and nodded to myself, because suddenly everything was falling into place.

Twenty years. The teenager was tall and thin, angular, so awkward you could still see it in a creased and aging photograph. With a touch of colour in her face. Twenty years on, she was less lean, less angular, certainly less awkward. Dark-haired. Fine-featured. She still had the touch of colour in her face, but that had nothing whatsoever to do with South America. Visually, there wasn't much to connect the teenager of twenty years ago with the woman of today.

Except the mother.

How stupid had I been? I'd had the photograph the whole time, there in the back pocket of a pair of trousers slung across a chair in a cold room in the First Quality Inn. I'd dug through my old files, in case I'd seen Sally Carson before, and I almost had. There in my room the whole time. Even while I was talking to the woman I'd known there was something out of place, and I'd jumped at pauses and odd little questions that didn't mean a thing. I'd felt something ringing a bell, or jarring, I couldn't figure out which. Turned out it was both. She rang a bell, and she jarred, all at the same time.

Sally Carson, twenty years on, was *almost* the image of her mother. Just *almost*. Not quite, and that was the jar. Her family had been killed that night, murdered by the same men who'd gunned down Milton and Ahmet to get at her husband.

Sally Carson wasn't in danger. Sally Carson wasn't Sally Carson at all, she was Chiara Moretti, and she wasn't running away.

Quite the reverse.

She'd gone to finish it all off.

25: Into the Darkness

I WAS BACK in the car but I was damned if I knew where the hell I was going. Not here, that was all. Not a field. *Restaurant*, Carson had said, but that hadn't been a *where*. It had been a *why*.

Carson. It was starting to feel like I was spending more time in his hospital room than the First Quality Inn, but he was worth another try. And his room was more comfortable, anyway. I could call on the way.

I turned the car around and started driving. Back towards the motorway, which would lead me to Manchester. Away from the field. In the twenty minutes I'd been there, walking around an empty rectangle of mud and grass and shouting at a phone, it had got colder and damper, and now there was no one else on the street. No people. No cars. Certainly no red Astra. The whole street, dead, as if it had died twenty years ago and nobody had ever come back to visit.

I narrowly beat a red light and dialled Malhotra's number as I shot past the football ground. This was where Brian Betterson had lost his phone, or so he'd said. Maybe it had been true. Thing was, he knew who'd taken it, and that knowledge had turned him from a shabby, strung-out chancer into a man with a secret so dangerous he'd left the country.

I had the phone to my left ear, taking the roundabouts at speed with my right hand at the end of an arm that had stopped throbbing and now just felt numb, as if it had been trying to tell me something and given up waiting for me to get the message. Whatever it was, it could wait a little longer. Malhotra's voice came down the line.

"Hello?"

"It's Sam."

"Oh good. I'm glad you called. I'm in the room with Carson. He won't talk to me, though."

He'll talk to me, I thought.

"Is Serena there yet?"

"No," she replied, and I sensed a hint of relief. Serena wasn't going to be delighted that there was yet another person in the room with her client and no lawyer there to defend him. Not that he actually needed defending any more. Or not from the police, anyway. Serena wouldn't be long, though. Not after the message she'd got from Gaddesdon.

"Pass him the phone. I've got something I want to say to him."

I heard footsteps, and rustling, and breath, but no voice. Carson was back in quiet mode.

"I know who Sally is," I said.

Another breath. No words.

"I know why she's disappeared, too. She's not running away at all, Thomas. She's running right at them, isn't she?"

Still just the breath, ragged, uneven, like a man who'd run further than he was used to and was waiting for the rest of his body to catch up.

"So what do you call each other when you're alone? Is it Thomas and Sally? Or Frank and Chiara?"

Finally he spoke, the words breathed out in a weary, desperate sigh.

"Where's Matthew?" he asked.

"Matthew's safe," I said. "The police have got him."

"I never meant... neither of us ever... it wasn't supposed to be like this," he said.

"What do you mean?"

A long sigh, again. The sound of a key turning. A lock clicking open.

"You're right. I'm Frank Grissom. I was Frank Grissom. I did some nasty things, back then. But I was a kid. And I never killed anyone, I swear it. By the time I was twenty I'd had enough, but I couldn't leave. You know what they did to people who wanted to leave?"

It was a rhetorical question. I replied with a question of my own.

"So what happened?"

"Chiara. She was a couple of years younger than me and her dad had this Italian restaurant where we used to meet."

"So he was part of it?"

"Christ no. He was just the poor bastard whose business got picked. There was nothing he could do about it. Chiara used to take orders and serve drinks and I couldn't help noticing her. She was something else."

"What happened?"

"Her dad. Luca. He'd had enough, too, but he wasn't smart enough to keep it to himself. I was seeing Chiara by then, and she told me, I said to him *don't be stupid, just play along*, but he wasn't having any of it. Said he was going to go to the police."

"He did go to the police."

Another sigh. "I know. And someone there must have seen him come in, some snitch, or some bent cop must have spilled the beans."

"Did you know what was going to happen?"

"Of course not. I'd have got them out if I'd known. I didn't hear a thing about it till next day when I went round to see Chiara."

And that was enough, for Grissom. Getting out might have been risky, but sticking around didn't exactly guarantee a long and healthy life. He got out, changed his name, fled to another continent. But he kept in touch with Chiara, who'd gone to live with an aunt in Italy. Four years, they waited. Four years, and then Chiara Moretti became Sally Grieves, went backpacking in Argentina all by herself, and fell in love with a handsome young man she met in the wilds of Patagonia.

"I never wanted to come back. It was Chiara."

"Why?"

"Because for her it was still home. And I thought, after all this time—"

I cut him off. I knew where he was going.

"You thought it would be safe, didn't you? You thought they'd have forgotten about you by now."

"I did. I was wrong."

"And when they found you, they were – what? They weren't even going to do you the courtesy of killing you themselves? You had to do it, right? You had to do it to yourself, or they'd go after your family."

A pause, a long, laboured breath, then, "Yes."

"So now she's gone after them."

"I think so."

"Where, Frank? Where's Chiara?"

There was what sounded like a stifled sob, then, "I don't know. I'd tell you if I did."

I wanted to believe him, but frustration was starting to creep in, frustration at the way every tiny detail had to be prised out of him like a pearl from an oyster shell.

"How can you not know?" I asked, half-spoken, half-growled. If he noticed the change in my tone, he didn't seem to care.

"Because back then there were only a few places we used. The restaurant, a room in the back of a warehouse, someone's flat. They're all gone, now. The restaurant burned down, the warehouse is an office and the flat's part of the college. Burnley. That's all I know. It'll be somewhere near Burnley."

"So you've got nothing?"

He sounded convincing enough. And yet. His wife had gone somewhere, and I didn't think she'd gone to stand next to a field and look at the grass. She'd gone to find the people who killed her family. She knew where they were.

Another one of those long breaths. And then a name.

"Derek Lyons."

I'd got as far as "Who's De—" when I heard more footsteps, a shout, and the unmistakeable sound of the phone being snatched away.

"Sam?"

Uh-oh.

"Hello, Serena," I said, trying to sound like I didn't know what was coming.

"What the almighty fuck are you playing at, Sam?" she said. Her voice was level and quiet and almost calm. I didn't believe that voice.

"I know what's going on, Serena. We were right – I was right. Carson *is* Grissom. The wife – Sally – she's gone after the people that did this."

"Enough," she said. The voice hadn't changed, but now I recognised it for what it was, a voice you didn't want to argue with, flat, restrained, just a hint of what it was restraining in the background. "It's enough. I'm here now, and the police are here. You can stand down and just go home or go back to your hotel or something. We've got a name. We'll find Sally Carson soon enough."

She was probably right, I thought. Malhotra was there, she'd be onto Gaddesdon and getting that name fed through every database in the country.

"OK," I said.

"Speak to you later," she replied, coolly, and ended the call.

I was done.

Derek Lyons.

I'd stopped the car and turned it around. I might be done, but that didn't mean I knew what to do next. I didn't want to go home, even if I could get myself there. I didn't want to go to Folgate, and I certainly didn't want to spend another night alone in the First Quality Inn. It suddenly occurred to me that if someone had suggested a night out in Manchester, I'd have taken it, a new city, a bit of life, a few drinks to dull the reawakened ache in my arm and wash the last few days out of my brain. But everyone I knew in Manchester was in Folgate police station or standing next to Carson's hospital bed waiting for him speak in some kind of tongue they understood. I thought for a moment and texted the name to Maloney, *Derek Lyons*, because Maloney had the kind of database Roarkes would kill for. It was a long shot, but it was better than nothing. And then, because I didn't know what else to do, I turned on the radio and drove north, into the darkness, out of Burnley.

The story had broken. The BBC had the CCTV stills and whatever else Roarkes had seen fit to give them, but even with all that there wasn't a great deal to say, not without throwing out more guesses than an idiot on a gameshow, and certainly not enough for an expert analyst to sink its teeth into. The BBC had expert analysts queueing up five hundred deep so they jammed one in anyway, a woman who'd clearly done this before, reeling off the complete range of motives from domestic to organised crime to terrorism, and seasoning all her suggestions with little pinches of caution like *ongoing investigation* and *must not prejudice* and *at this early stage*. It was a slow news day. Guesswork was better than dead air.

Hills rose ahead of me, fields either side. I hadn't even noticed the town disappearing. I folded myself into the darkness. Hill to wooded hill. Signs to villages with names like *Noggarth* and *Roughlee*, *Blacko* and *Barley*. Manchester might be rough, but at least it was twenty-first century rough. Burnley was staggering gamely out of the twentieth. These places still had some way to go.

My phone rang and I managed to find the answer button without looking. A familiar voice.

"Where the hell are you?"

"Roarkes," I said.

"You were supposed to be going back to your hotel and getting some sleep. But now I hear you've been in Burnley and you've been upsetting Carson and getting Serena all worked up, which doesn't take much, admittedly, and I don't know where you are now, but the one thing you're not doing is getting some sleep at your hotel."

He sounded calm enough. I felt calm myself, suddenly, the exhausted, done-in calm at the dead end of the dead-end road.

"Sorry," I said, and I was about to go on and explain where I was, and why I was there, because I was tired of hiding things and trying to second-guess everyone else. But then my phone gave a long solid beep and the call was dead. I glanced down and saw the signal had gone.

Too many of those wooded hills.

I drove on another half mile, looking for somewhere to turn around so I could follow Roarkes' advice and get myself a soft bed in a warm room, even the First Quality Inn would do, and then, to my surprise, my phone rang again. This time I looked down before answering.

Maloney. I toyed with the idea of ignoring it. I was tired and I wasn't involved any more. *Done.* I could ignore it if I wanted to.

I picked up the phone and hit "ANSWER".

"I've got it, Sam."

Maloney sounded uncharacteristically excited. Still like a fat, middle-aged man having a leisurely game of pool in the pub, but maybe a game with ten pounds riding on it. For Maloney, that was excited.

"Got what?"

"Got your address."

For a moment I didn't understand what he was talking about, and then it hit me.

"Derek Lyons?"

"The one and only. Didn't even have to call Crick. He showed up here himself a few minutes ago. Said he'd seen the guy on TV and there wasn't really anything to protect any more. Wanted a grand."

I whistled. The snitches were getting greedy.

"I gave him a hundred quid and said I'd tip him off if I heard anything about Lyons' people coming after him."

"So where is it?"

"So it's up in the arse-end of nowhere is where it is. Near Burnley."

"Oh," I said. Carson had been right about that, at least.

"I'll text it to you, OK?"

"Thanks, Maloney."

"You owe me one."

I'd given up trying to figure out who owed who what. If Maloney said I owed him, he was probably right.

"So do me a favour, right?" he went on.

Never say *yes* before you know what you're saying *yes* to. I waited.

"Hand this straight to Roarkes, will you? I don't like the sound of these people. You don't want to be going anywhere near them."

"OK," I said, and hung up. I'd seen what Derek Lyons and his friends could do to people. Maloney was right. I didn't want to be going anywhere near them.

A second later the phone beeped again, with Maloney's

text. The address.

Black Moss Farmhouse. Stang Bottom Lane.

Stang Bottom Lane. It was like someone had sat down with a toddler and asked them to come up with the street names.

Barley Road.

That sounded familiar.

Roughlee BB9 2RD.

I dropped the phone and turned to my left. There was a sign there, just behind me, wreathed in darkness. I backed up, turned a few degrees, shone the full beam on it.

Roughlee ¾m, it read.

I sat there for a moment, wondering what to do and who to tell, searching for a clarity that wouldn't come. The facts didn't help. It all comes down to instinct in the end.

I picked the phone back up and dialled Roarkes.

PART 3

BLACK MOSS

26: Chiara

THIRTY MINUTES, ROARKES had said. Thirty minutes and help would be on its way.

It was out of my hands now. I was done. That was what they'd said, all of them, Serena, Maloney, Roarkes. Sit tight. Hand it over. Piss off. You're not a cop. You're done.

Of course Roarkes had also told me to drive straight back to Manchester, and instead I'd driven down a narrow track in the dark with my lights off for the last quarter of a mile, and now I was standing next to my car looking up at a house where someone was probably going to die before those thirty minutes were up.

If they weren't dead already.

It was an old house, and an ugly one, a farmhouse with lean-to extensions jutting out on all sides, roofed in slate and plastic and aluminium and whatever else Derek Lyons might have found lying around. I didn't picture Derek Lyons as the sort of man who cared for the niceties of building regulations. There was one light on inside, upstairs, a bare bulb splashing stark white light onto a patch of exposed stone wall and a chunk of dark wooden beam. Shadows crossed the wall from time to time. There was someone up there.

There was also a familiar, cloying smell. It was something obvious, just a tiny mental hop away, but so much of my brain was caught up in the painful pulse in my arm, I couldn't think clearly enough make that hop.

I heard a ringing and reached instinctively for my

pocket, but it wasn't my phone. It came from the house. The ringing stopped and was replaced by a voice, and I pulled out my phone and switched it to silent, just in case.

The window was open. The window onto the room with the light in it. A man was speaking, and by some fortunate quirk of the wind and the channels cut through the air by all those slanting bits of roof, I could hear every word.

"Here?"

Silence.

"Well it's brave, at least. Stupid, but brave."

The accent was subtle, the kind of accent you wouldn't remember if someone asked you about it afterwards. The kind of voice that could dial 999 and talk shit about a man with a weapon and still, somehow, be as memorable as a blade of grass in a field.

"You screwed up. We'll talk about that later."

The person on the other end of the line clearly didn't agree, because there was a moment's pause, before the man cut in again.

"No. You listen to me. You take care of the loose ends where you are. We'll sort out the ones here."

A figure suddenly appeared between the light bulb and the window, and I saw him clearly. He was walking across the room, in sight for no more than a second, but it was enough: a man with a phone pressed to his ear, a well-built man, not short, not tall, not fat, just solid and well-built, a little grey, a lot bald.

Derek Lyons.

The call had ended, and now there was another voice.

"What is it?"

Another man, a thinner, frailer voice, a nervous voice. Or maybe that was just wishful thinking. I was terrified. Someone else being nervous would help.

"We're expecting a visitor. Get Mike, go outside and

see if she's here yet."

"What do you want done to her?"

"Just bring her inside. We'll figure it out then."

My body was frozen, and most of my brain, too, but part of it was jumping from question to conclusion before the rest of me had started processing what it had heard.

Lyons knew someone was coming.

Who?

She.

There was only one candidate, really, and now they knew she was on her way. She was, undoubtedly, a clever woman, and a determined one, but I doubted that would be enough with Derek Lyons and his friends all primed and ready.

And the police were still thirty minutes away. More like twenty-five, now. Nothing before that, because there were no helicopters available and there might be a single patrol car nearby, with an unarmed officer or two in it, but after what we'd seen on the CCTV footage no unarmed officer was going to be stupid enough to take on Derek Lyons.

That twenty-five minutes rested on one pretty large assumption, too, which was that Roarkes was on the level. That Roarkes hadn't been working all along with Tarney and Astra man and Derek Lyons and his friends. That Roarkes hadn't deliberately lured me out into this this cold, wet relic of the past, with its farmhouses and barns squatting on the earth like stone carcasses in primordial mud, to laugh at my stupidity and watch me die.

I stood there, in the stone and the mud, and I smiled to myself, because now I'd spelled it out, now I'd followed my thoughts to their logical conclusions, I could see how absurd those thoughts had been. Twenty-five minutes was a long time, and something still wasn't quite right, but whatever it was, I knew it wasn't Roarkes.

The voices upstairs had stopped, replaced by footsteps. I knew I had to move, but I also knew they'd be out in seconds and there weren't enough of those seconds to get back in the car, turn it around and drive away. I'd parked it in a patch of shadow by a corner of the house, but it wouldn't take much bad luck for them to walk out, turn, and shine a torch on it.

The footsteps faded into nothing, and then I heard something else, faintly, from the other side of the house. A splashing, the gentle tinkle of liquid on earth and stone. The hop was made. I knew that smell.

It was petrol.

Sally Carson was here, somewhere, outside the house, with a can of petrol and twenty years of revenge bubbling its way up. I wondered, briefly, whether she'd heard what I'd just heard, the phone call, the fact that Lyons knew she was there, and if she had, why I hadn't spotted her flying back past me to safety. Only briefly, though. Twenty years, and a can of petrol. Now she'd got here, Sally Carson wasn't about to leave before she was done.

I heard a door open round the far side of the house and took a few steps back, coming up against the reassuring cold metal and rust of the Fiat, and thanking a god I didn't believe in that whoever had come out had chosen the back instead of the front door a handful of yards from where I stood. There was just enough light for me to make out the contours of that door. It hadn't been painted in a while, and where it had, the paint had run into points and ridges of indeterminate colour. I looked at the door and it stared blankly back at me, a broken animal, a flightless bird, a dumb portent of death.

It was a front door. What the hell was I thinking?

I ducked down and watched it, not that ducking down would do much since the thing I was ducking down behind was a car that wasn't supposed to be there any more than I was. Just because the first bastard or two had chosen the back door didn't mean the next one would.

The front door didn't move. More noises round the back, footsteps, a shout.

"Can you smell that, Ray?"

Then a reply, the same voice I'd heard talking to Lyons.

"Oil. Line must be leaking."

No gas round here. Oil tanks in the fields and the gardens, and pipes through to the boilers inside. But I knew what oil smelled like, and it wasn't this.

I wasn't the only one.

"Use your nose, Ray. That's not oil. That's petrol."

"Are you – look, Mike. Over there."

More footsteps, faster now, and the sound of something metal dropping to the ground. Then another shout from Mike.

"Don't you fucking move, bitch."

I recognised that voice, now. I'd heard it only once, and briefly, but once had been enough. *Get your nose out of Thomas Carson's business*, it had said, and then the fist attached to the voice had come swinging back into my face. I remembered that fist. I remembered Roarkes telling me it wasn't much of a lead.

If I was lucky enough to get out of here alive, I'd be having a word with Roarkes about what *did* make a lead.

The footsteps had stopped, all silent and still. All except me. I hadn't realised I was doing it but now I was halfway between the car and the house, crouching low, rubbing absently at my arm.

"Turn around. What's that in your hand?"

"It's a cigarette lighter, boys."

It was Sally Carson, but it wasn't the Sally Carson I'd heard before, the one with the little eyes and the little nose

263

who didn't know what was going on or how it would all end. There was no emotion at all, not in the first four words, at least, just a clear, bland statement of fact. But that last word, *boys* – I turned the corner of the house as she said it and suddenly I could see her, squinting at the torchlight shining in her face.

Boys – if it hadn't been for the half-smile it would have been a hiss – and that was it, of course. The control, the hiss. A cat, toying with its prey. On the surface, it looked like they had her. One gun, maybe two, pointed right at her – and suddenly I realised where I was, that I was actually here, right in the middle of it, or closer to the middle than I wanted to be, and I inched back to the hard cold stone. But she had them, too. Petrol everywhere, from the smell of it, and a flame in her hand in the moment it took either of them to squeeze a trigger.

So this was what balance looked like. The moment of choice. The coin up and spinning, the instant between ascent and swift and brutal fall. But death on heads and death on tails, inevitable, inescapable, unless something new appeared, some hand to reach out and grasp it from the air. There was something new on its way right now, the police were coming, but not for as many as fifteen minutes, maybe twenty, so Sally couldn't count on them. There was nothing new for her.

I heard a noise above me, a window opening, and shrank back further into the stone.

"Have you got her?"

Derek Lyons. I'd heard that voice once on a recording, and a second time, just minutes ago, and there was still nothing memorable about it, but knowing who he was and what he'd done made the difference. I didn't think I'd be forgetting Derek Lyons' voice in a hurry.

"Erm, sort of," came the reply.

"What? Bring her up here, will you. I've got some

questions."

I stared at Sally Carson and tried to look through her, into her mind, tried to work out what she was doing and how much she really meant it, whether she knew her choice was no choice at all. She could drop the lighter and let them take her inside, and I didn't think it would be tea and biscuits waiting for her there. Or she could snap her fingers, burn to death, take one or two of them with her. I found myself sniffing the air, feeling something wet against the stone, bringing my fingers to my nose, moving an inch or two forward again. Realising that fifteen or twenty minutes might be too many, but there was something new here already, something that might tip the balance ever so slightly Sally Carson's way.

Me.

I stood there and tried to remember what ridiculous steps had brought me here, between the flames on the one side and the bullets on the other, and each step taken with a blind and wilful stupidity that could only ever have led me here. I remembered what Claire had said, *This is what Sam Williams does, and you're Sam Williams, so off you trot.* I remembered she'd told me I was wrong, I did have a say, there were still decisions to be made. I remembered I'd laughed, inside, at how wide of the mark she was. And then I remembered Sally Carson talking about her son, talking about her wedding, tricked into moments of forgetfulness and simple happiness, and I stopped thinking and decided.

I crouched down lower, felt around and picked up a handful of gravel. I hadn't thought it through, but some form of distraction seemed right. I drew back my left hand to throw it, upwards, towards the window on the first floor.

"Got you," said a voice, and I froze, but the voice wasn't talking to me. The voice was Lyons', he'd come outside without anyone noticing, which meant he'd come round the front door and I was lucky as all hell he'd decided to walk round the other side of the house. If he had done, if he'd chosen the shorter route, he'd probably have spotted the car, and even if he hadn't spotted the car he'd have fallen over me on his way past.

He'd come up behind Sally Carson and picked the cigarette lighter deftly out of her fingers before she'd even known he was there, and suddenly the balance was broken and even a tired, aching, terrified lawyer skulking in the shadows wasn't going to be enough to bring it back. I watched her swing round to face him, watched him grab her wrists and laugh, watched her spit in his face, saw the smile slide right off it.

"You have been a busy girl, Mrs Carson," he said, and sniffed. "We're going to have to torch this place anyway. Looks like you've done me a favour."

She was facing away from me, so I couldn't see her expression. I didn't want to, either. There's nothing pretty about defeat. She didn't speak. I couldn't blame her.

"Take her inside and tie her up," he said, and released her wrists, and the others stepped forward. The torchlight wavered and then went out entirely, and even though the darkness I was hiding in was no less dark, the sudden absence of brightness elsewhere left me feeling uncomfortably exposed.

Sally turned around to face them and held out her hands. She was standing in a patch of faint light cast from the upstairs room, still smiling, which was brave, but that was all it was. There was nothing behind that smile except the act of forcing it onto her face.

One of the men grabbed her hands. The other moved to stand behind her, a gun pressed to her cheek, and when they started moving I realised they weren't going for the back door. They were coming round the house, to the front, and unlike Lyons they were coming my way. They were going to walk right into me, or past me if I was lucky, and it was too late to do anything about it without making the kind of noise that would give me away as surely as standing up and introducing myself.

I crouched lower and tried to make myself as small as possible. Lyons had re-entered the house through the back door – and now I saw why the others hadn't, because it was narrow, two steep steps up to it and an awkward lip to get over, and then the body of the internal staircase in your way the moment you put your foot inside. They didn't want to take any chances with their prisoner.

They'd been walking towards me now for three, maybe four seconds, each of those seconds a million instants, each instant the possibility that one of them would glance in my direction. Then they were next to me, no more than two yards away, and I realised I was probably going to be OK, they weren't going to see me, and they weren't going to see the car either, because the one in front had to look where he was going and the one behind had to keep his eyes firmly on Sally Carson. The crouching position I'd been holding for what felt like an eternity was starting to give me cramp. The cramp wasn't a normal cramp, though, it was something sentient, a bastard of a cramp that had made its home in my right calf and combined in some kind of pincer movement with the bastard of an ache in my right arm so it took everything I had not to cry out in pain.

Instead I stretched out a leg against the gravel, which must have made just the faintest of sounds, because at that exact moment Sally Carson turned her head and saw me. She didn't turn her head far, she couldn't, what with the gun pressed into her cheek, and for much the same reason she couldn't do much with her facial expression, but it was the eyes I was watching, and the instant I saw it I knew it

267

was deliberate. Her eyes flicked up, and then to the right, for the briefest of moments.

Behind me. Back where she'd been dragged from. Where the cigarette lighter lay. Where Derek Lyons had let it drop, beside a shallow pool of petrol. Sally Carson was beckoning back to what she'd started, and her message couldn't have been clearer if she'd etched it on her forehead in blood.

Finish it.

27: Good Vibrations

THE IMPLICATIONS FLASHED through my mind one after another, fast, solid, like carriages on a freight train. A moment. That's all it would take. A moment, and they'd be dead, with luck, all three of the bastards, and Sally Carson along with them.

I could do it, too. Probably. A click of a cigarette lighter. A snap of my fingers. Even I could manage that.

There were shouts and grunts from the house, Sally fighting as she was dragged up the stairs, the light coming and going as Lyons and his friends passed in front of the window, tying her up, gagging her, no doubt, although what would be the point of that when as far as they were concerned no one knew where they were?

The police would be here in, what, fifteen minutes? Sally Carson didn't have fifteen minutes. If I did what she wanted me to, she didn't have five.

The window was still open. Lyons was talking.

"Mike. Get out there and see what the bitch has done."

A grunt of acknowledgement.

"Then get the gate open and get the car ready. If she found us the police won't be far behind. I want to be out by morning."

Footsteps outside. *Open the gate.* I wondered, foolishly, whether I'd shut the gate when I'd come through, whether it had been open already, and realised I didn't remember a gate at all. A moment later it hit me that it didn't matter, anyway, because Sally Carson had been through before me, and if I had left it open they'd assume it was her, and I was standing there wasting seconds while a man with a gun was heading my way.

And if, by some miracle, he didn't see me, he could hardly miss the Fiat. He'd have to walk right past it to get to the track.

I was back at the car ten seconds later, door open and in, thanking all the gods I could remember that I'd bought myself an old-fashioned manual so all I had to do was slip off the handbrake and roll back the way I'd come. If I managed not to roll into the stone walls six inches either side of the car, sliding backwards in the dark, and if Mike started off round the back dealing with Sally Carson's mess before he came round to sort out the gate, then with luck he wouldn't hear me.

I was due a little luck, I thought.

I'd managed all of four or five yards – there were probably two hundred to the gate, I reckoned, because now I did remember it, glimpsed in the dark, wide open and about halfway down the track – when a there was a burst of noise from outside the car. I hit the brake. *The police,* I thought, for a moment, relief coursing through me like a well-earned whisky. And then I realised the sound was coming from the house so it couldn't be the police, and it wasn't an engine or a siren or a loud-hailer or anything the police would use anyway.

It was the Beach Boys singing "Good Vibrations".

There was my luck. I didn't know where Mike was, he could be standing right in front of me, but I had to take a chance and hope he wasn't, and if that chance paid off then the music would mask the sound of me starting the engine.

I started the engine.

Thirty seconds later I felt rather than saw the track begin to open out to the right, and realised there was another track joining the main one. Before I knew what I was doing I was twisting the wheel, hitting the brake, killing the engine and waiting in what would have been silence if it weren't for the distant sound of the Beach Boys.

I sat and waited and wondered whether Mike had already been down, seen the open gate, come back up and spotted me. It was dark enough that I might not have noticed. He could be standing next to the window pointing a gun at my head.

Except he wasn't, because now I could hear the crunch and slide of his footsteps on gravel and mud. A beam of light shone against the wall right in front of me, and then down onto the ground. Mike had a torch.

The ground was uneven. There were rocks and puddles, you could twist an ankle if you weren't watching your step. If Mike kept that torch down and concentrated on his feet, I might be OK. If he happened to swing it round to his left, I was a dead man.

The footsteps drew closer and suddenly I could see his outline moving past, treading slowly and carefully, a splash of light on the ground and a shadow behind it.

The light stayed on the ground.

Then he was gone, and the footsteps were fading to nothing. He hadn't seen me. Yet.

Because he'd be coming back up, of course.

So I sat there a little longer and waited for Mike's return and the path the torchlight took, the next toss of the coin that would decide whether I lived or died. The gate wasn't as far off as I'd thought, either that or Mike was quick on his feet, because it didn't seem more than a minute before I heard those footsteps returning and saw the torchlight tracing drunken arcs in the darkness.

I didn't like the way that torch was swinging. Mike was obviously feeling a little more sure of himself, and there was less light on the ground than there was above it and on either side. The footsteps were closing in. The coin was back in the air, and once again I was waiting for it to fall. Waiting for someone else. Waiting to get shot or hit or told something that probably wasn't true anyway.

I could see the source of the light now, the torch itself, a moment of infinite black against the beam in front, and the outline of the man behind it. The torch was moving up, then down, then up again, then to the left.

One swing. That was all it would take. An idle flick of the hand to the right, and suddenly there would be a car where there wasn't supposed to be a car.

I'd had enough of the coin. I'd have enough of chance and inevitability and steps I'd taken without even knowing they were there. I closed my eyes and saw Fiona Milton and Naz Ahmet gunned down on a cold dead street in a cold dead November. I opened them again and waited until the outline was right in front of me and clear enough to be a human figure, and then I started the engine and brought the full beam right up on the bastard. He was still raising his hand to shield his eyes by the time I'd started moving, and when I hit him maybe two seconds later he hadn't taken more than a step.

I reversed a couple of feet and watched the heap on the ground in front of me.

It moved.

I couldn't tell which bits were limbs and which were just flaps of coat or trouser, but it was moving, and I thought maybe the part of it that was moving was a hand.

I released the brake and drove forward again until I hit the wall. I jerked up and then down into the seat, and let the car roll its way back.

Mike wouldn't be moving now.

I killed the engine and found myself considering how much damage I'd done to the car. "Good Vibrations" floated through the air. The headlights were still on, the heap on the ground motionless. I wondered what Mike had been thinking before he heard the engine, and after, whether he'd figured out what was about to happen, whether he'd been calculating his chances as he raised his hand to his face, whether he'd imagined a coin spinning down through the darkness, dead, alive, dead, alive, dead, alive.

Dead.

"Good Vibrations" came to an end and started up again. Derek Lyons was either a big fan or a man with a limited music collection. I turned off the lights and looked back up at the house.

Fifteen minutes. Probably closer to ten, now. I sat in my car, a dead bundle of flesh and clothes in front of me, and went through all the options, all the different things that the different people I was might do, burn, run, stay, come up with something clever, and ten minutes was nine and if Sally Carson wasn't already dead then surely she'd last the next nine minutes, wouldn't she?

Sally Carson screamed.

I was at the front door a minute later with Mike's torch in my left hand and his gun in a right that could barely handle the weight of it, and each individual Sam Williams shouting in my ear that what I was doing was stupid and unnecessary and was probably going to get me killed.

The door was open.

As I stepped inside a voice called out, "Took your time, Mike." The staircase was right in front of me, with a corner at the top, and there he was, turning the corner, the other one, the one with the nervous voice, the one who hadn't punched me in the head.

The one who wasn't lying dead in the track outside the house.

He saw me and started to back away, and entirely

without thinking I raised the gun and pointed it at him and squeezed the trigger.

There was a vicious crack, and then, for maybe half a second, an even nastier silence, broken by my own howl of pain as the recoil sent another burst of agony up my arm. Ray, who had, I hoped, actually been shot, made a gentle, questioning noise that sounded a little like, "What?" and fell down the stairs, tumbling shoulder to shoulder all the way until he landed at my feet. A moment later he started to get up, so unless there was more going on here than I'd imagined I hadn't shot him in the head or the heart. The pain in my arm wasn't easing off at all, which would have worried me if I didn't have more immediate things to worry about. I looked around frantically for something to hit him with. I couldn't see anything obvious, and Ray was on his feet now with what looked like a nasty cut on his hand. A nasty cut from a bullet, so I'd as good as missed him entirely. I was holding a gun. Ray had no gun, I could see it lying there all alone halfway up the stairs. There was blood on his forehead too, from the fall, no doubt, underneath a mop of bushy blond hair I'd seen before. I saw him look at me and take in the torch and the gun, and he opened his mouth and said "What?" again, but by that time I'd realised what it meant that I had a gun and he didn't, and I took it into my left hand, pointed it at his chest, no more than two feet away, and squeezed. There was the crack, again, which meant that this was a semi-automatic and I wasn't necessarily about to die. I opened my eyes, which I didn't remember closing, and Ray was back on the ground. I didn't think he'd be getting up this time.

The final "Good Vibrations" chorus started up, the one that builds and builds, layer on layer of voice and instrument, but even with the Beach Boys at full blast there was no way Lyons hadn't heard those two shots. I stepped over Ray's body – *body*, I thought, and marvelled briefly at what I'd done and that I was still functioning, still thinking and moving much as I had done a few minutes earlier – and sprinted up the stairs, trying not to think about the pain. There was a landing with four doors, and all of them were closed, but only one of them was on the same side of the house as the open window I'd seen from outside, the same direction the music was coming from, so I was counting on that being where Lyons was.

I waited and listened for a moment outside the door, and that moment was my mistake, because it gave me time to think, again. I found myself backing slowly away. I could turn and run, I realised. Lyons might come after me, but he probably wouldn't. The police would be here in six or seven minutes, and with his friends out of action, Lyons would want his hostage alive. I'd done my bit, I thought. The police could take it from here.

I started to turn, and then I remembered that Lyons didn't even know the police were coming, so as far as he was concerned he could kill Sally Carson and take out the intruder at his leisure. I stood there, frozen between two choices, and of all the things running through it, my brain chose to stop on the image of a child weeping at a funeral. Then Sally Carson screamed again, and I threw myself at the door, tucked into the shoulder roll I'd practiced with mixed results at the martial arts class, and prayed there weren't any sharp objects or large items of furniture in the way.

There weren't. The floor was just rows of unvarnished wooden boards, so now my left arm was aching too, but some way to go before it could match the right. The roll had worked, though, and I hadn't dropped the gun or accidentally shot myself in the head while I was doing it. I was up on one knee beside the open window, and I was looking into the face of Derek Lyons.

Derek Lyons was in the far corner of the room. He was standing behind a wooden chair – apart from the wooden chair and a stool on which stood a small, now silent stereo, there was no furniture in the room at all. Sitting on the chair with an expression of pure terror on her face was Sally Carson. Derek Lyons held a knife to her cheek. He looked older than I'd expected, older than he'd seemed on the CCTV, but then I remembered he'd been running the show round here for decades. That much crime can put the years on a man.

He was smiling at me.

"Sam Williams," he said, for all the world like an old friend he'd just run into in the pub. "This is most unexpected."

I kept the gun pointed at him, in a left hand that had never been my strong point, and tried not to shake or feel flattered that he knew who I was. I was James Bond, that was who I was, and he was Blofeld, only instead of a cat he had a woman with a knife jammed in her face and an expression of –

I'd been wrong. It wasn't pure terror. It wasn't terror at all.

It was fury.

"You don't scare easy, Mr Williams. We've been kind to you, as a favour, but I think the time for favours has gone."

I guess when you're used to shooting people for no reason at all, a punch in the face and a near miss with a car probably do constitute a favour. I couldn't imagine why I'd been lucky enough to receive it, but I wasn't complaining.

"Put the knife down," I said, and Lyons laughed. He didn't say anything, just laughed, and I saw the knife flick out a fraction of a millimetre, and then settle back, and now there was a thin line of red on Sally Carson's cheek, thickening as I watched.

She didn't so much as wince.

I realised suddenly why she was angry and who she was angry with. It wasn't Lyons, the man who'd killed her family, framed her husband and was currently digging a knife into her cheek.

It was me.

Sally Carson was furious with me because I hadn't finished off her work for her and set fire to the building. All she'd wanted was Lyons dead, and if I'd done what she'd wanted me to do, that was precisely what he would have been. As things were, he might yet live.

Sally Carson was furious with me and Derek Lyons was laughing at me, except now he'd stopped laughing and was shaking his head slowly with his mouth shut and curled into the smirk of a man who was about to show an amateur how things were really done, and suddenly I was furious myself. I noticed he'd stepped a few inches away from Sally, confident he had nothing to fear from an injured lawyer with a gun. I remembered what I'd been told years back, by one of my less savoury clients, about the stomach being the best bit to aim for, because of its size, and I remembered how badly my first shot at Ray had gone. The bigger the target, the better. And he'd just moved another inch away from Sally.

I squeezed the trigger.

The knife fell to the floor and landed next to the power cable for the silent stereo. I'd knocked out the plug when I'd come rolling into the room.

Lyons fell more slowly. The smirk was gone, in its place a wide-eyed astonishment. I looked for the wound in his stomach, but there wasn't one. His leg was bleeding instead. His right leg. I'd aimed for a stomach and hit a leg, and that was probably fine, because the important thing was that Derek Lyons was no longer holding a weapon, and I was, and Sally Carson was already up from the chair and walking towards me, no longer furious, just determined.

I tried to reach out my near-useless right arm to grab her and run, but she moved quickly down and inside and took the gun from my left. I knew what was about to happen, and I tried to say something, but I didn't know what that something should be.

She turned, and I followed her with my eyes, and I saw Lyons knew what was coming, too, and the wide-eyed astonishment was a desperate pleading fear. In the moment before the gun fired he shook like a child that had fallen from his bicycle. Then there was another deafening crack, and a large and bloody hole appeared in his head.

The police are on their way, that was it, that was what I should have said, I realised, as his body jerked and settled onto the floor. It was too late for that now. The room shifted, and I looked up, and Sally Carson was there looking down at me, which didn't make sense at all until I realised I'd fallen, too. My arm was no longer hurting, but it was pulling at me, dragging me down and keeping me pinned to the floor. I watched as Sally Carson bent down, put her arms underneath mine, and levered me up. She must have been stronger than she looked, because she got me on my feet without a hint of help from me.

"Come on," she said, and dropped the gun. I nodded, dumbly, and found my legs were now willing to follow instruction, suddenly vigorous, shot through with adrenaline. We took the stairs two at a time, Sally in front and disappearing through the back door even as I took the final step and vaulted the body lying beside it.

I was outside half a second later and round the side of the house before I realised I was alone. I turned to make my way back, and the rush that had brought me that far fell away. It was as much as I could do to stagger round the corner, my whole body telling me to stop where I was and drop to the ground. If I survived, so much the better. If I didn't, I'd beaten the odds so long it was only fair I lost this time. The number of things that should have killed me, or at least could have killed me – well, really, I should be grateful I wasn't dead already.

I tried not to worry about what was behind the silent surrender of my limbs and forced myself back round the corner.

Sally Carson was standing in the shadows, barely visible. She held something in her right hand, and I couldn't see it clearly but I knew what it was. There was a sudden brief flare of light, a tiny oval of flame in the darkness, and then a great rushing sound, and the tiny oval had grown vast. It was everywhere. It was all around me.

I was on my knees, my head in a dozen places at once, upstairs with Derek Lyons and his leaking head, downstairs with dead Ray and down the track with poor flattened Mike, in the hospital with Thomas Carson, in the police station with Gaddesdon, grinning from ear to ear as someone told him again what an idiot he was, in Malhotra's car as we bumped down another useless dead end, in my own flat, drinking coffee and watching Claire emerge from the shower, in court watching David Brooks-Powell dissolve from tyrant to nervous wreck, in the pub with Maloney and the cell with Tarney, and back further, in a bus, in a tiny office that stank of cigarettes, in another pub where faces loomed red and pregnant with laughter.

The scenes turned. My life unravelling before me, except I wasn't dying. I was all of these people and none of them, I was Sam Williams on his knees outside a blazing farmhouse and the brightness was unbearable. I couldn't be dying.

Everywhere was burning. Nowhere was dark.

Sally Carson appeared above me, again, and I felt myself being lifted onto my feet. My legs jerked back into life. My right arm, which had gone numb, now felt like someone had cut it open, inserted a lump of smouldering coal, and sewn it back up again.

I was definitely alive.

28: Falling Into Place

THE LIGHT FRACTURED into individual beams, cones of brightness, white, blue, the sound suddenly distilled from a solid roar into single, comprehensible noises. Shouts. Sirens. I opened my mouth to shout, stopped, collapsed to the ground. This time Sally didn't pick me back up. She didn't need to.

There were two of them, a police officer in uniform and a paramedic. Figures in brown and yellow rushed by. I looked up, my eyes following them towards Black Moss Farm, or what was left of it.

The paramedic was talking to me. I concentrated on his face, round, wide, lightly-bearded, red-cheeked, and topped with a little crown of brown hair. I looked at his lips and tried to work out what he was saying, and then I realised I could hear him, I could pick out the words even in all the noise.

"Can you hear me, Mr Williams?"

I nodded.

"Can you speak?"

"Yes," I said. It came out deeper and hoarser than I'd expected, but it came out.

"We need to get you to a hospital. I think there's something wrong with your arm."

Maybe there was something wrong with my arm. Maybe there had been something wrong with my arm ever since Russell Tarney had stamped on it.

"Wait a moment," said the police officer. "Is there anyone left inside?"

I nodded.

"Yes. Two of them. I think they're dead."

She looked up at the building, and then back down at me, and returned the nod. I didn't say anything about Mike. The police had made it this far, so if they hadn't driven past Mike on the way up then they'd driven over him. They knew about Mike.

"Come on, then."

The paramedic was smiling at me, eyebrows raised in invitation, and I luxuriated, briefly, in the prospect of an ambulance, with a bed, and drugs I could sink into until nothing mattered. I shook my head and looked around. Sally Carson was sat on the bumper of another ambulance nodding at another paramedic and another police officer. I tried to walk towards her and remembered I was sitting on the ground. The paramedic – my paramedic – shook his head.

"I need to speak to her," I said. He shrugged and helped me to my feet and even though there were a hundred thoughts buzzing around inside, I managed to keep that one thought, the thing I had to say to Sally Carson, front and centre until I was standing there murmuring to her and praying she could hear me.

She nodded. I wasn't sure she understood and I wasn't sure it was me she was nodding at, but it would have to do. I'd see her soon enough, anyway.

"Come on, Mr Williams. Let's get you checked out."

I nodded, dumbly, and then stopped.

I couldn't go to the hospital. I needed to see Roarkes or Malhotra first. I couldn't remember why, but I had to speak to them. There was something.

There was something wrong. There was *still* something wrong.

I looked over to the farmhouse and then across to Sally, who was being helped into the ambulance with a dressing pressed against her bleeding face, and I tried to figure out what was wrong.

I'd remember it when I saw Roarkes and Malhotra.

"No," I said, and tried to explain. The paramedic listened to me, still smiling, and told me I was suffering from shock and the police would be able to take care of everything. I shook my head.

"Malhotra," I shouted, and the police officer, who had started to walk back towards the phalanx of patrol cars and vans that had suddenly appeared, turned and stared at me.

"Can you get me to Folgate?" I asked. "I needed to speak to DI Roarkes. It's urgent."

She was still staring at me, tall and blonde and serious-looking with a frown on her like the hood on a cobra.

"What is it?"

I shook my head.

"I need Roarkes and Malhotra."

She held out her phone, and I shook my head again.

"I need to see them."

She sighed, and walked over to speak to the paramedic. I could see him argue, but he wasn't putting his heart into it. I blinked, and a moment went by, and he was in front of me, no longer smiling.

"You'll need to admit yourself as soon as you're done with the police," he said.

I nodded.

"Do you want anything for that?"

I nodded again. The arm was hardly bearable, a bastard bully of an arm, dominating every other thought I had. With something to push it back down, maybe I'd be able to remember why the hell I was so desperate to see Roarkes and Malhotra.

The journey was short and violent, the lights flashing and the sirens wailing and the pain still there, just a little further below the surface than it had been. I stepped out of the patrol car and found I could walk, one foot in front of the other all the way to the main entrance, where I was nearly sent flying by Serena Hawkes rushing the other way.

"Have you heard?" I asked, and she shook her head.

"Come with me," I said. She needed to know what had happened. I put my left arm across her back – as if I had the strength to move a box of tissues let alone another human being – and a moment later we were inside.

Roarkes had been told I was coming. He ushered us straight up to his office, where Malhotra was already waiting.

Roarkes began.

"Sally's in the hospital. She's going to be OK. Apparently she won't talk to anyone except her husband and we're still trying to figure out if we should let her."

"Let her," I interrupted. "It's over, Roarkes. Lyons is dead. They're all dead. No way anyone walked out of that house."

"Are you going to tell us what happened?"

"Sure," I said. "Just not right now."

"Want to get your stories straight, Sam?"

I forced myself to concentrate on his face, which was swimming in and out of focus like the memory of Saturday night on Sunday morning. He was frowning, and if he decided to take a serious interest in what had happened at Black Moss Farm then Sally Carson was screwed, and me with her. I'd have to cross that bridge before it burnt down.

"So they're really dead?" asked Serena. She was leaning against the wall of the office, pale, drained but relieved, like I'd just told her she wasn't getting hanged in the morning. She hadn't enjoyed the case, but it was over. Even after everything I'd been through, I found a moment to feel pleased for her.

"No one could have walked out of that fire, Serena. They're dead."

"All three?"

I nodded. No need to mention how Mike had met his end.

"So why did you want to come here?" asked Roarkes. "They said you weren't in great shape, and from the look of you they weren't exaggerating."

I paused. I knew there was something I needed to tell him, something we still had to think about, and I'd hoped it would come pouring out at the right moment, but it hadn't. I shook my head, at myself as much as Roarkes. Here I was in a police station with a bunch of clever people (I noticed Gaddesdon wasn't in the room), people who could crack anything if they put their minds to it, and I had nothing for them.

There was a muted buzzing and Serena fished her phone out of her bag, stared at it, and shook her head.

"Sorry. Got to take this," she said, and slipped out of the room. It didn't matter. If I couldn't figure out what had been bothering me, I might as well check myself into the nearest hospital and get some sleep.

It was probably nothing, I realised. It was probably just my brain playing tricks on me, a hangover from one of those other versions of Sam Williams I thought I was but wasn't after all, an idea some previous incarnation of me hadn't quite brought to fruition. I sighed and slumped down in the chair Roarkes had pushed me into, and sipped at the glass of water Malhotra had placed in my hand.

"I don't know," I said, eventually. "I had an idea something wasn't quite right, something didn't add up. But I can't figure out what."

Roarkes nodded. "Shock," he said, and even though it was dumb and patronising, and the one thing this wasn't was shock, I didn't argue.

We sat there, me, and Roarkes behind his desk, and Malhotra standing beside me like a portrait of a Victorian nurse. We sat, and stood, in silence, for all of thirty seconds, and then the silence was broken.

Gaddesdon didn't so much enter the room as bring it whirling into orbit around him, and where there had been peace and empty space, now there was Gaddesdon, panting noisily, and outside the room shouts and a loud, steady wailing that sounded like a very serious alarm.

"What is it, Gaddesdon?" asked Roarkes, clearly annoyed. Two more breaths, and he was able to answer.

"It's Tarney, sir. He's dead."

Tarney being dead wasn't the *something wrong* I'd anticipated, and part of me wondered whether it really counted as something wrong at all, but I pushed that part away and tried to see if this fitted into anything I knew.

Roarkes was shouting, and Gaddesdon was trying to answer, but every time he opened his mouth to say something Roarkes shouted another question at him. It took Malhotra bellowing "Stop!" at the top of her voice to bring the other two to a halt, and then she smiled, apologised, and quietly asked what had happened.

"Knife wound, says the doc. Knife in the neck."

Roarkes took one of those long, slow breaths through his teeth that sounded like gas escaping. Dangerous, explosive gas. When he spoke again, he was quiet, each word picked carefully out and released into the room.

"You were supposed to be watching him."

Gaddesdon nodded. "I know. I don't understand. I was outside the room the whole time. It doesn't make sense."

"When did this happen?" asked Malhotra. Gaddesdon shrugged.

"Doc thinks some time in the last hour."

Malhotra was still probing, the calm, quiet voice of sanity. "In his cell?"

Gaddesdon nodded. "Yup. Same one we had Carson in."

Roarkes was thinking aloud. "So Tarney knew something else."

There was a short silence. Three frowning faces, I saw, my own no doubt the same.

"What else was there to know?" asked Roarkes, to the room in general. I could see he was trying to stay calm. He wasn't doing a great job of it.

Something occurred to me.

"He was involved from the beginning, right?" I asked.

Malhotra nodded. "That's right. He was on custody. Shift records showed he signed in early, and now we know why."

"And nothing else unusual? Back then? At the start?"

She shrugged.

"I don't know. You could try asking Serena."

"Right," I said, and then, "so she was there at the start too?"

"I think so," she replied. "None of us got to speak to him that first day except Tarney and the arresting officer, and by the time I showed up Serena was already there warning us off."

"How long after he was brought in was that?"

She shrugged again. "Dunno. Half an hour, hour maybe?"

An hour. It was feasible, but it seemed fast. Unusually fast. And there was something else. Serena hadn't been appointed. Not by Carson, not by his family. You could imagine some chequebook lawyer rolling in like a greasy lead bullet when the local millionaire's son earned himself his first drunk in charge – I'd been that chequebook lawyer myself. But Serena wasn't.

"So who brought her in?" I asked, and Malhotra looked at Gaddesdon and Gaddesdon looked at Roarkes and Roarkes looked at all three of us, and even though none of us knew, we all knew.

"Tarney," I said, answering my own question.

"Oh," sighed Gaddesdon. It was a quiet "oh", but now the shouting had drifted away, and the closed door had turned the alarm into a faint background whine, it was a breath of revelation into a still and silent room.

"Oh what?" asked Roarkes.

"With Tarney. Just now. I was outside the room. I mean, yeah, I know you said no one could see him except the three of us, but she was his brief, so I thought—"

I finished the sentence for him.

"So you thought there wouldn't be any harm in Serena having a bit of one-to-one with her client."

Gaddesdon nodded, disconsolate. I'd spoken calmly enough, but now I was starting to see what the words really meant.

Serena had killed Tarney.

Serena had stabbed Tarney in the neck, in a police station, and walked out like she'd just been in for coffee and a chat.

I shook my head, hoping something else would come, some other interpretation, some other answer, but there wasn't one.

Roarkes was already on his phone and shaking his head.

"She's gone. We can see what the traffic cams have got, but she's been gone a few minutes. Priya, circulate a description."

Malhotra got up and left the room. Roarkes was back on the phone shouting at people. Gaddesdon was running around trying to find some footage of what had happened in Tarney's cell. I sat there in my chair, with the pain just out of range, thanks to the drugs, and my brain turning circles half a mile above my head, and I waited for everything to fall into place.

"All three?" she'd asked, and sure, she might have picked up the number somewhere else, but I was pretty sure I hadn't said it. No wonder she'd been pleased. Bar one man, everyone who knew what she'd done had died at Black Moss Farm, and that man wasn't going to be talking to anyone now.

I thought about Gaddesdon running around for the CCTV footage and remembered something similar happening after Carson's suicide attempt. Carson had been in the same cell. There wasn't going to be any CCTV footage. Whatever we thought we knew, there wasn't going to be anything solid linking Serena Hawkes to Tarney's death.

Someone, I realised, had known about my trip down to London, someone had set me up with a fist in the face in my own flat. Someone had told Derek Lyons he might find me outside the hospital, if he wanted to send me a little green car and a message no one except me would take seriously. And even I, it turned out, hadn't taken it seriously enough.

And someone had made another call.

That was it, that was the thing that had nagged at me and brought me here to the police station instead of staring at the ceiling of the Manchester Royal Infirmary, eyes-deep in morphine. That was the piece in the wrong place that I hadn't quite grasped, until everything shifted and I saw half the other pieces were in the wrong place, too. Someone had called Lyons and told him Sally Carson was on her way, and he'd sent Ray and Mike out to pick her up. "*You take care of the loose ends where you are,*" he'd said, and an hour or so later one of those loose ends had been knifed to death.

For most of the last twenty-four hours it had been Malhotra I'd thought of, rather than Roarkes, whenever I had something to tell or something to ask. Gaddesdon didn't count: he was just the messenger. Get Malhotra down there. Let Malhotra know. Ask Malhotra if. Roarkes had been on the edge, neither friend nor enemy. Serena had planted that seed cleverly, had watered it and watched it grow.

And it had been Serena all along.

They'd catch up with her, eventually, no doubt. They might even find enough evidence to put her away, although Serena Hawkes was a clever woman and she'd have covered her tracks well. But I didn't think they'd find her any time soon. I shook my head to clear it, and glanced at Roarkes staring silently at his phone. I couldn't afford to think about Serena Hawkes. I had some talking to do. Some stories to get straight.

I stood and waved to Roarkes, who gave me a nod in return and went back to his silent stare. I felt a buzz in my pocket, lifted out the phone, which had somehow survived everything, checked the display.

I recognised the number. I couldn't think what Mia Arazzi would want after everything I'd already given her. Maybe she'd have something for me.

"Hello Mia," I said.

"Sam," she replied. "I owe you one. Looks like there's at least one lawyer who can give a journalist an honest tip."

I laughed. And then paused.

"What do you mean, at least one?"

"That's why I'm calling. She's been feeding me crap all week, hasn't she?"

I stopped dead, halfway out of the room, suddenly

cold and alert.

"What do you mean?"

"All that bullshit about planning, all that crap about Argentina, she was taking the piss, wasn't she? Stringing me along while she had a good old laugh at the dumb journalist, right? So I thought I'd tell her to take a fucking hike. I tried to call her first but she's not answering her phone. Not to worry. I can wait."

Serena. Not Folgate. It had been Serena all along.

One thing. I needed to know just one thing.

"Where are you, Mia?"

"Well I'm at her place, aren't I? I'm standing outside her door freezing my tits off waiting for her to turn up."

"Get the hell out of there," I started to shout, but I'd only got as far as "Get—" when I heard another voice, clear and close, and even though I was hearing that voice down a phone line on the other side of Manchester I could tell the difference, the beleaguered provincial solicitor gone and in her place the woman who'd been playing me, playing us all, picking us up and moving us around her board like little black-and-white chessmen, twisting us to and fro like Roarkes' dead Lego police.

"Hello Mia," she said. "What the hell are you doing here?"

The line went dead.

29: Blue Sky, White Sky

THERE ARE PROCEDURES you're supposed to follow in a hostage situation, there are rules for approach, cordons, communication channels, media blackouts. We broke every one of those rules without a second's thought.

We went in one car, Malhotra driving, without her beats but still like the devil was behind her, and we'd been going five minutes with the sirens on and the lights flashing before anyone thought it might be a good idea to let someone back at Folgate know what was going on. There was a hostage, there was probably a weapon, there might even be a gun. Armed police would probably be needed. We almost certainly wouldn't.

By the time Roarkes got off the phone we were just three minutes from Serena's house in Marston and there was no way anyone was going to beat us there. I put down my own phone – Mia wasn't answering – and looked around the car. Malhotra in front, eyes glued so tight to the road you could have set a firework off in her face and she wouldn't have blinked. Roarkes next to her, stony-faced, poised and angry. Gaddesdon next to me, smiling nervously and cracking his knuckles.

They were detectives. They might not have been the first people you'd pick for an armed siege, but at least they might be some use when they got there. I tried to work out what function I might fulfil, when I could have been lying down on a hospital bed getting my arm looked at, or having my first honest conversation with Sally and Thomas Carson. The arm was hurting again, every sharp brake or fast corner releasing another wave of pain to roll up and down between my shoulder and my elbow. I wondered what kind of damage Tarney's feet had done, and why it had taken so long for me to cotton on to it. Whatever the medics had given me, it was wearing off. They'd assumed I'd be at the hospital by now. I cursed Roarkes for letting me come with, for letting his guard down and forgetting to tell me I wasn't a cop and I was done and I should just fuck off home.

We were there. There was no screech of brakes, just a sudden halt and the harsh silence as the siren died. We were there and we were out of the car, without noticing it, and following Malhotra across the road to a normal-looking semi-detached house with four windows and a garage beside the front door. Malhotra had left the lights running, so alternating blue and white bathed the whole street, shadows leaping up and lying down again, corners coming hard and bright and receding an instant later into darkness. And that feeling was back, the long-haul red-eye dead-brain blank-sky sense that none of it was real, that anything at all could happen now and it wouldn't matter, because we'd all just wake up in the morning.

That was the tiredness talking, I realised. Again. The tiredness and the pain and the lingering effects of whatever I'd been given to kill that pain. Flashing police lights don't make your problems go away. They bring them home.

The door was slightly ajar. Sirens sounded in the distance. Roarkes looked at Malhotra, who held up a hand to stop him. He shook his head and started towards to the house. Halfway up the driveway he stopped and called out.

"Serena!"

It was a sensible enough place to stop, I thought, although the only truly sensible place for any of us to be right now was a long way from here. There was an authority in his voice that didn't match his stance, still three or four yards from the door, elbows tucked in, shoulders tight, like he was expecting someone to walk up and throw a punch at him.

He stared at the house and the house just stared back at him. He turned and looked at the three of us, and I saw Malhotra shake her head. I was furthest back, still on the pavement. Gaddesdon took a step forward and went to walk past Malhotra. She held out an arm to stop him.

The sirens were getting closer. Gaddesdon pushed past Malhotra's arm, and as he half-turned in the act of doing it I saw his face bright in a flash of white light, jaw set, eyes locked on the door ahead of him. He took another step forward and then paused as Roarkes shouted again.

"Serena! Come out, please. And let the journalist go."

Silence, apart from the approaching sirens. They couldn't be more than a couple of streets away now, I thought.

"We can talk about this, Serena."

A window opened and a voice called out.

"Really? We can talk about it, can we?"

Roarkes looked up. The open window was directly above the front door, a patch of darkness against a different kind of darkness. He turned around to us, to me and Malhotra, because Gaddesdon was standing beside him now, then back again to the house and its occupants. He held out his arms on either side and called up again.

"We can work something out."

Serena laughed, and I pictured her face. A sad, bitter laugh, and an expression to match it.

"Don't you think it's a bit late for that, Roarkes?"

The quality of the light abruptly changed, there were cars in the street, more blue and white, and a moment later someone shouted "Go dark!" and the street lamps went out entirely. Doors opened, slammed shut again, more shouts, footsteps, all a blur and none of it meaning a thing.

"Just walk away, Roarkes. All of you. Fuck off and leave me alone."

I took half a step forward, like someone with something to do, or at least something to say, and then I stopped. I couldn't think of anything to say, and I'd run out of things to do. I'd been out for dinner with this woman, I'd sat in a car with her and told her everything would be fine. Nothing was fine.

"I said *fuck off*."

There was nothing menacing in that voice. I pictured her again and all I could see was desperation, a fish on a hook, a cornered animal casting frantically for a way out.

There was no way out. Serena Hawkes could look for a hundred years and she still wouldn't find one.

"I'll shoot you. I will fucking shoot you. Just back off."

Did she have a gun? Given the people she'd been working with, I wouldn't have bet against it.

"OK," said Roarkes, and started to back away, still looking up. There were more shouts behind us, serious, angry voices telling us to get out of the way. I was inclined to agree with them. Roarkes shook his head slowly, sadly, and turned, and Gaddesdon, beside him, took a step forward.

A step in the wrong direction.

"Get back, you idiot!" shouted a man next to me. He was wearing nothing but black and holding a long and nasty-looking gun, and I hadn't even noticed him crouching down no more than a yard from where I stood.

Roarkes turned back towards the house to see what was happening. Gaddesdon shook his head and took another step towards the house and Serena shouted "Back!", but all Gaddesdon did was shake his head again and take yet another step and now he was only two or three more steps from the front door.

The crack might have been loud, might have split the air and startled the birds and scared the shit out of Montgomery Street, Marston, but it hadn't come from nowhere. It had always been there, waiting and gazing dead-eyed from the end of the final step, not at the farmhouse but here, gazing not at me or Sally Carson but at Gaddesdon, as inevitable as the lights and the shouts and the footsteps and the blurs of the journeys that had brought us all here.

Gaddesdon rocked and fell to his knees. He looked down, and then up at the house, and then turned to look back at the street, at the armed units, at me. I wondered, briefly, absurdly, whether he was thinking the same thoughts I was, that everything had led to this moment, this point in the game where one piece fell and the rest stood and watched that fall, helpless and transfixed. He collapsed onto one hand, then both, then onto his side, as if he were letting himself down carefully and deliberately.

It hit me, suddenly, that this was no more inevitable than the throw of a dice. And I was more than a helpless spectator.

I ran.

The police were still shouting but I didn't care. I ran to him and sat down beside him. I could see him struggling to focus, and then realising it was me.

He smiled.

Blood was pouring hard and fast from his stomach. He was bleeding to death, he'd be dead soon, I thought, unless someone did something, but I didn't know what to do. I lifted his head and rested it on my legs and tried to remember whether I was supposed to put some pressure on the hole in his stomach or elevate his legs.

More shouts, from behind me, lights suddenly blinding as I turned towards them, lights pounding like fists onto the house. As I turned back to the window – *"Armed police!"* – I could see something now, dark shapes on a white background, the outlines of faces, one so close to the window it was almost out of it, and – *"Put down the weapon!"* – something in her hand, the light tinged with blue and her face now clear, looking down, at where I sat with Gaddesdon's head on my leg, looking up again, an expression of pure and obvious horror, the hand coming up – *"Put it down now or we WILL shoot!"* – and then the next crack, except it wasn't one crack, it was several, from directly behind me, from either side, from in front, the window itself, and I jerked back, because if she'd already shot Gaddesdon surely the next person she'd be shooting would be me, or maybe Roarkes, but either way I didn't fancy my chances.

The gun was still in her hand, poised for a moment, pointing in the direction it had fired.

Pointing at her own head.

Pointing where her head had been, at least, because the impact from the little gun in her hand and several more from the professionals had knocked that head back and away, and her own bullet at close range had taken a chunk out of it, so that frozen in that cold blue-white light against the dark interior of the house it was some strange, irregular shape, something unnatural, monstrous, not fit for reality.

The bullets might have killed her but they hadn't done anything to arrest her forward motion, the lean through the window, which was no longer just a lean, and down she came, in the glare of all that light, smack down onto the ground just a few feet from where I sat.

There was a moment's silence, and then an explosion of noise, sirens, shouts, the repeating thud of a helicopter close by. There were screams from the window, Mia Arazzi's screams, there was a broken body lying just in front of me, and a man bleeding to death on my knee. There were sobs so close by I looked up in surprise, wondering who was crying, felt my eyes blur over and sting, and realised it was me.

Blue and white washed over Gaddesdon's face. A shadow fell over it, over me. Roarkes. A hand on my shoulder. Malhotra was crouched down the other side of Gaddesdon, paramedics were rushing over, people were talking, to each other, to me, to themselves. I couldn't hear the words.

Blue sky.
White sky.
Red eye.
Dead eye.

Gone.

PART 4

AFTER THE FALL

30: Release

I'D PASSED OUT in the driveway. I'd been looking up cradling Gaddesdon's head as Serena Hawkes fell to earth beside me, and next thing my own head had been on the tarmac and the only thing I'd been looking at was the inside of my eyelids.

I came to in the ambulance, but I didn't remember any of that, either. When I finally got to see Malhotra, she told me the paramedics had told her I was shouting something about a car and a wall and swearing pretty inventively, and these were paramedics from Manchester so what they didn't know about swearing probably wasn't worth hearing.

I came to properly in a hospital bed with a needle in one hand and electrodes all over me, which they'd clearly only attached for the hell of it since the monitor they were connected to hadn't been switched on. Either that, or I was dead, and my arm was hurting way too much for me to be dead.

I looked around the room. A couple of chairs, no other beds, a door (closed) and a long glass window onto what looked like a corridor. I was alone in a silent room, but there was a big red button beside the bed, and five minutes of pressing it repeatedly brought a doctor to the door.

My arm, she informed me, was infected.

"Oh," I said. I'd assumed it was something more serious. She stared at me with her lips pursed and her eyes narrowed, an awkward cross between an angry headmistress and a cornered cat.

"You're receiving antibiotics by intravenous drip," she said. "You'll be OK, but it's a good thing we got to you when we did, because much more of this and you'd have been looking at amputation."

"Amput—" I began, but got no further.

"I understand from your colleague that you recently sustained an injury in that arm?"

I nodded, dumbly, and wondered briefly who that *colleague* might be. Roarkes, no doubt. She nodded back at me, and for a moment there was a hint of sympathy there. Only a moment, though.

"Well whoever looked at it should have their licence to practice removed."

"Why?" I asked. "Was it broken?"

"Broken?" She shook her head. "No, that's one thing it wasn't. But there was foreign matter in the wound, and it clearly wasn't cleaned properly, if it was cleaned at all."

I'd showered since then. But I didn't think that was what she meant.

"Really, it's hardly surprising there was infection at the site," she continued. "A nasty dose of septicaemia, that's what you've got, and that's more than enough to cost you your arm if it's not dealt with in time. If not your life. Frankly, you're lucky it's taken so long to hit you."

I remembered the doctor, in that very hospital, the comment about antibiotics and infection and the box of pills on the table. I'd been so bound up in my nose the arm hadn't even crossed my mind.

She disappeared for five minutes, and returned with a nurse and an orderly and a fitting for my drip. I'd be mobile now, I thought, and then I tried it out and realised I was about as mobile as an aircraft carrier in a supermarket car park. But that was better than not mobile at all.

"You need to rest," said the nurse, shaking her head at my efforts, and then I was alone and trying to fit it all into the same picture, septicaemia and *foreign matter*, and Derek

Lyons and Serena Hawkes and Charlie Gaddesdon.

The picture fell to pieces whenever I got close to Charlie Gaddesdon. Charlie Gaddesdon was too much to handle alone and in silence. My phone was on the table beside me, with my keys and my wallet, but the battery was dead, and I was all set for another five minutes with my finger on that big red button when there was a knock on the door and Thomas Carson walked in.

"Oh good," he said. "You're awake." And then he turned around and walked back out again.

He was back three minutes later, and he wasn't alone.

Sally was pale and there was a bandage covering her left cheek, but she was smiling. If the last twenty-four hours had taught me anything it was that I'd lost the knack of pinning people down, splitting true from false, but that smile looked real enough to me. I hadn't seen Sally Carson smile like that before. If I had done, it wouldn't have taken so long to recognise her mother in the old family photograph.

She stopped a couple of paces from the bed, and looked me up and down, the smile wavering, and then she rushed over and grabbed my hand – the one without a needle in it – in both of hers.

"You're alive," she said. I nodded, and all those who weren't flashed through my head again like the images in a child's flip-book. There was a pause, and then a quiet, deliberate cough from Thomas. He was stood with his back to the door, arms folded, staring at his feet.

"I'm sorry," he said. "I wanted to say that. I'd probably be dead if it wasn't for you. Sally. Matthew, too. We'd all probably be dead. And if it hadn't been for me..."

He trailed off. I got the feeling he wasn't a man to whom gratitude came easily. Or apology. But gratitude, as Elizabeth Maurier once told me, don't pay any bills. Me and the Carsons, we still had work to do.

They didn't know precisely what had happened since the fire at Lyons' farmhouse, so I kicked off there, with the truth about Serena Hawkes. I stopped short of Gaddesdon. I wasn't ready to look at that. After a moment's wide-eyed disbelief Thomas nodded.

"Makes sense," he said.

"How so?"

"All she ever said was I should keep my mouth shut. Don't trust anyone, she said. Even you. I thought she had my back. Guess I was lucky she didn't put a knife in it."

Sally, meanwhile, was nodding away like everything suddenly made sense. It did, too. Just not in a happy-ending sort of way. And then she asked me something I hadn't been expecting at all.

"So are you our lawyer now?" she said.

I blinked. Fire prevention, door-breaking, murder: I'd done all these and more for Sally Carson and her husband. But legal advice was something new.

"I am if you want me."

She looked at her husband for a moment and they had that *can we trust him I don't know* silent conversation I've seen take place between so many clients. The answer must have been *yes*, because after a moment Sally nodded, sharply, and turned back to me.

"I did what you told me to," she said. I nodded. What I'd told her to do, sitting on the bumper of an ambulance outside the farmhouse, with the sirens blaring and the fire raging, was keep her mouth shut until we had a chance to get our stories straight.

"I'm sorry you've been dragged into this," said Thomas. "But what the hell do we do now?"

"Lie," I said, and then I set it all out.

Thomas was Frank and Sally was Chiara, there was no getting round that, they'd have to come clean. But the more recent past, that was a whole different kettle of fish. I'd killed two men. Ray had been self-defence. Mike had been on the ground with my tyre-marks all over him, and then he'd stirred. The arm that had moved had been his left, and one minute later I'd been picking a gun out of his dead right hand, but nobody knew about that, and nobody ever would.

Sally's position was a little less straightforward. I knew why she'd gone to that farmhouse. I'd seen her shoot Lyons through the head while he was lying down injured and unarmed, and I'd seen her set fire to the house and destroy the evidence. She'd gone there to kill. She'd gone there for revenge. She'd got it.

Except, ladies and gentlemen of the jury, that wasn't it at all.

The new truth was this: Sally Carson had tracked down Derek Lyons and gone to his farmhouse to plead for her life, for her son's life, for her husband's, to swear eternal silence. Derek Lyons had laughed in her face, tied her up and cut her, and if I hadn't intervened she would have died, and Lyons and his friends would have been out of the country by midnight. She'd shot Lyons, true – the forensic teams would find a bullet in the ash and a hole in the skull to match it – but she'd shot him in desperation, in the act of escaping; she hadn't even seen where that bullet landed. Lyons, or Mike, or Ray, one of them had already lit the fire that was meant for her. It was a miracle she'd got out of there alive (and that was true in every version).

The old truth was one of those things the police didn't need to know, and it turned out I only knew half of it myself, because after I'd finished and the Carsons – I decided to think of them as the Carsons, it was easier that way – had sat in silence for a moment to digest my strategy, they spun me a tale of their own. It was the truth, the old, hard truth, and it went like this.

They'd been away for years. They'd become the Carsons. Nobody back home cared about Francis Grissom or Chiara Moretti, and certainly not enough to come looking for them. That was what Thomas had thought.

He hadn't reckoned with his wife.

Even before they'd set foot back on British soil, Sally Carson had started her search. The men who'd killed her family were out there somewhere, the same men her husband had been running from for close to twenty years. They'd burned her parents. They'd burned her little brother. She had names, details she remembered from her youth, snippets picked up from Thomas before he refused to talk about it any more. She had eight thousand miles of distance in which to make her discreet enquiries, and in the end all they told her was that the Corporation was a shell of what it had been, and two of the three men who'd run it were dead.

But the other one wasn't.

Derek Lyons was alive. Nobody knew much about Derek Lyons, he had half a dozen names and a face you wouldn't remember even if you saw it, which few people did, because Derek Lyons kept himself tucked away in his web and sent other people out when anything needed to be done.

Derek Lyons had made a lot of enemies. Thomas and Sally Carson were just two of them, probably the least important, certainly the furthest away. No doubt that was what Derek Lyons thought, if he thought about them at all. But Sally Carson thought about Derek Lyons. And she worked. She worked quietly and cleverly and nobody, not even Thomas, knew what she was doing. She found people who knew people who knew other people at the fringes of the web. She found people who developed sudden coughing fits or stammers when particular names were mentioned, and then went quiet and didn't return her emails or calls any more.

And then she came back to England, and those same people found it harder to ignore her when she was turning up and knocking on their doors, chatting to their neighbours, taking photographs of them from across the street. She was closing in on Lyons, working her way in towards the centre of the web. She knew who his colleagues were and where they lived. She knew what he sold and which businesses he used as fronts. She knew where he got his Chinese takeaways and his favourite brand of Scotch.

But she still didn't know where he lived.

She found herself getting impatient, being less careful, less concerned with covering her own tracks. Instead of whispering, she shouted. Instead of cajoling, she threatened. Word got back to Derek Lyons. In the end, he'd found the Carsons before Sally had found him.

So in a way, she said, a catch in her voice and all smiles forgotten, it had been her fault. All of it. Fiona Milton. Naz Ahmet. Russell Tarney. Serena Hawkes.

And Charlie Gaddesdon, I thought, but it still wasn't time.

And then, suddenly, it was, because there was a knock on the door and now it was me the police wanted to talk to, the same sergeant who'd done such a great job guarding Thomas Carson back when he'd been a murder suspect. She was polite and apologetic, but she was determined.

"Sorry, Mr Williams, we won't be long, but you're probably the best witness to what happened over in Marston."

"Apart from Mia Arazzi," I replied.

"Mia Arazzi's still in shock. She won't be talking to

anyone for a while."

I couldn't blame her. Mia Arazzi might have been a thorn in my side, and a poisoned blade in Roarkes', but she'd been useful, in the end, and she'd come closer to getting herself killed than most of us.

I asked the sergeant for another few minutes. She nodded and left the room, but I could see the top of her bob floating up and down through the window like a bad wig. A few minutes was all I'd get.

It was time to tell the Carsons what had happened. So I did.

Thomas stopped smiling right away. Sally frowned.

"Gaddesdon?" she said. I nodded.

"Charlie Gaddesdon, the boy who kept coming with you to Bursington?"

I nodded again. The frown deepened, and she shook her head, slowly.

"I don't think so."

Denial. Gaddesdon was the kind of boy who'd inspire that kind of feeling. And no doubt she felt a little guilty. She should feel guilty, I decided, she'd lied to us all and maybe if we'd known the truth—

I stopped myself. If we'd known the truth then what? Nobody had covered themselves in glory. If Sally Carson had told us the truth then she'd have wound up either dead or in police protection for the rest of her life, and so would her son and her husband, if he hadn't managed to top himself in the meantime.

"I'm sorry. I really am. But I was there. I saw him get shot."

I didn't know what else to say. I only knew what I'd seen.

Sally put her hand on my shoulder. She was still shaking her head, but she wasn't frowning.

She was smiling.

"I know he got shot, Sam. I saw him come in. I was on my way to see Thomas and they wheeled him past and he didn't look good, there was a lot of blood and every doctor in Manchester seemed to be running alongside trying to get to the wound, but he was sitting up and talking to them."

My mouth fell open.

"Wait here," I said, and I was out of that room as fast as a clumsy man in a wheelchair who has to argue with the police on his way out can move.

31: Hindsight

FIVE MINUTES AND half a dozen identical corridors later, I was face-to-face with Gaddesdon. They were prepping him for surgery. The painkillers had slowed him down and his speech was a little slurred, but he'd never been the fastest guy in town.

He patted his stomach and winced, and then he pointed at me.

At my arm.

"Still got your limbs, then," he said, and laughed, and fell into a fit of coughing. Even I could tell that "still got your limbs, then" was five words too many for a man who'd been shot in the stomach. I glanced up at the doctor leaning over him, a young man with an old man's face, or just the face of a man who'd been on shift since The Beatles had split up.

"Don't worry, mate," he said. "This guy's immortal. He's already been in once, got the bullet out, started to patch him up, heart rate went mental so we had to pull him out, and he's due back in theatre in five minutes. How the hell he's still awake is beyond me. But he'll pull through. How's your arm?"

How did this guy know about my arm? Did everyone in bloody Manchester know about my arm? I must have looked confused, because he carried on.

"Charlie here told us all about it. Blood pouring out of him, and all he can tell us is Sam Williams and his arm. We were all over you looking for a bullet, thinking she'd put one in you, wondering where the hell it was, we didn't know he meant someone's bloody stamped on it. But good thing he told us. Led us straight to the infection."

So Gaddesdon was the mysterious colleague. Gaddesdon, lying there with a hole in him, and he must have looked round and seen me getting wheeled off and remembered my winces and my whinges and Sergeant Tarney's boot. The late Sergeant Tarney, I reminded myself.

I'd been right in the end. None of it was inevitable. I was more than a helpless spectator.

And Charlie Gaddesdon was alive.

I was woken at eight next morning by Claire, who took the visiting hours about as seriously as an email from a Nigerian billionaire. She'd packed her bags and got herself up to Manchester the moment she'd taken the call from Roarkes, and she hadn't really known what she'd find there.

I wasn't sure myself. My arm was still aching, most of my body was aching in cruel sympathy, and thinking felt like walking waist-deep in mud, every step a struggle. But Claire was here, and she'd forgiven me, and that was one bright spot I could look at.

She took my room at the First Quality Inn and drove round dutifully for four days in a row to keep me company. I spent most of those three days linked up to the IV drip. My door wouldn't lock, the blind only covered half the window, and Claire had been told by the doctor I needed to rest and should avoid exertion, but for all that, it had been too long since we'd had anything more than a snatched few hours together. On the second afternoon I watched, perplexed, as she produced a doorstop she'd taken from the hotel and wedged it under the door. She taped a black binliner across the window and started unbuttoning her shirt, and for the next hour I forgot all about Manchester, Roarkes, Tarney, the

Carsons, and Serena Hawkes.

Mia Arazzi hadn't forgotten, though. On day three Claire brought that morning's *Mirror* along with her. It turned out Mia's inability to discuss what had happened in Marston hadn't extended beyond the police.

Mia had gone for Roarkes, which I'd been expecting, but she had a surprising take on Serena Hawkes. I spent two hours trying to get hold of someone at Folgate for any kind of confirmation before Malhotra walked in (knocking first, thankfully, and waiting outside while Claire pulled her jumper and jeans back on and kicked her underwear under the bed) and told me that as far as they knew, it was all true.

Serena Hawkes had been in from the start. She'd leaked lies to the press, tried to confuse the investigation, and told Carson to keep his mouth shut. She'd phoned Lyons and tipped him off that Sally was on her way, she'd stabbed Tarney to death in his own police station, she'd taken Mia Arazzi hostage at the point of a gun. I'd assumed she'd done it all for the money.

She hadn't.

In spite of everything, Mia's professional instincts hadn't deserted her entirely during the brief period of the siege. It had all started harmlessly enough, if rather unpromisingly. She'd fired unanswered questions at Serena's back for five minutes and got nothing except increasingly frantic requests to leave. Eventually she'd tired of watching a woman running around a house picking things up and putting them in bags, so she stood at the bottom of the stairs, down which Serena was attempting to drag a hold-all bigger than she was, and announced she wasn't moving until she got some answers. Serena had shrieked at her and disappeared back up the stairs.

Mia was still standing there with her arms crossed when a wild-eyed Serena returned waving a gun in her trembling hands and things took a more serious turn. But in the midst of the terror, Mia had managed to get a short and bizarre travesty of an interview out of her captor. She'd even had the presence of mind to hit record on her smartphone. The article quoted whole sections verbatim. And if you happened to be Sam Williams, it made for uncomfortable reading.

I'm sorry, Mia. [Serena Hawkes is suddenly calm. She has a hostage. The situation has changed.] *If you'd gone when I'd asked you to, you'd be sitting at home having a glass of wine or whatever it is you like to do on a Thursday night, and I'd be halfway out of Manchester. You slowed me down. You brought this on yourself.*

I don't understand any of this, Serena. What are you doing? How did you get into all this?

They threatened me. Derek Lyons.

How did you come across Derek Lyons, then? How did he come across you?

I was defending a lad. Drugs. Nothing big. Got him off, then I got a call asking if I'd be interested in working for the people who'd supplied him. I said no, of course, I mean, they're admitting on the phone they've actually supplied the drugs, that's not the kind of client I need, but they called again next day and when I said no they said go downstairs and there's a man standing in my garden holding a gun.

[Sirens sound in the distance. Serena moves us upstairs. She carries on talking, even as she's fiddling nervously with her gun and adjusting the curtains by the window.]

After that I said yes, OK, I'd help them, and I thought they just meant, you know, defending them if they were arrested, that sort of thing, but there was nothing for a while, and then I get a call saying

313

we might need your help shortly, and I said what for, and the guy said you'll know when you need to know. I said I want to know now and he said you'll be hearing from us and next day – Jesus Christ

[Sirens now closer, and footsteps outside the house]

You were saying?

There's a letter and in it there's just a photo, here.

[Serena reaches into her jacket pocket and pulls out a photograph of a girl, five, maybe six years old, wearing school uniform.]

Who is this?

And then Tarney, that bastard, do you know what he said, he said it didn't matter what happened with Lyons, not any more, or Carson. He said you'd better keep your bitch mouth shut or there will be trouble, and not just for you. For the little girl, too.

Who is the girl?

[As I look closer at the picture I notice it has been drawn on in red pen. A faint cross, right where the child's head is. A circle in the middle of her forehead. And a jagged line across her neck. I ask again.]

Who is the girl?

Tarney was an animal. The things he said.

[Shouts from outside bring the interview to a close. Less than two minutes later, Serena Hawkes is dead.]

After the third, or maybe the fourth reading, I put the paper down and closed my eyes. Claire reached out and put her hand on my shoulder. She wanted to know if I was OK.

Of course I wasn't OK.

The child was Serena's niece.

I remembered the call from her sister – *Everything OK? Is Bella OK?*

I remembered other calls, the way she jumped when her phone rang, the brittle breeziness when she answered.

I'd thought she was just that kind of person. Sharp.

Fragile.

I'd sat and spoken with this woman for hours. I'd sat there in Roarkes' office and smiled with her and watched her chew him up and spit him out. I'd sat with her in my car, listened to her tell me – what was it? – *I don't remember the last time I had a client I actually wanted* – and thought she was talking about Carson, just Carson, and I was giving her sound advice. I'd heard her on the phone, I suddenly realised, heard her talking to Lyons, heard her say *you shouldn't have done that* – and now it hit me what it was she was talking about. I'd just got back from London and a punch in the face. The day before I'd been given a scare outside the hospital. That was all. Just a scare. They were doing me a favour. They were doing *her* a favour, or they'd have shot me and that would have been an end of it.

I'd sat in that Indian restaurant with her and spent more time thinking about my unusually-hot chicken jalfrezi and where the evening might end up than I had thinking about what was on her mind and why. *It'll all be over soon*, I'd promised. A cast-iron, Sam Williams promise. I hadn't realised how right I was.

Should I have known?

Could I have done more?

Claire decided to take my mind off my problems by giving me chapter and verse on her own. She'd reached yet another dead end. For all the work she'd done, the police weren't playing ball. They'd listen patiently to her story, and then they'd come back to her after a few hours, or a day, and *their hands were tied*, or *there were other priorities*, or *departmental politics*, or *other factors to consider*. It sounded like bullshit to me, and Claire agreed, and I reckoned between us we had more than a decent nose for bullshit. But up here, lying around in a hospital, all we could do was smell it.

What it came down to was this: Claire had hit a brick wall, and she was anxious to get back to London and smash it down. She didn't say anything, didn't openly resent being stuck up in Manchester wasting time with a not-particularly-sick invalid, but I could tell. A selfless, decent man would have let her go.

I'd given up trying to be selfless or decent a long time ago.

It took them a week to sort out Serena's funeral and the whole time I wondered if I should go. I'd ignored half a dozen calls from Elizabeth Maurier and spoken to Hasina Khalil several times until finally she'd broken down and told me the truth.

There was no money. Her husband had spent every penny of it on his "other wives" and real estate in Cairo that had been expropriated by the army. So I told her to find herself another lawyer, and I washed my hands of her.

Except, of course, I didn't, because (as Claire would have put it), that wasn't what Sam Williams would have done. Instead, I listened to her crying and begging, and I realised that through all her lies, the one constant had been her desperation. That was real enough. She was stupid, and a crook, and she couldn't afford to pay me, but if I didn't act for stupid crooks without a penny to their names then my client list would have dried up a long time ago. She was desperate. She needed my help.

The funny thing was, she'd helped herself after all. I'd put in a call to Michael Slaney at the Home Office, and asked him if there was anything he could do to delay her next hearing, which was scheduled for two weeks' time. Not a chance, he told me, but it didn't matter: "between ourselves", the authorities wouldn't be fighting this one too hard. Hasina Khalil's opening gambit had paid off. Various organisations had got wind of her story, the *lesbian-fleeing-for-her-life* one, and the fact that it wasn't true wouldn't be enough to stop them shouting it out as loud as they could. The government didn't have the stomach for the fight. So there was no rush to get back to London, not for Hasina Khalil, and when I did get back I'd be bearing good news. Not perfect news, mind. Michael Slaney thought it might be a good idea for her to shave off all her hair. To *embody the role*, as he put it. That was Slaney's idea of a joke, in part, but only in part. He was right. It was a good idea. Hasina Khalil would hate it.

As for Atom Industries, I'd decided I didn't care. They could shove their job in one of their test tubes and heat it until it rained fire and poison down on the earth. I'd told Claire the truth about my temporary cashflow problem, and she'd smiled wearily at me, the way you smile at the drunk who's just introduced himself to you for the third time in fifteen minutes. She'd known. She'd always known. She wasn't an investigative journalist for nothing.

So there was nothing forcing me back to London, nothing urgent, at least, and now the Carsons were on the books I had a pair of clients I'd have killed for just a week earlier. But whenever I turned my mind to Serena's funeral, I found myself staring at the same two questions.

Should I have known?

Could I have done more?

I wondered, out loud, whether I should just skip the funeral and head back down south, and Claire said she'd stick around and come along with me if it would help. That was my chance to let her go. Instead, I smiled and said, "Thanks." I needed Claire with me. And then Roarkes showed up like a breath of stale air.

"About time," I said, and he gave me that reluctant half-grin with a long, slow nod of the head that told me things weren't perfect. Not by a long shot.

"I'm sorry, Sam. I really am. As you can imagine,

there's been a lot to sort out."

There was a man standing behind him, a man I didn't actually know, but certainly recognised, a bald man with glasses. Roarkes gave a quiet cough and beckoned him forward.

"This is Detective Sergeant Miller," he said. "DS Miller's a friend from way back. He had the misfortune to relocate up here a few years ago. I believe you've come across one another before."

Miller stepped up to the bed and offered his hand. Without taking my eyes off Roarkes, I shook it. Roarkes was watching the floor, and I was reminded of Gaddesdon, in this very hospital, avoiding Roarkes' own glare.

"Well?" I said, after a few seconds' silence.

"It was the flat. Your flat. I didn't like it. I'm sorry."

And then he explained.

It wasn't just simple, it was obvious, and far more plausible than all those corridors of conspiracy Serena had led me down. After I'd been attacked in my own flat, Roarkes had decided I might be in danger after all. And instead of telling me this, he'd mocked me when I made the same point, and asked the only friend he had in the area to follow me all over Manchester in his little red Astra, and beyond, and make sure I didn't get into the kind of trouble I wouldn't be laughing about a few days' later.

"Why didn't you tell Sam?" asked Claire, and Roarkes coughed again, and shrugged.

"Why?" she asked, a little harder, a little sharper, and I realised it wasn't my glare Roarkes was avoiding.

"I'm sorry," he said, finally. "I thought I had it covered. And it's not like you didn't need the work," he added, turning to me. He had a point. He was wrong, of course, because I might have needed the work, but not as much as I needed to be two hundred miles away from the fists and boots and bullets and guns that had come my way since I'd answered his call.

"Nice stunt that, in the car park," said Miller, and shook his head ruefully. "Boss here was fucking furious when I told him you'd got away."

Roarkes was still staring at the floor. Claire was staring at Roarkes, and I recognised the look on her face, fury softening to mere anger on its way down to frustrated acceptance. Detective Sergeant Miller was still shaking his head, but smiling, as he let the door swing shut behind him. I decided I rather liked Detective Sergeant Miller.

Claire was the least of Roarkes' problems, as it turned out. It had been bad enough before Mia Arazzi pointed the heavy artillery in his direction, what with the fire at the farmhouse and the man with the tyre marks all over him (self-defence, they'd bought that, so at least I was in the clear), what with Serena's death, and Gaddesdon's injury, what with Tarney's murder after Roarkes had taken personal command of his custody *to keep the bastard safe*. Roarkes had been getting heat from the men upstairs before anything had even gone wrong. And then everything that could have gone wrong did.

Malhotra was waiting outside the door, I spotted the top of her head through the window while Claire was listening to Roarkes with that sympathetic head-to-one-side look I'd learned to take as seriously as a used car ad. I levered myself up, hobbled to the door and told her to get the fuck in before Roarkes made us all kill ourselves. He heard me, stopped, and laughed.

Malhotra had news of her own. Tarney, it turned out, hadn't been the Corporation's first inside man. Operation Blackbird might have been clean enough, but DS McTavish wasn't. He'd left the force a year after he'd written that memo, in serious but unspecified disgrace. It didn't take too great an imaginative leap to figure out who'd told Derek Lyons about Luca Moretti's trip to the police station.

On a more positive note, Serena's family and friends were a little more forgiving than Mia Arazzi. Her sister and mother had been in touch with Roarkes directly, before he'd had a chance to contact them himself, to tell him that whatever the press were saying, they didn't see how the police could have been expected to prevent the tragedy, and then again to let him know that his presence at the funeral would be welcome. Malhotra was going, too. Gaddesdon wasn't well enough.

That decided it. I was going. Claire was free to go home and smash down her brick wall, I told her, when Roarkes and Malhotra had left.

"Are you sure?" she asked.

"Oh, OK," I said. "You'd better stick around."

She nodded, and then she saw the look on my face and snorted. We made love one last time on that high, narrow bed, with the door wedged shut and a binliner over the window, twisting our bodies around levers and bars whose positions had imprinted themselves into our minds as firmly as they had our backs and thighs. By evening, Claire was back in London.

The sun shone on Serena's funeral. It had been raining all week and most of the week before, and now I was walking away from a freshly dug grave with fifty other people and probably the same number of umbrellas, and there wasn't a cloud in the sky.

Roarkes broke away from the man he was talking to and walked towards me, gathering Malhotra on the way like a piece of plastic caught in a current. It was all a little unfair, I thought. Roarkes had been right on the dead ends, Argentina, the field. He'd known there was good meat on Tarney, but the idiots at Chetwood had shut the door and told him the kitchen was closed. He'd got no help from anyone at Folgate past Gaddesdon and Malhotra, and even then he'd managed to find Brian Betterson. Everything else had come from that. He'd come closer than anyone else to putting all the pieces together, and he'd ended up getting slammed for it. But that was the way it went. People had died. It had to be someone's fault. Roarkes would do.

"I see your clients have shown up, Sam," he said.

I'd been surprised to see the Carsons, but I shouldn't have been. Serena's sister and mother had been in touch with them, too. I was starting to feel a little left out.

The truth about Sally and Thomas Carson had begun to filter out – the new truth, anyway. But the press were being uncharacteristically quiet about Francis Grissom and Chiara Moretti. Partly because they'd got Thomas Carson so badly wrong in the first place. And partly because a certain foul-mouthed lawyer with a sore arm had been playing fast and loose with the libel threats. The police had confirmed the Carsons would be facing no charges, and all the newspapers had were dead Derek Lyons and a bunch of D-list twentieth century gangsters crawling their way into the twenty-first like beetles from under rocks, anxious to get their hands on a few thousand quid for a ghost-written column. They even had Boris Crick, who I recognised from his grainy silhouette, although he'd chosen the no-less-convincing pseudonym of Mister Zed. They could live without Thomas and Sally. In the space of a week, the Carsons had gone from being the biggest story in the country to last month's drunken one-night stand: some hazy memories, some bright spots, sure, but not really worth getting back into.

I still had some questions, though. I'd seen them three

times since we'd sat together and rewritten history in my hospital room, once alone, twice with the police. They'd both been discharged the next day, gone home, started to put their lives back together. They didn't really need a lawyer any more. They certainly didn't need me hanging around Manchester for them.

But I still had questions.

I made an excuse to Roarkes and Malhotra and ambled over to where Sally and Thomas stood, talking to Serena's sister Pauline and nodding seriously.

Pauline spotted me first, extended a hand and a genuine smile.

"Mr Williams. Thanks so much for coming. Serena would have appreciated it."

If I hadn't known the woman was dead I'd have thought it was Serena I was talking to. Less brittle, perhaps, I could tell that from all of three seconds' meeting, a year or two older, four or five years heavier, happier, more sure of herself. But for all the differences, it was like Serena was standing there in front of me, and for all the appreciative noises she was making, it was like she was asking those same two questions.

Should I have known?

Could I have done more?

"It was the least – I'm sorry for your loss," I stammered. I looked down and away, and found myself locking eyes with a child, a little girl I hadn't noticed at first, half hidden behind her mother's leg. The child gave a shy, awkward smile, which I managed to return, no less awkwardly, before looking back up at her mother.

Pauline smiled again. Her daughter's smile. Her sister's smile.

"I'll leave you to talk to your clients."

There was a quiet spot in the corner of the churchyard,

and we made our way there, to a bench under an ancient yew with the sun bouncing bright off the dewdrops still lingering around the graves. I didn't waste any time.

"Tell me about Alé."

Thomas set his mouth in a line and fixed me with a hard stare, and for a moment I could see the man he'd been all those years ago.

"You know about that. He disappeared."

"Like Grissom," I shot back. "Like Francis Grissom and Chiara Moretti, right?"

He shrugged. The hard stare hadn't shifted an inch, but Sally had a softer look on her face.

"We can trust him, you know," she said.

Thomas nodded and got up from the bench.

"Tell him, then. Tell him whatever you want," he muttered, and walked over to where Roarkes was standing alone. Sally noticed me watching him go.

"Don't mind him," she said. "Guilt. Survivor guilt, they call it. And he blames himself for keeping that bit of paper."

And then she told me the truth about Alejandro Lopez.

"It was the smugglers. They weren't exactly pros, Sam. The police found out what they were doing, customs found out when they were doing it, half the town knew, they might as well have put a Bat Signal up every time they crossed the mountains. They lost a shipment or two. They decided it was Alé's fault."

She stopped, for a moment, back there in border country with her friend's life in her hands. I took advantage of the pause to push things along.

"So he had to disappear, right? And who better to help him than you two. You'd managed it yourselves well enough."

She nodded.

"It took us a couple of days and we spent every second waiting for the bastards to show up at our door. But nothing happened. I guess we got lucky."

"And in return, he handed over the business, right?"

"There wasn't time for the formalities. We just had to hope his family wouldn't contest it. Again, we were lucky."

"And the monthly payments?"

"He had nothing. He left with a horse and a saddlebag and the clothes he was wearing. He'd helped Thomas get on his feet when he'd stumbled off the bus in Patagonia in a pretty similar position."

There was still the mystery of the coordinates hidden in the book, but I'd done some digging of my own, sitting in that hospital bed, bored, alone and waiting for Claire to arrive and liven things up a little. I knew what was there. Google Maps could pick up a tiny metal roof huddled at the foot of the glacier.

"There's something there," I said, and for a moment she looked blank. "There's photos of it on the web. Shitty little hut perched on the edge of a mountain."

She smiled. I was getting warmer.

"But there has to be someone else involved, right? Someone in town. Someone you can trust."

"Alé's best friend. Local copper. The only person who knew."

"And that's how you exchange messages."

"It's how we used to pass things on," she said, "in the early days, food, cash, before we sorted out the bank accounts, before he learned to manage on his own again. It's not like we need it any more. When you've got email and instant messaging and money in the bank, what do you need a dead drop for?"

I thought back to my trek into the Bowland hills with Malhotra.

"In the hut? Under the floorboards?"

"Under the floorboards. The way they did it in Burnley."

Old habits die hard, I thought. There was no body in the ice after all. I reached inside myself and tried to figure out how I felt now I knew the truth, whether I was angry at the time and effort I'd wasted on a spot of petty smuggling on the other side of the world. I found myself smiling. I wasn't angry. If anything, I was relieved that this time, no one had wound up dead.

They weren't your everyday couple, I thought, as I walked away. Thomas had drifted back to his wife, stopped to shake my hand on the way, and apologised. He needed to stop apologising. It was over. As much as anyone ever is, Thomas and Sally Carson were free.

I was done with the Carsons. I was done with Manchester. I walked back to Roarkes and Malhotra and said goodbye and asked them to pass on my regards to Gaddesdon. No one was mentioning Tarney. We were standing around paying our respects to the woman who'd killed him, but no one had mentioned his funeral or whether they'd be going. He might have died a police officer but it wasn't like he'd been killed in the line of duty. Tarney had no close family, no kids, one ex-wife who hated him. I found myself rubbing my arm, which still gave a twinge from time to time, and remembered what Serena had said. *Tarney was an animal. The things he said.* That knife in the neck was more than just tying up loose ends. The sooner Tarney was forgotten, the better.

As I made my way past the mourners and out towards the car park, still smiling at the thought of Alé and his bank account, I felt an arm fall on my shoulder. I turned. There was a man beside me, about my own age, short brown hair, long black coat. He looked vaguely familiar, but I couldn't place him.

He nodded at me, extended his hand, and without

thinking I put mine out and met him in a brief handshake.

"Thank you," he said, and as he turned to walk away I remembered who he was and where I'd seen him. Fiona Milton's funeral. Arms on shoulders. Lips pressed tightly together. Jaw trembling.

I hoped I'd managed to wipe the smile off my face before he'd spotted it. And I hoped this was the last funeral he'd see for a while.

I walked to the car, still just about driveable after all it had been through, eased myself in, waited a couple of minutes for the air to clear the windscreen. I wasn't supposed to drive, not for another four weeks, the doctors had told me.

They'd said something similar about having sex.

It started raining again as I drove out of Manchester. I smiled. It was done. I was done. No more stings in the tail. It was over.

Halfway down the M6 I stopped to call Claire, and for something to eat, and noticed another missed call from Elizabeth Maurier. As I opened the door to get back in the car she called again.

I still hadn't figured out what I was going to say to her. But then, I didn't know for sure what she was going to say to me. *Fook it*, I thought, and answered the call.

"Elizabeth," I said, but it wasn't her voice that came back.

"Who is this?"

It was a female voice, deep and somehow sharp at the same time. They say you can tell a lot about a person from their voice, and that's bullshit, but if it were true I'd have said this woman was pretending to be more important than she was.

"You called me," I replied. "And you called me from

someone else's phone. Why don't you tell me who you are first?"

I heard a deep breath, a sigh of frustration.

"This is DI Martins from Westminster CID."

I stopped, one foot in the car, one out. This couldn't be good.

"What are you doing with Elizabeth Maurier's phone?"

"Before I tell you that, I need to know who you are."

I didn't much care for her tone, but there was no point being obstructive. It wasn't like they wouldn't find out in the end.

"This is Sam Williams. I'm a lawyer. I used to be a colleague of Mrs Maurier's."

"Well, Mr Williams, this phone has been recovered from a crime scene and your number was the last one dialled. In fact, there seem to have been several recent calls to your number. We're trying to reconstruct events."

"What do you mean, reconstruct events? What's happened?"

Another sigh.

"I'm sorry, but I can't go into that now, Mr Williams. Can you tell us what you and Mrs Maurier discussed when you last spoke at – let me see – four o'clock yesterday afternoon?"

"I didn't answer. And I want one from you. What the hell is going on?"

There was a scuffing noise that I recognised as a hand being placed over a mouthpiece, and some fuzzy conversation in the background. A moment later Martins was back.

"OK, we know who you are, Mr Williams. Do you know what Mrs Maurier wanted to talk to you about?"

"No," I said, sharply, and then corrected myself. "Well, she's been trying to get hold of me for a few days. We had a falling out, years ago. I sued her firm last year. They had to settle out of court. She called me on – I'm not sure what day it was, I can check – and left a voicemail saying we had to talk. I'm not sure we've got much to talk about. Hang on—"

Something had suddenly struck me. *Wanted*, she'd said. *Wanted to talk to you about.* Not "wants".

"What's happened to her?" I asked, even though I already knew.

"I'm sorry to have to tell you this, Mr Williams, but Mrs Maurier is dead. She's been murdered."

I should have known. I should have bloody known.

There's always a sting in the tail.

A Message From the Author

Did you like it?
You liked it, didn't you?
You did. Don't play coy.
You liked it so much you're heading right over
to my website at joelhamesauthor.com to fill in
your details and join my reader group for
exciting offers and free books and the benefit
of my wit and wisdom. Such as it is.

If you did enjoy this book, please consider
taking a look at my other books, or leaving a
review on Amazon. Reviews are like gold
dust, only better. I can tell people how great it
is as much as I like, no one's going to believe
me. You, on the other hand, have impeccable
taste, and are as honest as the day is long.

Also by Joel Hames

THE ART OF STAYING DEAD

A prisoner who doesn't exist.
A lawyer who doesn't care.
A secret buried for thirty years.

Meet Sam Williams. Lawyer, loser, man on the way down.
Sam's about to walk into a prison riot. Meet a woman who
isn't what she seems. And wind up on the wrong side of
some people who'll stop at nothing to keep him quiet.

**Sam thought things were going badly yesterday. Now
he'll be lucky to see tomorrow.**

*Read what Amazon customers are saying about The Art of Staying
Dead...*

"A brilliant read for thriller action readers"

"The suspense is perfectly timed and believable, the
atmosphere and characterisation spot on"

"The well-thought-out plot moves along at a relentless
pace"

"A pacy thriller with a rich seam of laconic humour"

"Engaging, fast-paced and genuinely thrilling"

VICTIMS – A SAM WILLIAMS NOVELLA

The trick is to save one without becoming one

Young lawyer Sam Williams is riding high. He's got a job he loves, a girl he wants, and the brain to win out every time.
But Sam's about to find out that he's got enemies, too. And figuring out which one wants to hurt him most isn't as easy as it seems.

Victims introduces Sam Williams, hero of international bestseller The Art of Staying Dead and Dead North, ten years younger than we last saw him, and a lot less wise.

CAGED – A SAM WILLIAMS SHORT

Promises come with consequences.

Binny Carnegie doesn't want her *notorious* night club shut
down. Lawyer Sam Williams wouldn't normally care, but
it's his job to fix Binny Carnegie's problems.
Fixing this particular problem might be more trouble than
it's worth.

*Caged is another snapshot of Sam Williams, hero of international
bestseller The Art of Staying Dead and Dead North, back in his
formative legal years at Mauriers.*

Please note that Caged is a short story, not a full length
novel.

BREXECUTION

There are thirty-three million stories on referendum night. This one has the highest body count.

Dave Fenton sleeps by day and drives a taxi by night. As the counting commences in the most important vote in Britain's history, one passenger leaves something in his cab.
Something secret.
Something explosive.
Something so dangerous there are people who will stop at nothing to get it back.

From Downing Street to the East End via the City and a whole bit of the country that isn't London at all, BREXECUTION is a fictionalised account of the closing days of June 2016. Politicians, bankers, cabbies and crooks - some will win, some will lose - and some won't make it past the first day of Brexit.

From Joel Hames, author of international bestseller The Art of Staying Dead, comes a thriller you'll want to put your cross on.

BANKERS TOWN

The number 1 bestselling financial thriller, "A real page turner - a hugely enjoyable, often funny, always intense thriller of a book"

"This time everyone else had their ducks lined up and every last duck had "Alex Konninger" written in bold marker-pen on its forehead. If I didn't crack this fast, those ducks would be shot, shredded and rolled into pancakes before you could say hoi sin sauce."

Everything's going rather well for Alex Konninger. He's drifted his way into a big-money job in a top-tier bank, and if he doesn't always play by the rules, he's hardly the only one. Alex doesn't know it yet, but he's got a problem, a whole army of problems, in fact, and they've all picked this week to jump on him. He's losing control, his past is about to catch up with him, and he doesn't know who he can trust, because someone wants him out, and it looks like someone else wants him dead.

In a world of bonds, bodies and blackmail, not everyone will make it to drinks on Friday.

Welcome to Bankers Town, the explosive thriller from Joel Hames

Acknowledgements

THIS BOOK HAS been far too long in coming, but as a result has benefitted from the kindness and expertise of more people than I have a right to count as friends or ask for help. Listing every last one here would be impossible, but the least I can do is try.

John Bowen, whose advice and skill in writing and marketing and design have been critical to any success I've met with.

Joanna Franklin Bell, whose brilliant editorial knowhow has torn my books to shreds and rebuilt them word by painstaking word.

Ray Green and Rose Edmunds, fellow Mainsail writers, for all their help.

Tracy Fenton, founder of THE Book Club on Facebook, and Helen Boyce, indefatigable admin and contributor. These people are the best friends to authors and readers that any of us could hope for. The whole team at TBC are due my thanks and the thanks of many an author.

Christopher Little and Jules Bearman at Christopher Little Literary Agency, for the months of effort they put into this book.

Louise Beech, Susie Lynes and John Marrs, three incredible writers whose words of encouragement have been invaluable.

And finally: my wife, Sarah, for reasons too numerous to mention. My children, Eve and Rose, for their patience. And my parents, Valerie and Tony, for their unwavering guidance and support.

Printed in Poland
by Amazon Fulfillment
Poland Sp. z o.o., Wrocław